Walking the

GORDON LIDDY IS MY MUSE II

AN OWL BOOK
Henry Holt and Company
New York

Cat by *Tommy "Tip" Paine:*

A Novel by
John Calvin Batchelor

Henry Holt and Company, Inc.
Publishers since 1866
115 West 18th Street
New York, New York 10011

Henry Holt® is a registered
trademark of Henry Holt and Company, Inc.

Library of Congress Cataloging-in-Publication Data
Batchelor, John Calvin.
Walking the cat, by Tommy "Tip" Paine: Gordon Liddy is my muse,
II: a novel / by John Calvin Batchelor. — 1st Owl Book ed.
        p.   cm.
            I. Title.
PS3552.A8268W35   1995   95-14537
813'.54—dc20   CIP
            ISBN 0-8050-3789-6

Henry Holt books are available for special promotions
and premiums. For details contact: Director, Special Markets.

First published in hardcover in 1991 by
Linden Press/Simon & Schuster.

First Owl Book Edition—1995

Designed by Chris Welch

Printed in the United States of America
All first editions are printed on acid-free paper. ∞

1   3   5   7   9   10   8   6   4   2

The author acknowledges his debt to Field Manual 34-52:
Intelligence Interrogation, May 1987. Headquarters, Department
of the Army. Distribution restriction: Approved for public release:
distribution is unlimited.

Contents

(New York City, Singapore, Seoul)

"There never was such a country for
wandering liars; and they were
of both sexes."
—Mark Twain, *A Connecticut Yankee
in King Arthur's Court*

WALKING THE CAT

PART ONE

The Governess

1

Dear Rosie

I PLACE THE START of this trouble not with a date, rather with a clever, loving governess named Rosie.

When I first met her, she was picking trash outside my kitchen service door. I wasn't looking for love or cleverness or anyone just then. I was blinded by a bout of the winter blues, one that weakened me for an invasion of tricky folk from my own neighborhood and also from another planet—Rosie's home planet, Asia.

It was crude February in New York when I fell blue, 1990 if you keep a diary. You know that Manhattan these anxious days is an island divided between the elite and the mob, where pricey buildings like mine are fortress palazzos against the doomed who wander the streets howling and scavenging, the dim ages under sodium lights. The tone is smut; the politics are futile; anyone who laughs outside is drugged or mad. It's also claimed that, if you live there, you must claim you love it. Like libel, it's never not exciting.

But none of that was why I was blue. I'm not a tragic thinker, and there's no time for sermons. Truth, I didn't have a reason. I camped in my apartment on the Upper West Side, making strong tea and playing xenophobic computer games. A week of this is okay, but not the way I did it, refusing the phone and the mail, listening to the Knicks and Rangers on all-sports radio, staying up all night and sleeping until late, grim afternoon. This is a formula for illness. My imaginary best friend, McKerr, was away in California on a driving tour with his pal, Boone, the tv personality, so there was no one around who could just walk in and shake me loose. At night, I became Commander Paine of the Gato-class submarine *Admiral Dread*, patrolling the Pacific in search of the Imperial Japanese fleet. Asleep in daylight, I dreamed of a time machine from America's future that carried me back to the tenth century A.D., where I was Brother Thomas the Timid, pursued by the Danes and in search of the secret of alchemy. None of it now makes sense to report, since I'm sketching the blues. I wanted to run away from myself, a routine escape fantasy for a vain, prattling salesman like me.

The trash-picking incident that introduced Rosie did start me on a very long trip. Yet it was so minor an event, it's silly—no matter how messy and sad everything turned out, that first turn was silly.

It happened mid-afternoon, outside my kitchen door. I was just awake and making tea, around 3:00 P.M., when I heard banging in the service hall that connects my side of the fourteenth floor to the service elevator and the fire stairs. The building is as silent as a time machine, so I investigated.

It was a middle-aged oriental woman, dressed in a trim white apron over a blue wool frock.

At first, I assumed she was just stuffing the large cans with trash. Embarrassed in my robe, I spoke eloquently. "Hiya, sorry."

She hunched her big shoulders and ducked, as if caught at theft. At her feet was a giant black trash bag, and in her hand was a smaller white bag. When she looked up, I saw fear and rage— maybe not, just something long-term unhappy in her black eyes.

I said I lived here, that I didn't mean to spook her, had I? I said I wasn't snooping, which I was.

"No, no, please listen, it's okay," she said in an easy, maternal, American diction. "You're Mr. Paine, the—" She smiled with strong white teeth save for a prominent chipped canine, but she didn't finish her thought.

Surprised again, I chattered, and what emerged were happy facts. Her name was Rosemary Yip, and she was Korean, a tall Korean. She was the governess for my new upstairs neighbors, the Purcells, who I didn't know existed until Rosie told me. I live on half of the fourteenth floor. Above me is the floor-through penthouse. Due to highfalutin design, it's necessary for the building staff to climb the dead-end fire stairs to fetch the penthouse trash. I'd found Rosie come down from the Purcells' landing to use my trash cans.

Rosie spoke to me as if she'd seen me around, though I had no memory of her. My building is on Riverside Drive, where cooperative apartments are so expensive that the sort who can afford them don't hang around much. This goes more so for those wealthy enough to buy a penthouse (Riverside real estate is Park Avenue west). The servants come and go in the lobby and elevator, yet I'm shy in the public places, anxious I might sound like a layabout, which I am.

The other fact that emerged from that first meeting wasn't happy. What Rosie had been doing, when she dropped the plastic trash can lid with a bang, was picking off meat from a turkey carcass and stowing it in a small white bag. I saw this, and Rosie saw that I saw it. We decided to share our secret in silence.

Let this be a lesson to me: never share a secret with a soul from another planet. Unless? No, *never* share a secret. Blab it out, rid yourself of the burden. It's like saving someone's life; you get responsibility without control forever. I'll have much more to say of secret-sharing, since I'm no fan of it, regard it as the bugbear of the American busybody and the cause of all sorts of home trouble and foreign entanglement—it's troubled me more times than men or time machines have, and you wouldn't believe now the folly it brought me until I work up to it.

At the time, I vainly concentrated on why the penthouse governess should know my name. I flatter myself as notorious, but not in New York, where jeopardy squats and only your anonymity approximates security.

Also, once we'd parted with nods, and I was back at tea-making, I puzzled about Rosie's sneaky thrift. What kind of nasty folk could the Purcells be that their governess should scavenge turkey?

I found out a little more about my new neighbors a few days

later, a Saturday. I was off at twilight to the gym to challenge the treadmill in wind sprints. I packed up my kit bag with last night's rented VCR tapes and slipped out to ring for the elevator. At the last moment, I realized I'd left out *Run Silent, Run Deep*, a favorite even when I'm not playing submarine games obsessively, since Clark Gable gets to die on camera for the first time in his career, two years before he actually died. When I got back, the elevator had arrived, and there was Rosie in convoy with four youths—two boys in a double stroller and two stand-alone grammar school girls.

I was eloquent. "Hiya."

Rosie treated me like an old pal—her chip-toothed grin and then introductions to the kids. "This is Mr. Paine, children. Say hello."

The two buckled-up toddlers obeyed in the way of the under-five set, averting their eyes and yanking at their mittens. They were going out for a walk and had no interest in dawdling with grown-ups. The elder girls, Sharlene and Dorothy, curtsied to me and stepped back toward Rosie's hem. Crucial note: They were a most motley crew. The eldest, Sharlene, nine, and the middle toddler, Jeffrey, four, were fair, bright-green-eyed types, but Dorothy, seven, and Duncan, two, were black-haired oriental dolls.

I returned the kids my usual stentorian "Good afternoon," and saw once again why it's best I'm not a family man—the overbearing in me annoys children.

Rosie herded the children close in order to give me room, and then she started to me as if I were another charge. "You've been watching movies," she said, noting the tape containers sticking out of my kit bag. "I've seen your movies, all of them."

This didn't fit my idea of a tall, dowdy governess, but then, the heroic nanny Wendy had invented Peter Pan, like a proto-VCR.

Rosie continued, "Please listen. I like them, they're funny. I know the critics've complained about the violence, but it's a violent world, isn't it? You make it funny-violent. And they let you keep in a few jokes, don't they? I've guessed they must cut you badly, to have time for their car chases. But you like car chases, don't you, though I've read you don't drive."

I promoted Rosie to my top-ten critics list. Just to make sure, I prompted her, "You like my movies? All of them?"

"Don't you?" she said. "I know there're some lazy parts, but you have to do that, they give us a chance to buy popcorn, and you always get in something wackadoo. Isn't that what they call it—'wackadoo'? Like Sir Laurence Olivier playing Joseph Stalin as Prince Hamlet. I laugh harder each time. And that line, 'Has this fellow no feeling that he sings at grave-making?' "

"I put that in?"

"It's there," declared Rosie. "You don't have to write it in to get it in. I know how it works."

I puffed up and promoted Rosie to my top-five list. Nah, she was tops. I was greedy for more of her brilliant taste, and was preparing a list of needy questions to move her toward an Elizabethan analysis of my Hollywood hack jobs, when we were interrupted.

It was the beggar parade. By then, we were outside, turning onto Broadway to merge with the pedestrian flow and other toddler convoys. We were instantly targeted by the riffraff who patrol the corners waving chewed McDonald's cups for change.

I barked at a lunging offender. He challenged me with the ironic curse "God bless you."

Rosie deposited a dime in his cup, as if paying a fare, and said, "God bless you, too."

I was impressed, not embarrassed. I pay taxes scrupulously, and throwing coins at the living dead isn't for my temperament; it makes me feel evil.

Meanwhile, Rosie returned to keeping up both ends of our conversation. "Please listen, I go to the movies whenever I can, don't you?" She answered for me, "I guess that's what I like best. When I was growing up, I went to the movies every Saturday. Saturday is my favorite day, isn't it yours? Matinees, that was heaven for us, was it for you?"

Rosie talked like this, nonstop autobiography followed by intimate interrogatories. She told you what she was thinking, then she reached out to get you involved. I think now that it's why being with her made me feel like a member of her family. I saw Rosie as an illustration of the governess as hero. She governed the family, her family, the way a wise regent governs a golden realm. The kingdom of the family was what was worth living and dying for to her; and what she favored most about the realm were the familial virtues such as love, mutual trust, cooperation and teamwork.

I've learned since that the Koreans, who see themselves as one
big family, have many proverbs that apply to Rosie's philosophy
of life. The one I like best Rosie taught me soon after: "Even a
piece of paper is lighter when two people lift it." This is Confucian wit. Remember it above all else about Rosie; she wanted two
or three or a dozen of her charges to take hold of that paper with
her and lift.

All this makes good sense when you consider what I learned of
her childhood over the next weeks, as we chanced to meet in the
lobby or strolled the street or park with the toddlers. She had
been a war orphan, one of tens of thousands of babies abandoned
in the catastrophic refugee columns running away from the Korean War massacres.

Rosie was Dondi at middle age. You remember, the cartoon
character Dondi, who was brought back to America by a rich
man's son and never grew up, a forever child during the forever
Cold War that birthed him. Once upon a time, it had been Rosie's
fate, like Dondi's, to be rescued by Americans in Seoul. This was
after MacArthur's landings at Inch'on. She said she was turned
over to a Presbyterian orphanage in Seoul, where she was named
Rosemary by a nurse and given the Korean surname Yip, because
the good Presbyterians had a lot of Yips about. (Koreans only
have a handful of family names—Lee, Kim, Park, etc.; the given
name is what is profound.) Rosie grew up a mouth and number
on the American dole.

It was one of the miracles of history that she remembered her
lonely poverty so giddily. Rosie never got adopted like Dondi, was
never transported to America to enjoy a childhood. That was why
movies were so precious to her; they were what she had of joy in
childhood—especially the American movies shown at the orphanage in American-occupied Seoul. At forty-two, she dated
her birth to John Huston's *The Treasure of the Sierra Madre*,
which she didn't see until she was a teenager, yet adored because
it shared her birth year. Adored as a strange mimic—it's not
unimportant to the mysteries of her soul that she could do Walter
Huston's splendid monologues. A tall, dowdy, chipped-tooth
Dondi could twist her face and growl with rapturous conviction:
". . . We're goin' to a country very wild and dangerous . . . have
to cut our way through jungles and climb mountains so high they
rise above the clouds. Good. Glad to hear such tall tales, because

that means mighty few outsiders have ever set foot there. . . .
Well, let's get goin'. . . ."

That first Saturday on Broadway, movie-mad Rosie swept me
up into her governess version of the world, and by the time we
reached the supermarket I was feeling better than I had in weeks.
So good, I began to realize that I was indeed blue.

Heroic governesses can do this, it's their magic, take you by
the hand and say, "Why so sad, let me tell you a story—once
upon a time . . ." I felt that I wanted to trundle along with her,
listening to moviegoing tales. I wanted to take Jeffrey's place in
the double stroller, since he thought he was too big for pushing.

I came to my senses, however, and told Rosie I had to get along
to the gym. I said good-bye to the children in my overloud manner: "Good to meet you all, good day." I hadn't gone a block
before I realized that what I should have done was to ask Rosie
to go to the movies that night, something compelling like the
latest car-chase masterpiece. I rushed back and caught her at the
dairy counter reading nutrition labels to the toddlers.

"Oh, please listen, that would be wonderful," she said to my
proposal, "but not tonight. Mr. and Mrs. Purcell are going out."
She smiled affectionately at my disappointment and offered a
compromise. "Tomorrow though, after church, how about that?
I'd be honored to accompany a famous American moviemaker—
who wouldn't? "

Humbug, I thought, then caught myself. Remember where
she's been, where you are (I didn't know the orphan tale yet, but
guessed at a long struggle anyway). I also thought how clumsy I'd
been to ignore her station and mine. Nighttime was for the jaded
grown-ups. Rosie and I were the same age, yet I hadn't meant my
invitation as more than fun. A midday matinee couldn't be seen
as anything other than neighborly.

I didn't go to church next morning. It was a Herculean effort
just to get up in time to meet Rosie at the church door by noon.

She worshiped at the Broadway Lutheran Church at Ninety-
third Street, a tidy stone facade anchoring the corner of a fragile
neighborhood of run-down projects on one side and, on the other,
brand-new co-op buildings with hilarious monikers like the Co-
lumbia, the Savannah, and the Princeton. The Lutheran remnant
had rejuvenated their church by sharing its space with the bur-
geoning Korean Presbyterians. You might not know that upward

of a third of South Korea is Christianized. And the most successful foreign mission in Korea, after the Catholic, is Presbyterian.
Also, it's commonplace for upward-bound South Koreans to worship in the style of that grumpy Frencher John Calvin. You figure
it out, how Geneva plays Seoul plays New York.

What I saw that Sunday was well-turned-out families in tailored clothes and smart Italian footwear, the children like flower
girls and tiny Dauphins. These were not pinched immigrants
from walk-ups. The plates on their large sedans (Korean-Ameri-
cans favor Detroit, especially Chryslers) were New Jersey more
than New York. This church clearly had a pew that traveled to
gather together to sing from the rhymed Psalter. I figured many
of them spent their weeks working eighteen-hour days at store-
fronts; however, on Sunday mornings, they celebrated the American dream of middle-lordliness.

Rosie was dressed plainly in a dark overcoat and sensible boots
for the gray slush of a recent snow. She waved from the church
steps. She stood slightly down from a clutch of prosperous men
in pinstripes from Barney's.

"Please listen, Mr. Paine," she called, "please meet my
friends."

In quick succession, I shook the ungloved hands of Lee Tae
Ha, Lee Sang Ju and Lee Nam Paik, the three Lees of this yarn.
Keep your eye on them (as I didn't). They were shrewd, ambitious, vengeful men. For now, I'll tell you that nothing about their
immediate details was false: they did own an electronics import
firm, a chain of greengroceries in Newark, and an insurance/law
firm in Lower Manhattan, partners in a service-oriented con-
glomerate; and they did keep large, happy families across the
Hudson in Essex County. Then again, this wasn't the whole truth
of them. Don't guess; it's my job to reveal their clowning and
cunning; just accept the fact that, if you're guessing mobster or
gunsel, you're half wrong. They were *sincere* fools, who thought
more scrutinously of the many planets on earth than the bankers
do.

I figured Rosie was showing me off, maybe also getting their
approval for her notion to go to the movies with an American
nabob. The three Lees didn't have colloquial English like Rosie's,
but they approximated clarity with politeness.

"Miss Rosemary Yip has said," offered Lee Tae Ha, the elder

statesman, a grandfatherly, broad man with moles like freckles,
"it is the honor, with the American artist, the Dr. Paine."

Lee Nam Paik, bushy-browed, big-lipped and dignified,
added, "Miss Rosemary Yip has said, the Dr. Paine has the books
in the shops, and I am to have the books soon."

Lee Sang Ju, youngest of the three and radiant with a gender-
less profile, contributed the best grammar. "Miss Rosemary Yip
has said that you are the American Graham Greene, Dr. Paine,
the great author of the universities. You are tall, as the great
General Douglas MacArthur, and strong, as the great actor Mr.
Eastwood."

I was overwhelmed: an artist in the league of Greene, Mac-
Arthur and Eastwood all at once. "Dr. Paine" was manners; anyone who writes books is a doctor for Koreans. I missed that their
remarks were rehearsed, that they'd meant to puff me up. You
know that's easy. I made a show of flattering their august selves
and families; however, the dependents withdrew to the cars.
Korea, if you missed it, is a baronial culture, not unlike New
York's reigning immigrations, the Irish, Italian, Jewish and, truth
be told, Dutch and Yankee—women and children don't stick
around when the lords are operating on the church steps.

Why was Rosie so prominent, then? Because she was Rosie is
my answer for now. The three Lees obviously regarded her, and
I learned later she was also a favorite of the Reverend Park, their
Aberdeen-educated gospel thumper. At work, she might be Rosie
the governess in hired frocks; on Sunday, she was a church lady.
And she could talk.

"Please listen," crooned Rosie on our walk down Broadway to
the movie house. "I thought their tongues were going to fall out.
I told Lee Sang Ju's wife about you this morning—did you see
her, the one with the new mink?—but waited until coffee hour to
spring you on *them.* They were blown away! I did it in the Korean
way, meekly, as if offering you to them. It's face, Mr. Paine, you
know about face? It's our way. You Americans like surprises. We
Koreans don't. I told them quietly, and you know how the kids
say it on MTV, awesome! Oh, you've made me happy! You don't
mind, do you? It's not as if I'm using you, is it—since I'm telling
you? It's what you call being straight, isn't it?"

Yes, yes, Rosie, anything you say, hand out intimacy (and
dimes) and gather me closer. After this, the movie at Eighty-

fourth Street was anticlimax, though Rosie trilled about it as if we'd gone to *GWTW* meets *Raintree County*. We ate popcorn and smirked at the lumpy dialogue ("F——, why can't I get a break?" wheedled the heroine; "I'm yer break, sweet stuff," pouted the hero), and then we walked home, while Rosie rewrote the screenplay and reviewed the acting.

"Good of its kind, Rosie?" I asked.

"Bad, bad," she said. "Why don't they just pretend?"

Rosie got off on my floor and had me deliver her back to the service stairs.

I'd hoped to meet the Purcells by the front door, so I was disappointed. I'd quizzed Rosie just short of impolite to learn that the Purcells were native Californians who had only recently moved into the city from the New Jersey suburbs. Mr. Purcell, forty, was a banker who had been in East Asia (Singapore and Tokyo) for almost all of the 1980s. He was now working near Wall Street. Mrs. Purcell, thirty-six, was a fashion executive who was between jobs.

The four children were more intriguing. Fair Sharlene, nine, was Mrs. Purcell's by a previous marriage; fair Jeffrey, four, was theirs together; dark beauty Dorothy, seven, was an adoption they'd made in Singapore; and the baby doll, Duncan, was a recent adoption from Singapore. If you're wondering why I keep repeating the children's ages and origins, it's because they're clues to a crime wave in Asia that I didn't then know existed.

Rosie would have told me much more about her employment if I'd asked. The guarded Yankee in me kept my inquiry to surface details. I did learn that Rosie had been with the Purcells over a year, since first they'd arrived in New Jersey. This recent move to Manhattan had been Mrs. Purcell's idea. She'd regarded elite Ridgewood as an embalmed compound and wanted the excitement of the big town.

At the trash cans, Rosie was sweet. "Please listen, thank you so much, Mr. Paine, I've had a terrrr-ific time. I hope you have."

I thanked her so much too, and we parted, Rosie back to her golden family and me back to being Commander Paine of the Gato-class *Admiral Dread*. And also to being blue. But not so much that night. Thanks, dear Rosie.

2
Dead-Red Lila

I T WENT ON CLEVERLY like this for two weeks, me bumping into Rosie and chatting movies and autobiography. Then, on a Monday morning, I got to meet the Purcells after all, thanks to Rosie's skill at governance.

I was asleep, of course. A bad habit is a consort. I heard the front bell from inside a pious dream—medieval Brother Thomas the Timid hiding in a walnut tree to escape the marauding Danes —and I wasn't sure the bell hadn't been a call to matins until I opened the front door.

"Golly, I'm sorry," began Mrs. Purcell, the friendly Pam, a fair, long-nosed beauty, as Californian as previous lives. "We can come back," said the tsarina-countess-suffragette-starlet. "It seemed dumb to phone."

Before I could lie that I was awake and lolling around, another long-nosed woman leapt into my view from the elevator door. The new entry was sipping espresso and holding a Paris *Vogue* so that the inserts fell to the floor like petals.

Meet the willowy redhead Lila, older and taller sister to blondine Pam, with as diverse a style as believable between sisters. How diverse? The telling answer was dangerously, to me. I'll wait on threats and focus on immediate observations. Pam was bright and pastel, Lila primary and black. Pam was gregarious, Lila ironic. Pam was a nester, Lila a teaser.

"Don't scare him," Lila started in her smoky, smart voice. "I told her you'd be sacked out. Sleep days and party nights, what a life you writers have."

I panicked and spun sideways, realizing once again why a man should never answer his door without his pants on.

What I'm stumbling to say, just as I was oafish in my robe, is that Lila was the sort of woman who could beat me simply by showing up. I didn't know this yet. I felt it. Do you know baseball lingo? There are wondrous ways to say "fastball"—number one, heater, hard stuff, the cheese, smoke, beebee. My favorite is "dead red." Lila was a dead-red redhead coming at me and rising.

Meanwhile, Pam had started introductions. "I'm Pam and this is my sister, Lila. . . ."

I left them at the open door to flee to dress and soak my head so my bald spot showed less. When I returned, I was pretentious enough to have forgotten much of my first impression. I record it here because it's fun to admit that I never had a chance. Not one.

The sisters had moved past the vestibule and were appraising my digs, Pam in the kitchen and Lila nosing in the coat closet.

"Pam, you have to get one of these," Lila announced. "You see, goose down, a bang-around coat."

Pam ducked out and smiled at me. "Don't mind us, we're new to New York. Lila and I're from L.A., kind of tropical-minded."

"She means Singapore," Lila told me. "I live in Singapore, Pammie used to. You ever been there?"

"You've got a great place," Pam continued. "That's a fabulous stove, that microchip kind. I've got to check those out."

Now that I was awake, I could see that Pam was a knockout blondie. That Lila was attractive, handsome, striking, but she wasn't nearly as beautiful as Pam. Then again, not even Plato was all sure what beauty is. If it's how you look—Lila wore her red hair like a war bonnet and was that day draped in black everything over red bootlets, just in case anyone missed that she was dramatic.

Pam giggled playfully. "I am sorry, we did get you up."

Lila teased, "You said that."

Pam continued, "I'm Pam, this is my sister, Lila. And you're Tip, right, we're neighbors. You know, like from upstairs?"

"He doesn't know his neighbors," Lila teased. "This is New York. Everybody in bunkers, triple-locked with private cops."

Pam grinned spectacularly. "You met Rosie, right?"

"Sure," I managed, "your governess."

"She's just Rosie," Pam said, "and what a lucky girl I am to have her, it's like being free." Pam was a friendly knockout, I repeat, that was her nature, her soul: friendly. Coyness, coquetry, glibness, deviousness, all the other styles associated with cover-girl beauty were not hers. Friendly Pam walked forward into the living room that connects to the other rooms in a long run. "I love the view you have, all over the river. Our living room looks at the big bridge, the George Washington, right? But what a view!"

Lila pointed to naked Riverside Park and the windy gray Hudson and teased, "All the way to New Jersey."

I didn't like having Lila behind my bald spot. Fortunately, she walked through the room, so I could keep both sisters in view.

Pam camouflaged her mission with more patter until she came to a point: ". . . Well, we've been curious, we have, and when Rosie mentioned about you again last night at dinner, well, I just thought, Pammie, get down there and say hello. We're new, but I said that."

I'd missed something about why they were here. I tried a quick review of how much fun Rosie and I'd had at the movies two weeks back.

"What did you see, something artsy?" Lila teased, now toeing over the big rug to inspect the weave. "Where did you get this?" Lila asked. "Here in New York?"

"Uh," I said, "Persia."

"Yeah, you mean Iran, huh? That figures. Something sneaky, I'll bet." Lila spun around to study the other rugs. "You have a name or address I could write?"

I said it was a long story.

"I'll bet." Lila laughed.

Pam finally launched, "I'm giving a party this Saturday, Tip. Like an open house for friends of my husband, like work friends, and I didn't have anybody to invite because we're new to Manhattan. The thing is, this morning, I thought, how about your neighbor? Like is it okay, is this the way you are in New York, just go downstairs and ask your neighbor on short notice? In Singapore, where we lived before we came back to the States, well, you have to send servants to invite them."

I lied that it was okay in New York.

"Pammie, he's going to think we're yokels," Lila teased, parading through the French doors. Here came her warm-up speech. "What's happening is that Pammie wants to show off how she's done up her million-dollar co-op now that she's got the contractors out, and she planned this shindig, and sent out invitations for a Saturday night without knowing that, in New York, Saturday's a social Gobi. You follow me. Pammie's trying really hard, and now her guest list is short. I told her we'd round up the locals. Anyway, a houseful of bankers'll wipe me out. We're roping you in. Local."

Pam was on cue. "You don't mind, do you?"

I lied again.

"Great!" Pam declared. "Rosie said you were like this, kind of generous with your time. I wasn't sure. I've never met a writer before. They're bankers, like Lila said, I have to tell you, the other guests, but not boring—they call themselves high rollers." Pam gulped a breath for a confession. "My husband's a banker."

"Tip knows about bankers," Lila teased. "Don't you, Tip?"

"Uh-huh," I said.

"I was a banker before I wised up," Lila declared as if she were confessing lockup, hard time. "They're just guys who do big numbers and get names. Guys like you do big names and get numbers."

"Great!" repeated Pam, who was peeking once more into my kitchen. "Did that range come with the place? I've been working on my place since we bought it last Halloween, and there's been so much—have you lived here long? I hear it's a quiet building. I don't like quiet. Not that we're noisy."

"Four kids quiet?" Lila teased.

I saw my chance to look awake and flattered Pam for her four beautiful children.

"Thank you. I love them so much, it's been neat to be home with them. But now that the move's done, it's back to the grind."

I liked Pam for not being defensive about her mixed brood.

They were her kids, and she didn't choose among them. Still, I wasn't so awake I could make conversation.

The sisters paced around me once more. I could feel their heat and panicked again. I forgot to mention that they smelled wonderful, two mighty perfume scents with art-form paint. I chose between erotic splendor and safety, saying I had best not keep them.

"Like this Saturday night, right?" said Pam at the door. "And you can bring anyone you want. Great! I'm thrilled, really, and Rosie will be too."

"I'm thrilled too," Lila teased. She winked and added, "Don't bolt, Tip. I know you writers. Say yes and then you're in Cairo. I'm in Paris for a few days, but I'll be back in time. Maybe you'll ask me to the party. Want to meet in Paris and firm up our date?"

"She's just kidding," Pam said.

Lila teased, "He's probably leaving for Cairo tonight."

"No, no Cairo," I managed. Something was missing again, some explanation for this sudden invasion of Californians.

I asked Pam if her husband would be thrilled, too.

"Charlie?" said Pam in the way a wife invokes a husband's name, an important but not critical idea. "Why, he's your biggest fan, he's got all your books! We know all about you! When Charlie found out you lived here, he just sailed off to work. He'd kill me if I hadn't talked you into this. Charlie, he loves you!"

"We all love you, Tip," Lila said, that smoky voice rolling over "all" and under "love" to make "you, Tip" a denunciation. "Isn't that what you guys love? Love, love, love?"

Lila stepped up to whisper loudly in my ear, a balmy breeze of perfume and espresso. "My first husband was one of you guys, a screenwriter, he claimed, and he just lived on love. I couldn't."

I blinked.

Lila didn't. The dead-red redhead had showed her best stuff, and, like all stud starters, she must have known, as I did not, that my bat speed couldn't handle her.

Alone again, I retreated to the kitchen. *Phew!* was my major thought. It wasn't until I had drunk my tea and decided to stay awake that I sat down to review what had just happened. I was going to a banker soiree in the penthouse. No. I wasn't going and said that I was. No. I was blue and a couple of exciting sisters were scheming to entertain me. No. Rosie had told the Purcells I lived here, so it was Rosie behind this, Rosie who'd known about me before I'd found her at the trash cans, Rosie who'd dispatched two dynamos who could have fetched Bonaparte from Beelzebub. Why? Because Rosie knew I was blue?

I booted my ludicrous 386 and called up Commander Paine of the Gato-class sub *Admiral Dread.* Diesel-driving across the Pacific, searching for a carrier task force, I had time to puzzle out other matters. Three penthouse motormouths loved me; that is, Lila said they did. I wasn't thinking about baseball just then, rather underwater combat on a beeping monitor. I made Lila for a first-class destroyer bearing down on me with good sonar.

If you've ever ruminated like this, you know it's not possible to stay blue when you're sizing up a Lila. She said she lived in Singapore, said she'd been a banker before she "wised up," said her first husband, the screenwriter, had loved her inconveniently, said she wanted to rendezvous in Paris. I brilliantly decided that Lila had just opened fire. Crash-dive, Tip, defend your vanity.

Lastly, I pondered the odd incident that had started all this penthouse flurry—Rosie sneaking turkey at the trash cans. I'd figured by then what Rosie did with her secret thrift, since I'd spied her handing out not only dimes but also small cellophane gifts like protein canapés to the Broadway beggars. Still, it didn't fit. Why should Rosie sneak *anything* from someone as friendly as pastel Pam?

3

Charlie's "Terrible Thing"

Tᴿᴼᵁᴮᴸᴱ ᴰᴼᴱˢɴ'ᵀ ᴷɴᴼᶜᴷ. Then again, it's more fretful when it raps politely on the back door like a messenger from tomorrow. A few days later, a Thursday morning, I was snacking in my kitchen around 5:00 ᴀ.ᴍ., when I heard rap, rap, rap on the service door. I guessed early riser Rosie. What could Rosie want at five in the morning? Tell me it was sleeting outside?

"Hey, I hoped it was all right," he began. "Rosie said you stayed up all night, and I was just on my way out, so I thought it was time we met. . . ."

It was Charlie Purcell, a glamorous man who was dressed and coiffed glamorously for the bank. Rosie had told me he was Alan Ladd handsome. The truth was that Alan Ladd was Charlie handsome. Charlie was a male version of Pam, a knockout goldilocks—ruddy, mustached, bright-eyed, trim, graceful and an advertisement of his tailor's talent. (It was Lila's tailor, a tough clue I didn't know was a clue.)

I ushered him in and said it was fine, fine.

"It must be great to live like this," he said, gesturing to my kitchen's centerpiece, a red Leatherette booth McKerr had found for me out of a failed New Hampshire diner, "you know, kind of loose and all. Like what you wrote in that movie—"

He paused as if plucking my most immortal line out of Bartlett's.

"Vice is its own reward," Charlie performed.

He laughed glamorously and looked straight at me to make sure I was pleased. "I've wondered, I have, wow, great to meet you."

It wasn't choice flattery. It did sound heartfelt. I asked him if he wanted some of my vice-ridden tea?

"Had mine, the early bird, you know." He laughed again. For a moment, I thought he was going to admire my oven as Pam had. No, he had a separate domestic agenda. "Pammie told me you're coming to the party, and I had just had a call from Lila— you met Lila, yeah, my sister-in-law. She called from Paris to tell me I was to get down here and confirm your date with her. You understand me? Does this make sense?"

I admitted not even slightly.

"Wow, Tip, you know I've read all your books, twice! I love your books! It's wild meeting somebody you think you know so well. You're all those guys, aren't you? Captain Bartleby and Locust Niles, all of 'em. Wow."

Charlie was goofy, a fan's fan. Was he going to ask me to autograph a paperback? No.

"I've been kind of worried you might think me a jerk," Charlie continued, " 'cause I'm a banker and all, and Lila says she thinks you're opting out of the party. But, Tip, I've bragged to the fellows at the office you'd be there. My boss is reading *MacArthur's Ashes* to have something to say to you. We're bankers, but we're mostly all right. And we're not just bankers, we have lives, too. I was in the Army, like you. Not Vietnam though."

"Me neither," I said.

"Yeah, not Vietnam. I was too late for that disaster, thank God. It was Korea for me. You ever been to Korea, Tip? I was there, '73–'74. A Spec 4, like you, yeah? College-boy clerk fetching coffee for the lifers. Kind of shitty. That was a shit army."

I spotted that Charlie was about to make a confession.

How spotted? He started moving strangely. Swooping, swooping—I suddenly pictured glamorous Charlie as a carrion bird, a

small one, say a common crow. I was wrong about this; he wasn't
a crow. Yet he was a scavenger, that was spookily accurate. You
can't get this yet, so I'm telling you, he was a scavenger and a
screwup.

Charlie delayed his confession with a diversion: he glanced out
the window and observed, "It's lousy this morning Rosie wants
me to wear boots, but I never touch ground except to get to the
car and out."

I saw what I'd missed at first. He was agitated not just from the
confession he couldn't manage to get out. He was also high.
Drink? Drugs? What? It didn't make sense. I had to stop his jerky
motions.

"Have a seat," I tried. "Have some tea."

Charlie obeyed like a child, sitting instantly in the booth, on
the other side of the room from my bench.

"And I was thinking," he continued, fingering a hole in the
Leatherette, "maybe you'd like us better if you came in and saw
the shop. You want to go downtown with me this morning? You
ever seen Wall Street before dawn? It's dynamite."

Another invitation, I thought. These Purcells were an inviting
family. "Maybe I do," I said, "only thing happening around here
is a long patrol south-southwest of Midway."

"Huh?" said Charlie, not comprehending xenophobic game
talk. Then again, maybe he got the xenophobia aspect, because
he continued, "That's great, yeah, you want to come? We can
have breakfast, we have it catered in. And Tokyo's numbers are
all in, while the midday from Europe's running."

"Sure, Charlie," I said. I liked the sound of "Tokyo's numbers." But I didn't like his agitated style; he was making my
kitchen feel padded. Out of self-defense, I risked prying. "Charlie, are you okay?"

Here's when Charlie did the deed—*a non sequitur from hell*.
He put his delicate hand over his delicate mouth, tugged at his
golden mustache and lowered his head to the Formica.

"Tip, I've got to ask you," he mumbled, "have you ever done a
terrible thing that's so terrible you can't make up for it ever?
There isn't any way you can get out of the trouble you're in. And
it's terrible, really terrible, and you know it's coming for you and
it's going to kill you. And you have to wait and wonder when."

He sobbed. An intimate noise punctuating an intimate question, the kind only best friends might ask of each other, maybe not even then. The kind you only ask of yourself.

I guessed that the reason Charlie could ask me all of a sudden, on first meeting, was that, in his mind, he knew me like an old buddy, knew me from my books as if he were me. I know now that there was more to it—Charlie was a crybaby as well as a scavenger and screwup, and he cried over himself all the time.

Also, and significantly, Rosie was behind this morning's sobbing. She'd convinced him to come to me like a penitent seeking sanctuary. But I didn't know this yet. I waited, knowing he'd repeat himself.

"It's terrible, Tip, and I can't get out from under it. What would you do? Stall? That's what I've been doing. Stall?"

I still waited. I had no reply. He *was* high. I pretended he was ill and the raving would pass.

Charlie grabbed his mouth again and jumped to the kitchen door. I didn't want him to vomit. He said something about meeting him downstairs in five minutes at the car, and then he was gone.

I would have breathed easier if not for Rosie. Within moments, she was rapping at my service door, and, when I let her in, she didn't try to explain herself, she just said, "Please listen, Mr. Paine. Mr. Purcell needs you. Can you go with him this morning? Please?"

"What's wrong with him?"

Rosie said, "He's sick. Too many pipes, too many pills. I tried to stop him. He's been awake all night."

"Pipes, Rosie? What pills?"

"Uppers," she said like an MTV host. "After the opium, what gets him going again are those uppers." She didn't explain that either, just begging me, "Go with him. He'll tell you. Please."

There was minor repetition in our exchange, but the clear point was that I said I'd go with Charlie. Rosie thanked me and thanked me. She had to get back to the children, she said, they were upset by Daddy's noises. Pam, it seemed, had barricaded herself in the master bathroom, and Charlie had been on a rampage to get dressed. Rosie told me she had to go hold together the threatened little penthouse family.

"I *knew* you would," Rosie exhaled as she left, "I just *knew* it."

I pinned on my crisis face and, in not much more time than it took for the elevator, I joined Charlie at his limo door for a ride to Wall Street with an opium addict. Opium smoking, I'd heard, cuts down on your exhaustion and hard thoughts. I knew from too much reading that history is filled with creative men and women who have used it like a sable collar. It's a seductive disability—hallucinating, equivocating, usually erasing the border between man and madness. Yet this is big think about chemicals. I was much more afraid of the "uppers" Charlie used. Amphetamines are a death drug.

Thankfully, Charlie had gotten himself under control, perhaps with another drug, and the soft-lit comfort of the limo ride made him seem polite and gentle. He propped *The Asian Wall Street Journal* on his lap and asked me if he could listen to the financial news.

I expected New York radio, but his limo had a telephone link with a private service, and we listened in to London, Paris, Rome, Frankfurt, Hong Kong, Tokyo, Singapore and Sydney markets being interpreted by BBC-sounding announcers. It was an around-the-world trip. I was awed, asking if all was well this morning.

"The dollar price is what makes them happy," Charlie said. "It doesn't mean anything, but it makes them happy."

Limo cruising Manhattan before dawn is also happy-making. There were similar limos on the road as we approached Wall Street. I marveled at the financial brotherhood careening to their fourteen-hour days. The skyscraper lights to the east were hazy in the weather, the Hudson was black whiteness, and, as we fell under the make-believe circus tent held up by the World Trade Towers, I envied these bankers and traders.

No, I didn't.

I did broadcast some of my impressions to Charlie.

"Wow, yeah, it's like that, anything can happen out there."

I was grateful he wasn't going crazy on me again. I hoped we could get through breakfast as uptight gentlemen. The limo cruised off a ramp and into the catacomb beneath Battery City, a brand-new fantasy raised on a landfill that used to be the Hudson. It looks like a series of brassy building blocks—as up-to-date as a space colony, guided by microchips, manned by the elite, airtight and free-floating in geosynchronous orbit.

Charlie's bank was quietly named Horizon Pacific Securities

Company. This meant it wasn't a bank at all, rather an investment bank—bag-holding bagmen between the gamblers and the
gambled-upon. It quietly occupied a duplex floor-through in a
pyramid-topped tower.

"How's about that breakfast?" Charlie asked. "You like English heavy or Parisian light?"

We glided past the reception area and into spacious splendor,
much oriental furniture mixed with soft leather seats and, in the
atrium, what looked like an orchid garden fed by a fake skylight.

There were more mixed signals at Horizon Pacific than I could
tally. I didn't truly know what investment banks did. Since then,
I've learned to make that bag-holding bagmen remark. It's also
fair to say that investment banking is what used to be called
buccaneering, what modern prigs like me call scavenging.

I won't detail my morning with the bankers, because it was
bland, and I wasn't there to learn about the color of their sus-
penders, gleam of their jewelry, latency of their carnality. I was
there, simply, because Rosie had asked me to help Charlie. Yet
Charlie at the bank wasn't acting as if he needed help. He was
associate managing partner in the New York office and a shining
lord.

(I know, you've heard that by 1990 investment bankers were
bygone. Even the *Journal* had cracks about investment bankers
"knocked out of the box." History confides, though, that the best
time to stay with a trend is when it's past. Nobody new is getting
in, and, if you're still showing up at the pay window, chances are
good you're prospering in a Learjet 35 sort of way, as solid as
Manhattan granite.)

Nonetheless, there were clues that morning that all was not A-
OK with Charlie at the bank. For example, his glamour was
serenely purposeless; and he kept asking me, "What do you make
of that, Tip?" whenever he answered one of my simple questions.

The best clues to the trouble came from Charlie's boss, James
M. Flowers. After Charlie had played the excellent host in the
cozy breakfast room, he walked me through his vast corner office
and then through a gallery into Jimmy Flowers's vast corner office.

"What's happening, Tip, is the Pacific Rim. It's a boomtown,
like the Klondike. There's gold in them thar hills."

Those were nearly Jimmy Flowers's first words to me. James M. Flowers, the managing partner of the New York office, was a husky, muscular forty-four-year-old multimillionaire. You've all met or heard about guys like this—boisterous, precocious, slightly sweaty winners who love other winners and don't attend funerals; it's bad luck. Jimmy Flowers's particular nature had stuffed his vast corner office with bobsledding memorabilia from his Winter Olympics days. And, before I forget, he was a Dartmouth alum and trustee, much the same way Charlie was a USC boy. Dartmouth wasn't crucial to Flowers, it was just a club to brandish. Nor was his vague Carolina brogue critical to his character, just another club for him. I didn't like Jimmy Flowers right away, but not for regional prejudices. Okay, yes, for them, too. Truth, I didn't understand my instant contrariness. Maybe because he was one of those ex–Ivy jocks who like to flex their neck muscles.

Jimmy Flowers claimed to like me. "I'm reading your book, the MacArthur thing," he said. "Pretty good, I like all the spying, it's rough-and-tumble, a lot like this business."

I corrected, "No correlation whatsoever, Jim."

"How's that?" Flowers asked.

"Spying can't turn a profit," I joked. "All that's black is deep in the red. It's a sinkhole."

"I'll think about that," Flowers said. "You putting me on?"

"If it ain't silly," I admitted, "I can't remember it."

Flowers glanced at me as he might locate a pigeonhole in a rolltop desk. He had me stored in the kook slot before he guffawed. "Yeah, *heyyyy*, yeah."

Shoving my vanity aside, it was significant to me that Charlie acted afraid of his boss this morning. How? Charlie lowered his goldilocks whenever Flowers talked; Charlie squared his shoulders toward the exit whenever Flowers moved; Charlie flashed his pretty teeth in a fragile snarl whenever Flowers bothered to ask him a question. Maybe, I thought, it was routine office politics. Then again, I thought, it fit somehow with Charlie's sobbing in my kitchen. Folk aren't cloaked geniuses when they're in trouble; everything shows at once and involuntarily, as if they're being squeezed by thought police.

I'll pick up Flowers's palaver and Charlie's fear at the choice

moment. We were sitting around an oriental coffee table, surrounded by priceless Chinese prints and an ungodly postmodern
canvas, while Flowers boasted about banking.

"You follow the markets, Tip?" Flowers asked. "This New
York scene's old hat. The assholes on the Street are back to keeping their pricks limp."

I looked where he gestured, east toward Wall Street. And perhaps also slightly uptown, to the Jacob Javits monolith off Tom
Paine Park, better known as the Federal Building, blockhouse of
the FBI. I guessed, "You mean, they're scaredy-cats?"

Flowers guffawed. "Yessiree! The government made them
clean their balls 'stead of playin' with them. Pretty good, *heyyyy?*
You like it?"

I did; I didn't. He was a crude stand-up.

Flowers tightened his neck muscles as if throwing himself into
a squash shot; he asked confidentially, "You get me when I say
there's no SEC in Asia?"

"Lawless?" I guessed.

Charlie smiled unhappily.

"Cowboy country, the Wild East, the free market," Flowers
declared, "like our great-granddads had. The Rockefellers didn't
have an SEC on their backs. China's comin' wide open again,
you'll see, and the Japanese love cutthroat, though they talk a
straight game. Charlie tell you about Singapore? The crap that
goes on there is unbelievable. Taiwan's tame in comparison. And
Korea! You ever been to the Asian Miracle?"

Charlie jerked and changed the subject. "He was in the Army,
too, Jim. A Spec 4 like us."

"Yeah?" Flowers beamed. "Three vets sittin' around shooting
the shit, huh?"

"Accurate, Jim," I said. Flowers was a crudely exact man who
didn't screw up like Charlie. Flowers believed he knew what he
was doing all the time. It was his only weakness, this cockiness,
but it's my experience that it's a colossal weakness.

"Where were you, Tip?" Flowers asked. "The Nam?"

"Nope," I said.

"That's right, you were NSA," said Flowers, flapping toward
his desk and what I presumed was a copy of one of my paper-
backs. "Well, I wasn't a grunt either. Frankfurt for me. I had the
first Porsche 911 on my block."

Charlie laughed brittlely.

I asked Charlie, "And you were in Korea?"

Charlie's pretty eyes came back from far away and blinked.

"Charlie's our Asia pro," said Flowers, glancing at Charlie with the respect due custom-designed software. "He was all over Asia before he got out. Tell him, Charlie."

"Yes." Charlie obediently didn't tell me.

I asked if they were army buddies.

Flowers answered for them both. "We met at the Berkeley B School. We showed up for a seminar on the DoD's purchasing practices. And we were the only two there! It was '76, and our fellow boneheads thought the DoD was for losers. Were they wrong! In comes Reagan and—*shazam!*—the DoD's a f——in' bazaar!"

"So you and Charlie are B-school chums?" I asked. The trick detail was "chums." It was stone-written that they despised each other.

Flowers digressed to his memoirs. "Shit, the Army is a shithole. I went in thinking I'd punch my ticket for politics. Was I wrong. Politics, who does that anymore except pissant little heirs to some dandruff-shampoo fortune? The Army's gone cheap, too. With Reagan, there was serious money for the DoD. But now, since the f——in' commies blinked, *not no more.*"

The Prince of Darkness doesn't pronounce a verdict any simpler. *Not no more.* Gear-loose as he was, I favored Flowers suddenly, contradicting my instant dislike. *Not no more.* When they foreclose on me, that's what the horn-rimmed loan officer will say: "You've had your day, sir—*not no more.*"

Flowers primped for loopier prognostications. "You know what the big money is for 2000, Tip, and don't say bailouts or politics."

"Couldn't guess," I guessed.

"Tell him, Charlie," Flowers ordered.

Charlie's brain was absent again.

"Robotics!" Flowers boomed.

I figured he was doing stand-up again. Truth, I didn't believe him when he said it. This was a joke, wasn't it?

Wrong. Flowers made up more ad copy: "Androids, yeah? You write about them yet? Give me a robot with a 60 IQ, and it can carry water. At 80 to 90, it can see there's no water and fetch it. But at 100, it's smart enough to mix and fetch martinis, barbecue the ribs, fetch your wallet on the dresser. I'm not talking assembly-line drones, or even robot houses—I'm talking butlers, maids, gardeners, watchdogs. Stay-at-home robots, cuddly little critters, cartoon look-alikes. That's the future, that cute robot. And at 120, it's a single parent."

"Or a Spec 4?" I guessed.

"Now you got it!" Flowers said. "He's good, Charlie!"

Charlie touched his pretty mustache as if certifying it was attached to his face.

"Specialist Robot, *heyyyy!*" Flowers hooted. "I'll bet you could write a great story about him. Takes orders twenty-four hours a day and never eats or shits." Flowers did the banker turn, glancing at his watch and figuring what time it was wherever he had a conference call by satellite uplink. "Good, good, we go on like this I'm going to give away the data base. Robotics, that's where it's at, big, very big. What the photocopier and stereo and color tv and compact were for the sixties and seventies, the PC and camcorder and phone shit were for the eighties, that Stepin Fetchit robot's sure to be for 2000. You know why?"

Here came the sales pitch.

"Tell him, Charlie," Flowers ordered.

Charlie couldn't have told me his name.

"Because mothers are going to buy them!" Flowers prophesied. "Not General Motors. Mothers, the wealthiest consumers in the universe. Now that's a *sure thing.*" He leaned closer, his two-thousand-dollar rags ruffling golden threads. "I know Charlie's not told you this, because I'd have to kill him if he talked, but"—Flowers's neck was rigid—"I can tell you, since you like secrets, yeah? Put your money in robotics. Call up your broker and ask him to look. And here's a hint. Near the Sea of Japan. That's a hint, *heyyyy?*"

"Not Singapore?" I guessed, glancing at Charlie to see if he was up in smoke.

Flowers guffawed and added a routine fan question. "You writin' about us, Tip? Is this research for you? Just make sure you use my initials, so I can prove it's me to my wife."

Our tête-à-tête closed with more primping by Flowers and weirdness by Charlie.

You might think it strange that a walk-in guest like me could spend a few hours with the bankers and discover where they're bound with their Jolly Roger flying. But it's my opinion that professionals love to talk shop. If an amateur is standing around, they'll brag about their *sure thing* just as if it has already happened. As if the magic word *sure* does indeed attach to their *thing*.

The truth about things, however, is that men will cheerfully fight and die for nothing. Believe it or not, one of the things that's happening in this yarn is a bunch of guys going crazy about a *sure thing* called robotics.

(I'm not keeping this stupid secret of robotics from you, since it's too silly to have to remember. Ask yourself, right now, what sort of an idea is a Bugs Bunny robot in your bedroom? The correct answer is stupid. So outrageously foolish that you can't nix it. It just stands there, big-eared and fluffy-tailed, chewing the banker's line, "Eh, what's up, Doc?")

I didn't keep the stupid secret of stupid robotics from Charlie a moment longer than necessary either. While he walked me to the elevator bank and down to the waiting limo, I thought, Why hold back? All deals are the same. When they go bad, they go bad in the same way—lies, betrayal and, after a limo ride uptown to the Federal Building, plea-copping for genteel stir, Lewistown, Pennsylvania.

Charlie tried gratitude at the limo door. "I really appreciate you coming down here, Tip."

I speechified, "You're in trouble. And Rosie said you needed my help, and you'd tell me. Robotics, what about robotics and the Sea of Japan? What's your 'terrible thing'? What have you done? Fraud, embezzlement, insider stuff? So what? I hear there's no SEC in Asia."

Charlie lied. "No, no, it's not that." He also whined; the crybaby couldn't lie without sound effects. "Maybe we can talk later. Tonight, maybe?"

I told him to tell me now, because I didn't think I liked him anymore, and I was only there because I liked Rosie.

Charlie lied again. "Rosie shouldn't have done that. Honest, we can talk later. I need your advice."

I taunted, "If it's my advice you want, you can't afford me. I can't even afford my advice."

"Help, then." Charlie corrected one lie with another.

I let it go, since I was more cranky than curious. I was convinced he was stuck in that steamy place nicknamed big trouble.

I was also convinced he could wheedle his way free. He didn't need a friend, he needed a law firm of former U.S. attorneys.

Charlie's big trouble grabbed hold of him just then; it made him poke his head into the car for some crybaby antics. "It's Korea, Tip, it's about Korea."

4
Gargantuan Trouble

Right, charlie, sure, Charlie, I could've guessed that, too. So long, Charlie.

I reached home thinking that there was a good reason why I'd not become an industrialist like my brother Sam, and also why I don't gamble like that Barry Lyndon reproduction, Pete Rose—I can't get a serious breath when there's serious money around. It makes me want to read Mark Twain or watch a bone-rattler like *A Bridge Too Far* and just have fun.

Instead of fun, I got my sleep and was up by five that evening to get to the gym before Charlie or Rosie came calling.

I almost made it, just stopping off in the kitchen for an orange, when I heard more rapping on the service door. I opened it to find not Rosie or Charlie, but Lila in her sister's azure bathrobe.

"Hi, Tip," Lila began, "good to catch you."

She wasn't catching me, she was ambushing me. I said, "You're back quick."

"You know about air travel? Then there's Le Concorde, this baguette that whooshes."

I asked myself if she was as sexy today as I remembered her from Monday. Yes and no. Without fresh makeup, she was ordinarily redheaded, but her sleepy scent was a weapon. Once the mutt in me gets a scent, I'm owned by it.

"Tip?" Lila tried. "We've got to talk." She stealthily shut the door behind her. "I heard from Rosie there was a crack-up this morning. I got back just in time. Charlie, he freaked out."

I asked for an armistice, saying that I needed the gym, the whirlpool, and food before more consultations.

"That's a damn good idea. Take me along. I could use bubbles, and you've never seen me in a bathing suit. I'm a youthful forty-one." She smiled, not sure I was convinced, and also because she wasn't as nervy as she talked. "Wait for me in the lobby. I'll grab Pammie's stuff. It's raining, isn't it?"

We strolled down West End like strangers. In the dark, and with the city's stench overwhelming Lila's aroma, I was sensible enough to be suspicious of her. Lila clearly suspected I was trying to bolt. I ask myself, now, at what point I might have gotten out of the mess. When I had the best chance, Rosie popped up being needy. When I had the next best, Lila popped up being Lila. My excuse with Rosie was that I liked her, and my excuse with Lila was that I wasn't taking her seriously. This sounds flimsy even now. Have you ever done something stupid because of red hair, freckles and perfume?

At the gym, we separated for the locker rooms as Lila teased, "Don't dawdle; I might get hit on by a cute lawyer."

She meant the guys roaming around who looked like high-priced mouthpieces even in agitprop T-shirts. If that was the only problem there, I could abide it. Miserably, my gym calls itself a health club—there are ferns, mirrored walls and lots of enigmatic women strutting in colored tights.

Lila made the evening a trial. She wore one of Pam's too-tight pastel body stockings and tied up her war bonnet with orange ribbon. She sashayed around the floor to chitchat as if she were the leaser of the yacht. I ground out three miles on the treadmill in between her visits.

"Why's everyone so angry?" she would ask. Or, "That girl over there, she went to my high school!" Or, "What's the word for 'no way' in New York?" Finally, I gave up and declared I was showering. Lila said, "Whirlpool, you promised!"

That's enough explanation as to how foolish I felt bobbing in the whirlpool under track lighting with beefy lawyers and big-hipped bombshells of the Aquarian Age around me, while slinky, black-suited Lila floated her youthful forty-one close and started her strange report about brother-in-law Charlie Purcell.

"It's this. Charlie's coming apart on us, and it's my fault. I got them together in Singapore. Pammie was just divorced from a Silicon Valley nerd, and I'd met Charlie, since Singapore's a small town if you're not Chinese, so . . ."

I told her to delay autobiography and get to the opium pipes.

"You know about that? Did Pammie tell you? Rosie, huh? Well, he's been making Rosie set up his pipes for him like a damned *fumerie*. He was always a user, but he had it under control until the last couple of years. I haven't been around much, but Pammie's told me."

I urged her on to the "terrible thing." What did Charlie do in Korea that the hobgoblins are coming for him?

Lila clutched my shoulders for balance. We were simmering and had only minutes before the whirlpool made us soup.

"Charlie," she said, rolling herself up to my ear, hot breath on hot tissue, "sold some information to somebody when he was there. In the Army. Sort of army information. He did it for money and for kicks, he says."

She added, "He was young, and he did it. Sixteen, seventeen years ago. I got this out of him on one of his jags years ago."

I report that, while Lila whispered and clutched, I was thinking eloquently, *Oh no.* Get out. This is paranoia.

I did mumble one word. "Blackmail?"

Lila whispered, "You've got that right. He needs money, lots of it. That's why I was in Paris. Well, it's a little more f——ed up than that."

I bumped her aside.

"What's the matter?" she said. "I thought you wanted me to tell you this way."

"Out," I said angrily. "Get dressed."

We bought a good pizza on the way home, and I tried to keep Lila shut until we had some security in my computer room. Not that I seriously thought I was being scanned. It was the lingering paranoia—I needed to feel I had a safe house. None of my precaution interested Lila. Now that she'd started, she was the Tigris and Euphrates of confession.

"It's my fault, really, about Charlie," Lila would declare whenever she felt sorry for herself. "I got Pammie to marry him, and now what do I do? Charlie's such a jerkoff."

The important points of Lila's confession are worth reviewing. It's not necessary to quote her at length, since she botched many details and, when it involved her, she often lied. For example, I figured that she'd brought Charlie home to her own Singapore bed before she'd passed him on to divorced little sister Pam for matrimony. I could say that Lila only lied to make me like her. Then again, Lila lied all the time, just like everybody else when they're in trouble.

In any event, I am telling you the truth of what I learned at the time from Lila's noncandid report.

Sometime in 1973–74, Spec 4 Charlie got hooked by bad guys working on our doped-up soldiers in and around Seoul. The Vietnam War had wrecked our army; its esprit was negative numbers, and, when that happens, it's not an army, it's kids with guns feeling bullied and forgotten.

Lila didn't say it, but I assumed that the bad guys who hooked Charlie were working for North Korea. This doesn't mean Moscow or Beijing; the bad-guy world is competitive gangs buying and selling information. Just the price matters to them.

Charlie's bad guys hooked him with a bribe to marry a prostitute and ship her back to the States (the old Mata Hooker trick).

And then, for more money, they bought information passing over his Spec 4 desk. Lila didn't know what kind of information, or how it was done. Charlie had told her it was "chickenshit." My supposition was that Charlie had sold them operations material, useful for a short time. But what proved long-term useful to them was having this "terrible thing" on Charlie that they could use for blackmail.

According to Lila, the bad buys didn't squeeze Charlie for a long time. He left the Army, graduated from business school at Berkeley, took a good job with the behemoth Bank Pacifica. Soon he prospered in a banker way and signed on with a hot investment bank called First California, a breakaway from Bank Pacifica. Charlie went overseas like a good gofer, Manila, Hong Kong and Osaka in several quick years, riding out the late-1970s oil crises. Eventually, he sat fat in First California's Singapore office.

According to Lila, that's when the bad guys began the blackmail. Singapore, in the early 1980s. They didn't want cash, they wanted information.

"All kinds," Lila said. "You'll have to ask him, but I can guess, can't you?"

What was passing over Charlie's Singapore bank desk wasn't army secrets, it was paper gold. The bad guys had moved from black operations to greed.

Charlie paid them off whenever they asked. He didn't like it, but he learned to live with it. I figured the opium might have been part of how Charlie lived with it. Also, he became ever more childlike—pliable, self-pitying, given to tantrums and, of course, the satisfaction of being a playboy. That's how he'd met Lila. Charlie was a swinger. Lila was a swinger—twice divorced and, according to Lila's chronology, on her way to becoming a rag-trade queen.

In 1983, Lila hooked Charlie to her own purpose and got him married to Pam. Charlie and Pam adopted an oriental child; they acted the good burghers in Singapore society and tried several times to make their own child, succeeding in 1985.

Nevertheless, as Charlie flourished, the blackmail continued.

In 1988, Charlie made his break from First California. He became a partner with the newer, hotter investment bank named Horizon Pacific Securities Company, in their Tokyo office.

Lila wasn't certain, but she thought there'd been trouble again in Tokyo. Pam had called Lila one weekend, weeping that Charlie had disappeared. That Charlie had come home from the hospital claiming he'd been sick, and then he'd vanished. Pam was hysterical on the phone with Lila all that week. And then Charlie had returned from points unknown. No explanation as to why he'd been at the hospital or where he'd spent the missing week.

In the spring of 1989, Charlie had transferred to Horizon Pacific's office in New York. He and Pam had bought a house in Ridgewood, New Jersey, had adopted another oriental baby.

According to Lila, that's when the blackmailers had reached out again—spring 1989.

I asked Lila a trick question at this point. "When did Charlie tell you all this?"

"Last spring." She waved where she thought New Jersey was.

"Check your pocket calendar," I said. "You reported 'years ago' in the first scenario."

"I can't keep it straight sometimes," Lila said. "What's the difference when he told me? I knew something was weird with him the first time I met him. But who isn't weird sometimes? That act of his—poor, poor me. I didn't know it wasn't an act until last spring, when he went nuts one night. I was visiting Pammie to help with the move into the Ridgewood house. She'd been miserable on the phone for weeks. Marriage troubles, I thought, since they were back here without a houseful of servants, and all Pam had was Rosie."

I asked if Pam knew about Lila's romantic past with Charlie.

Lila flushed useful pink and ignored the question. "Pam knows about Charlie now," she said, "because I told her after he jumped me last spring. In the Ridgewood house. He went berserk! And when I hit back, he told me what I've told you. I should have thrown him out, packed up Pammie and the kids and taken us all back to Singapore until the divorce went through. Shit, who needs this! But—I guess because I feel like it's my fault and . . ."

This is Lila's Scenario Two, How I Found Out, What I Did.

I pushed Lila to make more guesses.

Lila guessed that Charlie had gone "berserk" because the blackmailers had reached out all the way to New Jersey. But then, after his outburst, Charlie seemed to calm down the following day. Lila guessed that Charlie must have decided to pay off his blackmailers again. Lila had acted as if Charlie hadn't told her anything, as if the trouble were Pammie's restlessness in Ridgewood.

Six months later, the Purcells had soothed their domestic upset with property—the purchase of the Riverside Drive penthouse, the renovation, the move into New York.

"I thought it'd be okay to visit again for Christmas, to help Pammie with the move again," Lila said. "It happened all over again. Christmas night, Charlie jumped me in one of his fits. 'They've got me,' he says. 'Help me!' What was I supposed to do? He told me unless I helped him, they were going to kill him."

I interrupted, "So you came up with the scheme to buy back whatever proof they have on Charlie, right?"

"Yeah," she said, "how did you know?"

"Blackmail. I've seen the movie."

It was odd, I thought, that Charlie hadn't come up with Lila's solution before.

Odder still that Charlie needed Lila's money. I asked, "Where's his money?"

"He's really rich," she said, "but you know bankers. It's not liquid with them."

She finished her tale quickly. Right after Christmas, Lila gave Charlie what he asked for—seven and a half million yen (about fifty thousand dollars). Then she went home to Singapore.

"He wanted it in yen?" I asked.

"That's the way we think in Asia—dollars are for knickknacks, yen are for deals."

January passed without news from him. Then Charlie called mid-February to say that she must come to New York. That he needed more money. That the blackmailers said his New Year's fee had only been a bona fides.

"So I came over, and he promised me this was going to be the last of it," she said. "I went to Paris. I raised the money. I mean, I'm going to be in hock for the century but—but yesterday, he called me in Paris and said it wasn't going to work unless I could get twice that amount. Twice. Tip, now he wants *one hundred and fifty million yen!* That's almost a million dollars!"

I stopped Lila's confession before she repeated herself.

Besides, her long nose was growing right in front of me. Don't bother remembering either Lila's Scenario One or Two, entitled How I Found Out, What I Did. They were later to be replaced.

It was nearly eleven. I went to make another pot of tea. I figured Charlie was home sucking an opium pipe to find the mood to come down and lie to me.

Meanwhile, Lila visited the toilet. From the kitchen, I got to hear one sorrowful sniff. This was a fake weep by Lila; she's a puncher, not a weeper.

To calm myself, I carried the tea tray back to my computer room, sat in my commander's chair, punched up *Admiral Dread* and decided to go fishing for the Imperial Japanese fleet. My thoughts were simple: I like dramatic redheads; I don't like them when they talk espionage and blackmail.

Lila returned from the bathroom in poor shape after a transatlantic day followed by (sort of) confession.

". . . but, Tip," she started in the middle of a paragraph, "what do you think?"

I clicked *Dread* on suspension and gave her my blunt opinion. "You've got gargantuan trouble."

"Shit, I know," she said, managing that glance that the camera loves—the wet eyes. In her case, wet chestnut eyes. "I listened to myself tell you. Boy, am I dumb."

It was easy to agree.

She plopped down on my executive officer's chair. "I'm afraid of Charlie—for Pam and the children. You've seen him." She snapped alert. "And what he wants—I can't raise that much. And if I do, what if they send him to jail? I've got creditors, I've got debt service. Do you know how much it costs to borrow a million dollars?"

"A lot," I said brilliantly.

"He *says* he's good for it. He *says* he just needs time, and, if I help him now, he'll make it up to me."

I didn't bother pressing Lila about where Charlie's money was. It was probably in the robotics, the stupid secret that Jimmy Flowers had advertised to me. Why speculate? There were too many unanswered questions already. Such as: Why is Lila here telling me anything? Why did Charlie spring his "terrible thing" at 5:00 A.M.? What do they really want from me?

The only answer I had was that they were all lying to each other, and needed me not to lie to. Not very much.

"You're smart, Lila," I began again, "so do the smart thing. At eleven o'clock on a Thursday night, do nothing."

"What the f——!" she exploded. "I married my little sister to a crook! And your great advice is nothing! Tell me to go to the FBI, tell me to kick Charlie out, anything. But not nothing."

I weakened. "Your Paris loan was transferred to Singapore, correct?"

"Yes."

"Call Singapore, make sure it's safe from man and machine, then go to sleep. We'll talk again tomorrow."

"Okay, I can do that," she said. "You'll be here, won't you? If Charlie goes nutsoid again tonight, you'll be here?"

I saw what I'd missed. "Lila," I asked, "when Charlie jumps you with his opium pipe and uppers, does he *jump* you? Pam in the next room and his kids asleep?"

"The word is rape," she said coolly, "and I'm not using it." Lila didn't look good when she didn't say it. "Thanks, Tip, but really, with you and Rosie around, I can handle that jerkoff."

Rosie, I thought, I almost forgot about Rosie. I asked, "Does he *jump* Rosie?"

Lila ignored the question. "Rosie can handle him better than me. She's great. After Pammie hired Rosie last spring, Charlie cooled right out. Rosie, she's"—Lila looked down and aside, eyes rolling quickly as if recalling a scene she'd witnessed, trying to decide again what she'd actually witnessed—"she's great, Rosie's a real tough lady."

I lit my pipe like a nosy shamus and asked a question so peculiar it surprised me. "Did Rosie tell you to come talk to me tonight?"

"Kind of. She likes you. She says you're funny."

Note this as I did then: Rosie the governess was working hard to make everything happy in her golden realm.

I walked Lila to the kitchen door and let her lie to me that she felt better.

Eventually, I went back to being Commander Paine. I knew the penthouse crowd was coming back, and there was little I could do but wait them out. Truth, it was my opinion then that however tricked up it was, what the Purcells had was family trouble, and I was not family, so there was nothing I could do for them.

No, it wasn't that tidy for me. I felt intimidated by them. If what Lila said was half accurate, Charlie was a dangerous man. How about confronting Charlie with a "Dear FBI" letter? How about me just running away to Cairo?

I laughed myself out of this. Was it then that Rosie came knocking again? Or was it after I made the telephone call? I can't recall exactly.

Let's make it this way—well after midnight, I heard a rapping on the service door. I was listening for it, since I'd told Lila to tell Rosie to come down when she could.

"Please listen, Mr. Paine," Rosie began, looking vigilant, "I came to tell you, for Mrs. Purcell, that everything's quiet now. Miss Schumann asked me to tell you thanks. All's well in Singapore, she said."

Schumann? Right, Lila and Pam Schumann. I didn't like how

shaky Rosie was acting, that she wasn't trilling and humming lullabies as usual. I decided that I despised Charlie Purcell.

"I've got to get back," Rosie said, "but thank you, please listen, for everything, thank you."

"Rosie," I said, "you get everyone down here like gangbusters if he tries anything *funny*, you got that?"

"He's sick, it's the sickness, I've—" Rosie let her thought go and then started another, which I've told you about already. She quoted me the ingenious Confucian proverb. "Mr. Paine, my people say that even a sheet of paper is lighter if two are lifting it."

She showed her chipped canine in a smile that was hopeful, like the surprisingly ambitious person she was. "Thank you," she said. "I'll see you tomorrow, maybe in the park? Thank you."

It was after then that I called, I'm sure of it. Seeing Lila worn and scared was fretful, but seeing Rosie grim and brave was time for battle stations.

I checked what time it would be in Colorado and called for professional help. Do you remember my baby brother? He's Captain Bunyan Paine, and he's married to Captain Kaelie Paine; and both of them serve in the U.S. Military Intelligence Corps. Correct, I called my brother and sister spycatchers. It was time to do nothing the smart way. In the end, you see, Rosie and I had the same governess version of the world. When the family's in trouble, call the family together and fight; that is, in this life, even a sheet of paper is lighter if two are lifting; that is, all happy families are the same, and if you've got one, use it.

5

"You Can't Spit on a Smiling Face"

(The Interrogation of Charlie Purcell)

CHARLIE TRIED the *funny* stuff called murder. Saturday night, at the beginning of Pam's housewarming for the bankers, Charlie murdered himself. Absent on opium, jagged on uppers, goldilocks in his tuxedo, he closed himself in Rosie's bathroom and swallowed a pharmacy of Valium, while making at least one slash at his Rolex band with a serrated knife. I detail all this because, being Charlie, he screwed up and didn't get close to death. He fainted.

I was home at the time, sitting in my commander's chair and chatting with Lila. She was black-gowned and pearl-choked for the soiree, a splendid Singapore garden under red. I was secure in my khakis, arguing about our date. My conviction was negative.

"You promised!" was Lila's conviction. She said she'd done everything I'd asked about Charlie, hadn't she? Thursday night, she'd locked her money in Singapore and refused to release it to him. Friday and Saturday, she'd endured his self-pitying rage and told him she wanted the weekend to think it over.

Tonight, she needed my support for this party, so did Pam, so did Rosie.

That's when Rosie came pounding on my kitchen door. She was bloody-handed but not hysterical, the opposite—a governess in command. "He's hurt himself," she started. "Please, come and help me. We can't let the children see."

We raced up the service stairs, through the caterers, into Rosie's bedroom—the maid's quarters off the kitchen. Charlie was twisted sideways on her slender bed. He was retching and weeping. Rosie had wrapped a wet towel around his wrist.

I could see right away that he wasn't going to die. He was going to evacuate his innards. I'd dealt with this kind of murder before, and, apparently, so had Rosie. She said she'd already made him drink an herbal concoction that cleaned out his system. What help she needed, she said, was to get him away from his children and guests.

While Rosie cleared the caterers out of the kitchen, I pulled the sheet over Charlie's head and manhandled 165 pretty pounds. Out the door, down the stairs, into my apartment. Lila grabbed one of the large trash cans for Charlie's insides. I threw him into the shower off my kitchen. Rosie showed up with sponges.

"Shit, Charlie," complained Lila, who exchanged her gown for a sweatshirt, "why didn't you just jump? It's far enough. Look at my hose!"

Rosie worked muscularly, cleaning and flushing around us. I lit my pipe to mask the vomit and worse, but it didn't work, and Lila and I took turns in the master bath to be sick ourselves. Soon, Charlie was sobbing like a frat drunk. I posted Lila to keep him from drowning himself, while I conferred with Rosie.

"I want to call a doctor," Rosie said. "I've given him penicillin but—" She held up the empty Valium bottle. "I don't think I should call EMS, do you? They'll take him to St. Luke's, and there'll be a police report. Isn't that the way?"

I said his stomach lining needed a doctor.

"I could call my pastor, he'd know," she said, "or better, my friends. You met Lee Sang Ju. His brother's an intern."

Remember the three Lees? I told you to keep your eye on them. Here they come again, and the best part of it was that I welcomed them.

Rosie had more good ideas. "Please listen. We've got to help Mrs. Purcell with the guests. Can you and Miss Schumann do that? I'll take care of Mr. Purcell. You could say he's sick, is that good? And Miss Schumann could calm Mrs. Purcell?"

I agreed to the assignment, and so did Lila. We were wobbly, very distracted, but we faked our way together. While I showered and dressed, Lila recovered her gown. ("No remarks," she said. "I'm without foundations and look at my face!") We walked arm in arm upstairs and through bright rooms full of shiny bankers and diamond wives. (Lila asked, "Do my hands stink, do they, Tip?") And then we lied to them inanely: Charlie's sick, he wants you to have a good time, he apologizes. Lila also handled Pam, getting her and the kids into the back rooms.

The whole farce couldn't have taken more than a half hour. As soon as the word got around that Charlie was a no-show, the partygoers abandoned ship. Lila and I stood at the door and waved good-bye. It's impressive how easy it is to handle bankers with big lies. They hear an iceberg crunch, they know the way to the boats.

(Citizen Paine said this better: ". . . The rich are in general slaves to fear, and submit to courtly power with the trembling duplicity of a spaniel.")

Jimmy Flowers was the last curly cur out. At the door, Lila teased him deftly. "Why don't you call tomorrow, *Jaaaames.* Charlie better explain this himself."

"Good," said Flowers. "He's good, though, *heyyy?* Bad stomach or what?" Lila looked beautifully blank. Flowers tried me. "Tell Charlie to take it easy and call me later."

I spoke up halfheartedly. "He's not a robot, Jim."

Flowers worked his thick neck.

I wish now that I'd added something nasty. Such as saying, He's not dead yet, worse luck for you, Bobsledder. I didn't say this, because I wasn't certain that Flowers was involved in Charlie's suicide. Not absolutely certain. I couldn't fit what Lila had told me with what Flowers and Charlie had told me (all this deception and double-talk) with the *sure thing* of robotics near the Sea of Japan. Still, when in doubt, I must remember that men like Flowers don't sweat in New York in February unless they're *not* not guilty.

Later, as the caterers packed up the remains of the Purcell

Titanic, Lila poured five milligrams of Valium into Pam, and we three prepared to face Charlie.

Pam was frightened, confessional. "He's tried this before. I told you, Lila. He did, right after we moved to Tokyo. He fibbed about it, but he came home real dopey one night, and he said he'd been to the hospital for stomach cramps."

I asked, "The week he disappeared?"

"You know about that? Ohhhh, it was just like this."

Downstairs, the Korean emergency medical squad had things under control. They'd moved Charlie into my second bedroom. Pam and Lila went in to goldilocks. I waited with the Koreans.

Radiant Lee Sang Ju stood ahead of his slim and so-called brother, the intern. I think of Lee Sang Ju as Youngest Lee. He acted tactfully embarrassed. "Please forgive our presence, Dr. Paine. It is an honor to introduce you to my brother, Dr. Lee. We are together reading your library."

His so-called brother, the intern, stepped up, bowed ceremoniously, offered me his business card. "Your friend is to recover, Dr. Paine, and I hope I am of assistance to you."

I pocketed his card. Good Korean manners would have had me return mine. Instead, I glanced to Rosie.

Rosie whispered discreetly to me, "They're upset that they came into your home while you were away. Tell them there's 'no problem.' Koreans like to hear 'no problem.' It relaxes them."

I obeyed. The so-called brothers brightened.

The significant result of this cultural exchange was that I insisted that Charlie remain in my second bedroom rather than return to harry his family.

Pam disagreed, until big sister persuaded her. I liked Lila for how she conducted herself throughout the crisis. I found myself watching her for my own lead. Lila was many negative things— covetous, libertine, greedy, devious, blockheaded—yet she was also boldly competent in an emergency, never brittle or reluctant, a team player who, whenever possible, bossed.

Neither of us matched Rosie's skills. By the time we'd done doubting, Rosie stood by to take the night watch at Charlie's bedside, ever alert, ever clever, Rosie the governess.

Also significant that night, and again Sunday afternoon, when I woke up, was that I again called my baby brother and his wife, Captain Bunyan Paine and Captain Kaelie Paine, of the Military

Intelligence Corps. I'll tell you about our conversations soon.
What you need to know now is that I had finally gotten myself
organized. There was a suicidal junkie in my second bedroom,
two fretful sisters upstairs in the penthouse begging me to help
them and a loving Korean governess standing tall, urging me to
help everybody.

And so I, the Puritan scold, began my interrogation of Charlie
Purcell. My method was first Lila, second Pam, work up to Charlie, repeat and repeat, then get them together and preach.

Lila had told me a deal already; there was always more to learn
from her.

"Why'd he try to kill himself?" she snapped back at me Sunday
afternoon. "Because he's a coward and I wouldn't give him the
money. I did what you said, nothing. And he tries to check out on
us. It's my fault, isn't it?"

Pam was a more delicate informant. "I don't know why he did
it," she told me at supper in her kitchen Sunday night. "Lila says
he needs the money for them, you know, the blackmailers. He's
already borrowed us all the way out, I think, and my jewelry was
next. He told me something about our will. . . . How long have I
known about it? Years, Tip. He told me, a long time ago, there
was something terrible he'd done, and he couldn't get away from
it. . . . Did I know what it was? I knew it was something in Korea.
Lila told me about the Army. But he was so young! He's a traitor,
isn't he? What happens to him if they find out? What happens to
me and the children? I don't want him to turn himself in, Tip.
I've thought about it, and I don't. He says he can't, that something
terrible will happen. Maybe I do, I don't know. . . . What should
we do? Yes, I blame myself, wouldn't you?"

I didn't approach Charlie until Rosie gave me permission.
Monday afternoon I got my first chance. Charlie remained in my
second bedroom, languorous and self-infatuated, either listening
to Beethoven's string music, watching VCR tapes or staring at
window and walls. He also read from my bookshelves. I caught
him flipping through my autographed BOMC printing of that
Cold War classic *I Led Three Lives*, by Herbert A. Philbrick. He
also ogled Armstrong, Collins and Aldrin's *First on the Moon*,
reliving great moments from our Cold War youth.

(No alternate life for you, Charlie, I thought; this is it.)

I knew much of his dreaminess was the opium. Rosie had

fetched him his pipes of courage, and I didn't protest. He was an addict. The poppies were his execrable consolation.

Monday at 2:00 P.M., I took a comfortable seat at his bedside and said flatly to him that I knew about the blackmail.

That I knew the chronology, too: Army, Korea, Berkeley B school, Bank Pacifica, First California, Singapore, Horizon Pacific, Tokyo and New York. That I knew he'd been paying them off for years with information. That now he'd tried to change the deal and buy back their proof on him. That he wanted a big sum from Lila. That he'd panicked last week when they'd doubled the big sum, and that, when Lila wouldn't cooperate, he'd tried supreme cowardice.

Charlie didn't like that I said I knew so much. He pretended it didn't matter, sighing and staring away. I'd solved his fey, enlightened manner already, when, a good snoop, I'd checked his library shelves Sunday night. He owned many fancy biographies and letter collections of fancy artists, especially the junkies, studying how to avoid inconvenient morality with narcotized narcissism. This is big talk for what Lila said of him: "Jerkoff." He was a pretty one though, *GQ* perfect in his peach silk dressing gown, azure ascot tucked to accent his dopey blue irises, a golden gentleman down on his luck and getting used to it.

He sighed deeper. "Why'd I do it?" Charlie lied. "Because I couldn't face it anymore."

"Gee, Charlie," I said, "you've faced it for years. Why did you try to get out Saturday night, in Rosie's bathroom, with pills and a serrated knife? What's different?"

"I haven't got what they want," he lied. "Lila won't help me anymore. I've done a terrible thing, and what's the use?"

I didn't waste breath telling him the use was his wife and children, perhaps what was left of his soul.

I presented the obligatory remark: "Turn yourself in."

"I can't," he lied, covering up with victimhood, eyelids shut like a corpse's, in case I was watching.

He presented me with another obligatory remark: "Are you going to help me? Lila says you can. Rosie says—please, Tip?"

I enjoyed myself. "Maybe."

"I'm not much to help, am I?"

"Let's review," I said. "You say: 'What's the use?' 'I can't.' 'I'm not much.' Is that all of it? Now we can try *facts*. Why did you suddenly decide to take Lila's suggestion to pay them off after a decade of passing information?"

"I don't know," he lied. "It seemed like a good idea."

"The gold standard's a good idea."

Charlie asked, "You think so?"

"Macroeconomics later," I said. "Let's get on to: How much, when, where, how, who and what are you buying back?"

"I haven't got it!" Charlie lied. This was acted with passion. He could turn his opiated serenity on and off like a radio. "I gave them seven and a half million yen right after New Year's. That was supposed to be it. But then they said seven and a half million yen was a bona fides. They said that 'to agree the end' would cost more, could I suggest a closing fee? It's like that with them, really polite, while they rob you. So I tried a surprise move. I offered them ten times the first payment for everything. Seventy-five million yen. It works with them, you know. They have this saying, 'You can't spit on a smiling face.' "

"Not bad, Confucius," I said.

"One big closing fee and I was out," Charlie lied. "I didn't hear back for a month. Then they telexed me they'd take the deal. It was going to work. I called Lila, and she came over, and she went to Paris to raise it, and she got me the money, most of it. But they were jerking me around. Because last week, last Wednesday, they telexed again that the closing fee was *one hundred and fifty million yen.* Twice what I'd offered! And Lila won't help me!"

"What's the problem?" I asked. "You've got a deal. All prices are negotiable. I don't have to tell you. Price is a frill when you've got someone ready to deal. You told Lila you're good for her share. Good for half, good for all."

"I will be," Charlie lied, too quickly, "but they want it now. They don't wait. It's like I'm a goddamned servant."

"Where's your swag, Charlie?" I asked. "How come you didn't have even fifty thousand bucks at Christmas? You could've raised that on Pam's rocks."

Charlie made a boo-boo then; he showed his pouty lip and talked the tv punk. "What d'ya think I am, hock my wife's jewels?"

At this, I got temperamental and showed Charlie that, if we were going to do tv, he was up against a Hollywood salesman.

"Suck it up," I advised, "and listen up."

I told Charlie what he should have been telling me. I said that the reason he had gone along with Lila's idea to change the arrangement and buy his way out was robotics. That he'd pitied himself for ten years about being blackmailed, yet he'd always paid them off when they'd asked, since it cost him nothing. A few facts, a lot of rumor, so what? There's no SEC in Asia.

"There's no SEC in Asia," I repeated, "not in Asia, not in Europe, not on the moon, not anywhere but a couple of blocks north and south of Tom Paine Park, Charlie, a couple of blocks, that's all, and that might be overestimating."

But now, I told Charlie, he wanted to change his no-cost arrangement because he was about to change, because he was about to get *sure thing* rich. That he'd always thought of himself as a mortgaged partner, a bagman. Now the bag was going to be his. And like most rich folk I know about, I declaimed, he felt more vulnerable at forty with the big bag he didn't have quite yet than he had at twenty-three, when he only had a uniform to lose.

"You're greedy, Charlie," I preached. "That ain't news. What might be news to you is, the more you've got to lose, the less you want to try losing it. I stole this proof. I'll steal again. 'Uneasy lies the head that *almost* wears the crown.' "

Charlie sighed and drooped as I blasted away Monday afternoon. Yet he didn't spill any more lies.

When Rosie came in to tend to his worldly needs, I broke contact. Charlie wasn't fragile; he was used to getting away with being fragile, and he needed to recharge with his pipes.

Monday night, I called Colorado again. I also conferred with Lila ("Shit, the shithead, he never told *me* that. Robotics? What's the company, do you think? . . ."), and I tried to console Pam ("I can't get through to him anymore, he won't listen to me. He'll listen to you, he likes you. . . ."), and, finally, I asked Rosie ("He's sick, Mr. Paine, and you're helping him get better and he knows that. You know it too, don't you? Thank you. . . .").

Tuesday afternoon, I returned to Charlie at the same time as on Monday. This is counterintelligence flimflam. Let the hostile intelligence source expect you, let him believe it's just one long squeal.

"It's like you said," Charlie lied. "If I don't get out now, I never will." He was more sallow today, in a new shade of silk dressing gown, salmon, as if to offset his fading ruddiness. "But what can I do? Do you know? I know you don't like me for what I've done. But what?"

Charlie tried the question that had probably made those new shadows in his face. "Are you going to turn me in, Tip?"

I said it was a smart question.

"You said you were going to help me. That's what Pam said this morning. Lila told her you said so. And Rosie says you're going to help me, she said so."

"*Maybe* is what I said," I corrected. "It's just you and me here. Let's leave the innocent bystanders out of it today."

Charlie bounced with his brainstorm. "You haven't got any evidence, do you? I've said things, but—"

I asked him if it was time to call his mouthpiece.

"No, no," Charlie lied, "it's that they have evidence on me, they say, but nobody else does, do they? I got an honorable discharge. I'm clean as far as . . . And in your books! You say that espionage, you know, trading secrets, is the crime without a weapon. What you call it, 'Gossip Writ Large.' That they can't prove it, not without catching you in the act, maybe not even then. . . ."

I let him cheer himself up awhile with his fatuous logic and some of mine. "Gossip Writ Large" was my sort of sci-fi/spy joke, yet Charlie was passing it back to me like a legal brief.

Charlie's display did make me feel better. It reminded me that though he was in bed in my home without any support beyond a faithful wife who visited him as if he were in a sanitarium and a heroic governess who lit his pipes for him, that though he was a traitor, coward, addict and quitter, he was still a banker who liked to wheedle and bluff. I perversely liked him for this. It cleaned my motives of pity. Thanks for reminding me, I thought. I despise you, Charlie, and I'm working on hating you.

"Let's get back to facts, Charlie," I interrupted. "Forget espionage. That's what you did once upon a time, and I can't spell 'espionage' correctly all the time myself. What they're doing now is blackmail, and I can spell that. We dealt with why and how much yesterday. Today it's how, who, when and where."

"Do you think there's a chance? Can we get the money? Will Lila help me? What's Pammie really say?"

"Facts," I said.

"I paid them seven and a half million yen January third," Charlie lied. "Like I told you. A wire transfer from Singapore to Seoul. Yeah, Lila's bank, mine too once. I still keep a dummy account there." Charlie preened a moment. "Singapore to Seoul, a commercial bank there, Bank of East Asia. It was a dummy account in Seoul, too, probably. Cutout, right? A week later, in the mail, they sent me the picture. I'd seen it before. It was the first thing they sent me back when it started. A picture of one of my meetings with Mr. Kim."

A major general of a fact. I saluted: "Who's Mr. Kim, Charlie? Who took it? Where was it? And what kind of picture? Snapshot? Telephoto lens? Blowup of a detail?"

"How the f—— should I know?" he lied. "Just a picture! You think I posed for it? It was in Seoul, along the river. It's me in uniform, okay? It's not important, it's just their little reminder."

"It's very important," I said. "Let's call it the Tableau of Treason. They began the blackmail with it in Singapore. They wouldn't use it again unless it was important. Seoul. The Han River. Tell me about the other guy in the picture. Korean, right?"

Charlie lied, "Mr. Kim is what he said his name was. Mr. Kim. Great help, huh, there's only like about twenty million Kims in Korea."

"There's only one Mr. Kim we care about," I said.

"He was nobody," Charlie lied. "Just a taxi driver they used as an errand boy."

"He's more than that," I said.

"What's that mean?"

"They began the blackmail with Mr. Kim," I explained. "The same Mr. Kim costs fifty thousand dollars in 1990. Mr. Kim sounds like a prominent player."

"A nobody!" he lied.

"Have you seen Mr. Kim since Korea?"

Charlie ignored the question.

"So I burned the picture and made the deal I told you about. Seventy-five million yen and finished. It's awful to wait like that! It's what I hate most. That's the way it is with them. I thought, after I left Singapore, they'd quit it. But it was the same in Tokyo. And after I got here, the same thing. What could I do? There won't be an in from the cold for me, huh?"

"Skip the palaver," I said. "How does it work?"

"They send me telexes from Seoul or Hong Kong or wherever, twice from Singapore to me at Singapore. Was that scary! They don't mess around, no code or shit. Just straight-out English, funny sometimes, like it's being translated. They don't say when they want a reply, but with them it means instantly."

He threw the bed covers back as if they were afire. "They said yes! Then they doubled the price! For the whole package, one hundred and fifty f——ing million yen!"

I didn't applaud; I lit my pipe and asked, "What is the package, Charlie? What have they got on you?"

Charlie lied, "I don't know, more pictures probably, maybe some tapes. All I ever sold them was some roster shit, like motor-pool assignments, who drives what colonel, where such and such a driver went last month. Like expense-account stuff. I was a clerk at battalion HQ. S-3, you know? Operations. Chickenshit. And they paid me maybe two thousand bucks all told."

"How many times did you sell them this 'chickenshit'?"

"I don't remember," he lied.

"When did you first sell to them?" I asked.

"What's the difference?" he lied.

"The difference is 1973 or 1974," I said.

"I did it," he lied, "that's all."

(If you're wondering about all the lies, don't. I knew he was lying. I also knew that, in counterintelligence, lies are what you get for clues. I didn't care to explore Charlie's trading-with-the-enemy scenario just then. Motor-pool assignments? Chauffeur gab? For two thousand 1973–74 dollars? There had to be much more to it. Also Charlie still hadn't figured out that whatever he'd sold them, the deal had included his soul.)

I did want to hear the routine of the blackmail from the beginning.

Charlie told me that first contact—the snapshot—was in the winter of 1981, *several months after he'd arrived in Singapore.*

Charlie had panicked; he'd hoped it would go away. Then the telexes started. A decade of them. The blackmailers wanted facts and rumors of facts. Charlie had access to First California's data. Also, since FC was a breakaway from behemoth Bank Pacifica, he could gain access to a gigantic financial network, ranging worldwide. The telexes wanted to know who was selling off a subsidiary, who was undervalued, overextended, leveraged, friendly, hostile, at risk. I didn't understand all this jargon and didn't care to. I knew it was banker bunkum, 1980s-style, the now-infamous decade of the scavengers.

I asked Charlie for a list of the companies the blackmailers had been interested in.

It was too long to write down. All kinds, public and private. I recall a lot of mining and shipping. And the public companies were from every exchange in Asia—Tokyo, Hong Kong, Singapore, Sydney, New Zealand. Later, they'd inquired about European exchanges.

I asked, "When did the European traffic start?"

"Eighty-five, maybe eighty-six," he lied, flicking his pretty fingers, catching his pretty nails on his pretty wedding band. "I remember inquiries from Helsinki, two of them on the day *Challenger* went down. About the Stockholm exchange."

I noted 1986 in Helsinki. The blackmailers lived on jet lag.

Charlie also recalled inquiries re Siemens on the Frankfurt exchange, also re a host of banks from the Amsterdam, Brussels, Zurich, Milan and Stockholm exchanges.

Just for fun, I asked after De Beers in Johannesburg.

Charlie laughed. "You like De Beers? What is it you have for diamonds?"

"I bought one once," I admitted, "and it was so magnificent I had to hire her a lawyer."

"Are you telling me why you live like this—a stylite?"

"That's a genuine compliment," I said. "So I'll tell you what you've already figured out: 'If my pants knew my plans, I'd burn them.' "

Charlie displayed what I'd not seen before, a sense of humor: "That a line from your movies? Or are you robbing graves again?"

"A cheap turn of Frederick the Great," I admitted, "and I like it because I don't understand it."

We bantered on, and I've included this much to demonstrate that my interrogation wasn't uniform flimflam. Before fate and the poppies, there'd been the makings of a citizen in him. When I spend time with strangers, I get to liking them for being so strange.

Eventually, we got back to the necessary tedium of facts. Money talk, banker talk, scavenging talk. Charlie did note that, in a decade, there had been no inquiries about American exchanges.

I asked him why.

"I don't know," he said. "You think they're prejudiced?"

In sum, what I learned that day was that Charlie Purcell was blackmailed as an investment counselor. Most well-to-do folk call up their broker. The blackmailers had telexed Charlie.

I did reach one logical conclusion, and it struck him hard. I asked if he had ever used his information for his own pocket.

"Never!" he lied. "There'd be a paper trail right back to me. That'd be crazy! I didn't care what they were doing. You think I'm that stupid? I damn sure never signed my telexes."

"How do they sign theirs?"

"I knew you were going to ask that," he said. "States, geography. Like 'Oklahoma,' 'Pennsylvania,' 'Maryland,' 'Tennessee,' no pattern I could figure. After I went to Tokyo, it was the same all the time, 'Oklahoma' or 'West Virginia.' Really comical. The last three times, it's been 'Arizona.' You think it means something or what?"

"Everything does," I said, "but this might just mean cute."

"Cute like funny?" he asked. "Or cute like dumb?"

"If we're debating brainpower, maybe we should wonder why they haven't switched to fax machines."

Charlie laughed. "I did wonder. They could've faxed me like a deli. Hold the mayo, pickles and Siemens projections." He laughed harder. "Maybe they're just behind the times."

Charlie was indeed in a brighter, more playful mood on Tuesday, so I didn't mention the obvious—that he'd participated in a scheme that was beyond the imagination of every sci-fi/spy salesman I knew: a completely brainless operation.

For a decade, he'd been run by greedy ops who'd taken no precaution whatsoever for their asset, Charlie Purcell. They telexed Charlie at the bank. Charlie replied by telex to Seoul. That simple, that inept. It had never worried either party that telexes are footprints, that the messages had been logged. I could suppose the risk to the blackmailers was minimal, since they were always moving around, and the Seoul address was what is called a dead drop. But the risk to Charlie had been galactic. Was it their joke that they'd signed their telexes after states? (I was overthinking and underestimating.) Anyone could have intercepted the telex traffic at the bank. It was Charlie's kind of luck that he'd gotten away with it for so long.

Then again, I could see that Charlie felt very protected from what he'd done. The single threat he could see was his original folly to sell army secrets. I tried to look at it as Charlie must. I reminded myself there's no SEC in Asia. And what's First California going to do now, fire him? And what's Horizon Pacific going to do, fire him? Maybe. But not if he's a principal deal-maker in the sure thing of robotics near the Sea of Japan.

Charlie felt secure, except for whatever the blackmailers held on him.

At the end of Tuesday's session, I tried to get past Charlie's security screen by doubling back over what I'd already learned.

I asked him how he'd met Mr. Kim.

"Really dumb," Charlie lied. "Through some hooker I was going to marry for bucks, you know, get her an American passport, really dumb. She introduced me to the Kim guy."

Another major general of a fact.

I asked, "What was her name?"

"Just some Seoul hooker," he repeated. "What do I care? She was nobody, just like Kim."

I went to attack speed. "Who are the blackmailers?"

"Who the f—— knows," he lied with xenophobic cunning. "One bunch of smart operators. They never had bad questions. I depended on them to point me in directions I'd never heard of. With what I told them, they could've made a lot of killings."

"Who is Mr. Kim?"

"Why do you keep asking? He was just a little guy. He looked like some kind of hustler. How old? Maybe sixty, though it's hard to tell with them. He'd be like in his seventies now. He was just a runner for the big brains, you know, *them.*"

I told Charlie to try again. That he'd made *them* happy for ten years. That they must have watched him. Hadn't he ever looked around in Singapore, in Djakarta, Seoul, Hong Kong, Tokyo, all those lunches with Korean wheeler-dealers, and wondered if it was one of *them?*

"I tried not to think about it," he lied. "What if they watched me? I did what they said. You can't suspect every Korean, they're all over East Asia. The Asian Miracle."

I made the hard point. "What about North Koreans? Mao-suited trade delegations?"

Charlie didn't like this mention of North Korea. "I never got a telex from P'yŏngyang. That's *their* capital. Never. I telexed the capital of *South* Korea."

"Why should South Koreans want 'chickenshit' on a motor pool?"

"I didn't ask," he lied.

"Then again," I said, "why should the North Koreans want it?"

"It was just some hustlers," he lied.

I tried again. "Who are the blackmailers?"

"Tip, they all look the same to us, don't they? Little yellow men. Who cares what they call themselves?"

I tried one last time to get past Charlie's defenses. "What's the telex address in Seoul?"

"No way," said Charlie. "I'm not telling you that. I've read your books; I know how you work. Find a fixed point and work forward or backward. Whadaya call it? Walking the cat."

"You're a good fan, Charlie."

"I've really read your books. I love your books. I love the crummy world in your books. You know, I told you. *'Vice is its own reward.'*"

Charlie grinned beautifully. Then he told me the truth for the first time and maybe the last.

"I don't want to find them. I want to get rid of them. And if Lila will help me, I can do it. Will she? Are you going to tell her to help me? She'll listen to you."

Charlie stood and took an invalid stroll around my second bedroom in his silk dressing gown.

"Because if you aren't going to help me," he argued, "I think we should just quit this." He coughed, acting sickly.

His act had some meaning. When he felt weak, he acted weaker. Telling one truth—that he didn't want to find the black-mailers, he wanted to get rid of them—had wobbled him.

Nonetheless, Charlie had finally called my bluff.

I was ready.

"Yes, Charlie," I said, "I'm going to help you." I got up. "See you tomorrow."

"Now!" he demanded, a finger at me, trying to close the deal. "I need help now or—I've got to get back to the office. I'm flying to Tokyo Saturday. I can't . . ." He wheedled the more.

Tokyo, I thought, why not? There aren't any rules. Pop Valium like cashews one week, jet the polar route the next.

I did have a guess. "Robotics," I said. "Want to tell me what you and muscle-neck Flowers are up to?"

"It's got nothing to do with it," he lied. "I do have a job, you know, besides being blackmailed. And I'm good at it."

I tried to turn him upside down on his vanity. "So you and Flowers are flying to Tokyo to close a takeover of robots? You're principals in the deal, and you're going for equity and board membership, right? A billionaire bazaar."

"If you know so much, you know I can't talk about it."

"What's Flowers got to do with the blackmail? Does he know?"

"Jim Flowers is an asshole. I'd never tell him anything. You're going wrong, this is out of his league." Charlie slumped to the bed. "It's such a bitch. I can't think about it like you. Please, just help me."

I accepted tactical defeat. I called for Rosie and the opium pipes, then went to the gym. I had a dinner date with Lila and Pam at a neighborhood restaurant.

I'll mention here that though I was up late Tuesday night conferring with Lila, I avoided compromising my status as a busybody with regard to her youthful forty-one. Not that she offered, not that I inquired. This is tv detail, for your information, and because I've intimated intimacy with her up till now and not shown you anything beyond my mutt nose. It was a comfortable decision at the time. I favored her style, not her themes. One liar inside my concertina-wired home at a time.

6
TV-Simple

THE FINAL SESSION was Wednesday afternoon. I brought in irritable Lila in ominous black and friendly Pam in motherly pastel. They were under orders to keep shut until necessary.

"What is this?" Charlie demanded. He was in a violet dressing gown today, the well-dressed crybaby. "Pammie, what? Are you going to give me the money, Lila?"

"Blackmail," I began pompously, "a crime of wealth."

I didn't bother reviewing Charlie's lies. I leapt to my tv-simple plan.

I told Charlie he was right to buy back the proof they had on him. He smiled.

I told Lila she was right to hold out on Charlie. She frowned.

I told Pam she was right to think of her family first and last. She sagged.

Rosie was in the park with the preschoolers, or I would have told her she was right to be Rosie.

Salutations done, I told Charlie that what he was going to do was telex Seoul and demand a face-to-face meeting.

I told him that in exchange for the agreed sum of one hundred and fifty million yen, Charlie was to have the "whole package" handed to him personally.

"I can't," Charlie lied. "I'll never get out. They'll videotape me. I'll be paying forever. I can't."

I quoted Confucius correctly: " *'Can one spit at a smiling face?'* You're the face, Charlie. You made the deal. They accepted. Don't spit, smile."

"It won't work," he lied.

Pam pleaded, "Listen to him, Charlie."

Charlie whined, "We haven't got that much. Lila's got only half. I can't raise any more."

Lila remarked, "Tip's got it worked out fine, Charlie."

Charlie glanced weakly to his wife, then guardedly to his sister-in-law.

"You've got it easy," I said. I tallied his penthouse less the mortgage. His limo. His wife's jewelry. Then I turned to Lila and tallied her nonmortgaged house and grounds in Singapore. All this, added to Lila's Paris loan, and Charlie had much, much more than the magic number.

"That's everything," Charlie lied. "Where'll we live? And— shit!—it'll take months to convert. They wanted it last week!"

Lila snapped, "It's a lot of my everything, you jerk."

Lila had agreed the night before, but until that moment I couldn't be certain her guilt was a strong enough motive to commit her house to rescuing her brother-in-law.

Charlie kept harrying us with half-sentences. "How . . . but . . . cash, I need cash. . . ."

Lila broke in with my lines. "You can convert in a day, if you have your lawyer call Tip's lawyer. *He's* got the difference, Charlie, and what we have to do is sign deeds over as collateral."

Charlie blinked at me. "You'd do that?"

I liked how he handled this. Slick goldilocks on the make. Charlie was a professional scavenger. At the bank, he scavenged blips for power; at home, he scavenged women for desire; from me, he'd just scavenged cash.

I interrupted before he started thanking me (or before he started questioning my motive). I said it wasn't that much. That he had five times as much, maybe ten.

"What?" he lied.

(Rust your robots, Charlie, it's just another deal.)

Charlie took his invalid stroll by the windows, stalling and dealing. "So you want me to sign over my co-op and all to you," he asked, "and for that you cover the difference?"

I asked him if he'd done well in school.

"What? Yeah, Phi Beta Kappa, USC, why?"

"I only trust smart guys. Are you a smart guy, Charlie?"

Pam and Lila badgered Charlie awhile. I lit my pipe and congratulated myself for selling my tv-simple plan so far. Everybody likes tv. It's so sociable when it's simpleminded.

Once they'd quieted down, I got back to telling Charlie what he was going to do: telex the blackmailers with a date and place for the rendezvous. A posh hotel in Seoul. Show up. Make the deal. Leave.

"By myself?" he asked.

I said I'd be there, that I didn't need two co-ops and a house in Singapore, I needed a smart guy to come back and pay off his note to me. I added dutifully, "Plus expenses and interest, at the usual credit-card rate."

I enjoyed how Pam and Lila were admiring me as a hero. I was thinking unheroically at the time, nasty notions such as, Charlie, you're getting a chance to screw up one more time, and, Charlie, my help costs and costs and costs.

Charlie lied more, but it's not worth quoting—about himself, his family, himself, his trip to Tokyo, himself, the customary Charlie blither.

The only important detail to fix was the time and place for our rendezvous in Seoul. I'd checked with Rosie about bank holidays, and with Lila about hotels. Next week was clear. The hotel that suited my plan was agreeably at the center of Seoul. I told Charlie to telex that the deal was to be struck at the Royal Chosin, the following Friday, March 16.

"I can do that," he lied. He produced his pocket calendar from his dressing gown and played banker. "I have a week of meetings in Tokyo, but I can get free by Thursday, and hop over. . . ."

He sat back down on my second bed as if at his own teakwood desk. Pam joined him. The troubled couple embraced. Pam asked, "Are you sure you're strong enough? It's only been a few days since—oh, Charlie, what are we going to do, why is this happening to us?"

Charlie concentrated on his new pal, me. "And you're coming with me, Tip, aren't you? I can't do this alone, I just can't."

"Tip will be there," said Lila. She pounced over to stand beside me, another couple with troubles ahead. "We're flying to Singapore tomorrow," she said, "to sign my share over to Tip. Right, Tip? And if we don't hear the right things from Tip's lawyer when we get there, Charlie, forget it. I mean it. We'll be landing Friday afternoon, your time. That's the day after tomorrow, get it, forty-eight of your hours from now. And when Tip calls his lawyer, the paperwork better be done. Don't blow it, Charlie."

We left Charlie and Pam alone to argue. I figured the likelihood he'd not blow it was as high or low as his mood. At some point, I knew he'd have a banker's chat with himself and decide the risk was outweighed by the gain. If my tv-simple plan worked, he'd be free of blackmail. And if he was free of that, there was nothing between him and his robotics plunder near the Sea of Japan except happenstance.

I'm not going to labor the rest of that night. Charlie tried to back out once or twice, Lila had to yell at him some more, and Pam wept and coddled. Since all this went on in my apartment, I tried the gym and the video-game pizza parlor for respite, and later I tried visiting Rosie in the penthouse.

Rosie was sturdy and true, the only one who considered thanking me for busybodying in another family's business. She'd cared for Charlie, cared for the children and Pammie, and still had energy to care for me.

"He's so scared, Mr. Paine. He doesn't mean most of what he says. I know you're helping him. I prayed that you would. Is this okay to tell you?"

"It's fine, Rosie," I said, "you're great."

She hesitated. I thought she was going to ask me if everything was going to be all right. Instead, she turned toward the windows, looking out to the GW bridge. "Please listen, Mr. Paine, do you know about the pagans in Korea, the witches you can pay to go into hell and bring back someone's soul?"

"A little," I said, "very little. I've read about it."

"It's mostly a trick," Rosie said, "you know, a scam, and I've always been ashamed of my people for it. They use it a lot, even the Christians, always worrying about spirits and demons."

"I would, too, if I could stop laughing at my Puritan fore-fathers."

Rosie bypassed my crack. "I was going to make a joke that you're a big, a very big witch," she said, chip-toothed smile and firm black eyes. "It is okay to joke about this?"

I liked her tremendously. "It's sensational to joke anytime."

Rosie looked sober. "Please listen. Tell me what I can do, what you want me to do."

"Get him on the plane, Rosie."

"Yes, yes," she said, her big shoulders tightened for burdens. "I understand, Mr. Paine."

Yes, you did understand, Rosie, and when I think back upon all the trouble and lies and deaths that Charlie caused, you are the one who still makes me smile, now and then. Me, the big, very big witch. Hired to go into hell to rescue a soul. What would Oliver Cromwell make of that? Who cares? It's clever, Rosie, and true, too.

Let's skip Lila's and Pam's needy speeches to me later that night and close with what I've not told you so far.

First, here's what I knew and they didn't.

Least interesting: I didn't have the cash I'd offered to loan. I'm a salesman, not a banker. However, my brother Sam had it; he's a captain of industry, not a salesman. Sam fussed when I offered the deal to him, but eventually he agreed to look upon my real estate as collateral. ("Don't lose it all, Tip, not all of it," was Sam's fraternal advice. "Yeah, that'd be big trouble.")

More interesting were my phone calls to baby brother Bunyan and his wife, Kaelie, in Colorado, my spycatcher siblings. I've been promising to tell you about those calls. You'll have to trust me a little longer for everything. The need-to-know-now points are these. Yes, the U.S. Military Intelligence Corps was interested in my report of what is called SEDA, subversion-espionage di-rected against the Army, whether it happened yesterday or two decades before. Yes, MI was checking on former Spec 4 Charles Purcell from birth to tomorrow. Yes, if former Spec 4 Tommy

"Tip" Paine said he could deliver Charles Purcell to a meeting with his enemy control officer (blackmailer) in Seoul, then MI was eager to drop by and chat until the stars fell. Yes, MI was taking all this very, very, very seriously, because this wasn't some banking hanky-panky to them, it was a scenario that could only mean Charlie was working for a HIS, hostile intelligence source. The bad guys. The Reds. North Korea. Threat alert. ("Don't start on this if you can't handle it, Tip," was Bunyan's fraternal advice to me. "Yeah, that'd be big trouble.")

Most interesting to me about what I knew, and they didn't, was that I was no longer blue. I was getting out of New York, winter, the Gato-class *Admiral Dread* and that tenth-century monastery surrounded by the Danes. And I was leaping into big, big—gargantuan—trouble.

Second, here's what I didn't know at the time or for some weeks and what you probably have figured out already, since I've not tried too hard to hide it.

Rosie was a heroic governess. She governed her golden realm of the Purcells the best she knew how. Sadly, Rosie the governess had other identities, and one of them made her Rosemary Yip, an agent of the South Korean KCIA.

Repeat this plainer? Rosie worked for South Korea's state security, called the KCIA. The acronym is an exact translation for Langley, East. It's a sincere, shrewd, stupid, fierce, black-minded organization. It regarded Charles Purcell very, very, very seriously, too. That's what you've watched happen behind and around me as I fancied myself a smart guy. *Rosie was an op.* Rosie recruited me, both as a way out for her golden family, the Purcells, and as a cutout to advance the plans of her control officers, the three Lees. Repeat this, too? The three Lees were KCIA control agents; they were Rosie's bosses. You've never heard of foreign state security operating in America? You don't think Cold War allies spy on each other's citizens? Fine. Your check's in the mail, chump, signed by Benedict somebody.

Yet Rosie's double-dealing was profound conflict for her, making her suffer with those fancy words, denial and reversion. I'm not speculating. Ask yourself, why did I find her scavenging turkey in the service hall? Why sneak from her own golden realm?

My answer for now is silly human nature. Charlie scavenged

poison when he was in trouble, a crybaby without a deal to count on. Rosie scavenged food when she was in trouble, like the orphan she was, without a meal to count on. Maybe not. Planet Asia is a vast, strange place where my vain solutions don't work.

PART TWO

Planet Asia

1
The White Girl

SINGAPORE EXPLAINED much about Lila Schumann. My
first glimpse was as our jumbo banked for a leeside approach to
Changi International Airport. It was a routine equatorial afternoon—the Singapore Strait a hot blue, the tropical canopy a cool
green, the burly central hills showered by vapor. Lila, in the aisle
seat, leaned over to share my portside view of Asia's portrait of
capitalism unbound.

"My hometown," she said. "Are you melting yet?"

I understood right away that this was an island republic, just
as Lila was an island woman. Once upon a time, she might have
been Venice or Manhattan. By chance, she was Singapore.

Singapore, you might not know, keeps its own rules, makes
money like ice cream and works prudently to convince every
stranger that it's brighter to play along than it is to take over (old
word, "conquer"). It's luscious, overbooked, tidy and restless. It
believes that if you get up early and sell all day, then your reward
is a just bed in a high rise. Its two and a half million folk, mostly
Chinese, are well pleased with their thrift, politics and bank ac-

counts. When I want to picture the capital of a lush alien planet, I think of Singapore.

The only important difference between Singapore and Lila was that, as eager and abuilding as it is, the island has a reputation as dull. No gambling, no whoring, no littering, no illiteracy permitted, and the perpetual government is a prig. Singapore's sobriety is a ruse, of course; it's actually wild-eyed profiteering—the bank's bank, the outlet's outlet. Wall Street as Equatorland.

Then again, Lila's dramatics were also a ruse. After forty-one years as a California girl, she figured, why not? Let men think she was unrequited, except for her checkbook; let women think she was lucky, except for her divorces.

The truth was that Lila was busy. Her vocation was the rag trade. When she wasn't worried about her family, she lived and dreamed for the profit in the wardrobe. The day we left New York, Thursday, she got up early enough to raid the midtown shops one more time before our flight to the Coast. During our six-hour layover in San Francisco, she convinced me we had to dine in town, in order to raid more shops. "Feel that!" she complained at one rack. "Taiwan rubbish. The buyers must be blind." Our Honolulu layover was the middle of the night; but, at Hong Kong, I had to convince her that there wasn't time to mount another raid.

On the plane, she roamed the aisles to gossip with stewards and passengers—something about the future trends in ready-to-wear. I didn't pay attention after the first few hours. Lila was a professional voyager. When she flew, continents fell away. Fastidious Singapore Airlines treated her like a Princess of Serendip. When the new crew stopped by our seats to greet her after Hong Kong, I knew she was a big deal in a big bird headed for the happy island Lila called "my hometown."

There was also business for me in Singapore. I was there not only to secure Lila's collateral, but also, private agenda, to find the truth of Charlie's blackmailed years on the island.

My general theory was based upon sci-fi/spy talk. It's called *walking the cat*. That wasn't just Charlie's fanzine joke. It truly is the way the agents speak of counterintelligence, of old-fashioned sleuthing: to walk the cat. The cat, in this case, is the undomesticated truth. If you want to know the truth of the bad guys—who they are, how they did it—you must walk the cat backward and forward.

For my purposes, New York was the end of the trail. Seoul was the start of the journey. Singapore was the fat-cat middle, where the twists upon twists of blackmail might provide lots of footprints, that is, good clues.

(Don't be impressed. I'm an amateur at everything. The pro ops might indeed walk cats, dogs too, following paper and people trails, employing huge secret budgets and subpoena power up to the gates of hell. I don't. It was a game for me. From the very beginning, even after I'd sold out Charlie to Uncle Sam, it was vanity.)

My first day and night on the island were for recuperation. Thirty hours in transit, most of them seven miles high, had flattened me. Also, my first whiff of Singapore's perpetual garden sent me into allergy shock. The aroma resembled Lila's mixed scents times a thousand, and it delivered me dizziness and exhaustion. I retired to my bed and a satellite-dish tv (CNN, BBC, West Coast ABC) at a country-club hotel called Kublai Khan. Lila didn't fuss that I wouldn't stay at her house. "You like your own place, huh? Not that I didn't expect you'd be *weird.*" My hotel was conveniently off the main drag called the Orchard Road. Lila saw me to the desk and then withdrew; she said she needed her telephone service and "three baths after one of these."

By Sunday morning (we'd lost a calendar day in transit), we were repaired sufficiently to meet for breakfast on my hotel's veranda.

If hotels are stars, the Kublai Khan was Marlene Dietrich. I listened to the sounds of tennis-ball thwacks, someone's gin glass tinkling at 7:00 A.M., servants mumbling and Australians bubbling, and those flutelike notes from the fauna that I shall always associate with Singapore's humidity working up toward that merciless high sun. Sixty miles north of the equator is either sweat or frigid air-conditioning.

"Charlie's such a jerkoff!" was Lila's breakfast news headline.

Her remark was based upon her early-morning phone call with Pam. Charlie, according to Pam, had completed the first and second parts of his assignment. He had ordered his lawyer to satisfy my lawyer as to his collateral, though he'd held out on signing over Pam's jewelry and his limo. Just the co-op. I knew this already, by phone with my lawyer. I also knew it was acceptable screwing up. The penthouse was plenty when added to Lila's Singapore deed.

Secondly, according to Pam, Charlie had telexed to set up the meeting in Seoul. However, he hadn't specified Friday. He'd just said he'd be there by the weekend. This was also acceptable screwing up. The important detail was to get Charlie to Korea.

What I didn't like was that Charlie, according to Pam, was botching the crucial third part of his assignment. He was refusing to get on the plane to Tokyo. He was still camped in New York, now moved back to his penthouse bed.

"I won't take his crying anymore," Lila said. "I told Pam to tell him he's on that plane by tomorrow or I'm done with him. Shit! I'm signing my house over to you to help him, and he's moaning and moaning, 'I can't face it, I just can't.' "

Lila fluffed out her fashionable black blouse, raised her right hand in a northwesterly direction and signaled with a finger. "Face that, Charlie!"

This concluded the breakfast dramatics. I was in a good mood and didn't want to debate Charlie's delinquency. I assured Lila that he'd get on the plane eventually, because if he didn't, we'd be free of him, and things didn't ever work out that neatly.

Meanwhile, I claimed I wanted to play tourist. "It says this is 'Paradise at the Equator,' " I said. "How about the highlights? I'm rested and curious."

"You sound ornery," she teased. "Like you are when you wake up. You slept there," she indicated where my seat/bed had been on the plane, "and I slept here. You snore, because you smoke too much. And you're ornery when you wake up."

I was downwind from her amazing perfume. I risked flattery that she was sensational all the time.

"Thanks," she said with a dimpled smile.

Her flirtation was followed by characteristic bossiness. "We must do something about your clothes. Khakis and ancient seersucker are convincing, but not you. I've got a factory full of tailors, if you're interested?"

"I'm not."

"At least get rid of that hat. No one's worn a Panama here since 1945."

My roll-up Panama might be the only reason I go to tropical climes. I tucked it on the back of my head, over my bald spot, and looked immovable.

"The hat stays, huh?" she asked.

"Fashion later," I said, "Singapore today."

"You really want to see it?" She waved to the palm trees, orchid gardens and commonplace bougainvillea. "Or are you just fooling around?"

Yes and no was the correct answer. I wanted to see all of it, where Charlie had lived and worked, where she lived and worked. I told her none of this. I said I wanted to order a weak breakfast and then to be dazzled. Also, "Let's go to church," I said. "Where's yours?"

"Church?" She looked confounded. "You are fooling."

"I'm Presbyterian," I said. "You're Lutheran? Methodist? Reformed Church? Californian?"

"Episcopalian," she sighed, "just like my *mother.*"

Later, after we'd dined and parried some more, Lila motored us quickly over the new roads that render the southern part of the island a suburban jungle sprawl.

"My factory's in there," explained my tour guide. "This is all an industrial park. . . . The racetrack's there. . . . That's the university. . . . Yeah, that's our skyline. It's called Chinatown. They built it over a long weekend in 1972, that's the local joke. I think it looks like everybody else's. A glass box is a glass box. . . ."

I did insist we attend church services. Lila led me to her parish, the imposing St. Andrew's Cathedral, standing like a Victorian museum near the mouth of the Singapore River. There aren't any old parts of the city left. East of the river is a theme park called Raffles City, a developer's fantasy that is spread around the palazzo of the Raffles Hotel, where Maugham had a permanent table. West of the river is the Chinatown skyline, a handsome beast if you brag about architecture. Modern Singapore isn't original, it's efficient—hired, wired and microchipped, and the folk work as hard as the phones.

It's a tourist gambit of mine to go to church, when possible, because you get a quiet hour with music to imagine what the city,

state, peninsula or island was like when it started, homesick set-
tlers and bedrock piety. Also, truth, I like to go to church when
I'm not blue. This churchgoing did worry Lila. As we joined a
stately ancient crew of Anglicans in the rosewood pews, she said
why.

"Everybody knows I don't go to church," she whispered. "I
know I should, but I don't. And this is a small town for Europeans, and for me, you know, American working girl, and now
I'm here with a strange man, oh, brother. . . ."

I enjoyed the second Sunday of Lent regardless. The priests
were correctly white-maned, and they read the Scripture with
wet-lipped punctuation. The sermon went over my head, as most
do, but the music was first-rate classical, a Lenten songfest. Lila
wanted to bolt after the benediction. Instead, I led her past the
parsons and into the catered social hour, superb tea and perfect
scones. It wasn't long before she was obliged to make introductions.

"Why, Lila, how surprising to see you," a handsome grandmother would begin.

"This is my brother-in-law's friend Tip Paine, from New
York," Lila would return.

I did little but flatter the ancients for their polished sanctuary
and bountiful island.

They gave me the colonial line, "It's only our little parish.
We're proud of it, you must understand, very, a national land-
mark, to be sure."

Amid the eye-misting, I made a lucky find. The sagacious
Major D. D. MacGrew ambled up to flirt with Lila and reconnoi-
ter me. He revealed that he was director pro tem of the Singapore
Sporting Club, where many local VIPs had a locker and a bar tab.
Bankers too. Charlie too, once upon a time.

"Charlie Purcell's your neighbor in New York?" Major
MacGrew asked. "Worked with me, did you know?"

"No, sir, I didn't know. At the bank?"

"At the club," Major MacGrew said. He didn't look his ramrod
eighty-four years, nor did his wartime internment at Changi
Prison show, except for in his dentures; and what a tall tale he
must be, I thought. "Member of the bar," Major MacGrew confided of himself, "mostly retired now, at Government House. Do
keep the hand in with lectures at the university."

I asked, "Charlie was an officer at the Sporting Club?"

"Miss his game," Major MacGrew continued. "Yes, do, he was seeded top three at the club. Court tennis. These Indian gentlemen beat the pants off us at squash. Lawn tennis too, don't doubt. Pardon, Lila."

Lila flustered at this "pardon." I wondered why.

"Have court tennis at the club," Major MacGrew explained. "You know the game, Mr. Paine? Drop by, show you how. Indoors, so it doesn't drain you like a tap. Tell Chik Ho, at the door, I sent you. Lila's likely to take you to the Yacht Club, but that's for the swishy set, weekend dances and so forth."

I loved him. And he carried a Panama three generations older than mine. Sure, he was a colonial popinjay (ret.); however, he knew Charlie, and that was a fair start.

I got unlucky, too, for after some more of this mixing with the ancients, Major MacGrew returned with a foghorn-voiced chum named Torrance.

"Tommy 'Tip' Paine, the spy fellow," Major MacGrew declared. "Should have said so, know your books, some."

Torrance growled to himself, "I knew it was him."

"My treat, we've a celebrity," Major MacGrew said. "Don't get many anymore, used to, gone now, air travel got them."

Torrance was a dapper gremlin who kept sliding sideways and testing my peripheral vision. "You've got to come to dinner with us," he growled. "Miss Schumann, he must."

Major MacGrew studied his pocket calendar. "Tomorrow at six for cocktails," he told me, "monthly meeting of the Ensign Ewart Society, some old-fool soldiers really, none with Wellington, promise. Clear the program for you, talk or whatever. Chaps will treat you right."

Lila appeared to love this. I supposed that Major MacGrew and Torrance stood for everything about Singapore that she was kept out of, the old-boy network, the old network, the boy network, and now she had something that they wanted.

Lila's reaction was actually more cluttered.

"The English," she declared as we departed, "the *English*, they should watch television. What've they done in the last fifty years? I'll tell you—they've watered their whiskey and beat the Japanese somewhere, not here, and now what are they? 'Bloody weepy.' I'd buy Nissan, except the Chinese would think I was insulting them.

Around here, Tip, the Japanese are loathed. And the English are sucked up to. The *English.*"

"They believe in hats," I countered.

Afterward, we motored again to maintain my air-cooled comfort. Lila drove a lemon Jaguar coupe, and she drove it much too fast.

I figured her Anglophobia wasn't genuine, something she'd learned in France. I was wrong. It had to do with Major Mac-Grew's hint of an Indian squash player.

Her lover's name was Rajeesh. Lila didn't tell me about him until after we'd again buzzed her factory and warehouse in the light-industry development of Jurong. She started about Rajeesh matter-of-factly, during the drive to the back of the island and the botanical park she called her house and grounds.

"He's married," she said. "Raj, I mean. I guess you guessed. And we've been on-and-off for *twelve* years." Lila sighed like the ex-smoker she was. "It's off for now. He's in London for a sabbatical year, with wife and many kids. He's a doctor in chemistry, Cambridge, the whole bit. Raj is a big deal. His family back in Delhi, they're big deals too, estates and polo. Hindu fairy tale. It's dumb."

She rambled through a familiar island story—American girl makes it the hard way and then gets ambushed by sentiment. This was Lila Schumann the Romance language major, shopping minor, who'd emulated Dad and joined a bank training program out of Berkeley. Divorce from a hipster (the Hollywood hack) followed. Banking practices took her to Paris to lend money to the rag trade. In 1977, she'd arrived in Singapore as the wife of a French entrepreneur she'd married in Paris. The Frenchman, Anton, soon fled back to Paris, where he remarried his first wife. Twice-divorced Lila, rather than return to America in defeat, had used her bank connections (and Anton's colleagues in Paris) to buy out a shabby Singapore sweatshop from a diabetic colonial.

In the past twelve years, she'd transformed herself into a Singapore cash machine. She had Chinese tailors, French partners, cut-rate suppliers in Indonesia, Malaysia and a new one in Bangkok. I never saw the books, but I'm guessing an eight-figure gross (American), and Lila's salary at a healthy six with equity. Her product was primarily for the European houses in a volatile industry now compensating for Red China's fickle entry. She was a transcontinental hit, a rag rocket since the mid-eighties, but, to hear her sputter about Rajeesh, she was an American goof.

"Years of it, the mistress," she said, "For them, the boys, they think it's acceptable. The white girl. What really ticks me off, I kind of like it. Liked it. I was too busy for babies, and you can't blow what you haven't got. That's my short version. I've had years of practicing it, on Pammie, and on my *mother.*"

We had arrived at Lila's house by this chapter of the autobiography. Her home was modest luxury that could have easily been a planter's house in the Carolinas—wraparound porches and breezeways. Lila's wealth showed in her owning a colonial house and lawn on an island where one acre is precious. Sleek condos were crowding her close, but nature's privacy is instant in the tropics, since tubular roses grow out of divots. Her house's local flavor was the Chinese doors and shutters and a spectacular view of the Johore Straits across to Malaysia's jungle.

As we walked through the air-conditioned halls, I admired the trappings. Lila liked my remarks and sweetly observed that her house was "perfect," except for the snakes.

"Snakes?" I asked.

"Yeah, king cobra and python and weirder. Mowing the lawn is a fright. I hire these maniacs and hide while they're at it."

I laughed. She didn't. On the screened rear veranda, we were served lemonade and tea by Lila's two Chinese servants (husband and wife).

"Aren't you going to make a remark about mistresses?" Lila asked. "We're all alike. Never the wrong time."

I got comfortable in an excellent chair and asked how Charlie and Pam had fit in here with all the snakes in the grass.

"That's your remark," she said. Lila tossed her red hair, a habit I now understood was from years of enduring a sweaty neck. "I did try to get away from Rajeesh, you know. Charlie was one of my many failures. Not so many. After I bailed out, I brought Pammie here to meet him, and it worked for her. I did get a family out of it."

I'd noticed the shrine of family pictures in her parlor. Her two nephews and two nieces were grouped in a gallery. Mother Schumann and deceased Dad were oil portraits. Charlie's and Pam's wedding pictures were overlarge. I assumed the photograph of Rajeesh, in whites, was upstairs by her bed.

Lila's was a twice-told tale. Her twist was her success. She was a Singapore sensation—"the white girl," according to her—painted and envied. I figured Rajeesh worshiped her, a Hindu love goddess with red hair and firm thighs. And she, I could see, loved him like heresy.

Later, in the car back to my hotel, toward the close of my first long day of snooping, I said, "I was wrong about you, Lila."

"How's that?" she asked.

I said that I'd figured her for subterfuge about Charlie and the blackmail.

"Subterfuge?" she teased. "You mean like being involved?"

I nodded.

"There is something I didn't tell you."

"That you took a side trip, Paris to London, last week?"

"F—— you," she snapped. "And I didn't. It's about when I first found out about Charlie. It wasn't last spring, like I said. It was and it wasn't. Way back, when Charlie and I were together, he told me then. He got high and weepy and told me. About the Army. And about the blackmail."

I made an interrogator's mistake and nodded as if I'd expected this, which I had, but it's rude to show it.

"I didn't make sense of what Charlie told me until last year. I thought it was mostly one of his stories. He's not the straightest man, but what did I know? The Army, Korea, it was a long time ago. And when he said there were people who wanted things from him, I remember thinking, This one's got an imagination. I thought he meant money at the time. Way back, '81. Then he pulled that Charlie bit, you know, presto-change-o, and he was just fine the next day and didn't mention it again. I sort of left out telling it to Pammie when I brought her in and introduced them. It was too weird."

"Like a dream," I said.

"Yeah, like I dreamed that he told me. You're going along with this dreamboat, and, all of a sudden, he gets weird and tells you he's a traitor and a victim and all, and then nothing, he's back to being dreamboaty and everybody loves him and you think, Did I dream that? How come nothing happens? It was like that. But it was rotten never to tell Pammie till last year."

"Unless she knew already," I said, "and feels the same way."

Lila frowned. "I never thought of that."

I thanked Lila for Scenario Number Three of How I Found Out, What I Did. It was premature of me at the time, but I accepted it as the truth. Poor decision.

"I feel lousy through the skin. I married Pam to him."

I said I was still wrong about her. I wanted to show off my apology. I found a quarter in my khakis and illustrated my pet theory about motive.

"There's only two things that make folk go crazy, Lila," I preached. "Greed or family, family or greed. It's like a coin with two sides. Family's considered a good motive. Greed's considered a bad motive. But it's hard to tell the difference sometimes. It's a coin." I tossed the quarter and covered up, pleased by my gimmick. "Flip for crazy."

"You serious?" she teased.

"Maybe."

"Where's love?" she teased.

"Maybe."

Lila liked double-talk. When she wasn't throwing herself like a fastball, double-talk amused her like a hobby. She peeked over to see how my coin flip had come up. "What's my verdict?"

I pocketed the quarter. "You're not doing this for greed. Charlie's not holding paper on your company; you don't owe the French mob your skeleton, either. You're mostly okay, Lila. You don't take dangerous men seriously, and you make too much of money for a grown-up, and my mom would say your mouth needs soap. But okay. This is family for you. You're a sentimental sucker."

"Your mom would what?"

"Delete."

"Whatever you say. I'm too old for babies, too young for California and just nuts about my sister and her kids." She exhaled her confession. "So what's this to you? Greed? Or what you call it, family?"

"I'm the hero," I lied.

"A crafty one. You're going to hold paper on my house and my sister's penthouse, thanks to dreamboat Charlie."

We were pulled up at the Kublai Khan. The sunset was sherbet melting all over the shrubbery. Sunset and sunrise clashed with

Lila's hues. I admit now, sentimentally, that I preferred her at any hour. Lila was Lila. In Persian, "Leila" means dark as night. That's a tough clue.

I smelled the last of the redhead that day. "Good night, Lila, work tomorrow."

"Love, you," she teased, "love, love, love."

2
Holmes Paine on the Trail

I WASN'T IN SINGAPORE to be wrong about Lila Schumann. I was here to get something right about Charlie's blackmailers and maybe Charlie, too.

Monday morning, I shunned thoughts about redheaded mistresses and got tricky. I'd told Lila she should go to work, and I'd ring her later. It was time for Holmes Paine on the case, pipe, hat and big nose. You remember him, my most vain alter ego, the compleat busybody, following the great S. Holmes's elegant maxim. Eliminate the impossibles, and whatever remains, no matter how improbable, must be the truth.

My first stop was Charlie's previous employer—First California Security Company's glass tower in Chinatown. Simple quest. Who had kept an eye on Charlie on the island? Secret agents conceitedly call this tradecraft. The blackmailers must have watched Charlie all the time they ran him. He was too valuable to leave unattended; he was too much a crybaby to trust. Someone(s) had gotten close to Charlie *early on*, in order to provide surveillance when the blackmailers had turned him on with that snapshot of him and Mr. Kim, the Tableau of Treason.

I had a generic list of suspects. Office workers, house servants, clubmen and a miscellaneous category that included everyone else Charlie had known in Singapore. Fussily, I kept Lila on the bottom of the list.

(I mention my modern technique. Holmes had Watson to scribble the clues in his notebook. I have a laptop computer, seven pounds of blips in a black leather case on a miracle battery. I'd stored what I'd learned from my interrogations on a file labeled "Goldilocks." Foolscap or PC, however, in the end it comes to the same thing: you've got to get out there and ask questions rudely.)

I rocketed to First California's executive suites. I asked for Mr. Jeremy Kepler. According to Lila, Kepler had been Charlie's right-hand man. Now he was the enthroned wunderkind at FC/Singapore. The receptionist played the "have a seat" dodge, so I waited while appraising the mounted antique Dutch map of the Java Sea.

Soon a tailored Ms. Solatoff appeared to lead me to the sanctum. Ms. Solatoff I liked right away; she smelled like mousse, her name was Helen, and she made the most of a square figure and an ivory chin.

"You're a friend of Charlie Purcell's?" she asked. "How's he doing? . . . Yes, he *is* a high roller. . . . He broke a lot of hearts when he made the jump out of here."

I asked if there'd been any special heart.

Helen Solatoff revealed her thirty years in a flush. "You know Charlie. When I got here, he was flying way high. You aren't a banker, I guess? That's a joke, you're obviously not a banker. Are you on vacation?"

I said I was Kublai Khan's happy hostage.

"Isn't that some hotel?" She laughed girlishly. "You know what I tell my friends? Singapore isn't Cleveland."

My surprise was that Jerry Kepler wasn't surprised to see me.

"Charlie called," he explained, as he shook my wet hand with his dry one, "and, boy, am I glad you came by. Boy, am I a fan of yours. This is Tommy 'Tip' Paine the screenwriter, Hel. I got buddies back home who *study* his stuff, boy!"

Helen Solatoff smiled at Jerry Kepler's double-breasted gooniness. Kepler was a new colonial; that is, he wasn't a colonial at all. At thirty-four, he was overseas to soldier for the bank in order to earn himself a posh office back home. Except that he wasn't concerned with going home. The satellite uplinks meant that he could score from anywhere, and out here he was a calendar day ahead of his rivals in California. Big-headed, slender, curly-haired, what the old tales called Levantine, he was an all-American promoter. I heard L.A. in his voice, via Grandma's Yonkers.

Kepler launched, "Charlie says whatever you want, I can do for you. He was my boss, y'know, before he went big time. Me, I'm still getting it together. I was supposed to be in Djakarta this morning." He patted his desk calendar. "Maybe later. Peanut kings got needs."

I took coffee from the slim executive secretary, a prim Singapore Chinese matron. Helen hung around the mahogany furniture, and it wasn't a hard guess that, as Kepler was the new Charlie, she was the new Kepler.

As for Charlie's aforementioned phone call, I assumed quickly that Charlie was scheming from his crying bed. He'd claimed he knew all about *walking the cat.* I took Charlie's precaution as good news. It meant there was something in Singapore that he wanted unwalked.

"Did Charlie tell you about us?" Kepler asked. He wanted to take off his suit jacket and ramble. He struggled to stay in his chair and imitate his memory of suave Charlie. "You see that big green one right across?"

I glanced out the window at the skyline.

"That's Charlie's work, the Rubber House," Kepler announced. "You been out to Jurong? Charlie's all over, he's a legend. What he did turned this shop around. You've heard that all this was built over a long weekend in '72? It's fact, 'cept they didn't finish it for ten years. Back in those days, it was fast and loose here."

"The Wild East?" I asked.

"You got that right. I'm handling leftovers."

I admired Kepler; he had a rookie's humility. ("Now Catfish Hunter, he could pitch!") I also appreciated Charlie the more, since I was thinking: Charlie, you gold-carded liar. Never used the telexes for your own pocket? No. You just used them to swell the bank's vault while you sowed the credit.

Kepler juggled his three themes—praising my trashy movies, then back to the exploits of Charlie Purcell, then on to the triumphs of Jerry Kepler.

I interrupted him by asking Helen Solatoff what Singapore was like for a lady banker.

Kepler blurted, "Boy, she's terrific."

"It's a good job," she said, "and I like to travel."

"Get up to Seoul much?" I asked.

"Of course, Mr. Paine," she said. "Have you been there?"

"The Asian Miracle," Kepler said. "We're in there big."

I was being overclever, probing the kid (Helen) to get at the suspect (Jerry). Kepler wasn't a prime suspect as Charlie's watchdog—the tenures didn't overlap—yet he wasn't impossible.

"With the Hong Kong operation sort of closing down in '99," Kepler said, "the Chinese money's coming in here like a pipeline. It's us or San Francisco. Out here, American banks kind of hung back and let the Europeans go to work. But since the Japanese started lending, well, the Singapore and Hong Kong Chinese see us as allies. They dump on the Japanese here. And they kind of resent the Europeans. The colonial thing. Boy, how's that for a twist? Americans and Chinese—I mean the capitalist Chinese—as a team?"

Kepler's economic revisionism luffed. I crossed him off my suspect list. He lacked not only opportunity (wrong dates), but also motive: Why work for alien agents? He was too young to have been bent enough by Vietnam to dabble in treason. The blackmailers couldn't have had any answer but cash, and Jerry swam in it already.

"I'd love to show you around," Kepler said, brushing scone crumbs from his tie. "How long you here? Can we have lunch?"

Time to be rude.

"Jerry," I said, "Charlie's in trouble. He needs your help."

Kepler leaned sideways.

Helen Solatoff went blank.

"It's the blackmail," I said. "I've got to know who was spying on him while he was here at the bank. I need the names of those who saw him daily—from '81 until he left."

"Holy—" said Kepler.

Helen Solatoff sighed.

"Let's pretend you never knew about it, Jerry," I said. "No

lawyers, no fuss. If you help, it can't get any worse for you, and it might get better. You'll definitely feel better."

"Who are you?" Kepler asked.

"The guy with the white hat," I lied.

Jerry Kepler's closing scene was unremarkable. He couldn't think of a reason to tell me the truth, so he used what he'd learned from watching trashy movies to fake his way out of the dilemma.

"Terrific to meet you," was the best he offered at the door.

Helen Solatoff walked me through the corridors to the elevator. She tried a farewell. "Well—"

"Call down to personnel," I interrupted. "Get me the names. Charlie's executive secretaries, for starters. Call me at the hotel later with the telex runners and office children."

"I don't understand," she tried, then dropped her eyes. "Whatever is happening—you certainly upset Jerry."

"It's high-rolling, heartbreaking trouble," I said, hamboning it up. "Call your lawyer, mull it over, meet me for lunch with the list. Someplace conspiratorial. How about the Sporting Club?"

"I shouldn't," she said, "and that's gentlemen only."

"At the aquarium, then," I said. "There's always an aquarium where there's always an England. One o'clock. See ya."

I hired a taxi and spent the rest of the morning inspecting Charlie's former addresses on the island. It was the rise of Charlie Purcell, from apartment house to condo to a penthouse near the Yacht Club. There was no pattern, so I crossed houseboys off my suspect list. Charlie's USC youth showed in the golf courses surrounding his early digs. At the end, he'd graduated to the marina. I strolled around the Yacht Club in the heat, imagining how Charlie must have entertained himself every weekend.

A Malay boatman at the gas pump helped my imagination. "Mr. Purcell? Yes, sir, I remember him. That was his, the blue cutter. See. The *O.J.*"

I love you, Charlie, I thought. You're so good at winning, you named your fiberglass toy for the greatest running back ever to grace the Rose Bowl. Rise early, toy with Pam, dress in whites, breakfast at the Chart Room, take the thirty-two-foot *O.J.* into the straits, make for the islet of Sentosa for cocktails. All the while congratulating yourself for another score. Why worry, Charlie? In this weather?

I stood on the balmy shore and tried to see the blackmail as Charlie had. Why not answer their telexes? Wire fraud was the temperate zone's zeitgeist. Not worth sweating at the equator. I told myself that it had taken the pressures of the big towns, like Tokyo in '88 and New York in '90, to make Charlie doubt himself, to balk at being squeezed.

(Holmes Paine suddenly tapped me on the shoulder. He was puffing his pipe even in this heat. And he was looking at me with that dyspeptic frown of his—Holmes, the peerless fussbudget.)

I understood his objection. I reviewed my morning.

Kepler had said, "Charlie called. . . ." Not, "Boy, Charlie called me out of the blue. . . ." Just "Charlie called. . . ." As if it was usual, as if Charlie called routinely. Get with it, I thought. Kepler not only knew about the blackmail, since Charlie blabbed to whomever he wanted to manipulate, but also had played the wire-fraud game with Charlie. Kepler might not be working for the blackmailers, but he was a corresponding crook. Kepler's meteoric career turned on Charlie's legend. And now? Was Kepler still involved? Did he still feed Charlie bank secrets? Go further—was Kepler in on the robots?

Singapore's aquarium is named for a Dutch pirate called Van Kleef, and it occupies a slight building in the orchid-rich Fort Canning Park, by the river. I inspected all the fish you'd never want to eat and dubbed my favorite Ms. Liberty, because it was red, white and blue with big teeth.

Helen Solatoff appeared ahead of time, another characteristic of Singaporeans.

"Jerry's really shaken," she admitted. "He called his lawyer and then flew to Djakarta."

I mentioned that there was no SEC in Asia.

"No, no," she emphasized. "He's scared about what you said. He lectured me about ethics. Then he started in about his Jackson Hole fantasy again. He wants to rent a house facing the Grand Tetons and write essays. It was absurd, but kind of sad. I like Jerry, Mr. Paine. Is he in trouble like Charlie?"

I asked her if she'd called her lawyer.

"My dad's my lawyer," she said (smile), "and he's asleep back home just now. Where? Houston. But I'm not a southern girl, really. We moved there from Cleveland."

She produced a green folder from her briefcase. "Could you tell me what this is about? You said blackmail, but what for?"

"Espionage," I said. "The Army calls it SEDA, subversion-espionage directed against the USA."

"Oh no," Helen said eloquently.

I opened the folder and flipped through the printout. With her help, I deciphered Charlie's former executive secretaries from the office children. Helen was thorough. I closed with a loose question: Is Kepler working on anything about robotics, near the Sea of Japan—maybe Tokyo?

"If he is," she sighed, "I don't know about it."

"Mention robots to Jerry. It's a sure thing."

"Can I ask you something, Mr. Paine? It's going to sound bad, but—should I have helped you, if I did?"

Like Jerry Kepler, I don't understand ethics, so I didn't have an answer. Instead, I kissed her on the cheek like a shamus and bought her an ice cream.

Later, I retired to the Kublai Khan to make laptop notes. There was a surprise at my room, a switchboard message from Lila that I was not to be offended by Mr. Chang. Who? The puzzle was solved when tiny Mr. Chang phoned from the lobby and then appeared with his assistant and a dolly holding a blue silk suit that just needed one fitting, said Mr. Chang, to be "very good" for me. I played along in my underwear; that was replaced, too. Lila's note in the box of blue shirts and banker ties was vintage rag trade: "Now you can look sensational all the time!"

While the tailors stitched in my suite, I went down to the pool to deduce. I quickly eliminated the office children on Helen's printout. They came and went without order, pages of them during Charlie's tenure. Of course, the blackmailers could have tried a tag team, but that wasn't a straight line.

I fixed on the obvious suspects, Charlie's executive secretaries. Charlie arrived in Singapore in November '80 and left in July '88. In ninety-two months, he'd had four executive secretaries. (Helen had explained, "Charlie's kind of tough to work for, I hear. I just saw him the last year. He is kind of demanding.")

Charlie inherited secretary number one, a Singapore Indian named Miss Naima Salada, born 1945. She was long gone from the bank, said to be employed at IBM.

When Charlie promoted himself to high finance (anything goes), he acquired number two, a Singapore Chinese named Miss Soo Yu-Yi, born 1959. She was also gone from the bank, said to be working for the government.

Number three had the longest tenure, forty-five months, another Singapore Chinese named Mrs. Mary Hsu, born 1950. She was still at FC, working for another honcho.

I had met number four that morning, Mrs. D. Kang, another Singapore Chinese, born 1957, whom Kepler had inherited from Charlie.

All four were highly rated by personnel: multilingual, college-educated, blameless.

Salada, Soo, Hsu and Kang—I tapped them into my laptop. Two married, two not. Three Chinese, one not. Two young, two not. Their home addresses meant nothing to me. Altogether, no pattern. And numbers three and four, who had been with Charlie for most of his tenure, were still on board. If they were to be measured by the slim Mrs. Kang, they were priceless employees.

I punched out of my search, for a swim and pampering in the steam room.

By 6:00 P.M., I was dressed by Lila's tailor and doffing my Panama to the doorkeeper at the Singapore Sporting Club, near the Parliament House, on the Raffles City side of the river. The outside was a Victorian manse. The inside was hardwood shadows, uniformed factotums, gold-inlaid writing desks, altogether Westminster in Asia.

I admired the oil portraits of dead pirates and stopped at the glass cases of trophies. C. S. Purcell won the court tennis play-offs in '83, '85, '86. There was an R. Nehru all over the squash bronze; I assumed he was Lila's complicated heretic Rajeesh. Lila had said his family was a big deal from Delhi, but Nehru big? That's a big detail to leave out, Lila. Saintly tales of the partition? Mighty backhand, hey, Lila?

The foghorned Torrance found me. "Mr. Paine, you don't disappoint, good chap."

Behind Torrance, Major MacGrew was in a light gray suit with his granddaughter's Christmas gift tie. "Show you the courts," he said. "You play? No?"

We descended to the locker room and toured the teakwood fields of combat. The difference I could see between the club's games of choice was that squash goes "whack" and court tennis goes "pong" in a bigger room.

Major MacGrew said, "Court tennis, good for the glands."

Torrance said, "Lawn tennis, no longer a gentleman's game."

"Nor squash," Major MacGrew said. "Perspire like Labour."

To get us moving, I mentioned that, in America, squash was the agreed-upon combat for the uppity bound.

"Same here," said Major MacGrew, "all sorts."

MacGrew spoke in sniffs. Yet I heard something overdone in this remark. I asked after R. Nehru, the club squash champ.

"Raj is untouchable, haw!" Major MacGrew said.

Torrance confided, "There's fair wagering with Raj away for the year. Everyone's a tout."

Should I have noticed something out of order in aged Tory class consciousness? I thought, All champs have antagonists. Dr. Professor Rajeesh Nehru was clearly the Sporting Club's protagonist. Bully for you, Lila.

Upstairs, in the long bar, the Ensign Ewart Society gathered their glands vigorously. There were fourteen of them, with a combined age that would predate the Plantagenets and a collective vigor that would still outrage Shaw. The chaps did treat me right. I hardly had to speak. They cut their whiskey just enough to keep fluent with war stories. Their pecking order was topped by those, like Major D. D. MacGrew, who had been interned by the Japanese at Changi Prison. Parallel were the China-Burma alumni, who had heard or seen Mountbatten on a cheerleading tour. After that came the deluge of roving campaigners, including one who claimed to have survived the Somme. "Let me tell you. . . ." it would begin. "Those days are gone. . . ." it would close.

We paraded to dinner in the Empire Room. Singapore boasts about its Chinese cooking. The menu that night also featured rack of lamb and other Australian treats, such as a puckering red wine.

Finally, I found myself outside on the club veranda, seated across from the orange sun setting behind Chinatown's towers. I was joined by host Major MacGrew, pal Torrance, and their chum, a loony 23rd Anglo-Irish earl.

"Spies, like you write about," Major MacGrew remarked, "gone now, all gone. Now it's done with satellites, mmh?"

"Snaps through the roof," Torrance growled.

"I like your kind of spies," the earl told me of my books. He wore his hair savage long, and he pulled it when he was tipsy. "Get their hands dirty, your kind. No offense, but you Yanks queered the game when you plugged it in like a toaster. My cousin was SIS during the war. We invented the game. You've got to get dirty in that dirty business. Boring too, somewhat."

The truth is that the nutty English invented signals intelligence, too, in 1914; they were the original Peeping Tommies. I let it go. I was having fun. I'd heard at least two whoppers about the Japanese that I aimed to steal.

I was so full of the glory in their colonial eyes that I sipped at my seltzer and started bragging about my next book, so I said. Set in Singapore, so I said. A banker being blackmailed by Red agents who weren't after state secrets, so I said. Rather they wanted plunder in world markets, so I said.

This is when my luck to find MacGrew & Co. paid off.

I asked the trio a hypothetical: If they were trying to keep an eye on a man in Singapore, say a banker, how would they do it? Secretary, chauffeur, boatman, clubman?

Major MacGrew said, "Only one way, if he's a gentleman."

"Same as we invented it," said the earl.

Torrance nodded vigorously. "The Eye-of-the-Morning."

"Margaret Gertrude Zelle," pronounced Major MacGrew lovingly, "Mata Hari herself. Now that was a woman."

"She wasn't ours," said the earl, "but the right idea."

"In Singapore," Major MacGrew declared, "every chap's got two balls, two countries and two ladies, if he's a gentleman."

(Holmes Paine tapped my shoulder again. He didn't have to say it. I understood. *A mistress, that's how they did it. Charlie had a mistress.*)

The colonial trio were off into tales of hanky-panky. Major MacGrew's taste for Eurasian dragon ladies took stage center. "Always a dancer," he told me. "You're too young to know, but dancers used to be the best a man could do."

Torrance complained, "It helps if they can cook."

The earl sighed and remembered, "The Chinese girls are loyal. Used to be. Stick like rosewater, don't you know."

Meanwhile, I was thinking, Did Lila know? Stupid question. Lila kept leaving out as much as I put in. I'd spent all day not thinking about mistresses out of respect to her self-pity. And so I'd circled around the apparent solution.

Soon after, Lila turned up at the club like a wife fetching her popinjay. A porter announced her at the door. The trio escorted me out. "Thank you for lending him, Miss Schumann," Torrance said.

Lila displayed an exciting black silk sheath. She hopped up the foyer step and made a show of bussing me on the cheek. "What a handsome man you are in my new suit." She winked at the trio. "Isn't he a man to tell Mother about?"

Major MacGrew declared, "Fine catch, Lila, jolly!"

"Oh, you're all such handsome men," Lila returned. The trio blushed and fawned. She overdid the flattery, while brushing make-believe lint from my lapel.

I understood that this melodrama was to do with the squash champ Rajeesh, whom Lila must have fetched here many a night before their disapproving eyes. I asked her for an exit.

"Nighty-night," Lila cooed to the trio, grabbing my wrist to yank my arm around her waist, love-dovey style.

3
Eyes of the Morning

O UTSIDE, LILA SHOVED ME into the Jaguar and ignited.
"Those tin monkeys! I'll bet you wowed them!" She U-turned in
traffic and accelerated to the East Coast Parkway, directly away
from my hotel and toward the airport.

I pulled down my Panama and asked if I was being run out of
town.

"I suppose you don't care that Charlie's still in New York?"
she demanded. " 'Tomorrow,' he says, 'tomorrow' he'll go to
Tokyo. Why am I helping him? My lawyer says to me, 'Please,
to sign over your house to a stranger, please, isn't there a way to
reconsider?' He's Chinese, my lawyer, the best damned contracts
man in town, and he's morbid about this." Lila stared at me.
"You tell me, what am I doing? This is f——ed up."

I asked if we could slow down.

"And you," she continued, accelerating the Jaguar in the
direction of the coastal lights, "you're just glad-handing
around without a worry. You're going to get my house in your
pocket, and you've got those old lechers for buddies, and

Pam thinks you're a hero. *You* think you're a hero. What a joke!"

Lila found fifth gear and her fury. "What'd they tell you? How Raj banged me on the court, and they caught me drunk in the steam room? That's a club story for you. I'll bet they didn't say how I told them off that night, dripping on their library, I screamed my head off. They hate Raj, and they hate me for having him. Raj says, 'Lila, you mustn't ruin their fun.' Like I'm some kind of game. Well, f—— 'em all, right, hero?"

We dropped off the parkway for the serpentine coast road, where Lila scared me with her macho driving tactics.

I couldn't account for her mood. Charlie's delinquencies hardly explained it. Stalling was his nature. And signing her house over to me as collateral was a threat to her, but not the murderous sort. Lila was volcanic. Why?

She seemed to calm down as she slowed down when we reached the northeastern corner of the island, near the airport.

"That's the Changi Prison," she remarked blandly. I glanced at what looked a brick factory. Farther along, out over the black water, a jumbo jet was on final approach. It roared over us as Lila eased through the village of Changi. We finally parked on a bank that overlooked the ferry basin to Malaysia.

I asked if I was supposed to swim for it.

"I'm not apologizing for what I said," she started.

I guessed we'd come to her choice brooding spot on the island, America directly northeast, a Pacific Ocean away.

Lila continued casually, "Why don't you tell me what you did today. I'll listen."

I thanked her for the new suit and accessories.

"It's a bad habit of mine, dressing up men. You should have seen Charlie's taste before Pammie and I took charge."

Rag-trade talk softened her tone the more, so I decided to risk it. I confessed my day. I mentioned Jerry Kepler, the marina, Helen Solatoff. I left out the reason for my snooping; I also omitted mention of the executive-secretary list. Then, because Lila didn't seem annoyed, I included my exchange with MacGrew & Co. Finally I asked, "Charlie had a mistress, didn't he?"

"What's it to you?" she snapped. "Right, I see. You're working up a screenplay, huh? Kind of *Golddiggers of 1990*, bang everyone and stay on top?"

"Who was she?"

"She? Won't you be surprised? Who are the she's?" Her cynicism returned. "And if I tell you, what do I get, guild membership? My first ex had it, like Bleak House credit. He ate my food, and I ate his fantasies."

"Don't tell me, then," I tried. "Take me there."

"You geek. Take you there? What am I? Chop-chop girl?"

I lit my pipe and waited on her mood.

"You want me to take you there? You want me to find you one of your own?" Lila's spite overwhelmed her suspicions. She lit the Jaguar and reversed into a spin, jolting me against the door. "I'll do it!" she raved. "I'm good at my job, matchmaker for geeks."

"Geek," I mumbled, "it's from the Latin for fool."

Lila raved on. "Why not? I'm just old Lila, wipe their noses and peckers, old Lila, good for a favor or a toss when you're in town."

Whatever had hold of her, it made her drive predatorily. I was too excited by the chase to figure out what had transformed her from self-pitier to punch-out artist.

But you can review her rough speeches for yourself. There's time while we recrossed Singapore on the Pan Island Expressway. The answer is loud: Dr. Professor Rajeesh Nehru. And not just his memory, rather close contact via satellite-uplink miracles. Lila had spent her day feeling usefully abused. At some point, furious in all directions, she had reached out for comfort to her twelve-year-long lover, who was eight hours behind us in a wet London flat.

I didn't learn any of this until after more surprises. At pursuit speed, with Lila popping on a CD of *Rubber Soul* to silence me, we skirted the central mountains and reservoirs and turned into a tidy village named Mandai, on the rail line to Malaysia. Lila pulled inside a condo village of new-built double houses, set neatly in a dell.

"Charlie's is the end one," Lila said, "left side."

I said that this wasn't one of Charlie's former addresses that she'd given me.

Lila explained, "You think he just owns one New York penthouse? He's got this, and a one-bedroom on the East Coast Road, and probably more. You know how it's done—dummy real estate company. He leases them out for a tax dodge. Condo lord."

I asked why Charlie hadn't offered them for collateral.

"Ask him," she said. "But my guess is he's already borrowed them out. That deal in Tokyo. Robots, right? That's our Charlie, always thinking of Charlie. But this condo, it's where he kept his stash. He'd spend Saturdays here, while I held Pammie's hand. He's not a sneaky guy. Pammie stopped asking on the honeymoon."

"Gee," I said.

"You are a sneaky guy," she said, "so why're we here?"

At long last, suspicion. I hopped out the door, moving quickly up to the condominium's porch light. It was misting, a sweet evening in a jungle beaten back by the genius of the developer. Lila didn't follow me. She lingered sidesaddle in her seat, with the car door open, her long legs poking out attractively. I figured that but for some expensive counseling, she'd be smoking a Gaulois and humming with the Beatles.

The name on the mailbox solved my search, or so I thought. "Soo," it read. Soo Yu-Yi was Charlie's number-two executive secretary, 1981–83. She was born 1959. If she had been Mata Hari, Charlie's Eye-of-the-Morning, then she'd hooked Charlie when she was twenty-three. She was now thirty-two.

My buzz brought a bright orange light and an open door.

"Yes?" asked a slim, young oriental woman through the screen.

"Miss Soo, I'm a friend of Charlie Purcell's. My name is Paine, from New York."

The woman opened the door and stepped back. The air-conditioning frosted my glasses. The hallway and front parlor were luxurious rattan.

"Did he send you?" she asked. "Is he here?"

I stared: sheer gray dressing gown, long black hair, dark eyes, a rosy complexion, with Chinese features or maybe not. Eurasian? Certainly gorgeous.

She glanced to the Jaguar. "That's Miss Schumann. Where is he?"

"If you mean Charlie," I said, "Charlie needs your help." I raised my voice for clarity. "It's the blackmail. I need to know who hired you to watch him."

No response. She watched Lila a moment more, then asked me, "Charlie sent you?" I assumed she was about to lie to me. Instead, she dumbfounded me. "I don't know you, do I? Have you been here before? You must want my sister Yu-Yi."

Mata Hari had just multiplied.

(Holmes Paine stepped on my foot and whispered, "*Sister mistresses, my dear Tip, now what do you do?*")

"Yes, your sister," I said. "Is Soo Yu-Yi here?"

"She doesn't live here anymore," said the wrong Miss Soo. Her English was singsong and carefree. She put her hands together and bowed submissively. "Are you staying with us?"

Prudery stole my breath. There was also a sweet scent in the house that I didn't immediately recognize as the cause of my light-headedness. Charlie, I thought, you are jaded way beyond my experience. Sisters. A safe house. And you send your touring clients here now?

"Miss Soo," I tried, "where can I find your sister?"

"She doesn't want any more trouble," said the wrong Miss Soo. "Are you staying with us?"

Another young woman glided down the stairs. She also had black hair, bright dark eyes, and showed beautiful legs in a blue dressing gown. "Who's there?" she asked.

"It's a friend of Charlie's," said the wrong Miss Soo. "Mr. Paine from New York. He wants to talk to Yu-Yi."

The newcomer was younger still and equally gorgeous. Another sister? "Yu-Yi moved out," said the second wrong Miss Soo. "Didn't Charlie tell you?"

"There's trouble," I said. "Please, give me her address."

The first Miss Soo scribbled on a notepad. Someplace called P.K. "It's down the coast," she explained. "Miss Schumann can find it."

The second Miss Soo said, "She won't want to see you. She moved out. She doesn't live here anymore."

The first Miss Soo asked, "Is it about Dorothy? Or Duncan?"

"Duncan is okay?" asked the now-rigid second Miss Soo.

I made a fair guess. "Your son is fine," I told the youngest sister Soo, "and so is Yu-Yi's daughter, Dorothy. Have I got it right? You're Duncan's mom? And Yu-Yi is Dorothy's mom?"

"Is Charlie coming?" they asked. "Tell him we're okay."

I retreated to the Jaguar.

"You get what you wanted?" Lila asked, slamming her door and starting the getaway.

"Dorothy and Duncan," I said.

"Leave them out of this!"

"Sure," I said. "It's just that the Soos wanted to know how their babies are doing twelve thousand miles away."

Lila coiled the Jaguar into a one-eighty and then sprang us into the mist. "Shit," judged Lila, "shit, shit, shit!" Her temper frightened me. At the main road, she leapt the light and took off. "Are we done f——ing around now? Have you had your fun? Turned every rock? How's the screenplay? Charlie's a worm, Pammie's a whoremonger's wife, I'm a sick f——ing aunt. Had enough? Home for the hero?"

I needed to get to my hotel suite and reorganize. Lila wasn't done with me. We recrossed the island quickly, mostly in silence, though Lila did slip in jealous remarks such as, "The Soo sisters, I hear they're off the charts. A touch of everything, I hear. Chinese dad, Indian mom, Malaysian ancestors, and, who knows, Dutch, English? They go anyway you can imagine, and their complexion doesn't crack or age."

At the Kublai Khan, Lila left the Jaguar to the doormen and led me into the lobby. "I want to talk," she claimed.

She meant fight. In my suite, she went to the toilet, slam, bang, flush, pow, sigh, slam, and then charged to the terrace balcony. I called room service for tea and Valium, ha-ha. I eased out to the terrace to take my blows.

"What is it you're after, Tip?" Lila began calmly. "I've been thinking—church, Kepler, the club, the Soos. Are you making fun of us?"

I told the truth. "I'm after the bad guys."

"Charlie told you he didn't want to find them." She scoffed, "Why listen to Charlie? What's he know but how to get his own way and make me and Pammie clean up after him? Dorothy and Duncan were just another deal for him, but they're *my* niece and nephew. They'll have a good life. . . ."

She justified herself a little more. I watched the revelers below us at poolside. After eight days in and out of Lila's company, I was getting used to her rhythm. I've joked about her as dead-red Lila, and it's not a bad metaphor. The slier truth about Lila was that she didn't have a reliable mood. Tonight she was a little lost.

Lila's remarks about Dorothy and Duncan were preliminary chatter. Now she introduced the hot theme, the one I'd overlooked all evening.

"I called Raj today," she began anew, "and we had a really ugly fight. God, am I an idiot, or what? I just wanted to talk. He's been gone almost a year, and we've only—shit, other than a birthday card and a couple of calls, I've been cold turkey. You're it for men in my life, what a f——ing joke!"

She slumped to the refrigerator bar and popped a beer can. It was confession time. She roamed the parlor, reviewing her affair with Dr. Professor R. Nehru. There weren't many new facts, but she mixed them with palaver from her two therapists over the years.

I didn't listen that closely, because I was still taking in the news about the Soo sisters and the adoptions.

I do remember that Lila said Rajeesh was a shameless bully, but also a man's man. She claimed he never lied to her, which she claimed she valued above fidelity.

"He doesn't lie, Tip," was how she double-talked herself. "You understand? He doesn't ever not tell me things, if I ask."

The sum of her reminiscences was that she loved Raj madly, and she missed him like love. Yet now she'd had an "ugly fight" with him via satellite, and she realized that she was just "the white girl" to him, whom he'd return to when he felt like it.

"What am I going to do?" she asked. "I should end it now," she answered. "I needed him to be nice to me. I mean, he's not out of this. He was Charlie's best friend, and—shit!—it was Raj that introduced me to Charlie. I'm not blaming him, but you'd think he'd care more than scolding me for being an old woman. That's what he said. 'Lila, you're hysterical like an old woman.' "

Should I have paid more attention to this news? That Rajeesh was Charlie's best friend in Singapore? That Rajeesh brought Lila and Charlie together, just as Lila brought Pam and Charlie together? That they were one happy, kinky family?

I see it now so clearly—Charlie and Rajeesh handling the Schumann sisters like prizes and the Soo sisters like rewards. At the time, in my hotel suite, I was cranky and dull-witted. I thought, Who am I to judge?

This moralism was a clue that I was feeling defensive. Lila

wanted attention, revenge, attention, spite. I was the available provider.

"I'm lousy about commitment," was Lila's mood-changing line, as she flopped down on the arm of my chair. She established her balance by grabbing my shoulder. She said, "I've got a thing about selfish men. Really selfish. Charlie's a pip-squeak when you've got my record. Raj is the standard. You think you measure up?"

Then, leaning down and twisting so that I was facing her knees, she added, "Raj is a f——ing genius, you know, he's the smartest man I've ever met. Seven languages, physics, chemistry, math, and, shit, the Chinese hired him to lecture them. First at Cambridge, first at squash, first at bed. Hindus really get into pleasure. I'm an idiot."

I muttered that she was drinking like one.

"What're you gonna do about it?" she teased back. "Do I invite me to stay or do you, hero?"

I muttered that heroes don't give out invitations.

Lila tumbled and clutched. I didn't do anything heroic, such as carrying her to the bed or a taxi. I held her just long enough for her to say, "Am I breaking your lap?" and then I failed my Puritan heritage and kissed her. A mistake. She kissed too good, tipsy and arrogant as she was; she put way too much glucose into her lovemaking.

What was I thinking? The Soos, the red hair, the right thing to do, the wrong thing to say, and also that I'm neither a geek nor genius nor man's man. My body was not obeisant. And I've already mentioned she kissed too good for a woman who smelled like pollination and ranted like Rosalind Russell.

Luck intervened in the guise of our anatomies. Our time-out for the toilet—her first, then me—meant that I found her in the bed, in one of my new silk shirts, setting my travel clock for 6:00 A.M. I refuse to humble myself by reporting details that resulted in my nonperformance. I excused me. Lila did too, after she'd inspected herself to certify that I was not, after all, an unquestionably heroic kind of hero. You go to the movies if you want successful choreography. I'll provide a peek that Lila had freckles for tan lines, latent double nipples, and a downy red tail on her coccyx that she wasn't sure was an acceptable frill.

Afterward, while we were supposed to be falling asleep like friends, Lila teased, "Tip, you're funny."

I tried lamely that I'd learned everything I knew from novels, and the best ones skipped this part, so I did, too.

"No, no, I mean very *funny.*" She unwound to burrow and, just when a smoker might have coughed, she slipped into persuasion. "I had a nightmare about you last week, when I was in Paris, and you're exactly the way you were in the nightmare except not so grouchy. Maybe this means I want to give up dreamboats."

Meanwhile, in my most grouchy mind, I was reviewing the day and setting my schedule for the following day. Sex and death are terrific for the imagination, as Dr. Freud and I have said before; and even nonperformed sex, such as the two of us in the bed, and not-yet-death, such as Charlie and the Soos sucking opium to oblivion, are useful inspiration.

My last credible thoughts before a restless night's sleep—I prefer a bed to myself—were that somewhere in my laptop notes was the solution to my search in Singapore. The who, why and how of the blackmail were right in front of me. As in all stories, the first glimpse is the solution to the mystery.

(*"Good deduction, Tip,"* whispered Holmes Paine, *"now get out there and earn my reputation."*)

4
First Murder

I WASTED TUESDAY recovering from Lila and the Soos. It was supposed to be my last full day in Singapore. Yet Lila requested that we delay departure for Seoul until Thursday. She had business calls "up the wazoo," she claimed, and needed the day to catch up. I agreed, figuring we'd still have time in Seoul to connect with Charlie and prepare for the meeting with the blackmailers.

Significantly, Lila wouldn't talk to me directly about our rescheduling. She let her male secretary boss me around on the phone. "Miss Schumann is in conference, sir, is there a message?"

I also failed to reach any of the local players by phone. Jerry Kepler was in Djakarta. Helen Solatoff was with him. The Soo sisters wouldn't pick up on their answering machine.

I endured a tourist kind of day—the crocodilarium, gift shopping for my nephews and nieces, too much tobacco. Without Lila, I was grounded. Truth, I missed her. She was a pest, but she was fun. After dinner, I sent chocolates to her house along with a picture book, *The Wonderful World of Snakes*.

Wednesday morning, I started again.

Lila's secretary was promising; he said that she said she would fetch me at 4:00 P.M. for the visit to her attorney's office, in order to make the property transfer. "Is there a message, sir?" he asked again.

I was polite. "Thank her for the clothes." Two more double-breasted suits had arrived for me at breakfast. "And tell her everything's fine but the boxer shorts. No way."

Jerry Kepler was back from Djakarta, but he wouldn't take my call. On the third try, his executive secretary, Mrs. Kang, stated, "Mr. Kepler is in conference, Mr. Paine, and will be with clients the rest of the day. Perhaps on Friday?"

By then I was lunching on the hotel's covered deck to avoid a midday downpour and to test the cellular equipment. I waited a half hour before I called Helen Solatoff.

"I shouldn't talk about it," she said several times.

Helen could answer questions. Yes, Jerry had spent last evening with his lawyer. Yes, Jerry had tried to reach Charlie, who was said to be in transit overseas. No, she was certain there was nothing cooking at the bank about robots in Japan. No, Jerry had never mentioned the Soo sisters to her. No, she knew nothing about the Soo sisters being on the bank's payroll as—what? Business entertainment?

"Geez," she whispered, "what's going on?"

I sketched the Soos luridly in order to entertain her.

"Does Jerry have a mistress?" Helen replied. "Does he? Not Jerry! He doesn't even go out." Her laugh loosened her. "I told you Charlie was a heartbreaker. He could have had anyone—you know Charlie. But Jerry? He's a nice boy from Burbank. I can't believe it. No! Opium, dragon girls, really?"

A fun call. It ended with Helen joking, "Jerry did mention Jackson Hole again. You think he's looking for a hideout?"

I punched Jerry Kepler's home number to leave a rude message on his answering machine. I was convinced that Kepler was dirty up to his tiepins—not with the blackmail, rather with its profitable by-products. It was also a fair assumption Kepler was secret collaborator in the robotics deal. I figured that Charlie must have brought all his cronies in on the deal in order to assemble a cash phalanx.

Do you know how takeovers work? No? Truth, I don't know either. I do know that if you're a principal in the deal, you can barter your central position for chunky equity and the sort of headline in the *Journal* that glows like the galactic center.

What was happening was a Great Robot Robbery. The Charlie Bunch was sweating out their wait for the paper train to glory. Call me Marshal Tip, the spoilsport. I did just that. Jerry's home machine spun a gossamer promise of callback, then sounded a gong.

"Tip here, Jer," I recorded. "Charlie says thanks for the help. You can reach him at the Royal Chosin in Seoul, care of my suite. I'll be registered as U.S. Marshal Paine. How's your cross-country? I hear Jackson Hole's still nose deep."

I was cellular happy.

I called Seoul, the Royal Chosin Hotel, to confirm my reservation for tomorrow night. Also to pick up any messages from my silent collaborators, U.S. Military Intelligence Corps, aka the good guys. There was a cute message from a couple of good guys you haven't met yet named captains D'Ambrosi and Cole: "All nominal." It was signed with Military Intelligence's code name for this operation, REDLEGS.

Short on telephone chums, I remembered my manners and called Major MacGrew at the Sporting Club, to thank him for the Ensign Ewart Society.

"Pleasure, what a show," Major MacGrew said. "Chaps were abuzz. . . . When will you be back? Next time with the wives. Hope Lila didn't feel left out . . . smashing girl."

No longer flummoxed by my naked night with Lila, I asked Major MacGrew about my faraway competition—the club squash champ, Rajeesh Nehru.

"Raj?" said Major MacGrew. "Don't get it wrong, fine gentleman, Harrow and Cambridge and that. Great-uncle was *the* Nehru, you do know. Distinguished family on the mother's side, too. Estates." Major MacGrew changed tactics, thinking I might be jealous. "Gentleman like you, wouldn't concern yourself. You Yanks do right together. Most welcome here, Mr. Paine, most welcome."

"Thanks," I said, "but is Raj as wealthy as they say?" A weak ploy; it worked.

"Raj doesn't want for money," he said. "Not a university salary he's spending. Bright chap, a chemist of some sort, and his family must have the wealth. We didn't leave India in that rough a shape; don't heed that propaganda."

Later, in my room, I booted the laptop and arranged what I knew and what I'd guessed.

I listed what I called the Charlie Bunch: Charlie and Jimmy Flowers in New York; Jerry Kepler and Rajeesh Nehru in Singapore. Charlie had divorced parents in California and a sister in Mexico City; there was no way to rule them in or out.

Lila was certifiably out, wasn't she? And as for Monday night, such a woman might hanky-panky in love, but not when her own house was involved. Yes? No. I couldn't cross Lila out of the Charlie Bunch, no matter how much I wanted to.

None of this dial-a-clue advanced my search for the blackmailers. Everyone in the Charlie Bunch must have wanted the liability of the blackmail removed.

The key to the blackmailers had to be the alienated Soo Yu-Yi. She had weapon (herself), opportunity (secretary/mistress) and motive. What motive? Cash? Maybe the Reds had something on her? But what could North Korea have on a Singapore dragon lady who sells her own sisters into condo slavery and her daughter into the American dream?

The answers were with Soo Yu-Yi. I had to make a sales call. This meant that I had to persuade Lila that she wanted to drive me to see Soo Yu-Yi. In "P.K.," wherever that was.

Soon after, I was dressed for the rain and waiting for the lemon Jaguar. It emerged from a rain shower at 3:55 P.M., Lila characteristically running ahead of schedule.

"How was your day?" she asked. I settled into my seat. She accelerated into the creek of the Orchard Road. "Mine was awful," she said, "so don't ask, but this f——ing around is costing me business, and now I'm going away again and I'll never catch up with my callbacks."

I knew I was already in disfavor. She didn't comment that it was two days since I'd seen her. Nor did she mention the box of chocolates or *The Wonderful World of Snakes* I'd sent her. Nor did she ask after the fit of my new silk suits. Worst of all: nor did she rant and curse when she told me that, according to her mid-day phone call with Pam, Charlie was airborne to Tokyo.

I knew this via Helen Solatoff. But I decided to keep Helen's confidences to myself. "Are you sure?" I asked.

Lila huffed.

"Good going, Rosie," I said.

Lila double-huffed.

I tried a reconnaissance into today's mood and flattered her black suit.

"This old thing," she muttered, gear change to cut off a bus. "I only wear it when it's soaking."

We parked underground and rocketed to her attorney's office suite in a Chinatown tower. Everything about the office said "Break my contracts, break your head." We sat at a glossy conference table. Lila had correctly portrayed her lawyer, Mr. Kao. He was morbid at this arrangement, and it didn't help that Lila had dressed me as a jewel thief. I signed where I was told. I initialed so many copies, they might have secured my organs for transplant.

At the door, the unhappy Mr. Kao held Lila's hand like a funeral director. "Please, my thoughts are with you, Miss Schumann." He also shook my hand firmly, remarking, "We have satisfied your attorney," the way he might have said "Thief! Thief!"

Back down at the car, Lila asked, "What do I have to do now?"

I started a preposterous lie about wanting to drop by Soo Yu-Yi's to ask about Charlie's work habits.

Lila cut me off. "I just do what I'm told."

"Gee," I said.

"F—— you, too," she said.

I gave her Soo Yu-Yi's odd address in "P.K." The Jaguar did the rest, wind-surfing the Pan Island Expressway and mounting the causeway over the Johore Straits at 120 kph.

Welcome to Malaysia. I entered it hugging my seat belt and wondering why the constabulary should overlook a lemon demon. The border guards winked, eager to answer Lila's inquiry about our destination. "P.K." turned out to be the fishing village of Pontian Kechil. We whirred through Johore Bahru's flooded streets and turned west.

Finally in the jungles of Southeast Asia, I understood what

Singapore had accomplished that long weekend in 1972. I saw colonial hodgepodge, native helter-skelter, anemic riffraff. The Malaysians are a prideful people, I'm sure, but the first impression is a soggy mix of lost relations to the lords across the causeway. It's a mean fate in a rich jungle that doesn't hide its monkeys. Lila didn't slow down for the peasants on prayer rugs, serfs on ox carts or children on overloaded buses. We were hard bound for the Malacca Strait.

"Jesus!" Lila yelped as she maneuvered a rock slide in the road, slammed the brakes, spun sideways, then righted us. Her new mood was reckless.

Pontian Kechil was shacks and squalor with a last-light profile of minarets, bell towers, temples, pagodas and a stumpy Catholic steeple. The streets were not marked, or if they were I missed it, and when Lila parked in front of a ramshackle storefront by the quays I asked her if we were lost.

"Maybe," she said, issuing me an umbrella, "but this is it, unless you say different."

I felt the genuine time traveler. We'd just reentered the Middle Ages, except that it had electric lights, a 1950s Pepsi sign, rusty Hondas and live chickens.

Before I continue, I should note what I didn't note at the time, that old bugaboo, a tail. I didn't see another car follow us from the Kublai Khan, didn't suspect that anyone would care where I went. Since I know now there was jeopardy to my travels, I can reconstruct. I recall a glimpse of another auto parking in the rain behind and above us. Pontian Kechil sloped to the harbor. The Jaguar was on a shelf between green hillsides and a minaret. That's it. I might have seen another car's headlights wink off as I got out of the car.

"Do you want me to come along?" Lila asked. "Or is this only for geeks?"

"Please," I said, feeling lost. It was the dinner hour. Blocky women and ragged fishermen waded around us, indifferent to our out-of-dateness. I took Lila's arm and led her into the row of shops.

The given address was a tobacco shop. I pretended I was at a Broadway newsstand and picked out two packs of gum before I asked the Chinese counter clerk in deliberate English for Soo Yu-Yi.

The clerk nodded and didn't move.

Just then, two ancients pushed past us, went through a curtain and started to climb narrow stairs to the top floor.

"You know what this is?" said Lila. "It's a *fumerie*, a real one."

I told Lila to wait in the car.

"Forget it," she said.

I put twenty dollars on the counter. It was the right price. We followed the woman up those narrow back stairs. The top room wasn't large, but then, wickedness has a feel of shadowy spaciousness. There were rows of triple-decked cribs, old men in boxer shorts and girls in logo jerseys. The smell was sour animal and sweet vegetable in an opiate stratocumulus.

I congratulated myself for having gone too far. If anyone pulled a knife, I wasn't going to get off for just my billfold.

A skinny girl in a Reebok T-shirt bowed to us. We were tourists to her, and she awaited our perverse pleasure. I asked again for Yu-Yi. The girl said, "Yes, sir," then pointed out a ladder to a raised platform.

"Look, then," said Lila. "You've paid for it."

I maneuvered through the wasted old men to the ladder. I'm tall enough so that I could peek from the first rung.

"I am Soo Yu-Yi," said the woman in the top crib. She was half naked in a sheath; she was kneeling on a straw mattress, holding out two pipes.

Lila shoved me aside and climbed up beside me. "You remember me, Yu-Yi," said Lila. "Mr. Paine wants to . . ." Lila swallowed her speech.

"Miss Schumann?" said Soo Yu-Yi, holding out the pipes I'd paid for. "It's a saying: 'Better when a woman prepares it.' Would you like a girl?"

The important detail is that Soo Yu-Yi was not with us. This was her ghost. At thirty-two, the ghost showed no resemblance whatsoever to Yu-Yi's gorgeous sisters. It was ghoulish of me to ask, but I knew there wasn't enough of a person there to visit, so I tried to get it done.

"We've come about the blackmail," I said. "Charlie needs your help, and I need to know who paid you. To spy on him."

Soo Yu-Yi's ghost said, "Is Charlie here?"

I could've bought ten pipes and not gotten a useful word from the former Yu-Yi. Ghosts are not romantical. This one was shrunken, blue-toned, unwashed; the worst effect was her swollen gums and what must have been several rotted-out teeth. No; the worst of it was something brightly perverted in her eyes. The eyes of a dying addict—puffy, bloody, pointless.

We retreated from the crib. Lila paused to fish in her bag. "Give this to the girl," she told me, "not to Yu-Yi—the girl, and my card. Tell her to come to me. How much have you got?"

The Reebok girl took the money without looking and then squinted at the card like an illiterate.

Outside, in the rain, there were children admiring the Jaguar. I felt very guilty and gave away my coins. This made me feel evil, too.

Lila started the car, then turned it off. We sat in wet silence too long.

It was time for me to tell Lila the truth of my snooping. "I'm trying to figure out how the blackmailers watched Charlie for ten years," I explained. "You remember Mata Hari," I explained. "Well, I've got this pet theory called Mata Hooker. That the way to turn a man is—"

"Shut up, just shut up."

I obeyed.

"I hate this," she claimed dramatically.

"I'm sorry," I said. "I kind of pushed it. Too much tv."

"I did this to her," Lila said. "I knew. I should have. When you let something go—that's Dorothy's mother."

"It wasn't you. You watched it happen, you didn't do it."

"Tell me what I did. If you're so smart, tell me."

My best remark was to get us back to Singapore.

Lila lit up the Jaguar and rocked us up the hillside and onto the black jungle road. Her unreliable mood had altered again, this time to melancholy.

My melancholy opinion was that this caper had just recorded its first murder.

There's no time for suspense either, yet our car wreck does require illustration. Remember that I didn't see anyone following us, and I'm still not sure there was. The return drive felt twice as long in the dark. I called out what I could see ahead of us, as if Lila were driving blind. At what should have been the fork onto the good road, into Johore Bahru, a car came up behind and beeped us aside. I figure that's when we missed the fork. Lila said, "Does this look right?" The Jaguar scraped a rut, and she gave it some gas to pull out. Another car came at us uphill from the front. Could it have been the car that passed us? The road was too narrow for two cars at once, so Lila pulled over to give passage. You've been in accidents, you know that one moment you're feeling lost, and the next moment you are. Lila did drive too fast, but it wasn't speed that got us, it was an incline that shouldn't have been there. Lila said, "What! It won't—" and then the Jaguar lurched front end down, rolling slowly sideways into a pond, headlights a foot deep in slime.

Lila sobbed for her sunken chrome.

I boldly opened my door. "It's okay, we can get out."

Her scream paralyzed me. "Snakes!" she cried. "Close the door, snakes!"

There weren't any snakes; there was worse, fear of the Wonderful World of Snakes.

It took hours for us to start laughing about it. It wasn't until we'd ruined our shoes and torn our shins, until several locals had come running, until we sat hugging each other in the ripped backseat of a Honda taxi in the wild hands of a Chinaman named Bud, that Lila and I started to giggle. Shock. We sat there giggling.

Bud drove his Honda one-handed. "Beautiful Jaguar, you ha-ha for beautiful Jaguar?"

I told Bud that the lady was laughing for no reason.

"Tip, Tip, that was so scary." Lila giggled the more. "Tip, look at us, Tip."

We stopped at the causeway bridge to report the wreck to the border guards. They took Lila's business card as a carte blanche.

Now that I'm recounting this folly, I realize that I didn't care if we were run off the road or if we just did it to ourselves, two middle-aged Americans who went too far and came back by luck. Why didn't I care? Because it was that wet night I started to fall in love with Lila Schumann.

About time. But what about the blackmail? True, I was getting nowhere with my search. It was my vanity that had advanced. I had Lila's deed in my pocket, her sister's husband on a long chain, her lover as a new target in my sneaky investigations, not to elaborate on the fact that I'd already handled what she had. All this, and it wasn't until we were back at her house, and I was padding around her bedroom in Rajeesh's robe waiting for Lila to finish her shower, that I decided I liked her a lot. Shameless confession, I get romantic when I'm in charge.

Lila emerged from her shower with her portable hair dryer blasting away. "I should feel terrible," she began. "But I don't. I feel like I've gotten kicked in the butt, and I'm going to do the right thing. Right, Tip? F—— Charlie. The Soo sisters are off his payroll. F—— Raj, too, if he doesn't like it. Yu-Yi needs a hospital and her sisters need total rehab."

Dramatic Lila plopped before her vanity mirror. She'd already removed the gold-framed photograph of Rajeesh. However, behind her bench was a rag-stuffed toy Bengal tiger in a siesta pose. The Rajeesh surrogate, old raghead.

"Forty-one years old," she performed, "and I've got to roll my car in bamboo shoots before I wise up. Steal babies, and it's okay, because their mothers're whores?"

As love-struck as I felt, I spoke sensibly over the whir of that hair dryer. "Don't boss them, Lila, it's what got the mess started. Bossing around."

"And what were you trying to do to them?" she asked correctly. "What was it you called it, the Mata Hooker theory? You think Yu-Yi was working for the blackmailers? Who's bossy now? She's in love with Charlie! She gave him Dorothy! Didn't you watch her when she said, 'Is Charlie here?' We girls'll really do it to ourselves for love. With Charlie, *yech.*"

Yech? Nice word, Lila, new to you.

I added, "And if she was Charlie's Eye-of-the-Morning, she's closed down now, gone."

"I've got to accept that?" Lila sagged and shut down the noise-maker. "I hate Charlie. And Raj, how could he have let that happen?"

I winked at the Bengal tiger and forced myself to ask, "What did Rajeesh say about the blackmail?"

"He didn't talk about it," said Lila, providing the Raj Variation of Scenario Number Three, How I Found Out, What I Did. "He and Charlie were best buddies, sailing, riding, clubbing—banging the same sisters—*all* the same sisters."

I should have made more of this. Instead, I asked the obvious: "So it was Raj who introduced you to Charlie?"

"I told you it was!" she snapped. "Do I have to talk about it right now? You've done wrong things too, yeah? It was my grungy time, only that explains how I could have tried Charlie."

The Bengal tiger smirked. I smirked back and tried another gambit. "Your Raj doesn't sound like the sort of man who'd overlook his pal's problems. Didn't they talk about the blackmail?"

"You'll have to ask Charlie."

"Your Raj—nothing, never, silence about the blackmail?"

"He never mentioned it."

"Is Raj a doper like Charlie?"

"Raj?" She smiled to the mirror and rotated dramatically toward me, offering her good left profile. "I look at you there, where he used to sit in his jodhpurs, you know—ride a horse, ride Lila—and what you lack to be him is, well—he is a *beautiful* man. And you're not, Tip. But mostly what you lack is a tumbler of Scotch whiskey. It's all Raj drinks, all he permits. Once in a while champagne, if he's being sociable. Otherwise, Black Label. He says"—she lowered her voice an octave to imitate Raj's masculinity—" 'Whiskey neat, Lila, neat and clean.' "

I thought in this order: Jodhpurs? Beautiful? Neat? Clean? *Black* Label? My excuse why I didn't think harder about Charlie and Raj was that I was jealous. I'll cite this often from here on. I was in love with Lila. I was jealous of Dr. Professor Rajeesh Nehru. I aimed to win her.

A mouse at play with Raj away now comes to mind, but at the time I was passing myself off as a man. I wasn't much of a man —dressed in my rival's stupid robe, seated on a brocaded ottoman at the foot of a comfy feminine bed, surrounded by doodads out of a damsel's fairy tale. Outside the Chinese shutters, the rainstorm was lapping the Johore Straits. Not to forget old raghead, whom I kicked to face the wall when Lila turned down the bedcovers.

I declared my vanity. "I'm not neat. I do like ice. I don't like whiskey. What I am is fussy, Lila, fussy and fussy."

This non sequitur delivered, I tried to show off my genius. "I'm going to get the bad guys, and I don't need your permission to do it. I don't need your permission, or Charlie's, or Raj's, at all. Well—" And that is all I'm telling you too; close the door, open the redhead.

Lila did protest in her way. "But don't we need to plan and pack? We're going to Seoul tomorrow. Tip? What about Charlie? You do think he'll be there?"

"Lights out, Lila, I'm in charge." (Ha-ha.)

5
Singapore Surprise

THE GRANDEST SINGAPORE SURPRISE was my last. Thursday afternoon, I was settled in the posh first-class lounge at Changi International Airport. It was 1:00 P.M., a half hour to board the punctual Singapore Airlines flight to Hong Kong and Seoul. My laptop was agreeable too, humming a new computer game I'd found in the shops, called "Midway": whack the Imperial Japanese fleet before its Mitsubishis whack my carriers, *Enterprise*, *Yorktown* and *Hornet*.

I hadn't resigned my sleuthing; I was just on a break. I knew I'd flubbed my search for the blackmail trail in Singapore, and I needed to rethink my premises. Perhaps it's more accurate to say that Holmes Paine was on a break. I was loose in love with a supremely exasperating woman with a downy red tail. "Midway" was lovely fun, too; try it. It even made me overlook that darling Lila was running uncharacteristically late.

Beep, beep, beep, said my laptop; this meant that my recon flights had just sighted the Imperial fleet, and it was time to weigh the commodore's decisions. Come to windward and launch all aircraft? Come about and close the distance before launch? Beep, beep. No suspense; attack. Several minutes later, I was vectoring my torpedo squadrons onto the enemy, when Lila sprang from ambush.

"Tip," she flustered, "well, Tip, there you are, I've been looking, well, and guess who—"

I returned from the wild blue yonder to behold misbehaving Lila introducing the man's man himself.

"You're Rajeesh," I said.

"Mr. Paine," he said, "Tip, please, don't get up, that's a fine machine. . . ."

Lila flustered the more. "Raj just turned up. I was leaving the office, coming here, and he called, and I found him at the baggage carousel, and, well, he flew overnight from London via Delhi, and here he is, well . . ."

I stood to shake the clean hand of a most handsome, most virile man. Six feet of Aryan features and Mongol strength, a bronze complexion and kempt posture. The pungent cologne I forgave him; we aren't all born American college boys. I'd met squash champs before, Cambridge Firsts in hard sciences, too; this one was a dazzler. Clad immaculately and not by Lila's tailors. A London tradesman: gray, pinstriped, single-breasted and double-vented suit over a mild blue candy-striped shirt and, most irritating of all, a hideous lemon silk tie.

I tried to match his scholarly baritone when I explained my laptop's beeping. "You remember the battle of Midway," I said. "The good guys won, sort of, by luck, sort of."

"Neatly put. I should learn those games. It's a dull business, crunching numbers on such a fine machine. You do work on them? Sorry. Writers must get that question frequently. I've read you, now, on the flight. One of yours." He pulled a copy of my *Goose Chase* from his carry-on bag. "Please, don't tell me how it comes out, but Stalin still does die, I hope?"

"I hope so, too."

Rajeesh smiled warmly. Ours was a manly exchange, entirely euphemistic and hollow. Our theme was timeless. Two boys, one girl, now what?

I'll start with my point of view of the triangle and admit that I admired Rajeesh instantly. He was charming, frank, smart, hardy, graceful, all the usual trimmings, and he was also that rare thing, a generous man's man. Generous Lila, generous Rajeesh, a well-made duet. I was outperformed before a hootenanny could begin. Also, Rajeesh had the good sense to prize my laptop, my wit and my salesmanship all at once. How could I not admire him? It was what he intended of course, and he earned another Cambridge First for manners that day. He wanted Lila. I wanted Lila. He knew Lila was leaving with me. I knew Lila was staying with him. We knew we knew. So did Lila. And yet Rajeesh's manners were so well honed that he could manage turning up unannounced as if this coincidence happened regularly to us on this kinky little island.

Lila radiated every possible temper as she explained to me, "And when he called, I tried to call you, well . . .

"And I tried to call Tip," she explained to Rajeesh, "when you, well . . ."

We were at the lounge bar by then, thanks to Rajeesh's civil suggestion. Rajeesh sipped his totemic Black Label whiskey and demonstrated the power of breeding. I imitated him, sipping a diet cola, nodding yes, yes, to milady and glancing at Rajeesh as if to communicate that gentlemen like us don't make scenes, doesn't she know that?

"Here now, luv," Rajeesh proposed to Lila, "I'll be fine here, do go on. I'll be here through next week. We'll have time to talk."

I imitated his generosity (but not the "luv" hooey) and told Lila that I was fine going on alone, she could catch up with me tomorrow.

"Well," from Lila, *"wellll . . ."*

Of major note, no one was mentioning Charlie or blackmail or why exactly it was that Lila and I were bound for Seoul. Jealousy explains our lacunae, true. Then again, I'm making excuses as to why I didn't pounce on Rajeesh with rude questions about his twelve years with Lila, his eight years with Charlie, his present circumstance to have turned up at Changi.

Lila's point of view was triangular paradox. I can't even guess at it. She twirled between Rajeesh and me right up until the omnipresent voice of progress called our boarding.

"Well, Tip," she said, "can I talk with Raj?"

I tiptoed away a distance. Lila spoke quickly to Rajeesh. He nodded wisely. Lila blushed. It was my turn.

"Tip, well," she said, taking my arm and walking me toward the lounge door, "I've made a mess, haven't I?"

I imitated Rajeesh's wise nod.

"It's not that I'm a deserter," she said. "Well, I have to be there, you need my share of the money, but I can get there tomorrow. We don't know where Charlie is, really, and I haven't seen Raj, and he's come all this way, well . . ."

I said I could handle Charlie.

"I *am* a deserter," she muttered.

"You've in love, dear," I said. The "dear" was impolite, but, what the heck, I'm no gentleman, she wasn't a lady, and Rajeesh, he wasn't my pal. I tried to cover up, telling her to call me in Seoul, that she didn't have to show if Charlie didn't.

"It's half my money, I'll be there," said Lila, reassuring me she hadn't lost her bossiness. She plucked an envelope from her handbag and placed it in my breast pocket. "It's the baggage claim. My luggage goes with you, and there's warm clothes there for you. And a trench coat, you don't mind? Seoul's wet and chilly."

She dramatized. "Shit, this is shitty, I'm really a shitty person."

"Call it *Singapore Surprise*," I joked. "Makes no sense, but it'll sell if we add ragas and a jungle pursuit."

"Sounds tacky," she said. "Thanks, anyway."

My vanity never had a better nanosecond. What I had to do was kiss the girl, lose the rival, make that clean getaway.

Rival first. "Good to meet you, Raj. Sorry there's not more time to chat Stalin."

"Yes," said Rajeesh, humble smile, fair handshake, "it'll be a good chat when we have it, about Stalin. And Mr. Paine, Tip—"

"Well, well," Lila interjected.

"—what you're about," continued Rajeesh, "I don't pretend to know, but what I do know—is there anything I can do?"

Beep, beep, I thought, threat alert. So why didn't I attack? You know, I was being the noble loser. I broke contact and tucked up my laptop to mosey to the gate.

Lila trailed along beside me, flustering, "Well, well," until it was time to plead superstitiously with the security guards that hard disks can't endure an X-ray scan.

"I'll work this out," Lila told me. "It's just something I've got to do. I told you, I got wised up last night. Raj is going to listen to me this time. It's finished."

I said nothing as if I knew nothing. I didn't even put an effort in the fare-thee-well kiss, since I don't like the aftertaste of the girl left behind. Her aroma wouldn't leave me alone, and I boarded the jumbo still smelling my defeat.

What was the first thing I did? Flirt with the stewardess, of course, a sparkling Oriental in war paint, twenty years my junior and eager to be pretty all the time. The second was "Midway" again, reboot and find the Imperial Japanese fleet. The third was to tell Holmes Paine—who was whispering, *"Tsk, tsk"* in my ear —to shut up and practice his fiddle.

Yet I'm not going to leave you there, with me pouting as we taxied to takeoff and got airborne thirty-seven degrees north for Korea and trouble ahead. I'm going to tell you what love does. It makes you stupid.

Let's review. There was my point of view, then there was Lila's. But what about Rajeesh Nehru's? How did he see the triangle? Had he taken Lila's needy phone call on a wet Monday morning in London and thought spontaneously, She needs me; there's another man; who is this Tip Paine; best to read one of his trashy books; I'll get Lila back; what an ass I've been! Had he arrived at Changi airport just as Lila and I were leaving and spontaneously girded his Cambridge loins to face me like a man's man?

The correct answer is fairy tale. Rajeesh was as spontaneous as I am, which is about the same as mummified Joe Stalin. Rajeesh was in love with Lila, I don't quibble that, but he hadn't come back for her. He was here because his family and greed were in jeopardy. He was the trail I'd come to Singapore to locate. Dr. Professor Rajeesh Nehru, Harrow and Cambridge, out of Delhi and partition, was a triple agent.

You'd better not be impressed. I've met plenty of these guys, though I'll admit Rajeesh was a most modern example, arrogantly greedy, a family man like his great-uncle had been—all for India, and, by the way, I am India.

First guise. Rajeesh was the station chief for the Republic of India's Secret Intelligence Service in Singapore. A secret agent, a dirty trickster, an op. I can hear you being impressed, and I forbid it, unless you're also willing to be impressed by agents of the

EPA, British Rail and GOSPLAN. Secret agents are still just civil servants. If you hang out in foreign air hubs, you're going to smell the shoe polish of all manner of con artists, hacks, runners and gunsels. Espionage is a job, and the banks will credit just any nation's account. Planet Asia doesn't have the bucks to maintain muscular shops like Langley and Moscow Center, or even clubby shops like London's SIS or Paris's Deuxième Bureau. Instead, the nonaligned nations, so-called, press-gang their diplomats as bagmen and recruit their jet-set plutocrats as secret agents. It's a shrewd compromise, cheaper and surer than grubbing ops from the dubious military class; it also tends to invigorate the patriotism of their voyaging boy wonders. Rajeesh was a treasure—famous paternal side, pedigreed maternal side, intellect courtesy of bleeding old England, posting in the hard sciences courtesy of Singapore University. Look at him again, the cut and humor of a player in what Kipling called the Great Game and we now call clandestine services. James Bhagavad-Gita Bond, and he lectured the Chinese.

Second guise. Rajeesh was free-lancing for Charlie's blackmailers, whom Rajeesh knew to be the Democratic People's Republic of Korea—the Reds. Keeping watch on an American banker, quid pro quo, for a fee. Who knows what Raj's bosses believed? Why not India's SIS and North Korea's State Security cutting a deal in Singapore?

I never did get the truth out of Raj; it's impossible to get a Cambridge-educated civil servant to speak candidly. I have to make a lot of guesses, and maybe you don't like guesswork. Read the newspaper accounts of espionage if all you want is the facts, and you will quickly understand that there are never any. Black lights are kept under bushels.

I can guess that Rajeesh befriended Charlie at the Sporting Club when Charlie got to Singapore in November 1980. Soon enough, Charlie got high and bragged about his exploits. Charlie was a screwup in those days, too, but there wasn't any blackmail yet, so I guess Charlie wasn't confessing about Mr. Kim, just trying to impress the worldly squash champ.

I can guess that it took several months for Raj to contact his Reds and set up the blackmail operation. To turn Charlie on with the picture of goldilocks and Mr. Kim, the Tableau of Treason. From early '81 onward, everyone's pockets grew fatter. The

blackmailers telexed Charlie. He replied. Rajeesh took his quar-
terly free-lance fees—it costs cash to run a station like a gentleman, and Delhi is a mean employer.

Not that I think the fees were entirely what motivated Rajeesh.
He's greedy like the rest of us, but he's also a family man. His
paterfamilias style drew pal Charlie closer and closer. By then,
Charlie would've spilled the blackmail to him. I can hear Charlie's woozy self-pity: "They've got me, Raj, what I told you, in the
Army, can you believe it, they sent me this picture of me and Mr.
Kim, what should I do?" It must have been a choice moment, but
then, look what else Rajeesh organized. He fed Lila to Charlie.
He yanked Lila back and substituted Soo Yu-Yi, who was more
reliable in Charlie's bed than in his First California suite. A great
game player, Rajeesh got fancy. He had Lila feed Charlie her
sister, Pam, entangling them all together with the Soos and baby
Dorothy, baby Jeffrey, baby Duncan. All through the 1980s, Rajeesh was running a fertile enterprise that provided cash, sex,
drugs, trophies and the sort of irrational obedience Hindu clans
write ballads about.

By 1988, I'm guessing, Rajeesh assumed the *third guise*. He
went renegade. He wanted his kinky little island family clean of
the blackmailers, so he urged Charlie to make a break and jump
to Horizon Pacific. Why? Perhaps Rajeesh was obliged to scatter
his flock because Charlie was getting too loose-lipped with flun-
kies like Jerry Kepler. Perhaps also (my favorite guess) Rajeesh
had grown in his job. James Bhagavad-Gita Bond wanted inde-
pendence from off-island control. There were other ways to pros-
per besides running dope-fiend assets.

In any event, Rajeesh encouraged Charlie to explore an offer
Charlie had for a partnership at a very hot new investment bank
called Horizon Pacific Securities Company. In 1988, Charlie got
out of Singapore for Tokyo.

The twist was the blackmailers wouldn't let Charlie go. To
them, he was a seer of an investment counselor. Business as
usual, the blackmailers telexed Charlie at his new desk with Horizon Pacific in Tokyo. This time, Charlie buckled. He didn't
have Rajeesh's hand to hold in Tokyo or Soo Yu-Yi's pipes to
smoke, and so he tried his own kind of escape, suicide. Of course,
he screwed up. (Pam's report of the night Charlie came home
from hospital, complaining of stomach troubles, suggests barbi-

turates to me.) Afterward, Charlie vanished from Tokyo for that unexplained week. When he returned, Charlie got out of Asia altogether for Horizon Pacific's New York office, in early 1989.

I also have to guess at the next sequence, because it's still from Rajeesh's point of view. How did Rajeesh see the continuing threat to Charlie?

Rajeesh went to London on his sabbatical, 1989–90. Late spring, 1989, Lila visited Pam at the new house in New Jersey. Charlie had jumped Lila with his "terrible thing" act. Lila immediately called Rajeesh. Rajeesh, by now Charlie's paternal brain, called Charlie to counsel that he should give in to the blackmailers once again. Meanwhile, Rajeesh had to figure how to get rid of the blackmailers at long distance. Lila claimed that at Christmastime she suggested the buy-back scheme to Charlie. Maybe. But I can also guess that Rajeesh had already planted that seed in Lila's red head and in Charlie's golden one.

Finally, New Year's 1990, Charlie had borrowed seven and a half million yen from Lila and sent it to Seoul to buy back their proof on him.

All seemed well for Rajeesh's scheme until the blackmailers called the seven and a half million yen from Charlie a bona fides, not an end deal.

Again, let's ask why renegade Rajeesh wanted to get Charlie free of the blackmail.

Family, yes, Raj wanted his strange brood to himself. Yet I have to believe that a major motive for Rajeesh, by 1990, was also a new level of greed. Rajeesh was part of the Charlie Bunch. He'd invested his own money near the Sea of Japan. But there'd be nothing robotic for anyone should Charlie go missing.

When Lila had called Rajeesh that wet London morning and told him that Charlie had tried suicide again, told him also that a stranger named Tip Paine had entered the family estate, promising to fix everything, Rajeesh had booked the flight to Singapore.

What you saw at Changi airport was the homecoming of a cunning, fretful triple agent.

Don't you fret about all this guesswork. It's neither penetrating nor very important, which is why I'm telling you now and not at some later heated moment of revelation. It's what had already happened, before my meeting with Rajeesh at the airport. It was of little help to me in Seoul.

Nonetheless, you're way ahead of me and my jealousy just now. So let's total up the waiting operators ahead of me in Seoul.

One: Mr. Kim was critical. Yes, there was a Mr. Kim, and he was at the nexus of the blackmail, the postman between Charlie and the blackmailers.

Two: South Korea's KCIA agents, the three Lees and their op Rosie, were also critical. I've already told you they were onto Charlie, and for very scary reasons.

Three: There was the Charlie Bunch—several competing factions who wanted a done deal. Keep your third eye on them—not just Charlie, but also the bankrollers for the Great Robot Robbery, a mob you haven't met, who do dwell near the Sea of Japan. And don't overlook that Dartmouth blowhard Jimmy Flowers, who was as crooked as the Han River.

Finally, four: There was me and my allies, the United States Military Intelligence Corps. You don't have an eye for us. We're the good guys; I know your heart's with us. We were starting well behind the others, because I'd bumbled in Singapore, lolling with Lila instead of sleuthing with Holmes.

I can hear Holmes now, however, and he's characteristically hambone: *"It is a most dark and sinister affair!"*

Calm down, Holmes, it's mostly lying, with some banking and cat-walking for color.

PART THREE

Walking the Cat

1

The U.S. Military Intelligence Corps

I SPENT A SOLITARY Thursday evening in chilly Seoul before trouble started again with a rapping on the back door. I knew it was the good guys as soon as I thought about it—no one truly hostile knocks before entering at 4:00 A.M.

My suite at the Royal Chosin Hotel was routine extravagance. I'd paid for a sixteenth-floor suite—a lookout post over the predatory roar of eleven million consumers. Forget Singapore. Seoul is where mad money has spilled since they raised the skyline on a long weekend in 1982. Everything is younger than me, and the few ancient palaces are disintegrating from subway vibrations. Picture L.A.'s smog towers and Mexico City's prefab housing crammed into natural bowls encircled by spiky mountain ridges; add a river as broad as the Ohio and an economy dizzily called "overheated." Three steps outside the hotel door and I was lost in an obsessed contest like nothing since gold rushes. Inside the Royal Chosin, I could hide in a plush, brassy and vast suite. Accordingly, it was a long, barefoot stumble from my bedroom to the kitchen and the back door. Time: 4:06 A.M. Date: Friday, March 16. Place: the Asian Miracle.

"Hello, Mr. Paine," said the slim visitor; he waved his billfold ID, showing the profile of the famous bald eagle.

"Good morning, sir, it's us," said the bulky visitor; he flapped his leather jacket at the elbows, like eagle wings.

I ushered them inside with a remark about the Ides of March having gone.

Meet the reliable pair of counterintelligence case officers it was my fate to need, abuse and finally cling to for the next ten days.

I have much to say of them, but foremost you must hear this. They were career army officers. If you know what this means, then you know what they thought of themselves. U.S. Army, all the way, U.S. Army. Trained to take orders and to get the job done.

The slim fellow, twenty-nine, was Captain John "Jesse" D'Ambrosi of St. Louis, rough-skinned, sandy-haired, with a wiry, six-foot-tall grace. The bulky fellow, twenty-nine, was Captain Louis Bonesteel Cole of Nebraska, ruddy, balding, genial, well over six feet and powerful. I've told you that, since New York, I'd been in touch with the United States Military Intelligence Corps. I've also mentioned that I'd been a telex pen pal with these two since landfall in Singapore. They were officially designated special agents. More grandly, they were captain spycatchers.

"This is first contact, Mr. Paine," said Special Agent D'Ambrosi, who was called Jesse by everyone but his mom. "We can't stay, sir," he said, "but we didn't want you to think we'd not been there at the airport, at Kimp'o."

"We followed you in from customs, sir," said Special Agent Cole, who was mercifully called Cole, though by Jesse the *nom de guerre* Boneman. "You settled in and all?"

"We can't stay, sir," Jesse repeated.

I teased them that I understood—the Military Intelligence Corps' official motto is "Always Out Front." The unofficial is "Always Out Back."

"I'm very glad to see you," I added, "but I do know the drill. You haven't been here, can't say who wasn't here, will have to shoot me if I ask."

Thankfully, this got a fraternal laugh.

"Yes, sir," Jesse said, "you do know the drill. Bunyan said you did." He meant my baby brother, with whom they were class-mates out of Fort Huachuca, the Army's MI institute in the So-noran Desert back home.

"Outstanding, Mr. Paine," Cole said.

I proposed that since they were leaving, since they were my case officers and were going to hang around the hotel waiting for me to wake up so we could debrief, since I slept better knowing they were wide-eyed on the job, then why shouldn't they leave my kitchen for my parlor? Fiddle with my laptop and read through my notes? Powwow after sunrise?

"Well, sir," Jesse said, glancing at his partner.

Cole smoothed his handsome bald spot.

They were caught between my breezy invitation and their training with regard to how to handle an intelligence source (me). I invited them a little farther inside and booted my laptop aglow. "It works on the 'incentive approach,' just like me," I said, "strictly Geneva Convention stuff."

This got another laugh and momentarily reassured them. I knew from Bunyan that all MI case officers worked according to Corps Intelligence Regulations, a tract of thou-shalts about spy-catching. In one of the appendices, there is a hilariously solemn listing of "approaches" to an intelligence source—"direct," "in-centive," "emotional," "increased fear" and so forth. I kid you not, the Army has no sense of humor about itself; that's why it's the Army. We civilians can laugh at the Army; we can tease, mock, patronize and Bronx-cheer the Army. Nonetheless, the Army will, like the family Labrador, suffer our mockery. It knows what it's for; and it figures that, if we're making fun, then every-thing's okay with us. Let a nasty stranger come within fifty yards of the front gate, and you will see what a humorless watchdog can do.

I left the boys tapping away on my laptop and drinking coffee cowpoke style, cradling hot mugs two-handed and ducking to sip.

Three quick hours later, I was napped out, showered, dressed, and I had thought to order us room-service breakfast.

"Howdy, boys," I said.

Jesse turned from the laptop.

Cole stood like a host. "This is a fine machine, sir."

"Yeah," I tried, "it'll do everything but eat dust."

The boys looked at me suspiciously. They waited on my next

non sequitur. I waved them to relax and went to answer the door-
bell. It was the hotel's superb bellhops. Breakfast was served.

An important detail for you to remember about this and sub-
sequent scenes with the boys is that I immediately liked them. To
me, they were boundlessly trustworthy. Also guileful, tenacious
and stalwart. I didn't underestimate their smarts either; underneath their clipped military tones and midwestern twangs was a
lot of intuition.

Another important detail is that this operation—code name
REDLEGS—was their first solo subversion-espionage case involv-
ing a "hostile intelligence source." They were rookie spycatchers.
Like all rookies, they were taking this assignment as seriously as
their lives.

This praise delivered, I must mention their bold fault. Like
professional soldiers everywhere, they were encumbered by con-
servative thinking. It's what they were paid to do, I know, to get
the facts and let their superior officers judge the facts. Still, their
methods often felt like chains on me rather than anchors for me.
So far from leaping to conclusions, they wouldn't leap anywhere
—one-step-at-a-time soldiers, meticulous, steady, guaranteed. I
did need them, so I tried to stay in step.

Why did I need them? Why did I like them so effortlessly and
trust them so unquestioningly? Good questions. I don't have good
answers. My guess is sentimental. They were the law, and I'm
not. They carried guns, and I don't. In sum, they were the U.S.
Army, and we Paines are an army family. We Paines have gotten
used to relying upon the Army just as we do on the family dog-
of-choice, the Labrador retriever. When I'm in trouble on alien
planets, I don't call the local police, I call Yankee Doodle.

I should also explain about my chatter with regard captains
John "Jesse" D'Ambrosi and Louis Bonesteel Cole—my saying
"Howdy," calling them "the boys," dropping in non sequiturs
like "eat dust." Why did I do this?

The truth was that they were very straight, very orthodox midwestern college boys, whom eight years of soldiering had made
into olive-green arrows. You might not be able to tell them apart
(Jesse's the fair, slim one; Cole's the balding muscle man). Your
confusion would be "all nominal" with them. They acted as in-
distinguishable from each other as possible, because that's how

they were trained—parts of a machine, ball bearings in the wheel, men at the sharp end of the stick.

Yet it wasn't enough for me; it didn't suit my sense of a game. And without a game to play, I drift out of focus.

So I made believe they were cowboys out of Hollywood's Wild West. If I had my way, I'd render all their talk funny. Lots of dropped *g*'s and arcane bluster, kinda real drawly and manly like. Yet they didn't actually talk Wild West, they talked polite and earnest American. I'm not going to let this beat me. I'm going to make a fool of myself and advance my case that, though they didn't know it, they were tin stars, deputy sheriffs, heroes in white hats on white horses.

It also comes to me now, recording my folly, to admit that I was in big trouble by the time I got to Seoul. And so I not only called on Yankee Doodle, I also called on the biggest whopper I could imagine: Hollywood horse opera.

Tea and coffee poured; rolls, ham, fruit, cereal and milk dished out, I settled down at the dining table with Jesse and Cole and began my debrief.

"Charlie's still not arrived," I said. "Last word had him in Tokyo."

"Yes, sir," Jesse said, making a note. "Mr. Purcell is in Tokyo."

"His latest dodge is a telex," I said. I indicated the telex cable that I'd left for them by the laptop; it had been waiting for me when I'd checked in.

If they had opened the envelope and read it, it didn't show.

I summated the telex. "Charlie says that he's delayed and will be arriving tomorrow, Saturday. He left my name with the concierge and asked could I please pick up his messages."

Jesse wrote fast on his notepad.

I said, "That's Charlie's way of saying that, if the blackmailers call, would I make excuses for him?"

Jesse observed, "You say that Mr. Purcell is arriving at Kimp'o tomorrow."

"Don't count on it," I said, "but he'll get here eventually."

"Yes, sir," Jesse said. "You believe Mr. Purcell intends to keep his rendezvous with the hostiles."

I knew that Jesse's diligent, reiterative patter was a test. He didn't want to lead me, or push me; he wanted to hear how far I would go on my own.

I raced ahead to show him I had already gone beyond ratting on Charlie to double-crossing Charlie.

I told them that I had half the money for the buy-back, that the other half belonged to Charlie's sister-in-law, who was scheduled to arrive from Singapore by this afternoon.

"She's the one I call 'the redhead' in my laptop," I added. "Her name's Lila, and she's about as reliable as a low card."

Jesse nodded; he asked the same question once more. "Is Mr. Purcell arriving here tomorrow, sir?"

I joked, "The worst-case scenario is affirmative."

They didn't react.

To entertain them, I presented my plan for the doublecross. It was tv-simple, I said. Charlie's suite was down the hall from mine. (Lila's was on a lower floor, to keep her free of Charlie's harassment.) I'd picked the Royal Chosin because it was the highest-class hotel in central Seoul, which meant that it was also Bribe Central. Suitcases of cash changed hands here all the time between all manner of foreign devils and local sharpies. I said that when the blackmailer, Mr. Kim, called for Charlie, we would set up a meet in the hotel's posh restaurant.

"Smiling face to smiling face, Charlie and Mr. Kim," I said. "The end for me. The beginning for you."

Jesse paused to make sure I was done blithering. It was time to advance the interrogation. He began softly, "As I understand, sir, you're saying that Mr. Purcell is coming here tomorrow, to wait for contact from the hostiles. You're saying that the hostiles are named Mr. Kim." Jesse accelerated. "Mr. Kim is operating alone? How do you know it's Mr. Kim? Did Mr. Purcell tell you?"

"Charlie lied to me first to last," I said. "He doesn't want me to find Mr. Kim, he wants me to get rid of him."

Jesse asked, "And you assume that Mr. Kim is representing whom?"

"Not representing," I said. "Mr. Kim is the bad guy. This is his closeout deal. If you're asking who pays Mr. Kim's salary, I say it's the Reds, which around here means North Korea. Charlie flopped all over my apartment room when I mentioned the Reds. 'Just some hustlers,' he said. Charlie won't look at the idea that he's been working for the reds. That he's P'yŏngyang's banker."

Cole spoke up. "This Mr. Kim, you are saying that he's the brains of the blackmail?"

"Correct," I said, "the brains, the postman, the Red agent. This buy-back is Mr. Kim's doublecross of his paymasters. Mr. Kim wants out just like Charlie. Mr. Kim wants one hundred and fifty million yen and out."

Jesse and Cole glanced at each other; they were unsure who was going to take the next logical step and interrogate me impolitely. You can't see this, but I did—Jesse squinted like a lawman confronting a dude gambler. Then he said, "How is it that you're certain, sir?"

Cole leaned forward in his seat. If he'd been wearing six-shooters, he would have tucked them tighter on his hips. He was naturally much sweeter than Jesse and looked relieved he didn't have to offend me.

I preached sci-fi/spy boilerplate: "*All successful secret agents are loners.* Mr. Kim is first-rate."

Jesse made a note. Cole listened for me to quote my text.

I talked faster. I said I didn't know how the blackmail operation had worked all these years: Charlie in Singapore, Tokyo, New York; Mr. Kim in Seoul; North Korea's trade delegates wandering the planet and telexing Charlie whenever they wanted information. I did know that it had worked most successfully. In 1974, Mr. Kim was the recruiter. Charlie was his asset. In 1981, when it came time to turn Charlie on, Mr. Kim became the postman, the go-between. And Mr. Kim had kept the blackmail going smoothly for ten years, a seamless shadow man.

And then, I said, Mr. Kim had revealed a weakness. He'd gotten greedy. He'd agreed to let Charlie go for cash. My assumption, I said, was that Mr. Kim was willing to risk his controls to make the deal.

"Renegade," said Jesse, using the correct slang for an op who gets greedy.

I added that we had one advantage on Mr. Kim. Mr. Kim didn't yet know we were onto him. That advantage would end when the buy-back was completed, because this was Mr. Kim's home turf.

"There'll be one moment," I said, "when Mr. Kim has to come to where we tell him to come. That's the only fixed point we'll have. Beforehand or afterward, this is his playing field. But at that moment, it's ours."

Jesse and Cole glanced at each other. I could see that my cocksure certainty didn't suit them. I sounded like what I was, a screenwriter making it all up.

Jesse introduced some reality. "We have to ask, sir," said Jesse, "are you going to pay him the money?"

"Yes," I said firmly.

"Whoa," exhaled Cole. "One hundred and fifty million yen."

(Hear that? "Whoa." Proof, I claim, cowboy proof!)

"Blackmail," I said pompously, "is a crime of wealth. But not mine. I'm paper-covered, with interest plus expenses, though"— I sighed for my brother Sam—"I do hope we don't lose all the cash, not all of it."

I added that my part of the deal was to deliver the money to Mr. Kim. It was their part to repossess everything.

Jesse studied my wire-rims, my posture, the cut of Lila's suit. I saw that squint again, and this time it was unmistakable that he didn't trust me.

"Do you know what you're buying back, sir?" asked Jesse.

"Paper for paper," I said. "Very likely the evidence that shows that espionage did, once upon a time, happen. There's one photo I know about, of Charlie and Mr. Kim standing beside the Han River. There's likely more, maybe tapes, maybe anything."

Jesse asked, "And how is it that you see us handling it?"

"By the book," I said.

"Yes, sir, but"—Jesse emphasized—"how is it you see us handling Mr. Purcell afterward?"

I declared what might be news to you and what definitely was to them. "Before, now, afterward, Charlie is your suspect. I'm not protecting him from anything but myself. He's yours. I told him back in New York that I'd help him. That's what I'm doing here. I'm helping him get free of the blackmail, forever."

I didn't say, though I believed it, that it wasn't up to me what the Army would do with Charlie. Justice is blind. I'm not. I didn't suppose the penalty would go all the way to Leavenworth, not if Charlie cooperated. Then again, after what I'd seen in New York and Singapore, Leavenworth might suit him.

I repeated myself. "Charlie's yours. Rough him up some, and he'll roll over and cry himself to sleep."

"We can't speak to that, sir," Jesse said.

Cole didn't trust me either, but there was less suspicion in him when he said, "It's not up to us to say what'll happen, sir."

Jesse nodded, lowered his head and whispered one of his punch lines. "We do have orders."

(How did I hear this? "Dead or alive!" That's what I made believe they were saying.)

I played along with more jargon. "Get rope, then," I said, "I'll hold the widow's hand."

"Yes, sir," Jesse said, as if humoring a madman. "But before we get to Mr. Purcell," he started again, flipping his notebook pages, "we'd like to ask you some questions. Then we can get on to these other matters, okay, sir?"

"Shoot," I said. Seated comfortably at the dining table, I lit my pipe and enjoyed myself.

Cole interrupted. "Thanks for breakfast, sir." He took another pastry while he poured orange juice. "It's sure better than stuffed chicken, dead of garlic, like this whole country."

Jesse started. "About the questions, sir—"

Cole interrupted again. "We've seen your movies, Mr. Paine. Great stuff. I love that flying boat chase."

"Boneman?" Jesse objected. "Now, sir—would you tell us the first time you heard of Mr. Charles Purcell?"

My fun was redoubled. The boys were following the book, Corps Intelligence Regulations. They had just deftly displayed a transition from the "direct approach" (". . . The advantages of this technique are its simplicity and the fact that it takes little time. . . .") to what MI actually called the "Mutt and Jeff approach." I quote from regulations: " . . .The first interrogator [Jesse] is very formal and displays an unsympathetic attitude . . . the inference is created that the second interrogator [Cole] and the source [me] have, in common, a high degree of intelligence and an awareness of human sensitivity beyond that of the first interrogator. . . . When used against the proper source, this trick will normally gain the source's complete cooperation."

My complete cooperation to bring Jesse and Cole up-to-date on my travels took under two hours.

I know it wasn't longer than two hours, because Cole only excused himself twice for the toilet, in order to change the cassette on his hidden wire. Their interrogation continued textbook.

Jesse did the aggressive asking, playing the doubter. Cole did the head-scratching regurgitations, playing the credulous pal who was also a fan of my books and movies. I could've reviewed the last weeks faster if I weren't a hambone and hadn't included sidebars about Rosie, Pam and especially Lila. The robotics talk fascinated them. The Soo sisters flabbergasted them.

"Three of them?" Cole said. "All three?"

Jesse regained control. "Could you say that again? A *fumerie?* And the oldest Miss Soo was what you call 'Mata Hooker'?"

"No," I said, "I blew that line."

"What exactly do you mean by 'Mata Hooker'?" asked Jesse.

"Not much. It's easy to remember," I said.

Jesse squinted. "And you say that Mr. Purcell might've been turned by a female companion?"

"Might've been *watched* by her," I said. "The turning was here in Korea, years before. Another Mata Hooker, a real one."

Cole was carried away by his role of being a fan of my movies. "Unless it was the redhead," he said.

"No," I snapped, "Lila Schumann couldn't work for anyone. She's impossible."

Jesse scratched a note. I'd finally given him something he could use on me, and I credited him for his patience. My jealousy had irked me to reveal a personal and unreliable motive.

Jesse pursued my revelation carefully. "What about this Indian national, sir? Mr. Rajeesh Nehru? You say he was involved with the *fumerie?* Do you have more to say of him?"

I said I only shook his hand. I was refusing to think where Lila and Raj would be shaking just then, but I got a glimpse of Lila's toy tiger anyway.

"You can't vouch personally for any of these names," Jesse said, "can you, sir? Mr. James M. Flowers, Mr. Jeremy Kepler, Mr. Rajeesh Nehru, Miss Helen Solatoff, Miss Lila Schumann—"

"Mr. Tommy Paine," I countered.

"That's our job," Cole tried, "isn't it, Mr. Paine?"

Even though I understood their technique, it still worked on me. I was worn down by having to recite the breadth and depth of my ignorance. I returned testily, "You have the rank, the assignment, the clearance and Fort Meade's data bank. What I have is the money and the time."

Jesse nodded as if I'd just admitted I was afraid of guns, which I am.

Cole offered, "I keep forgetting you know about us, sir."

I reinforced Bunyan's top-security clearance by saying I knew only what was in MI books tagged "Approved for Public Release: Distribution Is Unlimited," and that I always made up the good stuff.

"We've read *all* your books, sir," Cole joked.

I joked back, "I keep forgetting you know about me."

We were at a counterintelligence impasse. They'd showed me their authority. I'd showed them my lack of same. If I was going to advance my investigations, I needed their professionalism to be more than tight-mouthed. I needed their help.

"I've got questions, too," I said, "and I'd appreciate it if you'll shoot me quickly if I go too far."

They glanced at each other. As cowboys, they were self-assured; as rookies in a cheesy game, they were feeling their way.

Jesse deflected me cleverly by addressing Cole. "It's that kind of month, all incoming."

"The March madness, sir," Cole explained, "and I don't mean hoops." Cole pointed to the city. "Do you know what's happening out there next week, sir?"

"In one hundred and twenty-two hours," Jesse specified.

I hadn't a clue, so I guessed it wasn't the NCAA playoffs.

"It's maneuvers, sir," Cole explained. " 'Team Spirit.' Every year in March, we and the ROKs play soldier in the hills, and the locals play mob in the streets."

Jesse grunted with another of his punch lines. "It's their country."

Now I understood. March in Korea. March was the month of the annual joint military maneuvers for our Eighth Army and the South Korean Army, the so-called ROKs (pronounced "rocks"). Over two hundred thousand soldiers with amazing war machines and loading live ammo spent two weeks roaming over naked terrain for the entertainment of the general staffs and the engorgement of South Korean patriotism via the nightly news. Meanwhile, Korean riffraff took to the Seoul streets in tens of thousands to protest whatever they could think of, and that usually meant Uncle Sam—sort of Bastille Day with brickbats and CN gas. Our Military Intelligence was press-ganged into a flying squad of campus police.

Here I'd come to make even more demands of their attention span. I told myself nothing's as much fun as everything at once. I told Jesse and Cole I still had *questions.*

"Yes, sir," Jesse conceded reluctantly, "we can answer some."

Cole teased, "We'll shoot very friendly if we can't, sir."

I stalled them, strolling to the master bath, where I tightened my tie, took a meeting in the mirror.

My primary problem was that I trusted the boys, but they didn't trust me. That simple, that challenging. To them, I might be their brother officer Bunyan's big brother, yet I was also a big-talking New Yorker. Worse, according to Military Intelligence's regulations, I was an intelligence source. Maybe friendly, maybe not.

My secondary problem was Jesse and Cole themselves. They were too professional, too military. That's what Jesse meant when he said, "We do have our orders." The fourteen-year gap in our ages didn't help, either. My sense of the ridiculous struck them as arrogant and tricky, which it is, so that wasn't their fault. Still, their sense of duty was too solemn for me and the game of walking the cat.

In all, I had to figure a way to loosen them up—to me, to their task, to the mystery of Charlie Purcell. I asked myself for a plan and myself returned tv-simple. I went back in the living room to tell the boys I'd talk happier if I was moving, how about a drive, rush hour was done.

"Negative," was Jesse's correct response.

I argued that I was safer in their car than with a taxi driver on just anyone's payroll.

Jesse paused overlong, waiting for the cards to fall out of my sleeve. Finally: "Just a drive, sir?"

"You drive. I talk."

Cole joked, "All we've got is a Ford Tempo, not classy like in your books."

2
No-Man's-Land

SOON AFTER, IN their army-issue beige Ford Tempo, I urged us out of Seoul as quickly as possible. Cole, at the wheel, asked for a direction. I said Route 3, north. Jesse, in the shotgun seat, watched my smile in the rearview mirror.

I didn't tell Charlie, Lila or you, but the truth was that I'd toured South Korea a decade before while researching my book *MacArthur's Ashes*. Seoul had cleaned up a lot since my first foray. Still, it's most everything flashy of the Asian Miracle, a megalopolis astride the curly Han ringed by mountain chains that continue in all directions to make Korea appear a dragon of a peninsula. Seoul is the dragon's heart; Pusan is the tail. Since 1945, the dragon has been headless—the profile of the beast lost with thirteen million desperate souls north of the Thirty-eighth Parallel. Note that I don't mention a brain. Like dragons, Koreans don't require a centralized nervous system. They're happiest with decontrol. The ROK (South Korean) government is said to be a benign tyranny. The DPRK (North Korean) government is said to be a malignant tyranny. Yet neither is profound to the

Korean sense of identity. They're a shrewd folk, not a mass movement. They go about their business day by day, clannishly organized by birthplace or by neighborhood or, in modern times, by corporation. South Korea is a molten boom cycle; North Korea is a glacial bust. What's critical about these two governments isn't their ideologies. Rather, it's that they are in a perpetual state of civil war for the dragon's soul. North and South are the nicknames of the contestants; they're better thought of as one big nasty family. What happened forty years ago, 1950–52, was father-kills-mom-and-kids disguised as battle campaigns. You remember this, since Koreans never forget it. War is a stupid crime, and the Korean civil war was a massacre that was armed by the Reds and us for famously stupid reasons called the Cold War. Those naked peaks are also like chips on the dragon's shoulders. After four hundred years of suffering the exported crimes of the Japanese, the Chinese and the Cold War gang, Koreans have grievances the way you have whiskers. Hear me. What I had voyaged into with my tv-simple plan to bag blackmail was a land where they never stop wailing for vengeance. No one can remember what else they're fighting about.

I mention all this ancient history because, at my suggestion, we were headed for the so-called Demilitarized Zone, north of Seoul. We crossed the canal east of city center and picked up Route 3 to the DMZ, aka the Thirty-eighth Parallel, aka No-Man's-Land.

While we puttered in the traffic jams, I encouraged the boys to chat about themselves. Relieved I wasn't probing re REDLEGS, they shared army gossip about what a rough posting Korea was. They'd each done a tour in Europe and then reeducated stateside before this, their first tour in Asia. In Korea, we've got 42,000 GIs scattered in tiny pockets from No-Man's-Land to Pusan. The thanks they get is army pay scale and homesickness. South Koreans can be crude about our Army's expensive vigilance. The so-called radicals are Molotov-cocktail-throwing lunatics. Jesse and Cole had plenty of year-round horror stories about muggings, harassment of dependents, the usual xenophobia.

Cole said, "Sometimes I think they'd like us to go home tonight, and there're plenty of our people who are ready to go."

Jesse added, "Which'd leave this place to the mighty ROKs, and you know their rep."

"*Buuuuug* out!" Cole joked, though with cause.

Route 3 north is better known as the Highway from Hell, since it was North Korea's direct invasion route to Seoul once upon a time. I hoped the infamous bloody terrain would provide me a set piece to win Jesse's and Cole's trust. That was my most current tv-simple plan. I had to show off that I did, indeed, know something of the score as well as the drill.

We were across the Hantan River and passing through Yŏnch'ŏn on our way toward No-Man's-Land, when I changed my tone from cheery chucklehead to know-it-all. The chilly spring landscape, rolling lake country and rice fields, snow-capped mountains west and north, were good for intimate interrogation. Three guys shooting the breeze about Why We Fight. And also about Charlie.

"I've given you a lot about him since 1974," I began. "Why don't you give me what you can about his time here?"

"Yes, sir, we can do that," said Jesse, checking his notepad. "Mr. Purcell was a headquarters clerk at a battalion repo-depo."

I could see Jesse skipping whole paragraphs on his foolscap; he wasn't going to provide specifics.

"Stationed east of Seoul," Jesse continued. "He was in-country fall of '73 to fall of '74. Not more than a specialist. His performance sheet says competent, quiet. It doesn't say snooty. I read that in. A college boy pulling duty with other draftees. You know, leftovers from the Nam buildup. We'd pulled out of MACV and had all these plug-ugly draftees."

"Potheads, right, sir?" asked Cole as if using an antique word that suited my advanced age.

I didn't care that Jesse and Cole wouldn't provide me unit names and locations. I knew that, in Korea, our guys are the Eighth Army, which is braggadocio for a single infantry division, the famous Second, and attached units. I did care that Jesse and Cole didn't appreciate what a ruination our army had been after it pulled the ground forces out of Vietnam in 1972.

For the moment, I stayed with Charlie. I asked if they'd had opportunity to question Charlie's duty officers or NCOs, maybe his bunk mates?

"We can't talk about that, sir," Jesse said.

Cole added, "We can say we talked about it to them, sir."

Jesse and Cole had worked hard, researching Charlie's service record, telephoning Charlie's old sergeants. But they weren't helping me or the case with their broad stonewall.

I tried a gambit. Charlie had said he'd been hooked initially with a marriage scam—he'd taken money to marry a Korean prostitute so she could go stateside to join the Asian call-girl rings. I asked what Charlie's sergeant or CO had said when he'd applied to marry a Korean woman.

Jesse flipped to the correct page in his notebook but said nothing.

"He was turned down," Cole contributed, trying to skirt my question with army wisdom. "It's standard when our men ask now. Turn 'em down. It's bad news for them to marry, and we're not going to let it happen. We lecture and lecture, they just don't get it. To marry a local woman, it's bad news."

I thought, Turned down? Not Charlie. No one ever said no to Charlie, and if they did, Charlie scavenged what he wanted anyway.

I said I'd already assumed that Charlie had married the woman anyway. The original Mata Hooker. Had they found a record of the marriage?

Jesse conceded, "Yes, sir, we've got it."

My gambit started to work.

Cole said, "We located Purcell's sergeant. In California, now, he owns a nursery. He told us that Purcell married the girl in a Korean church. Just like that. When the sergeant found out, he scalped Purcell, but so what? Purcell wasn't taking the girl home with him. An in-country arrangement."

"It happens a lot, sir," Jesse said, "and back then, they were good to marry one at a time."

"Bad news," said Cole.

I didn't want a hygiene lecture, I wanted her name. It was my further assumption that she was critical to Mr. Kim's subversion. Why? Because she'd been there.

Jesse and Cole still wouldn't cooperate.

"We can't talk about it," was repeated several more times.

Meanwhile, Jesse turned to the safe parts of his notes. He reported the service details of Specialist 4 Charles Purcell. Charlie had been a clerk without a security rating, which meant that he'd not handled valuable information. Charlie's battalion was mechanized infantry. The sort of outfit that would exist only if there was war, and then only if reinforcements arrived before Seoul was overrun. The way Jesse pictured Charlie's battalion, I imagined it as a giant parking lot concerned with keeping its equipment in service and its men fed. Charlie's workweek would have been: rise early, sit around a shabby two-story office building, wait for 6:00 P.M. and a beer. In 1973–74, the big thrill in Korea was sneaking dope on a smoke break. Once a month, Charlie might have gotten a weekend free to hang around Seoul's drug bars, listening to the Doors croon that self-infatuated anthem "Nobody Here Gets Out Alive." You've seen the Vietnam style of this mind-numbing routine on tv. The important difference, in Korea, was that sex and drugs were the incoming.

Jesse said, "The hostiles must have recruited him in Seoul, in the bars."

I contributed. "He got high and the Korean hooker got him. They got married. They played house for a while. He got higher and sold out whatever he could lay his hands on. Is that the way you figure it?"

"Yes, sir," Cole said. "Not the last time it happened. And from what we hear about those draftees back then, there was much worse. You've heard of 'fragging,' Mr. Paine?"

"Yes, yes, I've heard of fragging," I said. Again, I had to bring them back to my aims. I asked if there was any record of missing files out of Charlie's HQ.

"We can't talk about it," said Jesse.

Cole added, "There's nothing to say, sir."

"For two thousand dollars?" I tried. "Charlie said they paid him two thousand bucks. That was a lot of money to him at twenty-three. They must have bought something that shows? No missing vehicles, either? Say a tank?"

"Sir," Jesse advised, "we just can't say."

Cole remarked, "What Jess *might* be saying, sir, is that they didn't keep much in the way of records back then. We only found out about the marriage because his sergeant remembered Purcell as a peachy asshole. Those draftees were *uggggly.*"

I was frustrated by their professionalism. I had playfully tried the "direct approach," and then the "incentive approach," and then I'd used what is called the "emotional love approach"

(". . . the interrogator can show the source what the source himself can do to alter or improve his situation"). All tricks that the
boys knew better than I did.

It was time to try an approach that MI doesn't acknowledge,
but that's truly my only vocation. Selling make-believe.

I asked if we could pull the car over and take a walk.

"Just a walk, sir?" Jesse asked suspiciously.

"Maybe also some storytelling," I promised.

My problem remained that Jesse and Cole didn't trust me. I
was somehow related to Charlie, and they were never going to
trust him. Charlie and I were old-time troublemakers to them—
potheads at best, treacherous boobs at worst. Jesse and Cole were
too young to appreciate the loony politics of the Vietnam era.
Their version of Spec 4 Charles Purcell was black-and-white—
he was a "plug-ugly draftee." Why ask why? Their version of me
was fuzzy, but still unattractive. No time for sermons, what Charlie did was idiotic, but it was brainless everywhere back then.
Remember the Watergate Caper? It was idiocy writ large, and
those guys were in charge of the Constitution. Two decades later,
if the boys were going to help me solve the blackmail, I needed to
color in their righteous view of trading with the enemy, 1973–74.

Cole waited until we cleared the bleak little village of
Ch'ŏrwon and then stopped on a turnoff.

We were within sight of the infamous Thirty-eighth Parallel.
Just north of us, we could see No-Man's-Land—desperate naked
hills rolling into a brutal, snow-capped mountain chain. The odor
was upturned earth and damp late winter. There was actually a
wooden fence on our side of the zone, like a cavalry stockade,
that was driven and walked hourly by our army and their ROKs.
No-Man's-Land is primeval, five kilometers wide, wired for infrared scanning and mapped for fire control. At the same time,
No-Man's-Land is like a former theme park—Barrage Land—
now returned to exotic flora and fauna, as if time had gone backward. We could see the peaks where the North Koreans maintain
their observation towers, and, back behind us, we could see where
we maintain our signals interception scanners. If you've ever
thought the world was flat, this was what the edge might look like
before you plunged into nothingness. I knew it was just my mood.
Still, it felt as if the temperature had dropped and the wet sky
were laced with nitrates.

Out of the car, lighting my pipe, I pointed way north, to North Korea, to the biggest, rudest mountains. "That's the Iron Triangle," I said. "Do you know the story?"

Jesse hesitated. "I've heard of it."

"It was a long time ago," said Cole, flapping his elbows, "and bad news."

"Once upon a time," I began as Tip the Long Beard, "the monster lived in those mountains. See the peaks, like dragon armor, the Iron Triangle."

My make-believe cowboys were suddenly round-eyed in curiosity at the campfire.

I told my story with a tv voiceover. The monster, I said, sent the North Korean Army across No-Man's-Land in June 1950 and kicked our ragtag Eighth Army down to the tip of the peninsula, at the port of Pusan, where we held on by luck. Picture a semicircle of fire eighty miles long held together by luck, courage, luck, luck. We reinforced from Japan with armor, Marines, and the star-crossed Second Division—Jesse and Cole's Second Division. That summer saw more butchery than imaginable. (I was two years old, I footnoted, toilet-training in Camp Hill, Pennsylvania, while my dad, and Jesse's and Cole's dads and millions like them, went off to war again.)

Then, in September, General MacArthur pulled off the miracle of the Inch'on amphibious landings, outside of Seoul. It was reckless genius that never should have worked yet did, since MacArthur was MacArthur, a warlord who cannot be solved. The Eighth Army saddled up and kicked the North Koreans not only out of the south but also all the way to blazes, overrunning P'yŏngyang and most of North Korea. By Thanksgiving, our advance elements probed to the Yalu River on the Manchurian border. A few of our brave children actually pissed into the Yalu.

The monster laughed. Late November, it sent several hundred thousand Chinese soldiers sweeping out of Manchuria, across the Yalu, south to ambush the American army. We were actually caught in winter camp, eating our Thanksgiving dinners. It was the worst American defeat since the Civil War. Jesse and Cole's division, the Second, was ravaged up north and fell apart as it fled down an escape route, the obscene "Gauntlet." Over at the Chosin Reservoir, we had to use axes to separate our frozen dead.

We retreated with our corpses on sleds. By New Year's Eve, our army had thrown up a brittle line south of the Hantan River.

The monster laughed harder and took up residence in those mountains, called the Iron Triangle because it was impervious to air attack. The peaks hid whole *armies*. The Chinese jumped off soon after. What followed was another slaughterfest. In seven days, our army was kicked way back past Seoul. The reorganized Second Division was flanked and savaged again at Hoensong. MacArthur, back in Tokyo, had lost his luck. He went looking for it in a nuclear locker. He wanted to use atomic weapons; he actually proposed to spread atomic ashes on the Yalu River, as a permanent barrier. Only President Harry Truman stood between MacArthur and a madness that the monster would have loved.

"What happened?" Jesse said.

"Listen to the wind," I said. "You can hear the Chinese bugles and our only defense, the bug out. The ROKs never held their ground, that's true. When they heard those bugles, they dropped their guns and ran like refugees. But so did our guys. Our firepower covered the retreat. It couldn't stop it. Quad 50s were drumbeats at a funeral."

"We held on somehow," Cole said.

I owned their attention now and wanted to give them a happy ending. But there was none in Korea, only more disaster. I told them that President Truman sacked MacArthur and his dreams of atomic ashes. I told them that a hard-ass, *very lucky* general named Ridgeway came to Korea and organized a defense worthy of mythology. If the Cold War has a Cincinnatus, Ridgeway's the man. I told them that their Second Division stopped the red hordes at Wonju, by sacrificing itself and by firing every shell it possessed at the blitzkrieg of two Chinese *armies*. The unbelievable, but true, quote was from Second Division headquarters: "Keep firing until the gun barrels melt."

"Whoa," Cole said.

It was called the 'Wonju shoot.' It was obscenity on earth; our pilots reported that the river actually ran red with blood. And if that doesn't make a man weep, check his pulse. Five thousand Chinese were left dead in the valley passes. The Second Division was naked with its losses. The Reds withdrew back there to where the monster was camped, in the Iron Triangle. The monster wasn't done, it was rearming. Chinese platoons went into battle carrying firearms for every other man; they counted on losses to rearm their attacks. The Chinese army was cruel and cruelly led, starving and killing on a snowy moonscape. And in the May mud, the monster sent them again at our line. The battle axis was right on their Second Division, in the mountains east of here, at a reservoir. An insane attack. The American army shattered it with firepower. Not before the Second Division was destroyed a fourth time.

The "Bloody Yo-Yo" continued. By mid-July, 1951, we had drawn our front line here again, north of Ch'ǒrwon, opposite the monster in the Iron Triangle. Yet for two more years, our children died for nothing in the mountains, at evil places nicknamed Bloody Ridge and Heartbreak Ridge, while general officers dickered at P'anmunjŏm over face. "Face," that's what it was called. Two years of barrages and bodies, in order to save face without eyes to turn and see the monster laughing.

I added an editorial. "The war never ended. They called a time-out. Bored, the monster took a nap. Up on the line, they used to claim that you could hear it snoring."

"Is that true?" Cole asked.

Jesse nodded, then asked the right question. "Why're you telling us this, Mr. Paine?"

"Because Vietnam," I preached, "Charlie's Vietnam, was another binge of the monster that once lived in the Iron Triangle. In Vietnam, that monster didn't just wreck divisions, it wrecked our country. Vietnam drained America for ten years. Charlie wasn't a soldier—he was a sacrifice. The monster took his soul. Fate sent Charlie to Seoul, because in '73 the 'Saigon shoot' was done. Charlie doesn't have any syndrome to explain away what he did. I don't excuse him. I'm telling you to think about what an easy target he was, with his repo-depo rinky-dink. I'm asking you to see how he needs our help to rid himself of the monster that's got him."

Jesse and Cole circled me, staring hard at the Iron Triangle. I'd puffed myself up and painted a fancy picture of the politics of the Cold War. They were so persuaded, they wanted to make sure the bugles weren't blowing and the hordes weren't storming.

"Mr. Paine," Cole asked, "what's the monster called, the one that used to live there?"

"Old name, the devil,' I said. "New name, the devil."

"Yes, sir," Jesse said, "yes, sir."

Cole asked, "You're an intellectual, aren't you, sir?"

"I have my weak moments," I said, "but not today. You're the good guys. The bad guys are over that line." (And kind of behind us, but I didn't say that.)

Jesse asked, "What do you mean, sir?"

"I mean that Charlie's stuck out there in No-Man's-Land, and he needs your help to get back. I do, too. I need it as much as you need mine."

Jesse pronounced his punch line. "We do have our orders."

I teased, "Yes, you do, pardner."

Cole grinned. "You're okay, Mr. Paine, okay, isn't he, Jess?"

"That's it," Jesse conceded.

I finally saw what I'd missed about Jesse and Cole. They were trained as a team—twinned deputy sheriffs working for Marshal Uncle Sam. Appeal to one of them, and the other would dutifully hold back. Appeal to them both, and they dutifully regarded you as suspect. But appeal to neither, just let yourself go and forget about what they thought of you, they'd listen, and they'd help you.

I'd sold and sold make-believe, and then I'd gotten carried away and sold myself on American history. I'd made believe about Jesse and Cole the cowboys, Charlie the scavenger, Tip the dude; then I'd shucked the tricks and wandered into a battlefield where they didn't make it up, where memory was real. It took me over and for a moment I wasn't a salesman, but rather a grateful citizen. It sounds hokey. It is. I don't know what Jesse and Cole saw in me when I soared above the Iron Triangle. Whatever they saw, it persuaded them that I was okay. Not outstanding, not superior or inferior, just American okay.

Returned to ground-level-headedness, on a dark gray day in Korea, I figured that, if they didn't trust me now, I should resign for the banks. We got the car turned around and headed back to Seoul.

They were excited by storytelling and wanted to chat more about the battles. I answered in colorful snippets and then risked my agenda.

"So tell me," I asked, "who was this devilish Korean sweetheart Charlie married anyway? And where is she now?"

3
The Apothecary Shop

THERE IS GOOD REASON to report what I learned about
Charlie's Korean sweetheart during the drive back to Seoul. For
soon the devilish black op Mr. Kim was to make his entrance,
and the only way to him, as it turned out, was through the sweetheart. But I'm going to skip ahead now, because it's all coming
back shortly and indubitably.

Friday, the day after the Ides of March, finished without much
sense at all.

Lila joined Charlie as a no-show. There was a telex from her
waiting for me at the hotel desk. She said that she'd talked to
Charlie in Tokyo by telephone; she said that she would be arriving tomorrow night, Saturday, about the same time as Charlie.
No apologies, no excuses.

I was mightily peeved, of course, yet enjoyed my frustration.
Only my kind of a woman would send a telex to confirm that she
was two-timing me. Also, she was treating me like a bagman,
which was even more annoying because it was true. I wasted the
rest of Friday sending off novelties to my mom and dad. I dined

at the hotel's plush restaurant to reconnoiter it for the rendezvous with Mr. Kim. By VCR time—I rented Bette Davis—I'd decided I was mostly just a sorry heart. Lila was a goldbricking bimbo, I sneered, who swooned away the moment her guru appeared.

You see how mature I was. I tore up a picture of the Taj Mahal in *The Economist.*

Saturday morning, the real grown-up in the game showed himself. I had a wake-up call at six-thirty. There was also a flashing light from the switchboard. It announced a message from the bad guy, Mr. Kim. The bellhop delivered it instantly, addressed to Charlie, forwarded to me by the concierge, as per instructions.

"Welcome Seoul," it read, exactly the way one would copy out of a Korean-English phrase book. "Listen please. Agree meeting the end?" It was signed "Arizona."

I couldn't reply without the telex number in Seoul. This wasn't a worry. I figured Mr. Kim was used to Charlie's herky-jerky business style by now and could be left hanging fire a few days.

Still, everything about Mr. Kim's message was informative. Of major interest, here was proof at last that my portrait of the blackmailers was mostly correct. Mr. Kim existed, was one man, one secret agent, who was nearby. Why? Because an espionage network doesn't break communication methods, what they call commo plans. And Mr. Kim had departed widely from the modus vivendi of the blackmail operation. His message wasn't a telex, it was a typewritten note on cheap, plain stationery. There were even routine typing irregularities. All this told me that Mr. Kim had stepped forward in person. He might have delivered the message personally to the hotel desk, though that was iffy. Regardless, I believed he was operating comfortably renegade. His employers were out. This buy-back was his private deal.

Then there was the wonderful signature "Arizona."

For me, this was Mr. Kim's sense of humor, as well as his gamesmanship. Also evidence that he was closing Charlie down. You remember that Charlie told me the telexes to him were signed by geography—state names such as Pennsylvania, Maryland, Nevada. Further, Charlie had told me that the last several telexes, the ones wherein Charlie proposed and reproposed his buy-back scheme, were all signed "Arizona." Why? I haven't mentioned it before, since I've had so much to brag about, but I'd idly solved the odd pattern of the signatures on the telexes all those blackmailed years. So had Jesse and Cole. They'd called me late Friday night. "Flash from us, sir!" Cole had claimed. "Nevada, West Virginia, Pennsylvania," Jesse had said in the background, "we've got it."

"Pearl Harbor," Cole had said.

"Hostiles've really got it in for us," Jesse had said.

"That's right, Captains," I'd said, "battleship row ablaze, December 4, 1941. Which was even before I was born. You get a B plus, good night."

Now, Saturday morning, with "Arizona" in hand I could assume that Mr. Kim was here for the finish, just as that bomb in the USS *Arizona*'s magazine had finished battleship suzerainty forever. (I did not ask the interesting question as to why a North Korean network should use a Japanese victory as a code. I still don't know the answer, other than to say that black ops can be nostalgic, too.)

How did I feel? I was giddy and so was Holmes Paine. The chase was afoot. It was even useful that Charlie and Lila were absentee. I could devote the day to what I fancied as my own counterintelligence operation.

First, I wrote domineering notes for both Charlie and Lila, to be given to them upon their arrival at the hotel.

Second, I called the correct Seoul branch of the Bank of East Asia and told the account rep there that I wouldn't be needing the cash withdrawal until Monday morning. And neither, to my knowledge, would Ms. L. Schumann. The account rep's name was Han, an agreeable clerk who was able to sound on the phone as if he handled discreetly questionable withdrawals like this every day, one hundred and fifty million yen in a Gladstone bag.

Third, I rang the boys at the apartment they shared like tin stars over a jailhouse. Cole answered sleepily. I fired him up with demands, asking if they'd cleared our day trip with their CO. "Yes, sir, but—" I asked if they'd found us a translator. "Yes, sir, but—"

"REDLEGS rolling," I said. "Fetch me."

Soon, we were eastbound, on Route 44, a two-lane traffic jam that connects Seoul to the northeastern province of Kangwon. We were traveling to farm country to try to locate a Korean woman named Mitsuko Koda at the farming town of Inje. The night before, the boys had secured permission from their CO and

had arranged for an ROK Army liaison to meet us at our destination.

While we're en route, there's time for review of the details I
learned the day before, and that I've delayed telling you. I want
you to understand what we were searching for at Inje.

Charlie's sweetheart, the Korean prostitute he'd married and
later abandoned in 1974, was named Mary Song. Jesse and Cole
had said her name was most of what they had, however, because
Mary Song was dead. And horribly. She'd died of complications
of peritonitis in 1979.

Mary Song. I knew a clue when I heard one. Her name was a
lot to have, and her death was a signpost. I'd pressed the boys to
tell me how they'd gotten so much.

Gumshoe was the answer. They had her name by following a
trail, but not through army records (which had long since been
misplaced or destroyed), rather from their care to follow Charlie's
sergeant's memory that Charlie had married his prostitute in a
local Korean church. Jesse and Cole had backtracked by searching for churches around Charlie's old battalion headquarters.
One doorway at a time. Most of the churches had been rebuilt
since 1974, in the general Korean aggrandizement. Charlie and
Mary Song, it turned out, had married in a local noodle shop that
back then had doubled as a chapel on Sundays. Since then, the
noodle shop congregation had merged with several others and
had built a modest house of worship. An independent evangelical
flock. Churches like this keep records forever. Eventually, Jesse
and Cole had located the registries. There it was, in Korean,
translated by a helpful parson—the record of the marriage of
Charles Purcell and Mary Song, Saturday, August 10, 1974.

After that, there was a blank trail, until Jesse's and Cole's
gumshoes had gotten lucky. They'd reasoned that Mary Song,
once Charlie had abandoned her, had gone back to the bars as a
prostitute. They'd further reasoned that Mary Song was the same
as the hookers working our army today—always in danger of
venereal disease. So they had tracked her name relentlessly until
they'd found a particular charity ward in Seoul. According to the
hospital records they'd bribed, she had died there in 1979. They
told me they never could have found her name, no matter how
much they'd paid, if not that the charity ward was a favorite of
the prostitutes working our troops.

"We've got an arrangement going there forty years," Cole had explained of the charity ward. "We provide the antibiotics and problems, they do the dirty work. Bad news."

The charity ward's piecemeal records showed that Mary Song had been a regular outpatient from at least 1966 until her death in 1979.

Three important facts remained behind. One, at her first recorded visit, in '66, she'd given her birthplace as the Kangwon province farming town of Inje. Two, according to the final admitting report, she had been suffering from advanced peritonitis, possibly brought on by hemorrhage of scar tissue caused by several badly done abortions over the years. Three, the final admitting report noted that Mary Song had forced cash on the nurses, though it was a charity ward, and that Mary Song had insisted that whatever money was left over after her bills go to a woman named Mitsuko Koda, with an address in Inje.

I'd asked the boys how much money was involved.

"It was in won," Cole had said. "Back then, about two hundred and fifty bucks."

I'd asked if they had this admitting report.

"No, sir, we just eyeballed it," Jesse had replied. "We did get a copy of the death certificate, though, and it cost plenty."

"Charity!" Cole had joked.

I'd further observed that the name of the inheritor, Mitsuko Koda, sounded Japanese.

"The Japanese operated Korea like a slave pen, sir," Jesse had remarked correctly.

Cole had added, "The Koda woman's probably a Korean, anyway."

I'd contributed my research of years before, that the Japanese occupiers (1905–1945) had taken Korean wives and produced mixed offspring. That most of the Koreans still bearing Japanese names suffered discrimination. That the Japanese-Koreans tended to band together like an ethnic minority. That, outside the cities, they were often the poorest of the poor, at the bottom of the pecking order.

"So maybe Koda's a relative?" Cole had suggested. "That'd make Mary Song some kind of alias. Who knows?"

I'd said that we should know, and that Mary Song was worth investigating further.

"Yes, sir," Jesse had closed, "I knew you were going to say that, sir."

Why Mary Song was important to me is because I have a simpleminded opinion of espionage. It's a labor-intensive job. People do it; people are it. The same for subversion. Recall the first recorded case. The devil-snake recruited Eve; she turned Adam; he stole the apple. We were after the devil-snake, Mr. Kim. The trail had to include Eve—Mary Song.

Jesse and Cole didn't like this palaver when I tried to sell it to them. They'd thought themselves professionally adept to find Mary Song, even dead, and now regarded her as an extraneous detail. They further thought a jaunt to Inje was a sidebar, that Mitsuko Koda was completely off course and would bring them nothing but paperwork and discomfort, since, to make the trip, they had to clear it with their doubting CO and the doubtful ROKs. The discomfort I would meet in Inje.

Saturday morning, when they picked me up at the hotel, Cole complained again. "This is a detour, sir. You can't learn much when you ask the locals. They don't like us. They just don't."

"There're other problems, too," said Jesse, not explaining.

I insisted anyway. I prodded them into action by reminding them that counterintelligence meant tracking every clue, every rumor. I flattered their gumshoe work; I told them they were great detectives; I said I was proud of them.

"Yes, sir, but—" Cole tried.

"Okay, Mr. Paine," Jesse said, "but you're not going to like it."

(Note the change in our relationship from Friday. While they still might not have fully trusted me, they were willing to follow my leads. Also, they bothered to separate me from Charlie, who was now just "Purcell," while I remained "Mr. Paine." I can't account for it. I do know I was happy for it. The deputies and the dude.)

Their reluctance about Inje, I assumed, was their textbook sense of counterintelligence, that is, they saw it as they were trained: get the facts, let superior officers judge. For them, if Mr. Kim did exist, he was part of a sophisticated spy ring. In any event, they believed that their job was to stake out the buy-back, and then, just like that, they'd have their Hostile Intelligence

Sources: Charlie and the blackmailers. Clear-cut, straightforward.

My opinion was contrary. Mr. Kim was renegade and alone. Now that I had a message from him, I was sure that unless we solved how and why he'd recruited Charlie, how and why he'd helped run Charlie for ten years, the chance of catching him was minimal.

I also confess that I was caught up in the great game, and my vanity was showing again. *Remember, I didn't then know about Lila's lover Rajeesh's manipulations.*

At this point in the chase, I felt closer to Mr. Kim than to anyone else. I told myself that, even though he was aged, corrupt, Red and greedy, I knew what kind of man he was. Successful secret agents are not only loners but also misanthropic, superstitious, hypochondriacal, voyeuristic, what the mind doctors now call sociopathic, though that's a vague diagnosis, because it applies equally to astronomers and campaign chairmen. I know this diagnosis to be true; it also describes me.

On the three-hour drive to Inje, we had much to discuss in all directions.

The hand-delivered message from Mr. Kim excited Jesse and Cole. They examined the paper for watermarks, criticized the grammar. When they tired of MI cryptography, they worked back through the notes they'd taken the day before, requestioning me about Charlie and Lila. Would Charlie back out of the buy-back? Did Lila suspect I was cooperating with MI? Should they wire Charlie's and Lila's suites? I answered no, no, no.

They remained agitated. As we entered the lake and river country leading to Inje, brown peaks to the east, wet green hills to the north, they complained again that today would have been better spent in Seoul, running background checks, prepping for Charlie's arrival tonight.

They also kept complaining that Mary Song was dead; why bother about her?

"There're thousands like her, sir," Cole said. "If we had to track every bar girl—"

"Well, sir," said Jesse, "she was bait, that's it."

I said I was disappointed in them. They'd had a night to study and still hadn't figured out why Mary Song was worth pursuit, even dead.

Their counterintelligence pride bruised, they exchanged mutters awhile, as if I couldn't hear them.

Cole finally asked, "She was a bar girl?"

Jesse carefully recounted, "Purcell wanted to marry her. His CO rejected. He married her anyway. Hostiles approached through her. After Purcell left Korea, she continued to work the bars, maybe for the hostiles, maybe not. What else?"

We crossed the Soyang River. In midday sunshine, the landscape was miniaturized New England during the mud season, particularly because the river valley to the north was planted for corn, cabbage and hay. I relaxed and gave the boys a Holmes Paine lesson in elementary cat-walking.

"Who took the infamous snapshot?" I asked. "The one I call the Tableau of Treason. Charlie and Mr. Kim, Han River foreground, Seoul background?"

"Did Purcell say?" asked Cole.

I reminded them that Charlie was a most uncooperative informant; he wouldn't even give me Mary Song's name. He'd mentioned nothing about the marriage. He'd claimed she was just "some hooker."

Jesse made a note. "Yes, sir, I understand you."

Cole added, "You think this Mary Song took it, but—"

Jesse asked, "Have you ever seen this snapshot?"

"Charlie says he's seen it twice," I said. "Once in Singapore, in '81, for free. Once in New York, last January, for seven and a half million yen."

"If we had it," Cole said, "we'd have Purcell, almost."

I asked, "Why did Mary Song work with Mr. Kim? Why did Mr. Kim use Mary Song to recruit Charlie?"

"Money, drugs, who knows?" said Cole.

I asked, "What's the penalty for espionage here?"

Cole said, "Extinction and then some."

Jesse summated in his soft, tidy voice, "You're saying that Mary Song took the photo. That she knew Mr. Kim. That she wouldn't have worked for Mr. Kim unless she had to. That he had something on her. That Mr. Kim wouldn't have used her unless he could've trusted her. She was his number-one girl. She was in on the recruitment. Maybe a lot of other recruitments. And if we could ask her why she did it, could ask her anything, we could find Mr. Kim. But since we can't, you want us to go through who she was, from Inje back to Seoul."

Cole said, "That's farfetched, sir."

Holmes Paine replied for me, "It's improbable but not impossible."

Jesse asked, "But what could Mr. Kim have had on her?"

I didn't answer, because I didn't know. All I had was my pet theory about the coin of family and greed, flip for crazy. Since espionage in South Korea is as crazy as you can get, there had to be something between Mr. Kim and Mary Song that was as intimate as family. Yet I didn't want to provoke Jesse and Cole further without demonstration that I wasn't just showing off.

At Inje, my vanity had to step alongside a mightier one. His name was Captain Kim Ilwon, and he was the ROK officer designated to be our liaison. He was also a special agent in the ROKs' MI, the allied equivalent to Jesse and Cole.

We arrived before noon, parked in front of a prefab town hall on the main street and got out of the car to wait for Captain Kim Ilwon. Inje was seated on a river, between hills and naked mountains—a compact, crowded, cheaply built produce center, like a New Hampshire village without franchises. Inje wasn't sleepy, it was risen from the dead, since it had ceased to exist in 1950 and was born anew, like Korea itself, after the cease-fire in 1953. It now served as a tourist depot, a gateway to the spectacular Sorak mountain range east of the river. We watched caravans of tourist buses rumble past and hordes of city folk crowd the local inns and noodle shops.

Meanwhile, the boys were filling me in on Captain Kim Ilwon and confessing their anxious ruse. "This might sound funny," Cole said, "but it's best not to talk too much to the mighty mouses."

"Mighty Mouse" is our army's slang for the ROK officer class. I prompted, "Mighty mouses?"

"You're going to meet one of the mightiest," Cole said.

"What we're saying, sir," Jesse added, "is that we gave out a cover story for you. Captain Kim thinks you're here to write a movie about the Army in Korea. About our army. We gave him that idea. It wouldn't do for him to know about Purcell."

"Serious bad news," said Cole. "We've worked with Captain Kim before. He's brutal sometimes."

Jesse concluded, "Let us handle it, sir. He owes us a favor from before, and, if we have to, we'll cash it in."

I kept shut and waited for the soldierly charade to begin.

Meet a mighty "Mighty Mouse," Captain Kim Ilwon. A ROK jeep emerged from the bus traffic and parked tightly behind our Ford. A young, muscular man in an off-dress tunic popped out and began in strange English.

"The ironic Dr. Paine," he said, a rehearsed salutation, bowing once, offering his card, then changing to western style and shaking my hand firmly. He ignored Jesse and Cole, as if they were my servants. "I have brought the copy of your General Mac-Arthur book. Please to sign it for me. My father knew him well. A decorated warrior, my father, like General MacArthur. Big, big anticommunists. Like the Dr. Paine. It is the honor to help you. These country people are not what you know."

I returned my business card—good Korean manners—and flattered him, his uniform and country, also good Korean manners. I credited him for knowing me via my *MacArthur's Ashes*, which had been translated into Korean years before.

Captain Kim beamed, straightened his tunic coat, expanded his chest. Mightiest of mighty mouses was a rude but accurate description of Captain Kim Ilwon. I perversely appreciated him. His theme was clear: I'm the boss, you're the guests, we do this my way.

He asked, "How can I assist today, Dr. Paine?"

Jesse and Cole frowned and started their deception. They said we were looking for Mitsuko Koda. She was possibly a relation of a Korean woman, now deceased, whose memory was the inspiration for my researches.

Captain Kim snapped his fingers. The driver, who doubled as an aide, jumped to alert with a notepad. Captain Kim asked, "A movie? A woman named Mitsuko Koda? You have the address?"

Jesse cautiously gave the address.

I helped the cover story. I said I was planning a love story. A Korean beauty and an American soldier fell in love in the spring-filled mountains. Eventually, he left her, promising to return. There was a child. She survived desperately as a bar girl in Seoul. He married in America. After many years, he found he couldn't forget his Korean bride, and he and his wife came looking for her. I added, "I'm looking for an ending."

"Sad, sad love story," said Captain Kim. "And *the* success in the movies. The Korean woman's name?"

I said that I knew her as Mary Song. That she had left Mitsuko Koda some money after her death.

Captain Kim asked, "The name of this American soldier?"

I said the real soldier didn't matter to me, because this was the Hollywood version. In the real story, I said, he never came back, and she died alone. For now, I was calling him Charlie.

"Charlie, yes, the American name." Captain Kim was excited in a sentimental way. Koreans love tv soap opera just like us. I figured if I had to, I could bribe him with a coauthor credit.

"I shall visit the authorities," he said. "It will be soon."

What Captain Kim actually meant was that it would take some time. I marvel now that I was so naive of Korean custom. Everything is done by hierarchy. It was necessary for Captain Kim to call on the police chief, for him to call on the mayor, perhaps even for the mayor to telephone his superiors. Something accounted for our long wait outside the town hall. The boys had been right—dealing with the locals was prohibitively frustrating. My genius to take a three-hour drive to ask a couple of questions of a woman named Mitsuko Koda was turning into a tangle of lies and delays. The only relief during our wait was a quick lunch at a noodle shop, cheap and filling, where the boys tried not to say "I told you so," while commenting on my deceptions about Charlie.

"That was great," said Cole. "He bought it whole."

Jesse finished his soda in a gulp. "How does it end?"

I told them that, in Puccini's original, Madama Butterfly chose suicide rather than further dishonor, but that I'd always thought that a flashy Italian gimmick.

Captain Kim returned in the company of a local policeman. "Listen, please," Captain Kim announced. "I have found Mitsuko Koda."

Jesse squinted and Cole flapped his elbows impatiently. We had, after all, given Captain Kim her address.

"Do you know of her?" Captain Kim asked me. "No? Do you know about the—*mudangs?*" He made a show of translating. "The witches?"

Jesse and Cole rearranged their posture as if trying to think up a way to get out of this. Lying didn't come easily to them. Harder, their professionalism was out of keeping with Captain Kim's swagger.

I interrupted this clash of cultures by saying that I knew something about witches, about Korean shamanism, but not enough, and was happy to learn more.

Captain Kim fell in beside me to explain.

We followed the policeman on foot, down the main street and then into an alley that led to the field of open-air stalls that was Inje's farmer's market. The tourists were a riot for the treats, squeezing produce, bartering in loud squeals. Our policeman cleared a path, and the farmers bowed correctly at Captain Kim's uniform. We were at the edge of town now, along a muddy street of shabbily built shops.

Our goal was a storefront. It had a narrow window filled with roots, deer antlers and what had to be dried snakeskins. It was an apothecary shop.

You don't know any more about Korea than me, and all I knew at the time was that Koreans are notorious worrywarts about illness. To call them hypochondriacs is to understate their fervor for herbal cures. The apothecary shops do make you feel good right away, because they smell of ginseng and wondrous herbs like mugwort and sow thistle.

Inside the shop, we mixed through the patrons. The ancient apothecary was startled by the policeman, and he clicked off the color tv that is part of Korean shopkeeping. The apothecary, a frail, indistinct old man in a sweat of obeisance, bowed to us so fast he crashed roots off his counter.

The policeman barked. The patrons scrambled out. The policeman deferred to Captain Kim, who broadcasted loud threats.

"He'll hit him now," Cole whispered to me, "stay back."

The policeman suddenly poked the apothecary's chest with his baton. The apothecary fell on his knees and bowed faster, gasping and weeping. The policeman whacked him on the back. The apothecary instinctively raised his arms for a shield. He didn't have fingers on his left hand; instead, a reddish, flaccid stump.

The policeman whacked the stump as if to break it off.

"Hey!" I shouted. "What's wrong here? What's he say?"

The boys yanked me clear of the fray and then the shop. Outside, they scolded me. "You wanted it," said Jesse.

"Not this."

"We can't call it off, we can't!" Cole said.

Jesse warned, "It's their country, sir."

The policeman jerked the apothecary outside. The old man was trembling but silent. They stumbled around the side of the shop, down a narrow alley to the back of the row of shops. Jesse, Cole and I followed Captain Kim.

There was a low-slung hut loosely attached to the back of the apothecary shop. The policeman shoved the apothecary inside the hut.

Captain Kim explained, "He will bring Mitsuko Koda to you."

"You could've just asked him," I complained.

Suddenly, several women in hiking clothes rushed out, glanced fearfully at Captain Kim and scattered. The policeman charged inside. I pursued.

What I found was the ruin of a folk ceremony known as a *kut*. Kneeling on a straw mat was an old woman in a white silk gown fringed with feathers. The smell was sickening incense. The hut was divided by screens hung with Korean scrolls. There were tapers burning on the stone table. And at the old woman's knees was a rack of bells and a large brass urn filled with paper ashes.

The old woman was the *mudang*, or witch. You could hire her like a soothsayer or prophetess. The anthropologists call this shamanism, and that means it's whatever you can imagine.

The battered apothecary was kneeling beside the witch, whispering heatedly.

Captain Kim strutted in and spoke abusively. The witch actually snarled at him and closed her eyes, as if she wanted us to disappear.

"This is Mitsuko Koda, Dr. Paine," Captain Kim said. "Ask her what you want. I will translate."

I know now that Captain Kim had violated every taboo in his country to deliver me to Mitsuko Koda. She was a repulsive, cunning, ancient woman, who was also a money-making witch. Saturday brought the wealthiest clientele from the big city. I puzzle now, safely out of her reach, if things didn't start going wrong for me in Korea because I chased away her patrons. The Koreans believe that every hill, every object, every corner has a spirit and that some of them are devils . Mitsuko Koda's job, as I understand it, was to negotiate with these spirits in favor of her customers. Significantly, she could also be hired to descend into hell and

converse with the dead, perhaps even rescue the dead and return
them to paradise. I didn't learn of this possibility until, after a few
stupid tries at apology, I asked her, through Captain Kim, if she
could tell me about Mary Song. Why had Mary Song left her two
hundred and fifty dollars eleven years ago?

Mitsuko Koda was smoking a cigarette by then, Korean style,
like sucking on a dart. She heard out Captain Kim's daring bombast, then grinned greedily with blackened and crooked teeth and
spoke sharply.

"She says," Captain Kim translated, "it costs you two million
won. She means a ceremony, you understand?" We were both
sweating in the hut. Captain Kim struggled to appear bold. "For
you, Dr. Paine. She will go to Mary Song and ask her the questions. Mary Song will speak to you with the *mudang*'s mouth."

I sighed. Two million won was about twenty-five hundred dollars, which I figured was foreign-devil rate to chitchat with the
soul of Mary Song.

I also assumed I'd been wrong about Mary Song's two hundred
and fifty dollars. It hadn't been a legacy for a relative. Rather, it'd
been for this witch to perform a posthumous ceremony—perhaps
the major stunt of retrieving Mary Song's soul from hell. This
genius assumption told me nothing more than that Mary Song
had died in fear of damnation.

I told Captain Kim I had no more questions.

Captain Kim misunderstood; he argued with the witch about
the price. She barked back. "Two million won," Captain Kim
said defeatedly, "not cheaper."

Do you remember Walter Cronkite's "Twentieth Century" tv
show? Once upon a time (I must have been in high school), I saw
an episode about what had become of the Korean cease-fire by
the 1960s. The theme was that it was a farce, with our side and
their side arguing over trivial violations of the armistice. The
show featured an example. The North Koreans had found five
rusty nails on the Freedom Bridge at P'anmunjŏm; they claimed
the nails were American sabotage against their vehicles. Major
generals argued about it for hours at the armistice table, a pouting, ranting deadlock.

That tv show was the first time I can remember ever thinking
about Korea. It was then considered a poor, luckless society,
propped up by American aid. What struck me at the time, as a

teenager, was that Koreans were a most surly and stubborn people, who argued strangely over nonsense such as rusty nails. Since then I've learned, as you have, that grown-ups everywhere argue over rusty nails. It's called politics by the big thinkers, but that's usually a euphemism for the way of the world. I say they're rusty nails, you say they're sabotage, let's fight.

What I'm saying, queerly, is that as confounding as the way of the world is—where a whole country can remain at civil war for forty years because no one knows how to stop it—nonetheless, the way of the world is the only thing I know about. I don't know about hell and don't want to.

If Mary Song was in hell, if her two-hundred-and-fifty-dollar try for deliverance of her soul had failed, and if she was available to be interrogated at my direction by a hired witch, my opinion was that my investigation in Inje was done.

I thanked Mitsuko Koda. She was not pleased to lose yet another fee and scowled at the five twenties I did put down on the mat, though she took them quickly.

I also thanked Captain Kim. He was so concerned to show he was not terrified that he assured me he could get more information out of her. I humored him out of the hut and away from the apothecary shop by saying that I'd learned a deal that would be useful in my "sad, sad love story."

I'm breaking off this episode. It's time to get on to Charlie. No tricks. You now know what I did after my jaunt to Inje. And if I'm not telling you more, it's because I've already put you ahead of me at that time, and what's the fun of walking the cat if you get the answers before the questions?

Still, I've reported Inje with detail because it wasn't as futile as I thought. Mitsuko Koda did have the ability to descend into hell and to ask dead and damned Mary Song questions. If you laugh at this, you're just like I was, too superstitious to throw away a penny, not superstitious enough to pay mind to witchcraft, when all it wants is a fair return on its strange labor.

You're also forgetting, as I did then, that Rosie had made me laugh that last night in New York by joking that I was a big, very big witch, who was going into hell to rescue Charlie's soul. It was funny, Mitsuko Koda and me in the same trade, flimflam for hire. Next time, I'm hiring the witch the first time I'm asked.

4
Powwow

CHARLIE AND LILA did arrive, separately, Saturday night.
Meanwhile, I was deliberately staying out late with Jesse and
Cole. I felt bad about forcing Inje upon them, so I treated us to
Italian food at the Hilton, where we chatted happily about spring
training (they were National Leaguers, Cards for Jesse and the
Redlegs for Cole; I pretended the Mets, then revealed my tattered
pinstripes; end debate). Lastly, I pleased myself greatly by guid-
ing them to the all-night bazaar district. I was shopping for an
update for my "Midway" game. At the electronics counter, I
spontaneously ordered them each a 386 clamshell laptop.

"Wait, sir." Cole stared at the black beauty the clerk displayed
for us. He turned to Jesse. "Can we take these, Jess?"

Jesse was polite. "It looks like a bribe."

I said the fancy word was "testimonial."

Jesse rejected. "Then negative."

Cole agreed. "We can't do it, but thanks anyway."

I waved off the salesclerk. Outside again, I bought us ice-cream
cones. Back in the car, I said, "I made a mistake. I'm sorry."

"Yes, sir," Jesse agreed. He spoke to both my bribe and Inje when he said, "No more detours, Mr. Paine?"

"Affirmative," I obliged. I was grateful they weren't holding my mistakes against me. At dinner, I'd learned enough about their lives to recognize that we came from the same circumstances back home—the middle-middle class, as my mom says, all sons of large families of vets, all high school jocks, baseball fans, lucky, healthy and blessed. Fate had pulled me into books and Hollywood. They had gone through state schools on ROTC scholarships, then chosen the Army as a career. Bluntly, I was an uppity faker, and they were steadfastly themselves. Also, their taboos were mine, and I had just violated a big one: I'd flashed my ludicrous bank account.

We drove quickly across town to the Royal Chosin. Jesse turned around to say, "You have our phone numbers, sir, at HQ, at the officers' club, at the apartment. Use them anytime you want. We're on duty straight through until it's done. And we'll be close by."

I apologized one last time. "I'm sorry about the laptops. I make a lot of mistakes, Captains."

Cole joked, "You called us, sir; that wasn't."

Jesse smiled. "That's it."

Relieved, I ascended back to make-believe. "Have yer lariats ready for lunchtime Monday."

Jesse and Cole were true pleasures. It was time to get back to my fake uppity class, where everybody lies and the doublecross is the drug of choice.

My suite's telephone was flashing with messages waiting. I knew they were from Charlie and Lila. I'd called the Royal Chosin desk from the Hilton to make sure they'd arrived. I took hold of my attention span, consulted Holmes Paine about how we were doing (he sniffed) and then called the desk to be entertained by Charlie's and Lila's latest demands. The desk didn't tell me that the messages were booby-trapped.

Charlie first. I rang his suite, just eighty feet down the hall, and prepared to tell him how to breathe, since I'd finally understood that the way to treat Charlie was to bully him.

Rosie answered. I lost a breath.

"Please listen," Rosie said, "oh, Mr. Paine, he's asleep and I shouldn't wake him."

I still couldn't speak.

"He got your letter, and he said to tell you he'll see you in the morning."

I rallied. "What're you doing here?"

"You told me to get him on the plane," she answered flatly. "Mr. Purcell wouldn't come unless I came. I had to. Mrs. Purcell is so upset."

"Are you all right?"

"It was a long trip," she said without explaining. "He's not doing well, Mr. Paine. You must be kind."

I made her repeat all this, in hope she'd ask for help.

Instead, she maintained her fiction that Charlie was asleep; she was jet-lagged; I must be kind. She repeated "kind, kind, kind," as if she had just met the word.

I remember thinking, *This isn't Rosie.* She didn't sound or talk much like Rosie. The governing maternalism was there, but the playfulness was gone, and her movie-mad American slanginess had deteriorated into acceptable diction. It was a fair guess that she was along to tote and fix Charlie's pipes. The heroic governess had become a junkie's Stepin Fetchit. There was nothing to do about it tonight. Except hate Charlie.

I told Rosie I'd see her in the morning. I walked around my suite. I drank New York seltzer. I watched the traffic lights color the intersections. I felt angry and bad, mostly bad.

Then, to make myself feel better, I rang Lila's suite four floors below me. She'd curse Charlie for me, she'd agree this caper was too dirty to play without a long bath, maybe together.

I was enjoying silly thoughts about washing that red hair, when Lila answered and announced that Rajeesh was with her.

This felt worse than I will admit. Rosie was a surprise. Rajeesh was threat alert. Wrong threat, wrong alert, but I felt the persecuted patsy anyway and returned a rude remark.

Lila protested gorgeously, "Who the f—— are you? Listen, you want to tell me how to live? You want to? Go ahead! I'm tired, I'm trying to do what everyone tells me, and Charlie's out of his gourd. I'm *glad* Raj is here. He can handle Charlie, I can't, and you—you! Where were you all night? It's midnight, and I was asleep! You want to yell at me, call in the morning, asshole."
Slam.

I stared at the receiver and did feel better. I wasn't offended, I was in love. Lila, Lila, Lila—how I'd missed her loose lip, as much as her red hair. I didn't like the lip image when I thought about old raghead's stand-in, the Cambridge man. I doubt if knowing why Rajeesh was really with her would have changed my opinion as to what I thought about where Lila was sleeping.

I asked myself what I wanted from Lila. The answer was that I wanted her back and would fight with whatever was at hand. Such as lies.

I called Lila back to apologize. "Forget my bad manners, Lila," I said, "and listen." In a few sentences, I'd updated her on Seoul and Mr. Kim's first contact and our money at the Bank of East Asia with Mr. Han. I deviously left out mention of Jesse and Cole and the famous bald eagle. I assured her I could get Charlie to set up the meeting with Mr. Kim for Monday luncheon.

"We can do this, Lila," I lied, "just as we planned."

There was sighing. "I'm just edgy, I guess," she said. "Can we go over this tomorrow?"

She repeated herself and I heard moving sounds, as if she was walking the phone into another room. "You should talk to Charlie as soon as you can," she continued. "He's deep into the dope and the pills. You know Rosie's with him? When I called his room —" She broke off. "Hey, where were you all night?"

I said I'd been at dinner over at the Hilton.

"My family's cracking up, and you dine out!"

"Tell me about Rosie."

"Okay, okay, Rosie. I called Charlie's room, and Rosie answers quietly. Like it's New York, and the babies are asleep. She tells me Charlie's in bed. Yeah, right, tucked up with his pipes is more like it. I demanded she put him on the phone. She refused with that sugary crap of hers. I thought, okay, Rosie's with him, and what the f——'s that mean? So I called Pammie. I should've called her last night, but I forgot. Pammie says Rosie just disappeared the day before yesterday. Whatever yesterday was. Rosie asked for a day off and then vanished. Pammie's strung out on this, so I told her to call Mother, and that *is* desperate for us. If I have to, I'm shipping Pammie and the kids to Mother until we're out of here. In fact, I'm definitely getting Pammie out of there. Why should she stay? Charlie's gone, gone, Tip, he's gone."

I asked for more about what Rosie'd said.

"Ask her yourself, you're her big buddy. I'm sure Charlie flew her into Tokyo with more dope. He's weird about her, watch it."

"How are you?" I asked.

"Who cares about me?" she said.

I didn't have to lie. "I do."

"I guess I'm all right." Lila spoke softer and slower. There was more about her mom, Pam and the kids. It was clear the Purcell family was "cracking up" like a piggy bank. It wasn't for me to fix. I concentrated on Lila's mood (edgy, yes, but high-powered and intuitive) and asked her if we could meet for lunch the next day.

She stalled me. "We'll work something out. I know, I know, it's a mess—"

"Miss me, Lila?"

"—thanks, Tip, you must hate us by now."

"Us, Lila?"

"I've said some things about me and Raj," she whispered, "but he's helping me. He talked to Charlie in Tokyo last night, and I don't think Charlie'd be here if Raj hadn't talked to him. Charlie will listen to Raj. He might be the only person who can get through. I'm telling you, Charlie's nuts. Even for him he's nuts. Something happened in Tokyo."

I figured what had happened was robots; I tried anyway. "What about Tokyo?"

"Ask Charlie. But I—I think Charlie got really rich—*really* rich. He's *craaaazy.*"

"I understand."

"I'm sorry. I am. It's a mess, and I'm tired."

"Me too, Lila."

I also felt bamboozled. I sat up with my laptop listening to Armed Forces Radio do a late-night report from the spring training camps around the grapefruit leagues. Baseball lingo always calms me, reminds me that off-the-field problems eventually get worked out at the ballpark. I thought: If Charlie was weird about Rosie, then what was Lila about Rajeesh, what was I about Lila? I typed up Inje. I recorded Rosie's and Lila's words just in case I'd missed something. Being what I am, pompous adult male, I didn't like that my tv-simple plan was suddenly encumbered by Butch Raj's personality and the Opium Kid's puerility.

No, that was thinking like a make-believe cowboy. I didn't like it because double-crossing is best when you don't fall for the sister-in-law.

No, that was thinking like a loser. I didn't have an explanation, and neither did my laptop. Rosie was here to help Charlie? Rajeesh was here to help Lila? Why not? Before I'd pushed my way into their lives, they'd helped each other to anything they'd wanted. I was the outsider, the rookie tryout, and they didn't owe me excuses.

I could go on excusing my idiocy by claiming that I wasn't on the same page as Rajeesh the black op. Nor as Rosie the black op. Then again, there were pages left out of their files, too. For the last time, *I promise*, I'm reminding you that I didn't know that what had just collected in the Royal Chosin's suites was a battle of Asian creeps over a golden junkie.

Seven hours later, dressed by Lila's tailor for Lila's theatrics, I strolled down the hall to Charlie's suite.

I aimed to catch Charlie before he could scramble his chemistry. Rather, I upset mine. I knocked, waited, knocked, waited. Rosie opened the door.

"Please listen—" she started.

She looked beaten, a scrape on her chin and a red mark on the nape of her neck. Her chipped canine suddenly suggested a sinister explanation.

I stuttered, "Wha-at's going on?"

Rosie hunched her shoulders angrily, the way she had when I'd caught her scavenging turkey. "Please, Mr. Paine—" She clutched her peach dressing gown (Charlie's) to cover the bruises.

I went past her, through the parlor into the hallway to the bedrooms. The second bedroom was rumpled, and I saw Rosie's traveling case on the bureau and wool frock in the closet. I told myself I must stay in control, no tantrums.

"He's asleep, please," she said behind me.

"Rosie, tell me the truth," I said, "did he hit you?"

Rose changed her lie. "He hasn't slept, I couldn't get him to. Please listen. He's very sick right now."

"Sick" was Rosie's euphemism for the dope. Or was it also for those bruises? I pushed open the door of the master bedroom.

"Whadayawannow?" said Charlie. Naked, he rolled over on the bed and pointed the opium pipe at me.

I vandalized the hotel's curtains for air and light.

Charlie flopped backward and laughed. "It's you, yeah, yeah. Wha' time's it?"

I kicked the bedclothes aside and barked back that it was time for him to pretend he was a gentleman.

"Here, let me help," said Rosie, rushing over to cover Charlie with another dressing gown. "You haven't slept, Mr. Purcell, and you said you would."

"Goo' ol' Rosie," said Charlie, "than's." Charlie steadied himself against the headboard. I watched closely to see if he was pawing her. Not really, just leaning on her shoulders while she covered his privates, an intimate scene suited to a nursery.

"He's going to be sick," said Rosie. "Please, help me." She was trying to get the beauty to the toilet.

I wasn't going to clean up after Charlie that way again. I said I'd be in the parlor. I said I wanted him showered, dressed and sick or well in front of me. "Pronto," I demanded.

"I'll take care of him," Rosie obeyed, struggling to keep him decent. "Could you call for his breakfast, please?"

While Rose struggled with Charlie, I stormed to the parlor and grabbed the phone, punching for Lila's room.

She answered hazily, "Yes, oh, Tip, what time's—"

I told her it was 7:13 A.M. and she was to get up here. Bring along the squash champ. And a vacuum cleaner.

"What?" Lila said. "Is it Charlie?"

I said it was the whole sick gang of them, and if she and Raj didn't show up fully dressed pronto, I was going to make another threat she wouldn't like.

Lila and Rajeesh did hurry. Charlie didn't. Meantime, the amazing room service delivered a breakfast cart, so that I had a chance to collect myself sipping tea and watching the soft Sunday traffic below.

I hadn't planned on a powwow this early in the day. Rosie's condition had panicked me a little. I couldn't decide if I was right that Charlie was raping her, or if I was just feeling the general degradation around me. I had, after all, let Rosie keep Charlie's pipes lit in New York, and who knew what he'd done to her there, behind closed doors?

What was different now? It was the bondage. I couldn't accept that she'd let Charlie treat her like a slave. Then again, wasn't she? The sum of this pep talk with myself was that I knew I must bear down and keep this matter-of-fact, no more sentimental spectacles.

Lila and Rajeesh came in looking the harried couple. "What's happened?" Lila said.

Rajeesh nodded to me paternally. "How bad is it, Tip?"

"No more than yesterday," I said calmly. "Please, have some coffee. Please, sit down. Please."

I continued to babble insincerely.

So did Rajeesh; he commented that he hoped he could be of help to me. He said that, last night, he'd had a good conversation with Charlie in Tokyo, that he was sure Charlie's condition was because of the stress.

Great word, "stress," I thought; they used to say "sin."

Lila sat by dourly, watching Rajeesh and me pretend we were discussing a delinquent younger brother. I was annoyed that she looked good to me. She looked even better sitting near Rajeesh. It's never promising when the beauty and the rival wear the same color scheme and cut—charcoal-gray suits this morning, him with a silver tie, her with a black shell and a sterling choker. Of course, I was wearing one of Lila's blue suits. A tailor-made triangle. I stayed at the table and lit my pipe so I wouldn't have to smell her.

Rosie and Charlie emerged eventually. Rosie was a governess again in her neat frock. Charlie was bright clean and dapper in one of Lila's uniforms.

"Good morning, Raj, Lila," he said. "Tip, I'm glad you're here."

It was a miraculous transformation. I knew this was chemistry talking; he'd popped some uppers and was now goldilocks perfect. I was relieved. It made my schemes seem possible.

"Well, now," said Charlie, "coffee, please, Rosie, sweet, you know. Those rolls look good, like not too much marmalade."

Lila clattered her coffee cup and sighed.

Rajeesh said, "That's better, Charlie. You've worried Tip here. Me, too."

"I said I'd be here, and I am," Charlie declared.

"Christ, Charlie," said Rajeesh, who annoyed me because he really was being a help with Charlie, "you promised me you'd lay off of it. Charlie?"

."I'm here," Charlie repeated. "Another sugar, Rosie. You know I like it sweet. Like, sugar's not gonna kill me." He laughed prettily, sat straight in his chair across from Lila and Rajeesh. "Now, an early meeting," Charlie said. "Good, I've had a week of them, it seems. How're you feeling, Tip?"

Lila whispered, "Shit."

I poked a roll with my pipe and began my dissertation. First off, I asked Charlie if he'd had any communication from Mr. Kim.

"Yeah, yeah, there's something," said Charlie. "Rosie, get it, will you, it's on the bed." Rosie returned with another plain white piece of stationery. "It was waiting for me when I checked in last night," Charlie said. "Signed 'Arizona' like before. You say it's who? Mr. Kim?"

Lila coughed and fidgeted. Suddenly she, the ex-smoker, had a cigarette in her mouth, and Rajeesh was lighting it.

I brought out the first message from Mr. Kim and compared number one with number two. Exactly the same: "Welcome Seoul . . ." Charlie, Lila and Rajeesh were watching me for any hint of trouble. I showed them my overbearing confidence. I told Charlie that his aged taxi-driver hustler, Mr. Kim, was, in my opinion, the very same "Arizona."

"That little guy?" said Charlie, laughing. "Incredible, that little guy? But he must have partners, yeah?"

"Shut up, Charlie," said Lila.

I told Charlie that the buy-back was going to be the next day. He was to reply to Mr. Kim by noon. He was to demand a meeting with Mr. Kim for the next day, luncheon at the Dragon's Gate restaurant, the big one downstairs. At 1:00 P.M.

"I understand," said Charlie. He pulled out his pocket calendar and wrote down my orders. "One o'clock tomorrow, Dragon's Gate. Good food, I've heard. Anything else?"

I didn't like it that Charlie was suddenly such an obedient victim.

"A lot else," I said. I appointed Rajeesh to be Charlie's keeper. No more dope, I ordered. Charlie was to stay in this suite.

"Yes, good idea," Rajeesh commented, "isn't it, Charlie?"

I expected Charlie to misbehave. No. He smiled brilliantly and wrote down something.

I appointed Lila to be the bagperson along with me. We would pick the money up in the morning. We would carry it in the Gladstone bag I'd ordered. We would keep it with us until the luncheon meeting.

"Okay," she said without conviction. "It's okay, Raj?"

"Yes, yes," Rajeesh commented.

Charlie was writing in his pocket calendar again.

I can remember thinking all the while we chatted that our powwow was going strangely well. Too strangely. That there was something off with Charlie's compliance, Rajeesh's paternalism, Lila's nerves. I talked slowly and repeated everything. They only spoke in order to assure me that they would do what they were told. How did I explain it? I told myself that they'd probably talked about all this among themselves on the phone, and that I shouldn't overthink their moods.

By about 9:00 A.M., I'd done my work as scrupulously as possible. I didn't feel any better, but that wasn't my job. This was spycatching, not a sauna. I got up to leave.

Lila demanded, "Where are you going?"

I suddenly knew where I was going and used it to taunt her. "Church," I said. "It's Sunday morning. Want to come along?"

Lila flushed. Rajeesh put a hand on her. Lila muttered, "Not now, Tip." She was being dramatic. We all waited her out. "I want—to call Pam," she said. "I should call Pammie." She addressed Charlie. "Shouldn't we call her, Charlie? Say something nice, like, How're you feeling after the D and C?"

Charlie said, "Sure, sure, Lile."

I'd heard what I'd heard. Pam had had an abortion? When? Why? I kept shut.

Rosie approached me. "May I go with you, Mr. Paine?"

Surprised, I said, "Sure. Happy to have company."

"Is it all right, Mr. Purcell?" Rosie asked.

Charlie flapped his princely hand. "I'll be fine, Rosie, you have a good time."

While Rosie raced for her coat, Lila whispered to Rajeesh. By and by, Lila came over to me at the door. She smelled terrific. I backed up. Her words were strained, since she was now lying to me like everyone else. "Do we still have a lunch date today?"

I noted Rajeesh's glance at his mistress's wavering. I weakened, grumbled, then told Lila we had a lunch date the following day, at one o'clock.

"No, no, today, can't we? I'd like to see this place before to-morrow. Dragon's Gate, downstairs, okay? Just us?"

I took the bait like the fool I was. Yes, Lila, lunch, Lila. She looked back to Rajeesh, who was smiling tranquilly. Rajeesh looked to Charlie, who was smiling tranquilly.

I smiled in imitation and ignored the fact that Lila was quivering. It was clear to me that they were a family team, and I was the alien.

So why didn't I yell at them? Perhaps because I was deceiving them as they were me, and the room was so full of lies that it was impossible to listen to my intuition that my tv-simple plan was already obsolete. The full answer might be that I wanted to be stupid for a while longer, rather than the kind of person who betrays everyone, including a woman he claims to love for her smell alone. What a laugh. I thought I was in charge? I thought Rajeesh was jealous, Lila was innocent, Charlie was too dopey to be dangerous? All this, and I never asked myself why, for people supposedly about to hand over one hundred and fifty million yen to a blackmailer, they didn't once say something normally fussy such as, "Gosh, Tip, is it really gonna work? Smiling face to smiling face?"

5
Rosie Lies

I NEVER MEANT for Rosie to be the one to pay for all the lies. That's the crucial truth here. Rosie was dirty, Rosie was running a nasty game. But. Excuses follow, but remember this: I blame everyone for Rosie's death, especially myself.

I do believe that Rosie went to church with me Sunday morning because she wanted to go to church. Yet she also had a dark mission. She wanted to get me out of harm's way, and she botched her lies that morning.

Up to then, Rosie's job for the three Lees had been to spy on Charlie. She'd been clever to rope me into the Purcell troubles back in New York. She'd been skillful to make Charlie so dependent upon her that he couldn't move without her. And she'd been devious to let me catch her being abused by Charlie that morning. Yes, that turn in the dressing gown with naked Charlie was a setup. She knew she was setting everyone against everyone else. Then again, she also knew what she wanted from Charlie.

For the moment, consider that, though I've told you Rosie was an op, you've never asked what her motive was. Just another civil servant? No. Were the three Lees holding paper on her? Not exactly. The truth of it was that Rosie Yip was a volunteer. This was family business to her. I've argued that she was trying to save the golden realm of her family, the Purcells. That she was trying to get help to lift that paper that *deviled* her loved ones. And it's true, she was.

Yet there was more to her sense of family than the Purcells. I've told you she was a war orphan, that her parents and siblings were dead. Consider also that Koreans have huge families, indeed, that they can think of themselves as one big family, and that the sort of paper they have to lift as a people is the death warrant called the unending Korean War. In sum, how come I hadn't ever thought to ask where Rosie was born in 1948?

Rosie did botch her lies that morning. We taxied to the Youngnak Presbyterian Church, a stone-built fortress not far from the hotel, in the fashionable Myŏng-dong shopping district. Youngnak might be the largest congregation in Calvinism; it's so big that it has to hold two Sunday morning services. We slipped into the packed upper gallery and enjoyed the third Sunday of Lent. Rosie found us an English-language hymnal, so that I could mumble along, especially my favorite, "We Greet You, Sure Redeemer from All Strife," said to have been written by John Calvin himself on a rare fair day at Geneva.

There wasn't opportunity for us to chat until afterward, outside, promenading under gray clouds. The worship service hadn't relaxed Rosie; she remained sad-eyed, pinched. I figured it was because of Charlie. I also figured if Charlie needed Rosie, then so did I. This was almost as contemptuous a treatment as Charlie's, so I didn't think about it. I tried small talk.

I learned that Rosie had joined Youngnak Presbyterian Church as a teenager, when it was holding its services in auditoriums.

"Seoul was mostly abandoned," she told me. "There were shacks and open fires, with beggars living in caves in the hills. You wouldn't believe it."

I asked where she'd lived.

"In a camp," she answered, "down by the river. A big camp."

This was radically different from the grateful-orphan version she'd given me in New York. Her childhood had been base poverty and fear.

"Sunday was always good, Mr. Paine," she said. "I got a job in the church bakery. It was my way out of the camp."

I asked about her time in the orphanage.

"That was when I was little," she said. "At the bakery, I was eleven by then."

I pictured Rosie scavenging garbage heaps, washing in the river, waiting for a miracle. I didn't like myself when I thought that nearly thirty years later I was letting Charlie pick at her, make her wash him by hand.

Suddenly, I disgusted myself for letting Charlie push her around. What was I going to do about it?

Rosie wouldn't linger at the church; she said she had to get back to Charlie.

I agreed and then did the wrong thing: I got bossy. I told her I wanted her safe and home. That if anyone needed her help, it was Pam and the kids.

"You should go back to New York," I bossed. "Charlie's okay with Lila and Rajeesh. And me. I'll arrange your ticket. You can get your sleep tonight and fly back in the morning."

"I'm all right, Mr. Paine."

"I'll get you a room of your own, for tonight," I said. "This afternoon, we can go shopping. In the market, we can buy the children every hand puppet they make, and the girls are old enough for computers. How about it?"

"That sounds nice," she said unhappily.

I hailed a taxi, thinking I'd struck a bargain.

Rosie curled in the taxi seat and spoke darkly. "Mr. Paine, please listen, what they're doing. I heard things in Tokyo. It's the money. You shouldn't trust them. They think they can buy you."

I gaped. "What are you talking about?"

"They don't know what they're doing. Mr. Purcell, Miss Schumann, Dr. Nehru, they don't know."

You might have said it more plainly, Rosie, but still, here's where I should have listened. I continued bossy.

"I know about the robots," I said, "and that Charlie's just closed a big deal in Tokyo. It's okay. I know he's rich and thinks he can buy what he wants. It's why I trust him about tomorrow. I trust his greed."

"What Mr. Purcell is doing," Rosie tried again, "it's very dan-

gerous." She looked at me intensely, affectionately, generously—
the governess in action. "This is Seoul. It's not what they understand. It's not like your movies. They can't buy what they want
here."

I wouldn't listen and made a stupid joke. "If you can't buy it,
it ain't dangerous, it's natural."

"No, no," she complained, "please listen. . . ."

No. My paternalism sounded worse than Rajeesh's. I told her
everything was going to be fine. I said that I would take care of
everything for her. I asked, as if coddling a toddler, if she trusted
me.

"Yes, I do." There were no tears. She was the grown-up.

I halfheartedly tried straight talk. "What is it, Rosie? What's
bothering you?"

She returned half-truth. "I think you should go home."

"You first," I bossed. "Please leave tomorrow," I repeated. "If
you go tomorrow, I promise I'll be home next Saturday, and we
can catch a flick together."

Rosie turned away from me. "I'll do what you say, Mr. Paine,"
she lied.

Would I have listened if Rosie had told me the whole truth?
Yes. No. No one knows the whole truth to tell it. Throwing money
at taxi drivers and clerks, toying with Military Intelligence and
Mr. Kim and Horizon Pacific, I was so pigheaded it was cruel.
Eventually, I'm going to have to tell you in detail how the person
my cruelty murdered was Rosie.

Back at the Royal Chosin, Rosie balked when I tried to get her
a room of her own.

"No, I have to stay with Mr. Purcell."

I renegotiated. "Then I'll have your plane ticket at the desk for
the morning. There'll be a car waiting."

Rosie bowed like a slave.

"Don't tell Charlie," I finished, "just go."

Rosie ran back to her master, her big shoulders hunched in
anger.

6
Just Business

PRESENTLY LILA WAS ANGRY too, when we met at the door of the Dragon's Gate restaurant. It was the money, lots of it, bags full.

Lila prepared me shakily. "It's a mess, I'm sorry."

I smiled and said I knew this was Charlie's idea—or was it Raj's?—our little tête-à-tête over soup and salad.

Lila wasn't fooling. "It's Flowers's," she said, "Jimmy Flowers. They cooked this up in Tokyo. And this morning before you called. Shit, Tip, shit."

"What?"

"I'm supposed to say there's been a change in plans. Because you like me, you're supposed to believe me. I'm supposed to say that your money, my money, that they don't need it anymore."

"Who?"

"Don't f—— around! You're onto them. That's what you were doing in Singapore, isn't it? You figured it out, you told me. The robots. Charlie, Flowers, that little nerd Kepler."

"Raj, too?" I guessed.

"You're acting as juvenile as they are. I told you Charlie's out of his mind. But, God, what they're talking about is sicko. I'm sorry I got you into this, I'm sorry, I'm sorry, I am."

Her display gave me my next line. "I'm not sorry," I bragged. "If not for them, I would have missed out on you."

She studied my insincerity. She flapped toward the main dining room. "You really want to go in there?"

"It's a major-league doublecross, isn't it?" I asked.

"They're serious!"

I took Lila aside, out of the flow of diners, so I could smell her in the privacy of a brass lobby. Jimmy Flowers wasn't a big surprise. But Lila was overestimating me. I hadn't expected that the Charlie Bunch could organize so quickly. Charlie must have had a very good week in Tokyo. He'd used a suicide attempt to hook me in New York. And now he'd used me to hook his cronies. I put the pieces together as I watched Lila light another of Rajeesh's cigarettes. This reminded me that I hated Charlie for using Lila like a hooker, too; and I hated Rajeesh for using Lila for whatever he wanted.

It was my jealousy that got me nasty. "Am I getting paid off or bought off or just bought?"

She puffed and dramatized. "I've had it with you guys!"

"Does that mean me and Charlie, or me and Raj, or all three, or just little old me?"

"F—— you! What do you care!"

We were having a good lover's quarrel. Nothing meant what it meant. You've been there—the soft carpet of the Royal Chosin made no difference.

"Get out, Lila," I said. "I'm sending Rosie home tomorrow morning. You go home with her."

"I forgot. You're a *hero*. You don't have to give a shit about anyone!"

Correct. I told her she was no help to me squawking. Then I exposed my true aim here. I asked who invited Professor Cambridge to butt in.

"You get out!" she yelled.

Patrons looked around at us. Was she going to hit me?

"I've warned you," Lila said, "that's what I wanted to do. And if you're such a big hero—you can figure out the rest." Lila flailed threateningly. "But don't you tell me what to do. Get it? I'm going to do what I want, and no one's going to tell me where to go." She led the way to our table.

Dragon's Gate was a gentlemanly restaurant built into the ground floor of the Royal Chosin like a tsarist throne room, with picture windows overlooking a famous ancient shrine outside. The trappings were discreet, the service instantaneous, the tables far apart, the clientele foreign and wealthy. Though it was Sunday, the main room was busy with VIPs just off the interplanetary flights.

It was the same at our table. Three salesmen—two Koreans and one Dartmouth Indian, aka the Horizon Pacific bagman Jimmy Flowers.

Flowers, in a magnificent light gray suit, stood to squeeze my hand in order to remind me he'd sledded at the Winter Olympics, once upon a time. "Good, good, right on time," he said.

"You too, Jimmy," I said.

His neck muscles strengthened his grin. "*Heyyy*, well, I guess you know why I'm here."

I said, "I guess it's the gold in them there hills, Jim." I was doing a poor job of covering my anxiety. I knew why Flowers was here, but who were the Koreans.?

Flowers scraped at Lila and introduced the two Koreans. Business cards changed hands like aces; the bowing was good but not obeisant. The elder, grayer, better-dressed fellow was Yon Han Ho; he was the guy who counted, since his card read Senior Vice President of the Han-gang Long Term Investment & Securities Company. This meant clients with war chests of hundreds of billions. I shall call them simply the Long Termers.

The younger, stouter fellow was a mere vice president of the Long Termers; he was also named Yon (no obvious relation), and his job was to speak excellent English and, for his boss, not to miss the idioms in mine.

"It's a pleasure to meet you, Dr. Paine," said Yon Junior. "And thank you for joining us today. Senior Vice President Yon asks me to extend the greetings of our executive board and our stockholders."

"Sure."

We had a small round table set for four. Flowers kept introducing Lila in the hope it would make her vamoose. Koreans don't mix women and business, you see, so Lila's presence upset the two Yons.

I stepped back to order a waiter to fix another place, between me and Yon Senior. We were all still standing. I pulled back the new chair and seated Lila.

I was showing off, because I thought I might be in trouble. Oops, I thought, *oooops*. The Charlie Bunch was bankrolled by *the Koreans*, not the Japanese, as I'd supposed. (Somewhere near the Sea of Japan: tough clue, Jimmy.)

In other words, I'd come to play doublecross on the home turf of the guys underwriting my target of opportunity. I suddenly doubted my genius. When in doubt, I know, be rude.

"Miss Schumann's with me," I told Flowers and the Yons. "And yes, that's real red hair. Magnificent, isn't it? Are you guys superstitious about it?"

"Bah," said Lila.

The Yons blinked and sat. Flowers coughed to get his neck muscles unknotted, then he bragged some about the menu.

I knew that Koreans don't do business while they eat, so I continued rude. "What's happening besides gold, Jimmy?"

Flowers began, "Well, Tip, I'm representing people very concerned that everything turn out well for Charlie."

Stalling, I asked him about the weather in Tokyo.

The Yons blinked harder at the mention of Tokyo.

I asked them, "You guys love Charlie, do you?"

Yon Junior translated for Yon Senior, probably the love part.

Yon Senior did have some English, and he responded to me cautiously. "Please listen, Dr. Paine. We know you to be the distinguished American author. And the friend. Of the distinguished Mr. Purcell. Mr. Purcell is the good friend. With us. And Mr. Flowers."

Yon Junior continued for his boss. "Dr. Paine, we're here to assist Mr. Flowers and Mr. Purcell. If you have questions, please direct them to Mr. Flowers. My superiors are most pleased with Horizon Pacific and its representatives."

My shock at the Korean bankroll was easing. I slowly puffed myself up. "Good double-talk," I told the Yons. "It means the same in American."

"Come on, Tip," begged the Dartmouth man, "it's just business."

I told Jimmy the last time he'd sales-pitched it to me, it was a *sure thing*.

Flowers brushed his curls, bit the tip of his tongue.

What I'd learned so far was that Flowers was sweaty. It was a seller's market. Glandular salesmanship makes me thirsty, so I asked Lila if she wanted a cocktail.

"No."

I ordered both of us New York seltzer while the Yons whispered together.

Flowers began again. "Charlie's important to us. If he'd made his position clearer before now, we could've taken care of it. He didn't, and that's that. Now, you're in a position to help him. And we're here to help you."

Lila whispered to me, "Don't do this."

"Easy, Lila," I said, "you're getting your house back. Right, Jimmy?"

Contrary Lila snapped, "I don't want it this way."

"It's your house, Lila," I said, "and maybe life without Charlie. This is a payoff."

"I know," she mumbled.

Flowers nodded. Yon Junior nodded. For all I knew the room nodded.

A bland young man appeared from the wall of diners behind us. He was carrying a big black case, the salesman's sampler kind that opens from the top with a flip; he stood behind me and placed the black case between my chair and Lila's.

"There's the agreed-upon purchase price, *heyyy?*" said Flowers. "One hundred and fifty million yen. We'll have it sent up to your room. Or anywhere you'd like. If you want"—Flowers indicated the bland fellow behind me—"this assistant's yours for the duration."

Lila was a treat. She just had to flip open the top of the black case and make sure the cash was there: one hundred and fifty million yen.

"Yeah, yeah," she said. "I've already washed my hands. I don't want to count it."

Talk of counting numbers made the Yons bend closer.

Flowers brought out paper from his breast pocket. "This is a bank draft for half a million dollars," Flowers told me. "It's yours if you take the meeting with Charlie."

"*With* Charlie," I asked, "or *for* Charlie?"

"Charlie'll be there," Flowers declared, "but we want you there also. Charlie's having a hard time of it, and you've been a help, I understand, back in New York and here and so forth."

I asked, "How much is there for me if I just go home?"

"If you're bargaining," said Flowers, "I'm happy to."

Flowers nodded again; Yon Junior nodded again; and yet another bland fellow appeared with another black case, placed at our feet next to the first.

"That's half a million cash dollars," said Flowers. "It's yours with this draft or"—he nodded again, delighted with the twentieth century and his place in it, and the original muscleman came out with a third black case—"you can have it all in cash."

Lila was spinning to flip open the second and third suitcases. "How much is there?" she asked me.

"One million American so far," I said. My nerves reached my bowels. I sipped seltzer and told Flowers to make the relay team and the black cases go away. "Make the fourth one vanish too," I ordered, "wherever it is."

Lila looked around. "There's more?"

"There's always more," I said, "it's 'just business.' "

"Good, Tip, good," said Flowers, glancing cheerfully at the Yons.

The black cases went back into the wall.

Flowers added a professional speech that the money was mine anyway I wanted it. For services rendered. That I didn't have to sign a consulting contract, they trusted me. That if I took the meeting with Charlie, they would be satisfied regardless of how it turned out. Just take the meeting. "Just business," Flowers repeated.

I said "yes" about nine times while he talked. When Flowers shut up, I addressed the Yons with the phrase Rosie had taught me that relaxed Koreans. "No problem," I said, "no problem."

Yon Senior said, "Please listen, it is said that—" He lost the English words for his proverb and consulted with Yon Junior.

Yon Junior translated Confucius. "Senior Vice President Yon

asks me to tell you that 'A quarrel is to be stopped, and a deal is to be closed.' "

"No problem," I boasted. "No problem, no problem."

"We do have a deal?"asked Flowers, neck muscles on idle.

There was a problem, however, and it had come to me while I'd listened to their bribe. I wasn't afraid of the Long Termers. This truly was "just business" to them—buy and pay until you get what you want. I trusted the Long Termers for the same reason I trusted Charlie: their greed was bankable.

The problem for me was that they'd all offended me. That simple: they'd hurt my feelings. The Long Termers were Confucian puppets; they avoided competition with compromise. Flowers was an American puppet; he thought competing meant everyone was for sale. But me, I was a Puritan puppet, and when I competed, I wanted the bosses to know it was not for a price, but because I wanted to.

My vanity flooded my brain, my mouth runneth over. So I made my speech, not because I had to, but because I wanted to.

I told them what they should have told me. It was somewhere near the Sea of Japan. Horizon Pacific Securities Company was an American investment bank. The Han-gang Long Term Investment & Securities Company was a Korean investment bank. "Just business" for them was called M & A, that is, mergers and acquisitions, what common folk think of as takeover (old word, "conquer"). Their target was toys, any kind of toys. The new Asian Miracle, Seoul, wanted the same thing as the old Asian Miracle, Tokyo, that is, to corner the market in toys. The Japanese had already picked off a lot of fun gadgets, so it was necessary for the Koreans to move fast on whatever was at hand.

I was going properly fast and speeded up into the sketchy part.

"Let's say the toys this time out are robots," I argued. "There're robot-making companies in Japan, in America and in Europe. They're cheap, because they've been losing money for a decade. Okay, step right up and M & A. But there are two obstacles. The first is flimsy—Koreans can't play on Wall Street until 1992, when everyone's agreed to open up Korea to foreign investors. The second obstacle is more troublesome—prejudice. The Japanese won't sell to Korea. The Americans raise the price when they're selling anything. The Europeans are nervous Nellies about everything, especially getting rich. So what's the solution? How to avoid hysteria in world capitals and keep the price down? I've got it! Find a front man, an American crew, say Horizon Pacific, and bankroll them. Begin mergers and acquisitions. Start with the American robots. Move on to Europe. Clean up with Japan. And then what you have is a smiling cartel. It's still losing money, but that's the short term. Crucially, it's a Korean cartel, since Confucius also said that when digging a well, stick with it for the long term and never share the shovel."

I repeated, "Long term."

I repeated, "Never, ever share the shovel."

Yon Junior was translating simultaneously for Yon Elder. Flowers was blank.

I finished fancifully. "All's well until the American front men develop a sudden new problem named Charlie. You can't lose him, because his problem is in moneybags Korea. And who knows how bad it could get if the problem grows a hundred heads at a fragile moment? Which is now. Maybe you can lose him. But it's not good business to have a principal blabbing to *The Asian Wall Steet Journal* and the prosecutors, at the same time. Maybe Wall Street would wink at you jumping the '92 starting gun. Maybe Japan and Europe would show maturity and forget a millennium of Korea-bashing. But are those necessary risks?"

I paused for Confucius. "So what's the solution? Maybe 'Eat a toad in the morning, the rest of the day looks easy.' "

I returned to Charlie. "If this toad had come to you before, you could have handled it discreetly. But no, he tries to kill himself in front of his New York partners. Then he comes to you ten days later and says, 'It's terrible, I've done a terrible thing and I can't get out.' "

I reiterated, "So what's the solution? Forget Confucius. This is 1990. The solution is cash. You tell him, 'Relax, Charlie, it's taken care of.' And here we are, 'just business.' "

Lila graded me. "You really are full of it, you know."

"Chatty Cathy amateur," I told Lila.

Before the bankers could reorganize, I told them, "No consulting contract, no fee, no deal. That first black case is yours to put on the moon. The other three are thrilling and flattering. But no thanks. No problem—no, no, no."

"No?" puzzled Flowers.

Since Koreans aren't really puppets, the Yons winced.

"Yes, Jimmy, yes," I said, "but my way, my say. I take the meeting because I take the meeting. I go home because I go home. Because I want to, yes."

Flowers patted his palms on the tablecloth. The pro in him couldn't understand me. He put himself on loiter and tried to close a deal that didn't exist. "I don't know what you're getting out of this," Flowers told me, "but I'm ready to shake hands if you are."

"He's the hero," Lila mocked.

Flowers used his neck to reinforce his face while he checked the smiles on the Yons.

I'd tried hard, but I saw you can't insult Confucianism when it's decided to stop a quarrel or close a deal. Flowers would have been ballistic if it had been his money I wasn't taking, yet as the bagman for the Long Termers, he was happy if the bankroll was happy.

I took Flowers's useless hand and dragged him up. The Yons sprang to bowing. I ignored their hands, since it's bad luck in Asia to touch genuine adversaries.

I assumed the middle-lordly position and bluffed. "Go away," I told them, "me and the redhead are in love."

7

"*Love's Love*"

LILA MADE HER SPEECH after they'd gone, plenty of rough verbs and nose-pointing. "You think," she asked, "we're what?"

I asked her if she wanted the soup du jour.

"Piss off," she suggested and then stalked off, but not toward the exit, rather back through the bar area to the ladies' lounge.

I was mighty pleased. Cases of cash, gangs of hostiles, lies like peanut shells, and now the beauty was off to dip herself in more tropical aromas. After she called in to Rajeesh, of course, whose Brit slang "piss off" was on her lips like his cologne. I'd promised everyone I was going to deliver. Truth, at that moment, what I really wanted was to postmark Lila. Could I have been that vain? Yes.

I ordered the soup and the salad and a phone. It was fifteen minutes since I'd chased the bankers, so their Confucian compromising should have advanced. I liked the way they'd handled me. Flowers had never lowered his head, and the Long Termers had listened to my report as if I were the KBS weatherman. What did they care if I was onto their robotics deal? There was nothing I could do about it, rain or shine; I was just another talking head. Do you like how I bluffed them anyway—that trivial detail about the 1992 deadline for Koreans playing takeover on Wall Street? And the bit about how Koreans don't believe in minority interests, that they're full-voiced on the executive board or they're not buying? I'd read it all in a glossy magazine on Singapore Airlines. It was my total knowledge of "just business" in Korea. If they'd asked me one question, I would have been exposed as a fraud. But no, they'd let me ramble. Partly cloudy tomorrow, Dr. Paine, well said, so what? Those guys are good, I thought, cinch up world markets, here comes another garlic-breathed beast, and this one doesn't break for the pope.

I called Lila's room to make sure the line was busy. Yes. Lila, I figured, was haranguing Rajeesh aplenty.

I called Charlie and got Rosie. "He's asleep in his room," she lied. "Should I wake him?"

I asked if there'd been any phone calls.

"You said Mr. Purcell wasn't to make any," she said.

I asked where Rajeesh was.

"Dr. Nehru was here, but he left."

I asked if Charlie was sucking his pipes.

"No," she said faintly.

I told Rosie to tell Charlie that there was a couple of million dollars in black cases floating around that impressed me. Not too much. I told her I'd call Charlie later, and we could chat golden parachutes.

Note that Rosie didn't ask, What black cases? She didn't say she was worried; she didn't add anything suspicious; she just said, "Yes, Mr. Paine," and then she rang off.

Lila was still away pouting and primping, so I squeezed in a call to Jesse and Cole at MI headquarters. The switchboard put me right through.

After I'd explained, Cole hooted. "They offered you—how much?"

I reported the handsome sum and said anything less would have been disenchanting.

"Now, that's a bribe, sir," Cole joked. Cole said that Jesse was downstairs in the communications center, trying to get answers to his background checks on the players. "Like we said, sir, it's not a good weekend for us. Things are popping. The March madness."

Translated, this meant that, with three days to the annual war games, MI was on full alert for pranks like C-4 sabotage.

I gave Cole the new names for MI's researches: the Long Termers, Yon Senior and Junior. I asked what they'd found out about Jimmy Flowers.

"The Korean nationals are kind of outside what we can do," Cole explained. "Mr. James M. Flowers, though, we're running him down. A service record from Germany, you said. Dartmouth, Berkeley Business School, you said. Jess will get on it. You think Flowers is hostile?"

"No, just too much beef in his diet."

"Better than garlic and red pepper," Cole said. "How's the redhead?"

Cole entertained me a lot; he was in love with Lila entirely by reputation. I told him REDLEGS was fine. Mr. Kim was so close I could hear him blinking. "More later," I added. "The redhead's popping, too. Warpath."

Cole closed, "Stay loose, sir,"

The soup arrived without Lila. The waiters fussed that it would get cold, so I chased them off with an order for more seltzer. Many minutes passed. I was now fairly sure Lila was leaning to my side again; otherwise, why should it take so long to call in a report to guru Rajeesh? I drank my New York seltzer like vodka. Only in five-star Asian hotels can you order anything you want out of a Broadway deli.

I thought, Stay real loose. If espionage is gossip writ large, what's a love triangle but espionage writ hot?

The proof of the heat was the first thing Lila said when she stormed back to the table in a perfume cloud. "Don't ever—ever! —tell me things are going to be all right. Ever!"

I heard this as a reply to Rajeesh. Lila was in a spatting mood, and any lover would do as a target. She pointed at my head, the dead red on its way: "And you make one of your wimpy cracks about girls, and you're finished."

I mumbled that boys were such emotional creatures.

"Bullshit." Lila sat down as if she was leaving.

I got back in the batter's box. "How's Raj, Lila? Soup cold, Lila?"

"Go ahead and ask me what you really want to know," she dramatized. "Does he snore like you?"

I struck out. We were not going to dine cozily, so I quit the intimate luncheon scene and asked her please, please, would she take a walk with me? It was a hokey trick, but I felt very threatened by the guru and couldn't figure how to counter his pride of place without falling back on flimflam.

"No tricks," she ordered, "just a walk."

It was raining lightly; that didn't stop me. We borrowed her a raincoat and umbrella from the concierge. Soon we were across the City Hall plaza and strolling two feet apart through the Tŏksugung Palace grounds. It's an oasis of ancient Korea, walkways and evergreens, featuring five-hundred-year-old pagodas with diplomatic names like the Palace of Virtuous Longevity and the Hall of Central Harmony. I played know-it-all. Lila harrumphed at my fairy tale that a boob prince lived happily ever after here with his favorite three hundred concubines and their older sisters.

We left the park and headed north to another tourist trap, the Palace of Shining Happiness. The rain had cut the crowds but had also attracted other distressed couples like us. We circled a pond that surrounded an ancient pavilion. Royal Korean ruins are shabby when you get up close, padlocked to keep out riffraff. I bought a diet cola from a hard-luck vendor.

We were now sufficiently cold, wet and diverted to resume our quarrel, if only for warmth.

Lila started at last, "You know what really gets me? Do you want to know? That you all keep telling me it's going to be all right. I hate it! They put two million dollars on the floor! This is me! I've been around. When men in white shirts put two million dollars on the floor, it's *not* going to be all right."

I said that we'd only seen one and a half million in cash American so far. Another half million was said to be offstage. Not to forget a million dollars' worth of yen. "There might be more," I added. "The Yons are bottomless Confucians."

"Shut up!" I thought she was going to belt me. Instead, her voice became level and confessional. "I told you Charlie and Raj were scheming. What I didn't tell you was that they're using you.

Raj says you're predictable. He says he knew you'd give the money back and that you'd *like* giving it back. He says you believe in baseball, apple pie and fair play. He says that you're doing this as research for another of your dumb movies."

"Baseball?" I said in honest surprise. The Cambridge man understood me profoundly. "Did he mention a team?"

"Aaaaah!" She swung the umbrella, not much of a weapon when open. She dropped confession for taunting. "You know what Charlie says?"

"That I'm in this for you?"

"Charlie actually said you'd kiss anything to get to my ass."

"Crude," I said. "Accurate," I said. "He should know," I said. "We three Boy Scouts do have your lovely rump in common," I said. "What do you say?"

Lila measured my jawline to see if it was hiding another crack.

"I think," she said, "you'd really like me to believe that you turned down two million dollars for my ass. I think you'd do anything to impress yourself. I think you're an uptight cheat and a pretentious pinhead who's too dumb to go home. I think," she said slowly, enjoying herself, "you're either having a breakdown or you're just pathetic, like Rosie."

"What about Rosie?"

"Rosie, Rosie, pathetic little Rosie," said Lila. "She's not little, I guess, just pathetic. Following Charlie around like that. It's sickening to watch."

Lila noticed my dumbfounded stare and added, "After that poor Yu-Yi, I hate it. It's really, really sick."

I tried again. "What about Rosie?"

"Rosie!" Lila insisted. "Charlie's latest love slave. He calls them his 'little yellow women.' I know the Orientals have a rep for it, but, shit—the way he laughs at her and jerks her around, how can men do that?"

"Little yellow women?" I said. "Love slave? What?"

"Stop saying *what*. Rosie, your pal Rosie. You've seen it. I told you she was weird about him."

"No, you didn't," I protested. "You said he was weird about her."

"They're weird about each other," Lila corrected. "Dopers in love. What do I have to do, draw it? I used to think it was sad, strange but sad, but she's going too far. There's masochism and then there's that. Wash him, shave him, dress him, feed him, stand around waiting for him to burp."

I tried, "Rosie's in love with Charlie?"

"Of course she is! Pammie says it was like that with them from the first day they were together. Why do you think I was a commuter from Singapore last year? I was on the phone or on the plane to Pammie because of it."

I turned toward the glass towers of central Seoul. Lila was telling me something I'd never considered. That abuse was love?

Lila tried, "You really didn't know?"

I said, "It's impossible."

"What's the matter," Lila taunted me, "love only counts when you're white like us? Shit, Tip, grow up. Love's love. Charlie's got a *thing* for his 'little yellow women.' He's always had it. He says he married white, but he dreams yellow. When I was with him in Singapore, he couldn't get it up unless we went to the nightclubs to watch the Chinese girls dance. Pammie says he keeps pornography on them. And he's not exactly healthy about Dorothy, which we're not going to talk about, because if he ever tries anything with my niece, he's going to jail forever. He can have his porn books and movies, but—Tip, what is it?"

I asked about Pam's abortion.

"You didn't know about that either. Forget it, it's done. Her decision. I didn't disagree with her."

I asked what Charlie'd said about it.

"He's a fertile bastard, and he doesn't deserve feelings." Lila softened. "I'm the last one to talk about abortions. I've had my day, and Pammie's had hers, and this isn't the time to be a little mother for that motherf——er Charlie."

I wanted to ask her if she'd ever aborted one of Charlie's, but then, I didn't want to know. I was genuinely upset. Everything I'd figured out was suddenly in the trash. Friendly Pam was alone and bleeding in New York. Loving Rosie was alone and enslaved in Seoul.

Lila came close and mothered me a little. "What is it?"

I didn't have an answer, so I kissed her forehead to stall, and somehow was immediately getting kissed back.

"Tip," she tried in between, "it's all right."

We walked around together for a while, halting now and again to kiss. I don't remember what we talked about on the way back

to the hotel. We should have separated at the elevator bank. But
we didn't, not that soon. Long walks in cold rain around ruins in
foreign capitals are usually enough for anyone's hormones. There
was also my *thing* for red hair. Who knows what was Lila's *thing*.
I asked her three times to come up to my room. She didn't argue,
not outside, not inside, nor in bed, in the bath, in bed again.
What I'm skipping is routine weirdness sometimes called love. I
was in love with her, I could tell. She couldn't yell anything I
wasn't interested to hear and when she bossed me around I felt
happy. We napped without debate. When the afternoon became
twilight, I ordered us snacks via room service, and we stayed in
bed watching the hotel's movie on the tv, a boilerplate romance,
starring either James Woods or one of the Bridges—I can't remember, since I got hooked by the plot. It had Hollywood's
trendy new ending: the dame did it, but the shamus doesn't send
her over. I applauded its credits by patting my hands gently on
Lila's priceless rump.

"I've got to go," she said.

We avoided the obvious while dressing, and then we did separate at the elevator bank, she back to her guru, me back to my
laptop. But will she love me tomorrow?

Don't think about it, I thought, play dial-a-doublecross.

Jesse and Cole were unavailable to my call, off defending
America, so I left an "all nominal" message with the MI switch-
board, and also on their answering machine. I resisted calling
Lila's room.

I did call Charlie. His line was busy, according to the hotel
switchboard. I didn't fret. I typed up the day's shenanigans before
I forgot the best quotes, and then I wrote a monograph to myself
about "little yellow women."

I truly could not believe it about Rosie. I convinced myself that
I could do something to protect her. I called the hotel desk and
bought an open first-class ticket Seoul to New York for Rosemary
Yip and told the desk I wanted a car for her tomorrow morning,
and that the driver was to wait until she showed up.

If I hadn't needed Lila for the bag-holding the next day, I
would have arranged the same kind of embarkation for her to
Singapore.

It was near 9:00 P.M. when I called Charlie's line again. Still
busy. It didn't make sense. This time I did try Lila's room, to see

if Rajeesh was chatting with Charlie. No answer. At least, I com-
forted myself, Lila and Rajeesh might break up over dinner, before he tried to fall on her apéritif. Wretched stuff, jealousy. I
punched on another flick and got lucky with space opera, an alien
intelligence masquerading as a union organizer at the Mars colony, go Lefty.

That's enough. There were more calls and some backtracking,
but within three hours I had caught on. Lila wasn't missing, she
was indeed out to a nightclub dinner with Rajeesh to discuss
existential meaning and whatever else a forty-one-year-old needs
when she's being chased by two forty-two-year-olds.

It was Charlie who was gone. Rosie, too.

I made sure they were gone when I did panic and called Jesse
and Cole after eleven for an emergency break-in. They came
running as only the U.S. Army comes running. Jesse hacked the
hotel's computerized lock.

Charlie's suite was deserted.

Otherwise, it was crammed with clues.

The first significant item was the third communication from
Mr. Kim, on the dinner table, with the remains of a room-service
supper. The plain white stationery read, "Welcome Seoul. Agree
meeting the end. Monday. Dragon's Gate. 1 P.M."

It was signed, "Arizona."

More clues: The Chablis bottle was a quarter full, two glasses.
The phone receiver in the master bathroom was in the toilet bowl.
Charlie's wardrobe was in place save for one empty suit hanger.
His luggage was monogrammed Mark Cross, shaving kit was
monogrammed Paul Stuart, aftershave from Gruene's. There was
a sterling-silver pill case containing a multicolored pharmacy.
There was an Impulse Af Polaroid on a chair, five shots gone.
The master bath trash basket produced two unfocused snaps of a
naked woman bent over adjusting the bath faucets, with a man's
Rolex-banded hand squeezing one cheek like a sponge. (You ask
how come I'd never seen this kind of *thing* before? Because I
wasn't looking is my weak answer.)

We searched on. Rosie's wool frock and wool coat were gone;
her traveling case was left open to show a copy of *Esquire* with an
article on Anjelica Huston torn out. Rosie's nightgown was still
packed—bought at Macy's, same for her underwear; her hose
was generic, her shoes from Alexander's. There was one silk scarf

with a Tokyo label. Her toiletries were franchise, minimal makeup, no diaphragm, no pills besides Tylenol. We stripped the beds to find the opium stash and pipes in Charlie's pillowcases.

Jesse and Cole got scrupulously MI and swept for surveillance bugs. None. I called the desk and pretended I was Charlie in order to check the billing. This was a long way around to find little: A call to Horizon Pacific's New York office—probably the telex to Mr. Kim at 10:32 A.M. An earlier call to New York, probably Lila's to Pam at 9:17 A.M.

The desk also gave me the log of room-service orders. There was my breakfast order. Charlie's lunch order at 12:40 P.M. Charlie's supper order, 5:04 P.M. Another question got me the pay-tv order of pornography films on the hotel's in-house service—logged all night, every two hours, nothing all morning, again that afternoon, the last at 5:30.

There wasn't time or access to check American Express for a log of any plane tickets Charlie might have ordered. The desk said it hadn't handled any taxi or limo orders.

The final clue was the matter of the money.

There were *eleven* black cases on the parlor floor. Stacked like lost luggage. The biggest with a hundred and fifty million yen. Ten matched others, each with half a million in mint-new hundred-dollar bills.

At the end of our search, Jesse said, "Purcell ran out on you. Do you know why?"

My stupid joke: "I know I'm left holding the bags."

Cole's intuition was superb: "Something's wrong here, sir, very wrong."

It was near 1:00 A.M. I circled the black cases. (And six million dollars of paper does indeed glow negatively, like a black hole in your face.) I waved the three messages from Mr. Kim, "Welcome Seoul . . ." I glanced at the porn snapshots of Rosie. I kicked the phone again. I'd called Lila's room eight times before I'd reached her twenty minutes before, when she'd been tipsy and muffled, just back from fumbling with Rajeesh. "What's wrong?" she'd asked. "Is it Charlie?" I'd hung up.

Now I argued with myself. If this was the Charlie Bunch's plan —bribe me, divert me, stiff me—then it did not figure that Charlie and Rosie would have skedaddled like this, evacuees from a cash flood. It also did not figure that Lila and Rajeesh would have returned, tipsy, in heat, to the scene of the skedaddle. None of that figured, did it, Raj, did it, you swelled-headed Cantabrigian?

Here's what I figured that night: Charlie and Rosie were gone. Maybe they were coming back. Maybe they'd moved to another hotel. Maybe Mr. Kim had turned up, and they'd gone for a stroll around the Palace of Shining Happiness. But without the money?

I reviewed my day to Jesse and Cole, including the "little yellow women" revelation, and Pam's abortion, and my hanky-panky with Lila.

I was so agitated I couldn't stop circling the black cases.

"Go easy on yourself, sir," Jesse said.

"Yes, yes," I complained, "but what are we going to do?"

Cole looked at the black cases, at least twice as much cash as he and Jesse both would earn in a lifetime. And it wasn't hot, wasn't marked, wasn't wanted back by man or state. Cole said, "This is bad news, Jess."

Jesse said, "We do have our orders."

"Orders aren't going to do it," I complained. "They bought me. And it doesn't matter to them that I said no. You can't say no to them. They lay their money on you and walk away."

Cole watched my hysteria and asked a strange question. "What would you do in one of your movies, sir? That's what we've been wanting to ask you for days."

I joked stupidly again, "Hollywood's 'just business' like everywhere else."

Just then, my stupidity revealed a plan. I waved the messages from Mr. Kim and argued, "Wait. We've got a buy-back deal with Mr. Kim. Correct? Let's keep to it. In twelve hours. 'Just business.' Smilingly."

Jesse objected, "Purcell's not coming back."

"Hear me out," I countered. "We've got the yen, the time, the manpower, the know-how. All we need is another plan."

"Hostiles won't show unless Purcell's there," Cole said.

"Yes, yes, and I've got a plan anyway. Will you listen to me before you say 'negative'? What I'm thinking is sort of Hollywood."

(If you're keeping score: Mary Song was dead. Soo Yu-Yi was living death. Pammie's fetus was aborted. Rosie wasn't dead yet, still the heroic governess out there, serving her master and his golden realm.)

8
Lunchtime Reds

HOLLYWOOD HAS NEVER had to negotiate with Lila Schumann. Lies failed, bluster failed, the truth would have failed, too. She was as implacable as Krakatoa (goddess of redheads) from the moment I started lying to her about the Dragon's Gate buyback.

"Forget it," she commanded. "If you're going to be there, I'm going to be there. It's half my money, more than half. I'm going to keep one hand on the bag and the other . . ."

If I hadn't been the same pighead she was, I could have finessed Lila out of harm's way somehow.

For example, I could have used the Long Termers' one hundred and fifty million yen, in the biggest black case, and thereby wouldn't have needed Lila's yen.

The ground rules Jesse and Cole established forbade it. Not just because they didn't even want to ask their CO if they could use unclaimed millions to advance their investigation, but also because the black cases had momentarily shaken their professional self-control. ("The interrogator must have an exceptional degree of self-control," reads MI regulations, "to avoid displays of genuine anger, irritation, sympathy, or weariness. . . .") As I saw it, the black cases had brought out their whiter hats and whiter stallions.

"It's Mr. Purcell's property, that's it," Jesse had concluded about the black cases. "And I mean it, sir, that's it."

So my buy-back plan stayed out of grand larceny and in the tv-simple.

No surprises: it was the old Hollywood stand-in. I replaced Charlie with Captain John "Jesse" D'Ambrosi, fitted by the hotel tailor into one of Charlie's suits, with his sandy hair coiffed banker style, his duplicity from MI training ("Always Out Front"), his nerve from St. Louis.

I'd argued my latest tv-simple plan to the boys this way. What could Mr. Kim know? He'd seen Charlie sixteen years ago. Maybe he'd seen Charlie in bank photos or in person since. Still, one fair-complected, six-foot Alan Ladd look-alike looks like another. If Jesse buttoned his lip and loosened his muscles, faked the hectored victim, what could a greedy aged op know? Mr. Kim wouldn't be looking at Charlie; he'd be fixed on the money. The money was the message; the smiling was the medium; the table at the Dragon's Gate was the rendezvous. What we wanted was Mr. Kim's paper on Charlie, and maybe Mr. Kim, if we were quick and lucky. That was my plan. Yes, simpleminded, as I've admitted.

Why did Jesse and Cole go along with me? The truth is, I don't know. I'd like to think that underneath their "all nominal" orthodoxy were, you know, hambone long riders. Whatever their orders were, could they have been broad enough to include such tomfoolery? I've checked the MI books since then, and nowhere is it written that you can masquerade as a crybaby.

Then again, I have found this ingenious army humorlessness: "An interrogator must adapt himself to the many and varied personalities which he will encounter. He should try to imagine himself in the source's position. . . . He must also adapt himself to the operational environment. In many cases he has to conduct interrogations under a variety of unfavorable physical conditions."

My role was as tough as Jesse's. I had to adapt myself to the "many and varied personalities" named Lila Schumann. I had to secure Lila's half of the swag and then blow her off like a water lily. I had to convince her that I could take the meeting *alone* as Charlie's pal. I had to do all this without mentioning my base trick, MI. In all, I had to lie so basely that I had to write it down beforehand in my laptop, like a treatment.

What chance did I have against Lila? Ginseng is more.

For example, I'd argued with Lila at 2:00 A.M. and failed. "Charlie ran out on us!" she'd yelled. "That bastard!" I'd told her we still had a meeting tomorrow, and maybe a chance to pull it off. "Pam's going to Mother!" Lila'd yelled. "That bastard!" I'd told Lila to sleep on it, not Raj.

Further example, we'd renewed our telephone spat at 8:00 A.M. We'd continued it in Lila's suite, with Rajeesh looking on. There'd been more of the same later in the taxi to the Bank of East Asia, where we'd watched blank-faced Mr. Han count out one hundred and fifty million yen and stow it in our Gladstone bag at eleven. We'd returned to Lila's suite to spat some more, with Rajeesh looking on.

Throughout, Rajeesh was professorially cunning. It was his gambit to convince me that he was disgusted with Charlie for running out, that he thought me shrewd to carry on with the buy-back regardless.

(The truth was that Rajeesh had urged Charlie to flee. The truth was also that Rajeesh truly did not know where Charlie had gone or why. The doublecross had double-crossed itself, and Dr. Professor Rajeesh Nehru, I enjoy telling you, was in with me in big trouble.)

"It's bold, Lila," Rajeesh had told her during one of our spats, "and it might work. Tip's right. All they want is the money. Why not try it?"

Lila had dramatized her endless protest. "Am I the brains for you two? They won't even show up if Charlie's not there. Why should they? Because it's Charlie's table? Hey, where'd you learn blackmail etiquette?"

"Tv," I answered.

"It's dumb," Lila had asserted accurately. "You want to give my house to a guy dumb enough to think you're Charlie's pal?"

I'd declared that, as dumb as it sounded, it was my plan. I told Lila she should just go off on a shopping raid with Raj and trust me.

"Yeah, yeah, the hero's gonna make it come out *soooo* happy," she'd returned. "I almost forgot you're the guy who says no to their two million one day and wants to go solo with my half million the next. What's happened in between? You let the pillows do the talking?"

She'd fiendishly grinned at me and Rajeesh, a lady who could handle men and merchandise with bathwater and a change of lingerie.

I'd distracted her logic then by saying that Charlie was good for her loss; we'd seen the kind of money he could raise with his crybaby jag in Tokyo. I hadn't wanted her to ask any more about the black cases, which remained, untouched, in Charlie's suite.

She'd declared finally that I was to forget it, she was going to keep one hand on the Gladstone and the other—she actually said, " . . . I'm going to keep one hand on the bag and the other on my pants, just in case you try anything funny, y'know, you're so dumb you might trade them my pants."

I'd glanced at Rajeesh. He at me. Puritan and Hindu lust jaw-to-jaw, no smiling allowed. Then I'd cut yet another double deal.

Now you know why, eventually, my lies had to include the concession that Lila could accompany me to the meeting at the restaurant table. Rajeesh, too, if she wanted.

Lila wasn't a genius; she was an American girl; she knew you're never all wrong if you know where the money is, if you are the money.

Lila also knew never to shut up when you're not in charge.

"Where are we going to sit?" she asked me as we arrived at the door of the Dragon's Gate.

"At our reserved table," I said. It was 12:30, Monday afternoon, thirty minutes to showdown.

"Is it really okay if Raj sits with us? How will we know it's Mr. Kim? Do I get to talk to him? I'm Charlie's family. I should talk, don't you think?"

"Yes, Lila," I said, "fine, Lila. You can tell him anything you want. He'll like you. You look sensational, Lila."

"I don't think so," she said, primping. Lila was dressed for blackmail in a black pantsuit and black beret. She also had the black-ops stinker at her arm.

Rajeesh was all politeness, since he expected nothing to happen but lunch.

I'd made no rules for them. I thought them ridiculous pains that I only had to divert from the real buy-back, which was to happen across the room at Charlie/Jesse's table.

Here's my further plan. *There was no further plan.* I was so worn down by my lies just to get the money to the restaurant that I hadn't bothered to worry my plan past 1:00 P.M. If Mr. Kim did show, the majordomo had been bribed to lead him to Charlie/Jesse's table. After that, I'd let MI work.

You don't like this? You're right. But then, you know much more than I did at the time. And I didn't like it either. I told myself that sometimes you have to admit you're no different from every other smart guy who's gone too far, and so it's time to trust luck and the U.S. Army.

"Keep the bag right there," Lila ordered me about the Gladstone as we sat down. "I want to feel it."

"Yes, Lila, happy to, Lila, hungry, Lila?"

The wine steward and waiter arrived, both looking harried by the lunchtime crowd. Two jumbo jets must have landed on the roof for all the double-breasted entourages in the room. I told the waiter I wanted New York seltzer and soup du jour, pronto. I tried to act the CEO while scanning for Jesse's entrance.

Rajeesh ordered an overpriced Pouilly something and duck pâté. "Nothing for you?" he asked Lila. "Are you sure, luv? You merely pecked at breakfast. Seafood perhaps?"

"How can you eat?" she snapped, kicking at the Gladstone. "Oh, all right, what's the soup?"

Another point to my side. I felt better and eavesdropped on the next table, where three Italians were arguing like gamblers about private-school bills. "At ten apiece," said one, "the nuns in Tuscany would be cheaper." His comrade said, "Contraception is cheaper," and they laughed.

Jesse appeared at 12:44, according to my glimpse of Rajeesh's ludicrous Rolex.

I studied Jesse as he came up the two steps from the entrance. He truly did look like Charlie from the distance of about sixty feet. No, he didn't. I couldn't be sure. Jesse walked like an infielder, head cocked, loose-jointed for range in the holes. In comparison Charlie was a stick.

I sipped my seltzer, then drained the glass to keep my tongue working.

Please pay attention. I'm recording what I saw, heard, smelled. Yet I missed something, and I missed it badly. I've noted the Korean waiter and wine steward, the cheery Italians at the next table, Lila on my right, Rajeesh on my left, my field of vision straight over five boisterous tables of executives to Jesse's table, along the wall at the busboy station. I can also record that the soup du jour arrived soon, an attractive carrot concoction with a curry flavor and the omnipresent garlic. What did I miss?

Simply put, I was poisoned. How did they do it?

Rajeesh was one of those wine experts; he tasted his choice and asked the steward to pour three glasses. "It's a soggy-day wine," he advised. "You'll like it, Lila. We first tried it in Bangkok two years ago."

"I'm not going to like anything today," she said.

"Hey, you," she addressed me. "This isn't going to work, is it? The three of us here—we'll scare him off?"

"Just smile," I returned. "Without Charlie, we're a free market. If we don't like Mr. Kim's deal, we walk."

"Shit, you're acting funny again," she told me. "Doesn't money make you nervous?"

We jabbered some more. Lila finished her second glass of wine, then took mine, which I'm sure I didn't touch.

"One o'clock," she said. "Maybe I'm fast. Hey, excuse me," she asked one of the Italians. When he smiled, she used her Italian. "What time do you have, please? Oh, thank you, thank you. Yes, it's Parisian."

Lila meant her perfume. The Italians were hitting on her as if this were Firenze in July.

I stopped eavesdropping when I saw Jesse flinch up.

The majordomo, the guy we'd hired, had just brought Jesse a note on a silver salver.

Jesse read it, made a show of reading it, and dropped his napkin.

I knew an alert when I saw one: white flag for "abort." I hurried across the room.

"It's the hostiles," Jesse began calmly. "They want to play hopscotch."

He showed me the note from the silver salver. A phone-in message for Charles Purcell, telling him to take taxi No. 4041 to the Pagoda Park.

I asked, "Where's that?"

Jesse answered calmly, "About a mile around the corner. We've got fox-trot teams high and low. No wires in case they have counters. It's show and tail."

This was MI palaver. Translated, it meant that Jesse was swaddled in cover, and it was armed; "fox-trot" means fire team. I didn't know what electronic counters he meant and assumed "show and tail" meant no arrests were planned, only surveillance.

I asked, "What now?"

"I want to try the Pagoda Park," Jesse answered. "There will be more hopping ahead. These are pros."

"But?" I asked.

"I need the bag with your money," he said, "and now, sir. I have to say that this will get chancy, and it's your money. Brush me at the main door. Are you still in?"

Vainly, foolishly, I said, "Affirmative, Captain."

"I'm moving now," said Jesse.

I knew what I wanted when I returned to my table. I wanted to be middle-aged brave. It was exciting, you must understand, more exciting than I'd ever imagined, and I thought the twinges in my bowels were routine fear.

"What was that all about?" demanded Lila, gawking to see where I'd been. "Who's that you were talking to? Over there? Who is it? Hey! How come he's in one of my suits?"

Rajeesh sipped wine. "Easy, sweet."

I took hold of the Gladstone.

Lila jerked down and kicked at my hand; she grabbed the handle too. "What're you doing? Who's that boy?"

"That boy," I speechified wackily, "is the hero you wait for, out of the sunrise and into the sunset. That boy is High Noon. Get it, Lila, that boy is one of Uncle Sammie's deputies, and you are to take your hand off the bag, real ladylike."

"Well, f—— you!"

One of the four best soliloquies of my life, and Lila wouldn't let me get it said without scratching and squawking.

I did outweigh her by eighty pounds. I started back across the room with the Gladstone. Lila wouldn't let go, so she was half dragged. Diners parted like elephant grass. The majordomo frowned at our lover's quarrel. Lila got in front of me to yank my tie. I swept her around left-handed, and we clinched at the entrance.

"You can't do this!" she commanded. "What're you doing to me?"

"Leaving," I said.

"What's 'High Noon'? That boy's what? He's a cop? FBI?"

"U.S. Military Intelligence Corps," I said. "Spycatcher to you. And we're cooperating with our government like good citizens."

"We're what? You sold us out?"

"Affirmative," I said, and for no reason I pecked her cheek.

Lila fired back, "Has he got Charlie?"

"Negative."

"What's happening?" she demanded.

"Maybe a photo op in the Oval Office."

"Holy shit, are you nuts or what?"

"What." I freed the Gladstone. "Adios."

"That's my money!"

I left Lila and her scent behind in the lobby tangle.

Jesse was a sentry outside the main door; he had Charlie's trench coat on his shoulder, his umbrella like a baton. I brushed Jesse's backside. Jesse made a graceful flick at the sky as if testing the drizzle. I was having so much fun I was woozy. The doorkeeper whistled to fetch us a taxi from the line that served the Royal Chosin.

Jesse waved the doorkeeper off and chose the fifth car in line, a standard green taxi coupe, No. 4041.

"Hey!" shouted Lila. She jumped between Jesse and me and grabbed our belts. "You go, I go. I'm going to fight, and I will, you know I will."

What would you have done? Correct. Lose the redhead. But when she's threatening to de-pants you? I think she was also feeling around to Jesse's hip holster.

I did what I had to, and we three were in the taxi straightaway. Lila and I sat in the back. The Gladstone sat at Lila's feet. Jesse rode shotgun up front.

Lila howled and scolded on the ride. I didn't pay any mind, because I wasn't just feeling woozy anymore, I was feeling sick. Those twinges in my bowels were stronger; if I'd been anywhere else, I would have returned to the hotel.

Lila broadcasted, "Tell me the truth."

I was queasy enough to ignore her for once.

She went at Jesse. "What are you trying to do to me? This is my money! Who are you?"

Jesse watched the traffic.

I was seriously uncomfortable by the time we rounded the corner at the Lotte shopping center. You've felt like this; you know it's embarrassing; except that it's not. But poison, how could I have figured that?

What I remember next was crucial, yet it was dim to me at the time because of my gas pains.

Presently, our taxi driver, a teenager in a gray satin "U2 World Tour" jacket, spoke to Jesse in Korean. (I think of our taxi driver as U2.) U2 used words that must have meant traffic jam and police.

We understood him despite the language problem.

There was a mass demonstration ahead of us. What we could see, from two hundred yards, was that Chongno Boulevard was blocked off by a phalanx of blue-helmeted riot police. Shields raised, visors lowered, the police were waiting in practiced ambush for a demonstration coming up the boulevard.

This was a routine Seoul occasion, as Jesse explained. "It's lunchtime Reds. They brown-bag their Molotovs and run around for the cameras."

"Who are you, really?" Lila asked Jesse.

Jesse didn't respond. He had another problem. We had to cross Chongno Boulevard to get to the Pagoda Park. However, the riot police were diverting traffic left and right into the east-west traffic jams.

Jesse directed U2 to make the next right, a bypass to the west. "We'll try to feel our way through," Jesse told me. "Otherwise, we'll have to double back. Way around City Hall. These things don't last long. Except sometimes there's trouble, and they're using live rounds these days."

"March madness," I joked. Talking up made me feel worse. I was in pain, and I put my head in my hands. I was sweating badly and told myself that it was nerves, just nerves.

We never got out of the traffic jam.

I remember firecracker sounds and the police phalanx ahead of us suddenly scattering. I turned to look out the back window to see a mob coming at us. It was a breakaway demo trying to flank the riot police.

That's when I remember Jesse kicking open his door and jumping out to signal for his fox-trot teams by waving his arms.

Lila protested, "Get back in!" She yelled at me, "What's he doing? He's got a gun!"

Jesse leaned back inside, across the front seat, with his Beretta pointed at U2's head.

U2 jerked and squealed.

Jesse ordered me, "Get out now." He stared back at me. "Go, go, it's a hit, go, both of you."

Lila howled, "Tip, don't go out there!"

The back window of the taxi shattered. Something big struck us from the front, perhaps another vehicle. The impact threw Jesse out of the car. It began to rain rocks, bottles, asphalt, smoke bombs.

I heard dull popping. The riot police were firing at range, shotguns and tear gas lobbed over us pell-mell.

U2 put the car in gear and backed into the mob. The open front door clipped a demonstrator in the back, and he yowled as he went down. There was the thud of bodies off the bumper. The taxi swerved backward until it bashed against another vehicle. We were pinned against a truck on Lila's side.

Lila yelled, "Tip!"

I opened my door. I got one step out when I found I didn't have strength in my limbs. My gas pains imploded, and I fell. It wasn't death, it was diarrhea and vomiting, similar to what you suffer from bad food.

But that was poison, I'm sure of it, poison.

Then I was in the fetal position on the street. Tear gas rolled around me. Demonstrators ran over me. I was kicked. I crawled to get clear. I glimpsed the green taxi between the running legs, and then I lost sight of it. I heard lots of screaming, something like, "Yankee devils, go home!"

9
The Three Lees

I LOST JESSE AND LILA and the Gladstone, but I never lost track. Poison does steal time as well as nerve endings, however, so I can't report the next ten hours accurately.

What happened, in sum, was that I was taken off the street by agents of the KCIA. This wasn't clear to me at first. I concentrated on my life. I was too scared to do more than stay within myself, asking questions of my body such as "Am I dying?"

A stretcher arrived, and I was scooped off the pavement. The back of the ambulance smelled like disinfectant. The talk was professional Korean. They stripped and washed me, and there must have been an injection. Then I was on another stretcher and the lights were bright. I recall a tube in my mouth, though that might have been many fingers working to pump my stomach and keep me breathing. There was a stopover at a hospital, perhaps two hospitals, and then I was in another van and very dopey. Flat on your back, you see fluorescent lights and pale ceilings. That must have been the stopover at the infamous NSP building.

It doesn't signify, because eventually it was nighttime, and I was in an apartment tower on a hill on the north side of Seoul.

That's when they woke me up and told me I was safe. How I felt was tired. It wasn't the first time they'd assured me that day, but it was the first time in English. Indeed, I was safe. I'd made up enough of these places to recognize a safe house when I was in one. Pine furniture, indirect lighting, beige walls, strong drapes, closets full of household supplies, male R.N. and male housekeeper. And finally, when I was alert, showered and dressed in a warm-up suit, the resident ops.

It was the three Lees. They came into my room like visiting relatives. I sat on the side of the bed and gaped.

You remember them—grandfatherly Lee Tae Ha, the bushy-browed Lee Nam Paik and the robust Lee Sang Ju. I told you to keep an eye on them. Yet, since I've also kept you busy with other tasks, it's fair-minded to admit that, though you've not seen them much, they have been hanging around like diligent creeps. In their white shirts and maroon ties, their dark suits from Barney's and cordovan wing tips from Italy, they were the well-turned-out KCIA control officers—field men, black ops, now come home from their American fronts and New Jersey lawns to advance their counterintelligence operation, to seek their private vengeance.

This is the major detail: it was family trouble to the three Lees. They were in it to right a Lee family wrong.

It was why they appeared so organized. Usually, black ops are humdrum, doing boring tasks repetitiously that they botch like any other civil servant. Don't believe my horsefeathers about secret agents, or Maugham's and Greene's guilt-soaked romances, or even le Carré's moody fairy tales. Espionage is dull, witless, pointless work that attracts like-minded boors who care more about career perks than patriotism. What did the three Lees usually do? Keep lists of Korean troublemakers in New York, launder money, clip the newspapers, make a payroll for their various disgruntled assets—the usual lifeless dross.

However, this time out the three Lees appeared energetic and focused, because they were family crazy. They didn't admit this to me for some time. Rather, they started out to me as Confucian puppets.

(Watch them closely: When they were comfortable with my blarney, they nodded, apologized, bowed and obliged. When they were uncomfortable, they went silent.)

The first thing they told me was that they knew everything, which was far from true, but they said it politely.

"Please listen, Dr. Paine," explained Grandfather Lee, "we are most unhappy for the unhappy trouble."

"It was the unhappy error, Dr. Paine," said bushy-browed Lee Nam Paik.

Youngest Lee, with the most sufferable English of the trio, added, "We should have closed up when Miss Rosemary Yip did not report to us yesterday. Unhappily, we should have."

"Rosie?" I muttered. "Rosie, Rosie, Rosie?"

"The great patriot," said Grandfather Lee.

"The agent," said Lee Nam Paik.

"Miss Rosemary Yip works for us," said Youngest Lee. "She was to report yesterday. The Youngnak Church. She did not."

"Church? She was with me. Report to you?"

"We were at church also," said Grandfather Lee.

"An excellent service, you did like it?" asked Lee Nam Paik.

"Miss Rosemary Yip chose not to report," said Youngest Lee, "when she was with you, Dr. Paine."

I won't labor my surprise; there were too many surprises. And if you're wondering how I felt about learning so much trickery all at once, the answer is spooked. But after being poisoned and dumped in central Seoul, rattled around in ambulances and police vans, plopped into the company of black ops who once flattered me as Greene, MacArthur and Eastwood, I should have been prepared for all sorts of nonsense. I wasn't. Remember the rusty nails on the Freedom Bridge at P'anmunjŏm? The three Lees were the kind of guys who might have planted those nails, thinking they were sabotage. When they're not dullards, black ops are clowns. Have you ever met one? Sporting-goods clerks are vastly better informed about history and do far more productive work. Black ops deserve laughter. Instead, they have secret budgets and bozo notions that get sober attention.

I gave them mine. "You guys are creeps."

I talk very fast and easy when I'm in trouble; life becomes simpler for me when I've been mugged. I was weak but not weak-minded, not too much, and found my New York rudeness. "Creeps," I repeated. "I'm an American citizen." Then I asked a necessary question. "Am I a prisoner?"

"No, no," said Grandfather Lee.

"Lying creeps," I said. "Why am I here?"

"We need your assistance," said Lee Nam Paik.

"Who's 'we'?"

The three Lees nodded and apologized, bowed and obliged. "We need it, we," said Grandfather Lee, "we are cousins. We."

"What kind of assistance? Creeps."

They didn't answer me directly; instead, they communicated a major threat alert.

Youngest Lee said, "You know, Dr. Paine, that due to our unhappy errors, your good friend Miss Lila Schumann is now not to be found at your hotel. And it is our unhappy belief that Miss Lila Schumann is a prisoner of our enemies."

This got me up and moving and cursing. My tongue was pure Lila. "You assholes." My jargon descended from there.

Educated by tv, I expected answers, but that's not the way when there's no script. Black ops dump lies on you and then wait to see if you're shaken enough to tell them something new. I tried to control myself. Still it came out noisy.

All the while, the three Lees nodded and apologized, bowed and obliged.

Soon, we moved out of my room and onto the enclosed terrace. The squat lights of Seoul were below us, pink and blue. They'd provided me comfortable sports clothes and a new pair of made-in-Korea Air Jordans. I didn't feel like eating, but they served me tea and toast on a tray that included a new Irish pipe and a tolerable tobacco.

After I'd exhausted my vulgarity at their persons, their country and their treachery, I manufactured about *seventy* good questions. They answered me evasively.

You already know most of what they said. Rosie was their op. They were onto Charlie. They had used me as bait. They wanted to roll up Mr. Kim, who did exist, who was one notorious enemy agent, who was their enemy out there.

Further, yes, I had been poisoned and ambushed. No, they hadn't poisoned me. Yes, Lila had probably been abducted by the

U2 taxi driver. No, they had lost his trail in the demonstration. Yes, they had secured my release from the secret police (NSP). No, I wasn't a prisoner, I was free to go anytime I wanted.

I made them repeat that. Yes, I was an American citizen; my passport was in my billfold in my pocket; I was free to go to the hotel, home, anywhere.

My *seventy-first* good question—why they wanted Mr. Kim— was most important, but working up to it took much talk.

It was near 11:00 P.M. when we began, and they offered to delay the powwow until the morning. I said maybe, talk faster. I repeat again that they offered to take me back to the hotel, to let me call the American embassy, to book myself a flight out of Seoul. At no point did I feel a prisoner. They were cordial and sincere. As rude as I was, as stunned as I was by their revelations, I never felt frightened of them. This was my vanity. The KCIA has a rotten reputation worldwide, and it's deserved. It's a violent, ruthless network; it is to our CIA what a wild boar is to a bunny rabbit. No time for sermons, but it's up against an even cruder gang to the north of Seoul. And the lot that had swept me up from the street, the NSP—the South Korean goon squad—are mobsters, torturers and killers, who work alongside the KCIA. Alongside, not with—two competitive gangs of thugs that our country, dear America, calls allies. If you want to blame, there's plenty of cause. Nonetheless, the three Lees were gentlemen to me that night. They did want my help, so they had reason to act civil.

I want you to follow along with our powwow, and with the chat in the car early the next morning, when they did indeed return me to the Royal Chosin. Yet because a four-way conversation is hard to recall and even harder to present matter-of-factly, I'm going to divide my questions and their answers into discreet groupings.

Firstly, what did the three Lees and I know together? They said that they knew everything Rosie knew about my interrogations of Charlie in New York, about my trip to Singapore with Lila. And also about my doublecross with U.S. Military Intelligence.

By the way, they said, captains D'Ambrosi and Cole were at the moment looking for me and Lila at NSP headquarters.

By the way, they said, would I make a phone call to captains D'Ambrosi and Cole to ease their excited inquiries?

"Negative," I said. "Tell me how Rosie found out about MI."

Youngest Lee said, "By your telephone calls in New York, Dr. Paine. Miss Rosemary Yip was in your apartment. With Mr. Charles Purcell."

"You bugged me? A wire?"

"No, no," said Grandfather Lee, tapping his ears.

Lee Nam Paik said, "We are not the powerful ones."

Youngest Lee added, "It wasn't of necessity."

Right, I thought, why wire when the source has a big mouth? I told them that since they knew about MI by eavesdropping, then they must also know I wasn't going to make any further phone calls near their big ears.

"Your friends are the great patriots," said Grandfather Lee of Jesse and Cole.

"Allies of the Republic of Korea," said Lee Nam Paik.

Youngest Lee said, "It would help them to know you are safe."

I didn't counter, What's it to you? I figured quickly that not my passport but rather my cowboys were my fortress. That I wasn't going to be a prisoner as long as MI was out there looking for me.

I told the three Lees I wasn't calling off the Unites States Army until I was home in New York watching tv, and maybe not then.

The three Lees nodded and apologized, bowed and obliged.

I'm leaving out much of my contrariness. I've claimed I wasn't frightened of them. At the same time, I might have been and covered it up with fury and arrogance. Rosie is what? You used me for bait? Lila is missing? What are you doing about it? You guys are messing with Uncle Sammie! Lila is an American citizen! Charlie is an American citizen! You are messing with American citizens! I mouthed off like this throughout. Why reproduce it? I was a fool, fooling around with hostiles, and you don't need proof.

Secondly, what did they know that I didn't? Again, they said they knew what Rosie knew. That Rosie was a trusted KCIA operative. That Rosie had inserted herself into Charlie's household in Ridgewood, New Jersey. That Rosie had stayed with Charlie from New Jersey to New York. That they were Rosie's control officers. That Rosie had reported to them at church socials. That, with their approval, Rosie had used me to solve Charlie's dilemma. That, with their help, Rosie had covered up

Charlie's suicide try. That Rosie had traveled to Tokyo and on to Seoul to keep Charlie moving toward his rendezvous with the blackmailers.

At this point, I asked harder questions.

"Rosie is your only watchdog on Charlie?"

Silence.

"And you don't know where Rosie and Charlie have gone? You don't have them? They're gone?"

Silence.

"Lila's gone, too?"

Silence.

"Does Mr. Kim have all three of them?"

Finally, a break in the silence: "Ah, Mr. Kim, the enemy, yes, the enemy," replied the three Lees.

"We need your assistance," replied the three Lees.

Lee Nam Paik said, "It is unhappy to consider that our enemy, Mr. Kim, has them."

I lengthened their list of unhappiness. "Do you know Charlie's been beating Rosie for as long as they've been together? That he regards her as his 'little yellow woman'? Do you know Rosie might be in love with Charlie?"

They nodded and apologized, bowed and obliged.

"It is the path," said Grandfather Lee. "You must not watch the tree you cannot climb."

Lee Nam Paik said, "Miss Rosemary Yip is the great patriot. She has known the risks."

I doubled back on their double-talk. "You say you've been Rosie's control officers for over a year? That you let Rosie get battered and raped and used like that?"

"It is the path. . . ." began Grandfather Lee.

"Confucius later," I interrupted. "It stinks around here. Open the window."

Obedience.

The delay gave me time to recognize a major general of a fact. I pursued it: "Okay, whoremongers," I said, "how did you get onto Charlie?"

"We have had the sources," the three Lees answered.

"Who's 'we'?" I asked.

Silence.

"What sources?" I asked.

"Mr. Charles Purcell is the suspect many years," they claimed.

"Not good enough," I said. "How *exactly* did you find out about Charlie?"

They replied inexactly, "A source, Dr. Paine, more than a year ago. Naming Mr. Purcell."

"Do better," I said. "Who told you Charlie was being black-mailed by Mr. Kim? And when did you acquire this source? And who is it? Informer? Big ears?"

After some fussing, Youngest Lee said, "A letter, Dr. Paine. These letters are common to have and to investigate."

"A letter?" I said. "A rat-fink letter? Shred your letter. You want my help, then you tell me. How? When? Why? Who?"

Black ops know when to flow and when to divert. They diverted me with news like a beaver dam.

"Miss Rosemary Yip is not the single agent on the path," tried Grandfather Lee.

Lee Nam Paik explained, "Yes, Dr. Paine. I am certain your friends in the Military Intelligence would tell you. Dr. Rajeesh Nehru is the foreign agent."

Youngest Lee helped them. "Dr. Nehru is Indian SIS, you must learn. Dr. Nehru is on our list as a foreign agent. Singapore station, Indian intelligence service. Like us. You must learn."

I was out of my chair and ranting. "Raj is a pro? He's dirty? You knew this and didn't close him down? You used me as bait, knowing Lila's boyfriend is an op? Does Lila know? Does Charlie? Does Rosie?"

"It is the path," said Grandfather Lee, repeating Confucian logic. "You must not watch the tree you cannot climb."

Lee Nam Paik repeated his logic. "We are not the powerful ones."

Youngest Lee explained, "Dr. Nehru, his arrival here, it was not known to us. When did we learn? Yesterday."

"What?"

Youngest Lee continued, "We knew not of Dr. Nehru until we searched our lists, Dr. Paine. And when your friends the American captains search their lists, they will find Dr. Nehru."

I lit their pipe and risked their tobacco. I was blithering sci-fi/spy jargon. "Roll him up, beat him senseless, make him talk!" I was so enraged that I solved a lot of Singapore all at once. "He's the one! Raj ran Charlie in Singapore! Raj might be Mr. Kim!"

"No, no," said the three Lees. "Mr. Kim is the enemy agent. Dr. Nehru is the foreign agent."

I told them their jargon was hooey. That if they couldn't see that Raj was so dirty that he was either the link between Charlie and Mr. Kim, or was Mr. Kim himself, they should enroll for remedial spookery.

I yelled louder: "Charlie and Rosie are gone! Lila's gone, along with one hundred and fifty million yen! I'm left for street cleaning! Your operation is trash too! Let's go cattle-prod Rajeesh Nehru!"

"No, no," said the three Lees.

"No, no? Why?"

Silence.

"Resources?"

Silence.

I thought about it a moment. I put all the Koreans into one urn. I made a good guess.

"It's the Yons, isn't it? You can't mess with Raj, because he's a pal of Charlie's, and Charlie is a pal of the Yons. Of the executive board and stockholders of the Han-gang Long Term Investment & Securities Company. The bankroll's bankroll."

"Senior Vice President Yon is the great patriot," replied Grandfather Lee.

Youngest Lee conceded, "Senior Vice President Yon would be unhappy if our errors were known to him."

The three Lees' Confucian witticisms had collapsed. I now understood the institutional basis for What They Knew That I Didn't.

It was "the powerful ones," aka the Han-gang Long Term Investment & Securities Company, aka the Long Termers.

The three Lees worked for a public agency called the KCIA; the three Lees were not "the powerful ones." They couldn't touch any of those trees they couldn't climb, that is, they couldn't manhandle us foreigners—Charlie, Flowers, Rajeesh, Lila or Tip. And all this was true, not because the three Lees were truly polite gentlemen, which they weren't, but because, if they did, the Long Termers would manhandle them.

Bluntly, if the Charlie Bunch got hurt, the three Lees did, too.

The three Lees didn't say this straight out. They wandered around obtusely.

I interrupted their palaver and rudely. "Let's review," I preached. "Listen up, and I'm not saying please. More than a year ago, you received a letter that said a foreigner, named Charlie Purcell, was being blackmailed by an enemy agent. You don't know who sent the letter or why. Do you?"

Silence.

"Instead of doing your homework," I continued, "you decide to spy on Charlie. How did you do this? You say you got a frumpy governess named Rosie into his bedroom. How'd that work? Rosie just showed up in Ridgewood and applied for the job? 'Position Wanted/ Little Yellow Woman/ Care-giving and Dope Smoking, Heavy Abuse/ P.S. I'm a spy!' Answer me! How did Rosie get her job? Did you sell her to Charlie? Do you guys run a call-girl service on the side?"

Silence.

"Whatever and somehow," I continued, "Rosie got inside, and she spied on Charlie for a year. Her job was to track down the blackmailer, named Mr. Kim. Meanwhile, you didn't investigate how the blackmail was done. You just waited over coffee and doughnuts at church socials. Eventually, Rosie told you that Charlie wanted to pay off Mr. Kim. Rosie told you that Charlie's sister-in-law was raising the cash. Rosie told you that she'd found a sucker named Dr. Paine to help Charlie get himself to Seoul. Rosie told you everything. You did nothing. Nothing! How come you guys sit by like fans? Where's your initiative? What's Rosie, your slave too? Do you own Rosie?"

Silence.

"So finally everyone arrived in Seoul," I continued. "You have to look us up in some spook glossary, because you didn't do your homework. And what do you discover? Charlie's pal Rajeesh Nehru is a creep like you! Gee. But do you do anything about it? No! You wait at another church social to chat with Rosie. What's Rosie to you guys? The brains and the brawn?"

Silence.

"Now you've got nothing," I continued.

Silence.

"Worse," I continued, "you've lost Charlie, and Charlie turns out to be a very good friend of a Korean bigwig named Senior Vice President Yon. You didn't know that until yesterday, did you?"

Silence.

"You've been spying on Charlie for over a year, yet just now you discover that Charlie travels in the company of a guy who is so big that he makes you wish you were back in Essex County mowing your lawns. Because if Senior Vice President Yon finds out what you've done to Charlie, and how stupidly you've done it, he will scalp your little wigs just like a lawn."

Silence.

"That's why you need me," I continued. "Senior Vice President Yon and the Long Termers hired me yesterday. For six million bucks. You figure that means I must be okay with 'the powerful ones.' And you also know that I might be able to provide the information you've botched or ignored, so that, somehow, you might be able to find Charlie and Rosie and maybe Mr. Kim."

I summated, "In sum, you three are watching that tree you can't climb and wondering when it's going to fall on you, since, without Rosie, there won't be advance notice. Just a loud crash. The end."

"It is unhappy," offered Grandfather Lee.

I taunted, "Unhappy's where you've been."

I wasn't satisfied with taunting.

"You guys are liars," I concluded. "You've lied to me from the first black moment I met you on the church steps on Broadway. I've waited for the truth, but you're just employees. And what offends me most, Messrs. Lying Lees, is that I've traveled here to track down Mr. Kim, and you still think you can treat me like dragon bait. I'm stupid for being here, but I'm not a sad sack you can bounce off the wall and get whatever you want."

Nods, apologies, bows, obliges.

"This chat was useless," I finished. "Take me to my hotel. If Lila is missing, if Raj is dirty and Charlie is gone with Rosie, if those aren't more of your lies, then it's the U.S. Army's turn at bat, and you creeps are banned with Peter Rose. Move it. Now."

10

"Thy Silly Face Be Done"

Rude enough? maybe not, but it worked. It was after
1:00 a.m. when I commanded. Their faces were no longer earnest
masks. Koreans don't believe in hiding their emotions. Angrily,
trickily, fiercely, the three Lees obeyed and took me back to the
Royal Chosin. Their angry trick was that we didn't go directly,
and we didn't travel in a car all the way. Instead, the first part of
the trip included a Bell helicopter.

I was impressed and more intimidated than I've let on to you.
We exited the apartment and rode a sedan across a park to a
concrete LZ. No guards, no guns, just KCIA business, all of
which reminded me that these fellows were state security, not
Jersey entrepreneurs. It wasn't good flying weather, so we lifted
off bumpily and rocked in head winds east over the suburbs, over
highways and scrubland, over a smaller city.

You can't talk in a chopper, and the ten-minute ride was their
trick to wow me with their muscle. We were still near Seoul when
we landed behind a Shell station and were met by another sedan.

Soon after, we turned off a single paved lane and bumped over trash piles to stop beneath a train trestle.

My thinking at this point was not dramatic. I saw village lights behind us, a railroader shack and switching tower a half mile to the left. A passenger train had passed as we approached, stainless-steel cars in a shadowy green. I thought about yelling but decided to keep shut and let them perform. If I hadn't been so tired, I might have imagined anything; then again, why should thugs bother to fly you to the Korean version of the Jersey wetlands to get tough?

"Dr. Paine, you are not wrong," began Grandfather Lee, sounding fragile and most untough, "you must learn the truth."

Youngest Lee ordered the driver to take a smoke break outside in the rain.

Lee Nam Paik, sitting beside me, flipped on the reading light and passed a folder to me.

The paperwork was in Korean. Atop the pile was a portrait photograph of a middle-aged Korean in military uniform, a light colonel; his insignia was the famous Capitol Division's.

"This was my brother," said Grandfather Lee, "Lee Tae Sang."

"My cousin," said Lee Nam Paik.

Youngest Lee turned around from the front seat. "He was my dad, Dr. Paine."

"The great patriot," said Grandfather Lee, "the war hero, decorated by General MacArthur. The D.S. and C. when twenty years. You know the war. Your book. The Capitol Division."

They paused in their collective mourning. I remembered to be rude. I said the war was forty years ago, and if this was going to be a long story, they should skip the anthems.

I thought I'd gone too far when they remained silent as another train flew past. No, they were waiting on the eldest to begin again.

"The brother," said Grandfather Lee, "was killed. Here!" He meant the railroad trestle. "The sixteen years past."

Youngest Lee told the story.

In the summer of 1974, his father, Colonel Lee, was being driven to a rendezvous in Seoul. It was late Saturday afternoon. Colonel Lee's car was ambushed, and he was abducted. Two days later his body was found hanging from fishhooks on this trestle.

When he was murdered, war hero Colonel Lee was the head

of a special unit he had organized in the Capitol Division; the special unit's job was to track down war criminals.

"Like the SAS," Youngest Lee boasted, "like the Mossad."

Colonel Lee's unit had been a quick success in the late sixties. But then the sources had dried up. He suspected he'd been penetrated by enemies. The politics of the period obliged him to push his luck and take meetings with bad sources.

The Saturday he was abducted, Colonel Lee was on the trail of a war criminal whose *nom de guerre* was "the Fisherman."

During the war, the Fisherman had been a fifth columnist in Seoul. He had assumed political command of a section of the city when it was captured by the North Koreans, the summer of 1950. The Fisherman had massacred hundreds of captured soldiers and civilians before MacArthur recaptured the city in September. His *nom de guerre* was based on the fact that his victims had always been bound by fishing line before they were shot or drowned.

Until Colonel Lee had received a tip that the Fisherman was living in South Korea, he had been presumed killed in the war.

That Saturday, according to the later interrogation of Colonel Lee's driver, Colonel Lee was diverted from a direct route to the rendezvous by an antigovernment demonstration in central Seoul. The city was still shabby then, dank alleys, no tall buildings, barely a million citizens. The driver chose a shortcut in order to avoid the city-center traffic jam.

"Poor tactics," Youngest Lee claimed.

What happened next was a professional hit.

A canopied American jeep came out of an alley and weaved slowly in front of Colonel Lee's car. Presently, the jeep pulled over and stopped and a Korean woman leapt or fell out. An American soldier jumped out after her. Both were acting drunken or drugged. The American soldier began pawing the woman, forcing her against the jeep.

Colonel Lee ordered his driver to halt. He got out to help the woman. Instantly, a taxi came up from behind and rammed the colonel's car. The driver got out to investigate and was bashed down; he never saw what happened to Colonel Lee. Jeep, taxi, American soldier and Korean woman disappeared along with Colonel Lee.

"Now you have learned," said Youngest Lee, finishing his story bitterly. "My dad was assassinated."

Youngest Lee got out of our car and walked away in the rain.

I'd heard enough, and you have too, to answer my seventy-first question: Why did they want Mr. Kim? But because I was cranky, I tried more questions about What They Knew That I Didn't.

I asked Grandfather Lee and Lee Nam Paik if they believed Colonel Lee had been set up by his own side.

Silence.

I asked if Colonel Lee's special unit was disbanded after his death.

Silence.

I asked why I should trust anything they said.

Silence.

I asked if they weren't the same KCIA that had routinely jailed, tortured and murdered thousands in its forty years, including assassinating their own dictator in 1979.

Silence.

"Let's grant you're only half lying," I said, "and get to the unhappy present. Tell me why you think Charlie was the American soldier at the ambush."

"The letter," said Lee Nam Paik, reaching over to the folder and pulling out an envelope.

I wasn't surprised, and you won't be either, to discover the letter was actually a black-and-white snapshot. The Tableau of Treason. It pictured Charlie in uniform, smiling gorgeously. The Han River and Seoul riverfront in the background. A gray day. Charlie on one side. Mr. Kim on the other—small, old, indistinct, face turned away from the camera. Here at last was the snapshot that had hooked Charlie to blackmail in 1981, that he said he'd paid fifty thousand dollars for in January.

I turned the snapshot over. I was surprised to find that, printed in careful English letters, was, "Specialist Charles Purcell 8.10.74." I checked the date again. August 10, 1974. It was Charlie's wedding day, when he'd married the now dead hooker, Mary Song.

I asked the two Lees, "The Saturday they kidnapped Colonel Lee—it was this, wasn't it? Saturday, August 10, 1974?"

Silence.

"Tell me how you got this," I demanded.

"Received by me," said Grandfather Lee, "the year past."

"Who sent it to you?" I asked.

Silence.

I indicated I wanted out of the car.

Youngest Lee was smoking nearby, and I moved over to him.

My thoughts were simple. So, Charlie, the devil really got you. Your two-thousand-dollar "chickenshit" was a dowry. And your part of the contract included conspiracy to murder a war hero. I was never sending you over. You're already there.

My next thought was black. So, Lila, if you knew, you're—I let that go.

I stepped under the cover of the trestle and lit their pipe, waiting for Youngest Lee to speak.

"It was the Fisherman," Youngest Lee said slowly, nodding toward the trestle. "It was his way. They hung my dad from there. They cut my dad like this." He made an evil motion.

Youngest Lee was the worst sort of intelligence source, entirely too close to the operation. Yet I needed more information.

I asked, "What's happened to the Fisherman?"

Youngest Lee shrugged.

"The Fisherman's dead, isn't he?" I said. "You're in this to revenge yourselves on whatever's left alive from that Saturday. You're doing this for face. No one cares but you and your ugly Lee faces. Isn't *face* how you excuse plain old serial murder?"

Youngest Lee lowered his shrug an inch.

"You think we're all Charlies, don't you? Greedy suckers you can turn and then persecute for a lifetime, because we're greedy suckers. Am I right, creep? Where am I right, where am I wrong? Say it aloud, creep."

Youngest Lee was a rock on rainy Planet Asia.

I'd blithered enough. You can hear my exhaustion and my fear, even if I couldn't just then. I sucked their pipe and asked, "Do you know the name Mary Song?"

Youngest Lee spun back. "No, Dr. Paine, who is it?"

"A dead woman who took a lot of answers to hell with her."

Youngest Lee held out his hands. "I will find her there."

"Clever," I said. "What are you going to do when you find Mr. Kim on this side of hell?"

To his rotten credit, Colonel Lee's son did not answer.

Back at the car, I told them that I'd had enough of their creepiness. "Take me to the hotel," I ordered.

They nodded and apologized, bowed and obliged. But not before they reintroduced their single-minded ambition.

"Will you help us, Dr. Paine?"

"I'm going to help myself, and that might mean Charlie, and it definitely means Lila and the money."

"This is the path," lied Grandfather Lee.

"We will not make you unhappy," lied Lee Nam Paik.

"You won't see us again," lied Youngest Lee.

At the very last, I remembered Rosie. It was impossible for me to think of her as their op.

"What about Rosie?" I asked. "She's a war orphan. Does that mean she's in this for revenge, too? To find Mr. Kim? To settle a score, just like your whole silly half country? Why pretend you're still fighting a forty-year-old feud? It's face, that's all you're doing. What do you guys get out of Presbyterianism—'Thy silly face be done'?"

Silence.

"No more lies, Lying Lees. You take the chopper, I take the car and driver." I growled, "Now."

If you're taken aback that I could get away with such vanity with the KCIA, so am I. That poison must have rotted the high centers of my brain where all those rules about baiting beasts dwell. Nevertheless I did it, said it, got my way. And that it happened was not really because they were declawed by my bluster. No, the truth was they needed my help any way I wanted to give it.

For there was that third topic.

What did I know that the three Lees didn't? You know most of it. You're still ahead of me. I'm catching up, though, and am about to pass you. Last chance to walk the cat before I do.

Six trick questions: Who's Mr. Kim? Why did he do it? How did he do it? Where's Lila? Where's Rosie? And easiest of all, where's Charlie?

PART FOUR

Good-bye Charlie

1

"All Nominal"

(The Interrogation of Rajeesh Nehru)

I'M RUSHING PAST MY REUNION with Jesse and Cole, my yelling to them about losing Lila, our excited debrief, more of my yelling about losing Lila, their negotiations with MI headquarters, in order to get to one of my good moments—the interrogation of Rajeesh Nehru, aka James Bhagavad-Gita Bond.

Here's what you need to know. It was Tuesday night. We were in Lila's suite at the Royal Chosin. Rajeesh was cooperating, sort of. We were holding him prisoner, sort of. I was without a plan of battle, sort of. Also, I'm joining the interrogation in progress, toward the end of the second hour. And finally, what you need to know is that we captors haven't yet told our captive that the KCIA was on the scene like ringers from hell.

"You understand, sir," Jesse began again to Rajeesh, "we do need to know the whereabouts of Mr. Charles Purcell and Miss Lila Schumann."

"Bugger off," Rajeesh advised.

Jesse nodded. Cole adjusted the directional microphone. This was their version of what MI calls the "repetition approach."

("Repetition is used," reads MI regulations, "to induce cooperation from a hostile source. . . . In employing this technique, the
use of more than one interrogator or a tape recorder has proven
to be effective.")

Rajeesh's hostility was showing; so was his talent. "I've told
you, I don't know," he advised. "You know I don't. Charlie's gone
away. I told him to go. Who knows where, and who cares? As for
Lila—I've told you it was a cock-up. As I see it, the buggers took
Lila, meaning to get you. You, Tip."

Rajeesh glanced to me at my laptop.

I typed his word for Mr. Kim—"the buggers."

"Examine what happened," continued Rajeesh professorially
to me. "You were queering the works. Snatching you was their
response. These're a bloody lot. You tried to dustbin them, they
did you. It's no wonder you don't like it, but wagging at me won't
fix it. In this game, you understand, we don't emphasize our
failures."

I thought, Good advice, Raj. In "this game," you win or you
don't talk about it.

It was mid-evening. We were spread out sloppily in the parlor.
The GI tape recorder and microphone were on the coffee table.
My Japanese laptop was on the big table. We'd brought the
eleven black cases of cash down from Charlie's suite and stacked
them near the best chair. We'd shut the drapes and turned on all
the lights. The tv was on, a soundless satellite feed of "Good
Morning America" (West Coast edition). I was rested. Jesse and
Cole were motivated, alert, patient, controlled, adaptable, perse-
vering and other MI attributes. Rajeesh was one bold, tricky professor of black operations.

Jesse and Cole had been harrying Rajeesh according to the MI
textbook when he'd lost his Cambridge cool a few degrees and
started with the "bugger off" recommendations. Though it might
have just been his guileful exasperation.

This was, indeed, a game to Rajeesh; and he was good at it.

I was trying to like Rajeesh. It was my vanity again. "Love thy
enemy" I hear as a challenge. Rajeesh was a wealthy, beautiful,
intellectual aristocrat. He was also the sort admired by the media
as expert, well-traveled, ruthless and devoted to conquest. How
do you like such a creature? He had cheated, stolen, lied,
screwed, abused, wasted and abandoned everyone in the course

of his bloody-minded duty. It was frustrating to admit that he was a hero to his side. And to admit further that Lila was in love with him, and I could see why. A libertine prince of men, who lectured the Chinese.

Of note, our interrogation of Rajeesh included the first and second degrees. The first degree had been holding him in Lila's suite all day; the second was our seminar of a chat. There was no threat of the third degree. MI forbids it, not only because it's wrong-headed, but because it doesn't work. ("The use of force, threats, insults, or exposure to unpleasant and inhumane treatment of any kind," reads MI regulations, "is prohibited by law and is neither authorized nor condoned by the U.S. Government. . . . Additionally, the inability to carry out a threat of violence or force renders an interrogator ineffective should the source challenge the threat. . . .")

Then again, I admit that I was lawlessly curious what it would look like if a cattle prod met a Cambridge First.

Then again, the Cambridge First was cooperating, sort of, and his gentlemanly bunk was giving me the time I needed to invent a plan, sort of.

"We are going to find Mr. Purcell and Miss Schumann, sir," Jesse said slowly, "and your cooperation is appreciated."

Rajeesh interrupted, "You really are such schoolboys. I'd've not believed it could be as they say. Overpaid, oversexed and just over, done, finished, debts called, tin cups."

Cole remarked, "Could you speak this way, sir, it's a directional mike."

"Incomprehensible," said Rajeesh, lighting another cigarette, rearranging his immaculate posture. He looked back over at me. "I'd appeal to you if you'd do more than peck your machine. I've told you and told you. The buggers meant to grab you, because they knew you were doing a dirty. How they knew is a good question. But really, once I'd chased Charlie off, it didn't take extraordinary brains. And the way you're carrying on, you must suppose American soldiers come and go unnoticed. Your security on this operation? Schoolboy. I imagine you've been bootjacking around the hotel for days, plotting and so forth. And your scheme to trick them in the restaurant was lunatic. It might have fooled you, but these're professionals."

Jesse said, "You're a professional too, sir."

"Thank you, Captain," Rajeesh said, "but not this time. I went to luncheon. I was happy to let Mr. Paine make an ass of himself. Your appearance, Captain D'Ambrosi, was unexpected. I say it hadn't come to me that Mr. Paine would have such entertaining mates. I have told this twice. When you all vanished, I meant to finish my luncheon. Until Captain Cole introduced himself clumsily."

Cole explained, "I asked you to remain on the premises, sir. You were checking out."

"Obviously not," Rajeesh said. "You queered it, they queered it. Think a bit, Tip, instead of pecking. They didn't want Lila. She's worthless to them. They're keeping hold of her because it might back me off. Yes, yes, me. They know I'm here by now. I *am* registered with Lila. They're not geniuses to know about all of us. We've left footprints like dogs at the river. And they're right, it does back me off. As soon as I leave, Lila's free. Too easy for you? You can't box me. You know you can't. You're beaten. *We're* beaten. Admit it. Back to your tin cups. Finish."

Jesse scratched a note and asked, "Sir, what information do you have about the disappearance of Mr. Purcell and Miss Schumann?"

Rajeesh sighed. "We both know this game—your trivial inquiry, repeat, repeat, it's flagrant. I've answered fully the few good questions you've had. Why shouldn't I, she's my—" Rajeesh sucked his cigarette. "I'm to blame, you're to blame, Lila's paying the penalty. If you cared so much about her, you'd hear me as a friend of the family."

I liked this cliché the first time I heard it and typed it dutifully into my laptop: "friend of the family."

Cole picked up on it too. "Friends help each other when someone innocent like Miss Schumann needs us, sir."

"Really?" Rajeesh replied, grinning touchily. "You can't be as thick as you seem. Innocent? A captain in the United States Army? Try to think it through."

Cole didn't even blink. "Yes, sir."

"Now that I've got you thinking, gentlemen," Rajeesh continued, "consider that it's not going to cover your backsides to pretend this is an investigation of a kidnapping. And if it was, where's your liaison? This is Seoul, not San Diego. I know the paperwork as well as you. It's a local matter, not military. Lila's a civilian, not one of your teenaged enlistees. I'm a foreign national, on a valid visa, cooperating with your inquiry openly. I would prefer access to my embassy, but that's a fine point. Have you got all that? You'll be filling out forms until you retire."

Jesse asked, "Do you have knowledge that either Miss Schumann or Mr. Purcell are being detained by the Seoul police, sir?"

Rajeesh mouthed a silent "Bah," and turned to appeal to me. "Where do you find such children?"

"That's a tough question, Raj," I said, enjoying myself, "but they just keep turning up."

It was suppertime. I asked Jesse and Cole for a time-out. Their "repetition approach" was increasingly futile. ("The repetition technique must be used carefully, as it will generally not work when employed against introverted sources or those having great self-control.") Rajeesh was testier than two hours before, but he was showing no sign of quitting his lectern. I was less angry than I had been at the start, yet I still was not getting what I wanted out of the interrogation—a plan of battle.

Soon after, room service delivered a cart. Cole gave Rajeesh a supper tray (no wine) and guided him into the back bedroom. I sat down at the coffee table with the boys for cold cuts and a powwow.

Jesse said, "We're only getting what he wants us to get."

"Cambridge," I said. "They're all like that, and the ones who aren't are worse."

Cole snapped a carrot. "Have you figured him out, Mr. Paine? Or any of it?"

"Nope," I said. "How about you two?"

Jesse spooned mustard on a turkey sandwich and remarked, "I think we've gone as far as we can without an overall. We can't hold him indefinitely. He's right about that. Last night, it was still hot pursuit. But with you back, sir, that won't do. We have to let him go soon. Tonight."

"Overall" was Jesse's word for what I called a plan of battle.

I let them eat a few bites and then tried a risky subject. "I want to scare him with the Lees," I said.

"Negative," Jesse said.

"I know, I know, but you have to believe me," I argued, "it will work. Class is everything to Raj. He's several classes above us, and we're what he's never been afraid of. We're Americans. To

him, we're baseball, apple pie, fair play, and none of that scares
him. But the KCIA—"

"Negative," Jesse repeated.

"I'm not saying we invite in the Lees," I argued. "All I want to
do is bring them up. Like a conversation piece. And if it doesn't
work, it doesn't work. Just tell Raj and let him decide."

"We can't make threats, sir," Cole said.

"Negative, sir," Jesse repeated. "That's it."

At this point, while we chow down on sandwiches, kosher
pickles, macaroni and potato salad, I'll explain that the reason
I've rushed past my reunion with the boys to get to one of my
good moments—the interrogation of Rajeesh—is because I
didn't have many good moments left.

Also, at this point, I'll admit my uninvented plan of battle was
guesswork. Holmes Paine, who hates guessing, had quit me for a
nap. In my defense, I argue that I was still eliminating the impossibles. The improbable truth isn't software that pops up on command. It takes gumshoe patience.

What I did know was slow-footed. Charlie and Rosie were
gone, and Rajeesh said he'd sent them off to stop the buy-back.
Lila was gone, and Rajeesh said she'd been taken by accident,
that Mr. Kim ("the buggers") had meant to take me but had
failed.

What I wanted to know was not fast afoot. If Mr. Kim had
taken Lila, what did it mean?

Jesse and Cole wanted facts. I doubt they truly believed they
could solve the mystery. Their one-foot-at-a-time soldiering kept
them plodding—steady, certain, guaranteed.

I needed leaps. I needed to figure not only why Mr. Kim had
taken Lila, but also why Mr. Kim was holding on to her.

It could have been as Rajeesh said, an accident that scored the
redhead with the Gladstone. This had some logic. If not for
Jesse's wits and training, the ambush at the Lotte shopping center
would have worked perfectly. Maybe. I didn't like this explanation entirely. I'd been set up and poisoned. But hadn't I also been
dumped and abandoned?

I repeat that Rajeesh was one bold, tricky professor of black
operations. He'd accepted detention as if it were a prank. It was
his opinion that we were "finish."

Accordingly, Rajeesh had spent the first hour of the interrogation (which I've skipped) boasting to us how he'd set up the blackmail in Singapore, how he'd run it for eight years, how he'd arranged to get Charlie out of the game.

"Charlie was played out," Rajeesh had explained earlier that evening. "It's mine to know when to shut down. Yet it's been two years now, and I've yet to get rid of them. The buggers are like flies, they won't shoo."

I've already told you all this, along with my suppositions. Remember—*it was what Raj believed to be true, not necessarily what was true.*

I'd taken Rajeesh's breezy telling more as a message that he was willing to accept his defeat than as evidence to be reexamined. Rajeesh was thinking "Good-bye Charlie" prematurely. Rajeesh had actually said, "Tip, if your lads here knew their work, they could've fetched up my dossier long before this. It's marvelous how beggarly you Yanks are that it took so long."

The truth of it was that Jesse and Cole never would have solved Rajeesh's identity if I hadn't returned from the three Lees to tell them. MI is a big, hard-wired outfit; but out there in Korea, it's more frontline than well-informed.

Then there was the further fact about Rajeesh's exposure, the one that he didn't know. I wanted to scare Rajeesh with the three Lees. To my certainty, Rajeesh knew nothing about my evening with the KCIA.

I reintroduced my lawless scheme to the boys as we finished our supper, Rajeesh out of earshot. "Sit him down and let him have the news. 'The KCIA is onto you. Call your embassy, pack your bags, taxi to Kimp'o. The KCIA is on your tail.' What's the threat in that? It sounds to me like brotherly advice."

"Mr. Paine," Jesse said, "do we have to cite you 'Prohibition Against Use of Force'?"

I've quoted this caveat to you already. I didn't want Jesse and Cole to get all red, white and blue on me, since, when the Army starts citing regulations, you are up against the immovable.

I changed tactics. "We need to make a deal with him then," I said. "I believe it falls under the MI rubric about 'Helping the source to rationalize his guilt.' "

Cole laughed and Jesse smiled.

I'd found a tiny seam in the armor. In my cowboy terms, their tin stars were five-pointed, and I'd just fixed on the point that says "Get your man."

"What sort of deal, Mr. Paine?" Jesse asked.

I sneakily didn't answer. Rather, I brought up the goal of my unrevealed deal. "We need Mr. Kim's telex address, and I'm sure Rajeesh knows it," I said. "If we get the telex address, we can set up another buy-back, smiling face to smiling face."

"It didn't work the last time," Cole said.

"Yes and no," I argued, eager to divert them from the deal to the goal. "We got something. Mr. Kim showed himself. We just don't know what he showed us. I think he took Lila for a reason. And just because Raj says *not*, we can't rule out that Mr. Kim's also got Charlie and Rosie."

"They wanted you, sir," Jesse said. "It was a mistake."

"No," I argued, "I don't like that. Mr. Kim has a style. And it includes daylight hits in central Seoul with taxis and demo diversions. As far as we know, he gets what he wants. I say he didn't want me—he wanted Lila with the money. And he got Lila with the money. Why?"

Cole frowned. "I hope it's not for those fishhooks."

Jesse frowned. "Leave it alone, Boneman."

"Sorry, Mr. Paine," said Cole, "I'm really sorry."

They thought they were being sensitive about me and Lila. I took advantage of their sympathy by strolling back to my laptop, as if recovering myself.

I was actually stalling to figure how to get around their sensitivity to Professor Black Ops. I let them think I was upset, while I typed more loose thoughts. I'd told Jesse and Cole everything I'd learned from the three Lees. They had winced at the KCIA, but they hadn't panicked. Nothing panics a Labrador retriever, and nothing panics the U.S. Army. Hear me loud and clear, home boys and girls and alien allies and enemies. Nothing, no one, nowhere, nohow. Not even defeat (cf. Korea, Vietnam). Jesse and Cole had listened to my recounting of my evening with the three Lees and had gone off to consult with their CO. I was not consulted and expected to hear that, with the KCIA in, then MI was out. Instead, they'd come back to me to say that Operation REDLEGS was "all nominal."

That's why I was typing hurriedly into my laptop. It's strangely giddy to have such power at one's table and yet not know how to use it, because it has orders that rule out lies, fakery, double-crosses and nastiness.

I started another outline. The only thing I could figure was to overwhelm their black-and-white rules with red-light violations. It was time to push it, bluntly.

"Your call," I said to Jesse and Cole. "Do we go for another buy-back or not?"

Jesse had his notebook open. "Explain to me, sir, if we can convince Mr. Nehru to provide us the telex address, what would we be buying back and with what?"

I gestured to the eleven black cases. "Lila and whatever else Mr. Kim's selling," I said.

"That's a definite negative," Jesse said.

Cole had the tape recorder running.

I countered with double-talk. "Charlie owes me, and he owes Lila. It's Pam's money, too, and I think she'd want us to use it to get her sister back. Maybe Charlie back, too."

"Sir," Jesse said, "we've permitted you to participate so far because it's believed that you have information vital to our investigation, sir."

"I'll mind my manners," I lied.

Cole said, "This doesn't work like your movies, sir, but it does work."

"No more Hollywood," I lied.

Jesse squinted again, right between my treacherous eyes. "We'll try with Mr. Nehru once more, and we'll ask for the telex address. But no threats."

"Sure," I lied.

2
"We Know All" Approach

COLE FETCHED RAJEESH. The man's man was splendid in a fresh charcoal suit and pink striped shirt, hideous lemon tie. He'd shrewdly used the break to shower and change and was now gleamy for the contest.

Rajeesh told Cole to bring him more tea. Cole obliged. Rajeesh showed an inch too much confidence when he held up his cigarette for Jesse to light like a factotum.

Jesse ignored Rajeesh's move and returned to the "repetition approach" as if supper hadn't happened. "We have reason to believe you know the whereabouts of Miss Lila Schumann and Mr. Charles Purcell, sir."

"I do not," Rajeesh replied.

Jesse added, "And we also have reason to believe you possess the telex address of the hostile known as Mr. Kim."

"Do you?" Rajeesh replied.

My turn. I could have waited another empty round or two, but what the heck, I'm an impatient fool. "I'm offering you a deal, Raj," I said. "Straight swap. You help me, I help you."

Rajeesh smiled. "Much better," he said. "Mine's a young nation, and we hear out American deals. What is it we're trading with? Dollars?"

I waited a pause to make certain that Jesse and Cole wouldn't interfere. I was sure they wouldn't. I'd solved their dilemma by ignoring it.

"It's just us here, Raj," I said, typing as I talked. "The 'royal we' is not invited. I. You. Deal. Trading intelligence."

Rajeesh blew smoke.

"And it's a real straight swap," I said. "You give me everything you know, I don't give the KCIA you."

Rajeesh didn't stop smoking, but his manhood reconsidered. "The KCIA is it?" he said. "Your bloody hired hands—excuse me, allies." Rajeesh rotated to engage Jesse, then Cole. "That sounds like a threat, Captains; what does it mean?"

"Just you and me, Raj," I remarked, addressing the directional microphone. "Captains D'Ambrosi and Cole have been called away. Duty and all."

Rajeesh smiled.

I smiled.

"I've been hoping we'd get an opportunity to talk alone," Rajeesh told me. "We never did have that chat about Stalin you promised, did we?"

I saw that it was working, that for the first time the professor hadn't told me what to think and do, rather he was asking me questions. I left the laptop humming. I tried not to meet Jesse's or Cole's gaze as I sat opposite Rajeesh's throne. The tape recorder was rolling.

For your notes, my approach was what MI calls the "we know all." ("There are some inherent problems with the use of the 'we know all' approach," reads MI regulations. "The interrogator is required to prepare everything in detail, which is very time consuming. He must commit much of the information to memory as working from notes may show the limits of the information actually known.")

I told Rajeesh about my evening with the three Lees. I talked too long, but I had to emphasize the choice parts, such as revenge,

Rosie, fishhooks and the blackness in Grandfather Lee's eyes when he said that Colonel Lee was his brother. The train trestle was useful color. I even imitated Youngest Lee's motion when he showed me how to cut a man like a fish.

Rajeesh continued grandiose. Maybe he did smoke a little too fast.

"You say you're a 'friend of the family,' " I proposed to him. "I like that. But if you're such a friend, then how come you never asked Charlie what happened on his Korean wedding day, Saturday, August 10, 1974?"

Rajeesh flicked ash.

"How come you never even got the name Mary Song out of Charlie? His first 'little yellow woman.' Mary Song, Raj. Ever heard the name?"

More ash.

"How come you ran Charlie like a puppy all those years, while swapping girls and squash shots, yet you never bothered to find out the truth of the 'terrible thing' he can't shake? One hard question, Raj. You say you know 'this game,' but you never asked, did you, Raj?"

He touched his teacup.

"You've got a wife, kids and status at home, feudal estates and family connections. For kicks, you've got a redheaded mistress, 'little yellow women' like pillowcases. You're right, we can't box you. You can shrug us off, as you shrugged off Charlie and Lila and Pammie and the Soos. How many more? Gee, Raj, you want to walk? Walk."

Rajeesh examined the glitter of his Rolex.

"Don't sweat Lila," I said. "If she comes back, she'll come back to you. A little love, a few lies, she's yours again. She already thinks you're cock of the black walk."

"Is it Lila?" he asked me. "Is that why you're doing this?"

"Are we getting tender about Lila now?"

"Then why are you doing this?" he asked.

"I'm with you, Raj," I said. "I'm a 'friend of the family' who got played for a sucker. We're mates, Raj. Same family. Same girl."

"Petty, Tip, petty."

"I like you, Raj," I boasted, feeling very petty and proud of it. "So let's walk together. Me back to New York. And where do you go when the beggarly Yanks aren't covering your back-side?"

"You're enjoying this," he said.

"Gee, Raj, I enjoy blackmail, slavery, poison, losing four hundred thousand dollars of my own money and evenings with the KCIA. It's never dull. The Lees are your kind of guys, very gentlemanly. I figure they'll be gentle to you, too. They told me as much. I believe them, don't you? I told them they should cattle-prod you. They said no, you're a foreign agent. Why not believe guys who settle family feuds with fishhooks?"

I credit Rajeesh a lot. He never looked away, never appealed to Jesse and Cole. He sipped tea once more and surrendered.

"That's sufficient," he said, just like that, no fuss. "We can help each other," he said.

"Yeah," I said, " 'friends of the family.' "

"Please yourself," Rajeesh said. "I've been trying to get rid of these buggers for two years. If you can do it, I can help you. Isn't that our deal?"

"The deal," I said, "is what I say it is. Now, give me Mr. Kim's telex address."

"You're convinced I have it?" Rajeesh tried, a squash back-hand trick—hit it when it's by you.

"I'm sure," I said. "You've probably had it for years, since Charlie spills everything when he's high and horny. But you cer-tainly helped Charlie send the telex last Saturday morning that confirmed the buy-back, because you needed that prospect to scare Charlie away."

Rajeesh tried the squash-court flattery trick. "Good, you're good for an amateur."

"Thanks, pal."

(Lila was right, I really was full of myself.)

"And what have we here?" I pretended to look around the room as I spoke loudly into the directional microphone. "Cap-tains D'Ambrosi and Cole have just returned from duty and all. What luck. It seems the United States Military Intelligence Corps has more to say to Dr. Professor Rajeesh Nehru, Indian SIS and international stinker."

Rajeesh lowered his beautiful Aryan head. "I did want to say to you, Tip, I've not seen your film but I've heard—Olivier was all wrong as Stalin. You got carried away there."

3

"Friend of the Family"
(Holmes Paine Solves the Case)

JESSE AND COLE TOOK the rest of the evening to wear out Rajeesh with their textbook approaches. He gave us nothing new, besides the telex address, but he gave it sincerely. Listening in was like eavesdropping on a forced march, since this time they combined the "repetition approach" with the "rapid-fire approach." ("The rapid-fire approach involves a psychological ploy based upon the principle that everyone likes to be heard when he speaks, and it is confusing to be interrupted in midsentence with an unrelated question.")

"When did you tell Mr. Purcell to flee?"

"You don't mind if we inspect your luggage and your clothes?"

"What's the telex address again?"

"Your full name?"

"Have you communicated with Mr. Kim in the last seventy-two hours? Two weeks?"

"What did you order at luncheon?"

"Do you have an intimate relationship with Miss Lila Schumann?"

"Where did you get that wristwatch?"

And onward, keep the hostile talking, double back, triple back, don't argue, stay on the attack. Just get the facts, others will judge.

However, while I listened, and no matter how often Rajeesh patiently restated his revelations, I kept coming back to that cliché of his—"friend of the family." Good homely image, Raj, what's it mean?

Presently, my fussbudget alter ego Holmes Paine came back from his nap and leaned over my shoulder. I showed him what I had. "Friend of the family." It felt like a clue. I told Holmes I still hadn't solved the case, but I was hewing a woodpile of impossibles around the improbable truth.

One. It was impossible that Mr. Kim had taken Lila by accident, for no reason.

Holmes poured himself tea.

Two. It was impossible that Mr. Kim had penetrated us so thoroughly from outside. That he knew what I would do, what Rajeesh would do, what Charlie would do. Mr. Kim seemed to know everything, down to the detail that Lila was the bridge between me and Rajeesh and Charlie. Was that why he took her? To back us off, scare us?

Holmes sniffed; he's the original counterintelligence officer; he never met a black op whose pants he couldn't drop. I got competitive.

Three. It was impossible that there wasn't a mole. That's op talk for a "friend of the family" who isn't.

Boffo, I thought, how'm I doing, Holmes?

Holmes yawned.

I punched up my list of players and asked who the mole was. This was a crime wave, and crime-busting insists there must be weapon, opportunity and motive.

Weapon was easiest: a mole is a weapon.

Opportunity meant that the name of the mole had to fit the facts. That the mole had to know everything, from Saturday, August 10, 1974, to date. Know not only about Charlie and Mary Song but also about Lila, Pam, Rajeesh. And about me and my double-dealing with MI. Did the mole have to know about the Long Termers and the three Lees? Yes, and that meant the mole knew about Rosie spying on Charlie. Knew that it was necessary to get Charlie out of the way before the buy-back so that the three Lees would be blind. Knew that, when Charlie went missing, I would force the buy-back with a tv-simple plan. Knew that Lila wouldn't let me carry out the buy-back without her dramatic self. And also knew that I was going to be poisoned and that my dumping would freeze MI from close pursuit.

Okay, the mole couldn't have known all this ahead of time. The mole just had to be in place, very close to the players—in other words, a mole.

In sum, the mole I was looking for had to know everything Mr. Kim knew and everything Mr. Kim needed to know to grab the money and Lila and get away.

Bluntly, the mole had to be working with Mr. Kim.

All this had to be true to explain the weapon and opportunity of the crime.

What of the tough third requirement of crime-solving, the motive? What was the motive for the mole? The money? Was greed enough to explain so much? What else? Family? What name was a friend of both Mr. Kim's blackened family and Charlie's golden family?

It was well near midnight. I looked over at Rajeesh. He wasn't fresh any longer (his suit was wrinkled at the back of the knees), but his posture made him tower over the slogging boys. I didn't like it, but I had to say it. Rajeesh had to be the mole. He was a liar's liar. Nothing he said was true. The name was Rajeesh Nehru, yes?

Holmes lit his pipe.

I lit my pipe.

I felt ridiculous competing with a make-believe fussbudget. I left my laptop and wandered through the suite. Into Lila's bedroom.

Holmes trailed me like a scold.

I opened the closet and was overwhelmed by Lila's scent. Her pricey suits, her excellent shoes, her fantasy lingerie. I picked up her clothes brush and waved it at Holmes.

"See that, great detective?" I said (I wasn't actually talking, I was arguing with myself, wasn't I? Maybe I was talking). "She's a redhead. What do you know about it? It's red and it's silly, but it means something to me. And that jerk out there is why I've got nothing unless I've got the name. Yeah, I'm jealous, why not?

Wrap it up neatly. Raj did it. Let's hang him and I get the girl. Too simple for you? It's damned American. I win."

Holmes glanced at Lila's wardrobe. He stepped into the master bath.

I followed.

I was angry at Holmes and yanked open Lila's toiletry bag. I spilled vials, tubes, makeup kit, brushes and whatnot on the counter.

I also found what I'd half expected, not one, not two, but *three* diaphragm cases. The modern woman.

I arranged them into the shell game.

"Here's Raj," I told Holmes, "and here's me. And here's a modern woman's backup, labeled Whom-It-May-Concern. That's romance. See, Holmes, get out your magnifying glass, watch. Lose Raj and what's left is me and Whom-It-May-Concern."

Holmes waited me out.

I stepped back. What was I angry about? Not Holmes—he was make-believe. I was frustrated. I so much wanted Rajeesh to be guilty of everything that I'd forced the solution. Jealousy had made me stupider than usual.

Lose the jealousy, I thought. Lose the first and second diaphragm cases from the shell game. What's left? Whom-It-May-Concern. What did that mean?

Start again with the diaphragm called Rajeesh. If Rajeesh was the name of the mole, if he was working with Mr. Kim, why hadn't he escaped us, why was he in there being worked over? If he was the brains of the hostiles, as well as being the mole, why had he allowed Mr. Kim to take and hold Lila? I had no answers.

I returned to my first impossible. It was impossible that Mr. Kim had taken Lila by accident, for no reason. So why?

Yes, yes, yes, I thought. So simple. Mr. Kim had taken Lila not to back Raj off, not to back Tip off, not even to scare us. *But to divide us.* To set the two "friends of the family" who could solve the case, me and Raj, against each other. Which was what was happening.

I put the diaphragm called Rajeesh next to the one called me.

If I now teamed up with Rajeesh, I thought, instead of trying to lose him, then—

I picked up the third diaphragm case. Whom-It-May-Concern, I thought, who are you? Who's screwed all of us?

Holmes frowned at the props.

I told him to forgive the hambone and listen.

I declared that Rajeesh wasn't the only name that wasn't impossible, was he? I tried again without the negatives. There was another possible name who was a "friend of the family."

Holmes yawned.

Silly as it is to report, that's when I vainly *walked the cat.*

I knew the improbable truth, who'd done it, how it was done, why it was done, who Mr. Kim was and how to find him.

Holmes didn't help me. I did it. Okay, we both did it, his mocking and my busybodying. There was this too, I hated the walking. It was so stupid, so sad, so obvious. It disgusted me.

I was a Puritan avenger by the time I returned to my laptop. I typed out my guessless plan of battle.

Eventually, I interrupted Jesse and Cole again.

"Just a few questions," I told Jesse.

Jesse squinted at me.

"If I cross you again," I teased Jesse, "you can arrest my laptop."

The boys continued to surprise me: "You want us to take another walk outside, sir?" Cole joked.

"Duty and all," Jesse teased me back.

"Not necessary," I said, "but thanks."

I addressed Rajeesh. "You see, it turns out that you're right, Raj, I do get carried away."

Jesse watched to see if this was another trick.

I explained, "Raj doesn't know any more than he's already told us. You're a bad boy, Raj, but you really have been as stupid as you say. You're not the one I've been looking for."

Rajeesh started his third pack of cigarettes and eased back. He did look that wonderful English qualifier—"shirty." I don't know what it means, but I've always wanted to say a Cambridge man looked shirty.

I addressed Rajeesh. "You've never met, seen or in any way identified Mr. Kim, have you?"

"Certainly not—he's your fascination," said Rajeesh. "I've had nothing whatsoever to do with the Seoul leg of the enterprise. Compartmentalized, that's standard, you know that."

"Exactly," I agreed. "And back in '81, when you first contacted the Reds about Charlie, did you tweak them, or did they tweak you?"

"Tweak, Tip? What a god-awful idea. Little wonder Lila says you're a—"

"Come on, Raj, I overdid it before. I'm sorry, okay? I'm jealous. Confession enough? Just tell me—did they contact you or you them?"

"Bit of both," Rajeesh said. "You don't have tea with your opposite number. My dealings began with their agent in Singapore, I've told you. After that, it was by dead drop. I kept Charlie in line, I got paid. A tidy quid pro quo for eight years. When Charlie left Singapore for Tokyo, my task ended and so did the pay envelopes. They've been squeezing Charlie since for free."

"Exactly," I agreed.

I changed directions. "Tell me," I asked Rajeesh, "how much do you figure Flowers, Kepler and you transferred to Charlie for the robotics deal over the last year? Not only your own money, but also what you could get hold of from the banks. Loans on your credibility. More than ten million? Less than a hundred million?"

Rajeesh didn't pretend I was wrong. "What's that to do with it?" he said.

"More than twenty, less than eighty?"

"I don't know," Rajeesh complained. "Charlie handled it."

"He sure did," I teased.

Rajeesh complained, "You're off the point. The deal's already signed."

"A sure thing," I teased. "A done deal. Bugs Bunny for moms everywhere."

Rajeesh smiled.

I smiled.

For fun, I changed directions again. I asked Rajeesh, "Charlie said nothing to you about where he was going with Rosie Sunday night? No hints?"

Rajeesh answered calmly, "I didn't care. I just wanted him to go away. He didn't argue. You know Charlie, he was soaring. He said something like, 'I'm out, Raj, you betcha, out.'" He leaned toward me, the weary professor sensing a crucial turn. "Why do you ask?"

I ignored him for more hambone. I told Cole to point the directional microphone in my direction. I bragged, "I'm going to tell you how yesterday's victim is today's crook. You too, Raj, listen up."

"Sir," Jesse interrupted, "I'm advising you again, you must not make threats. I mean that."

"None, Captain," I promised, "though I do have another plan, and if it works, you get Charlie and Mr. Kim and the end of the trail."

Jesse saw me glance at the black cases and tried to head me off at the pass. "No threats and no deals, sir."

Cole adjusted his six-shooters. Rajeesh tucked in his shirt. And me, I walked the cat out loud.

4
aka Mary Song

THE NEXT AFTERNOON, Rajeesh and I entered Dragon's
Gate restaurant in tandem. Two gentlemen joined for luncheon
and counterintelligence. It was Wednesday, March 21. We'd set
the new rendezvous with Mr. Kim for 1:00 P.M. We were ahead
of schedule, in order to show each other how middle-aged brave
we were.

Also, I've shown you my good moments. What's left to be done
is to illustrate the bad ones.

I ordered the same as Monday lunch, New York seltzer and
soup du jour.

Rajeesh bypassed the duck pâté for mushrooms, chops and
another of his worldly wines.

The adjoining tables were Swiss, Czech and Kiwi. The room
was subdued. The VIPs were packed and primed for their jumbo
jets launching home later in the afternoon.

"It must've been the waiter," Rajeesh teased about my poison-
ing, "unless you've just a wretched colon."

I drank the bottled water. I knew who'd poisoned me. I didn't know how, but I knew who. I wanted everything the same as Monday except that detail; just in case, I didn't touch my soup or seltzer.

"Must eat something," Rajeesh teased. "Blood sugar is courage."

I had the waiter clear the setting beside me so I could prop up my laptop. To imitate Rajeesh's suave, I called up "Midway" and continued my hunt for the Imperial Japanese fleet.

Thirty minutes of this beeping bravado was enough. The majordomo appeared on schedule, just past one, to deliver, on a silver salver, a message from Mr. Kim.

Rajeesh read it first.

"Welcome Seoul. Taxi No. 1031. Tongdaemun Market." It was signed, "Arizona."

"Predictable," I said. "Does it bother you, Raj," I teased, "how predictable your game is?"

"Don't make too much of it," he said, "though I see you must get carried away again."

"Lit crit later, Prof," I said, waving the message. "Are you satisfied by this?"

"I suppose, the buggers. It's your show. So far."

I corrected him. "It's Charlie's show. We're bagmen."

Rajeesh teased back, "Does it ever bother you that you must crush things into gaudy categories?"

"Yeah, but they're easy to remember." I listened to what he'd just said. "Is that 'so far' a crack?"

"Certainly not," Rajeesh replied. "In this game, even when they do what you want them to, it's never quite satisfying."

"There's this," I teased in return. "The worst-case scenario is that we get our redhead back to bash us at teatime."

"That's worst enough for me," Rajeesh said. "Lila's not a lady to waste her breath on fools."

"We must be talking about two different redheads. My Lila wastes more than that. I've still got her house, and you, poor sod, you've got twelve years of her attention span."

"You're *generous* comfort."

Rajeesh sipped wine and laughed politely. I liked him for his nervy manners. Today, I liked him genuinely. No, I didn't. It was confusing. His savvy was first-rate, but his conscience was either missing or that of a strangler. He had convinced me that he would oblige me as long as he stood to gain advantage. In "this game," he was the pro, I was the amateur. I was mostly genuinely jealous of him. Let the lady choose the tiger or the mortgage.

We signed our chits and departed the restaurant. I passed my faithful laptop to the majordomo, telling him to let no one touch it, the bad guys were trapped, ha-ha.

Our matching trench coats waited at the concierge's desk. So did our matching bellhops, handling the eleven black cases.

Outside, we both overdramatized, checking the drab spring sky. I also checked my bowels and my heartbeat. How did I feel? Keen. As if I was in charge. As if I'd just found the Imperial fleet.

Taxi No. 1031 was fourth in line.

We ordered the bellhops to load the black cases into the trunk, and then we both overtipped, though, I noted pridefully, they were happier at my American dollars than Rajeesh's Singapore dollars.

The taxi driver was another teenager. This one wore a California Angels windbreaker (I think of him as Teen Angel.) The gas gauge displayed a full tank. Teen Angel's wristwatch displayed a four-minute difference from the digital clock in the dashboard. I took all this as evidence that Teen Angel was not working the day shift. That he was a hired hand in a car meant just for us.

Teen Angel weaved us into the traffic flow. Rajeesh lit a cigarette. I lit my pipe. According to my map, the Tongdaemun Market was east of us, about one and a half miles. I relaxed some as we passed the scene of my Monday undoing at the Lotte shopping center. We gained the teeming Chonggak Boulevard and then circled, passing the Korea Development Bank's tower twice. Teen Angel was stalling correctly, waiting for the demo du jour to get organized.

So far, I thought, this is predictable, predictable, predictable. Presently, I spotted parked police vans and then, in the distance, the blue-helmeted line of riot police, forming up to intercept the phalanx of a mob.

We crawled a few yards at a time, hemmed in by a fleet of taxis, buses and vans trying to avoid the demo gridlock. There was no real danger if we wanted to jump out.

That wasn't our aim. Rajeesh and I were playing counterintelligence with Mr. Kim. No rules. No panic. Smile and wait, wait and smile.

Today's mass demonstration was ahead of us now, coming up the boulevard toward the Pagoda Park, a bobbing mass of lunch-time Reds waving banners and singing songs.

Teen Angel cut out of the traffic line and veered to the parallel elevated road, picking up speed.

Rajeesh addressed me. "I'd expected torn asphalt and tear gas, perhaps a water canon. I'm quite disappointed."

"Me, too," I said.

"You know, Tip," Rajeesh offered, "it's much jollier when you don't anticipate."

I grunted. Cambridge phlegm, phooey.

Teen Angel turned off the elevated road and turned back into the pedestrian swarm. This was the Tongdaemun Market, a mile-long bazaar of open-air stalls. Moms and kids were everywhere, bargaining for foodstuffs, clothing, hardware—midweek mid-afternoon shopathon.

Teen Angel bumped over the curb and eased into a vendor-lined lane. Our path was filled by a parked convoy of delivery vans. Judging from the smell and chopped ice on the ground, this was fishmongers' row.

Yes, I thought about fishhooks. I also thought, *So far, so far.*

We left the fishmongers' row for another lane. This one extended into an herbal-medicine arcade.

I pointed. "Apothecary row."

"Yes, yes," Rajeesh snooted.

The ambush happened routinely. Predictably. Expecting it, I felt it was sluggish. Teen Angel dropped into reverse gear and jolted the taxi backward beneath the canopy of a stall. Several teenagers surrounded the car. The trunk was opened and the black cases pulled clear.

The Monday taxi driver—the teenager in the "U2 World Tour" jacket—climbed in the front seat and stared back at us. U2 jerked his hand, thumb out.

According to my tv-simple plan, it was time to bluff.

I played my part. "We came for the redhead, creep."

U2 shouted, "Out! Fast, fast! Out!"

Rajeesh played his part better, but it was the more manly role. "The woman first," Rajeesh said. "No woman, no deal."

"Out!" insisted U2.

Rajeesh blew smoke at him.

I listened to our bluff and thought how flimsy it was. How could this work? They had the money. Why should Mr. Kim follow through and meet us, smiling face to face? I knew why I thought Mr. Kim would, but still, why? Was the crooked mind as simple as tv after all? I thought contrarily, Take the money and run, boys, do it, don't look back, run.

Contrary worked contrarily; the crooks did exactly opposite; they went along with the simplest trick I could imagine.

"Okay!" U2 ordered.

I checked. "We get the woman, right?"

"Okay! Two guys! Out!"

"I suppose this is it," Rajeesh remarked.

"It's gonna work," I said, "it's really gonna work."

"As I say, jollier." Rajeesh took a last tough-guy drag and stubbed out his cigarette. "The thing is, I feel we're about to get what we're paying for. It is what we want, isn't it?"

For the first time since I'd planned our day, I considered that it wasn't what I wanted. I bluffed myself. "Gee, Raj," I said, "gee."

The teenagers opened both passenger doors. They wore made-in-Korea junk; their hair was clipped to spiky crew cuts; important teeth were missing. None spoke English. I saw no weapon; their actions were forthright tv menace.

"We're coming along, chaps," Rajeesh told them.

Rajeesh glanced to me. "Any parting wit, that sort of thing?"

"See you on the other side, pal."

Rajeesh teased, "I'd hoped for something of your cinema, such as 'Take me to your leader.' "

We took a six-hour ride in a ginseng-smelling van. This was overlong, but then, they were teenagers, and countersurveillance tactics are endlessly fun.

While we're bouncing along, en route to Mr. Kim, I'll take the opportunity to tell you my prattling solution to the case.

Yesterday's victim was today's crook. Who was the "friend of the family" who had screwed everyone? The improbable answer was Charlie. The knockout goldilocks, the Alan Ladd screwup, the hophead scavenger, he's the name of the mole and the leader to be taken to.

I don't know all of it, I never got to ask, but the easy points are very easy once you know the correct answer.

The seven and a half million yen of Lila's money that Charlie had paid Mr. Kim on January 3 was a bona fides, all right. A retainer, a transaction fee. Charlie had hired his old nemesis, Mr. Kim, to run a sting operation on everybody—Lila, Pam, me, Rajeesh, Flowers, Kepler, the Long Termers and the three Lees.

How? You've been watching how.

Why? Charlie himself answered this best when he quoted my movie line: *"Vice is its own reward."*

Charlie wanted out, all the way gone. Good-bye family, job, mortgaged splendor and glamorous troubles. Hello "little yellow women" and the sort of worldview available to a multimillionaire sucking an opium pipe.

What multimillions? Didn't you ever wonder where Charlie's cash assets were? I did, and I convinced myself he'd invested it in the robotics deal. Nope; he'd cleaned out his private swag and stowed it somewhere Asian. He'd also scammed a lordly sum from the Charlie Bunch, who'd thought they were putting it into the robots—Flowers's money, Kepler's money, Rajeesh's money (a sweet trick, since Rajeesh's wealth included what he'd earned all those years of running Charlie). And then Charlie had added Lila's money and my money (a sweeter trick, since it was against property Charlie was abandoning; let the Schumann sisters eat carrot cake).

I don't know the total sum that Charlie scammed. I can only guess that it was less than a hundred million and more than ten million. Charlie had robbed everyone; he'd also taken what his pals could raise from the banks, supposedly to sink into the robots. In any event, it was eight healthy American figures.

It was also crooked genius. Everything Charlie had done over the last year had been to set up and trick everyone he'd ever known. When he vanished Sunday night, it was a clean getaway.

That's what I'd told Jesse and Cole and Rajeesh Tuesday night, in Lila's suite. Screwed by a screwup.

"Whoa," Cole had said.

Jesse had asked, "Are you sure about this, sir?"

And Rajeesh, he'd laughed and said, "It doesn't sound like Charlie, but that's the point, isn't it? When you turn the tables, you're a new man sitting there."

Good line, Raj, I'd thought, "turn the tables." I had further admired Charlie's table of fools. "It's over. We're beaten. Charlie's won. And he's free to go. The Army can't touch him on the '74 crime. There's no evidence of a crime, so no crime. Right?"

Jesse and Cole had nodded.

"As for Jimmy Flowers, Jerry Kepler, Raj here," I'd said, "they can't touch him. They gave him their money for a deal that wouldn't interest a court, and what court?—there's no SEC in Asia. And the banks, who's going to listen to them crying about personal loans they made for a robot cartel in Seoul?"

Rajeesh had sighed. "Bloody."

"As for me and Lila," I'd said, "we forced our money on him. Lila out of guilt for siccing him on her sister. Me to double-cross and bag him. So what charge could we make?"

I'd pointed to the drapes and Seoul. "And even the Long Termers don't care. They've decided to compromise to get what they wanted. The robots are theirs. Charlie and his bunch of rascals are a closed-out account."

I'd closed, "As for the three Lees, they don't want to hurt Charlie. They'd sooner hang themselves on fishhooks. To their mind, Charlie is a permanent friend of Korea. They'll say prayers for him forever. They'll even like the idea that he's gone and not coming back to rat on what they tried to do to him for a year."

I'd laughed. "That's the treat. What we all did to Charlie is what Charlie wanted us to do. Charlie's good, Raj, he's very, very good at this."

Cole had asked, "What do we do about it, sir?"

I'd suggested applause.

"We do have our orders," Jesse'd said.

I'd told them that Charlie had gone where orders were meaningless. "He got even, got ahead, got away."

Jesse and Cole had sat ramrod still. "We will get him soon enough, sir," from Cole.

Jesse'd said, "That's it."

"Not soon enough for me," I'd said. "I want him right now."

That's when I'd told them my plan of battle to lure Charlie before he left the tables he'd turned. It was again based upon my pet theory about the coin of family and greed, flip for crazy. Charlie had used family on us. So why not use greed on Charlie? Having won, perhaps that crooked genius of his couldn't resist one parting score. He'd not been able to take along the eleven black cases when he'd fled. It would have exposed him as the mastermind too soon, before the bogus buy-back at Dragon's Gate, before he'd had Lila taken to confuse and divide us. But it was *his* money, six million in cash, all Charlie's, a booby prize from the Long Termers.

"Let's offer it to Mr. Kim in exchange for Lila," I'd proposed. "Just as if we were hornswoggled and all we knew was that Lila was a hostage."

"Sir," Jesse had protested, "it isn't ours to trade."

"It's Charlie's," Rajeesh had laughed. "We're returning it to him."

"For the redhead?" Cole had asked.

That was the message we'd sent to Mr. Kim's telex address Wednesday morning.

We'd proposed that, in exchange for Lila, we were offering five million American dollars and one hundred fifty million yen, smiling face to face, Wednesday at Dragon's Gate, 1:00 P.M.

Yes, there were problems with it. Jesse and Cole had raised them dutifully. Such as, if I was right, the likelihood that Charlie would ignore us and leave the country.

But, I'd argued back, all that didn't allow for Charlie's new-won vanity. He'd won, he knew it, and he'd gotten away with it. *No one's vainer than a man who's gotten away.* I knew all about vanity. It's not a reasonable talent, it makes you go too far, say and do too much, turn back to preen when you should just walk. I'd argued that Charlie's vanity wouldn't let him leave us without taking a chance to brag and bully.

There was also this: once a scavenger, always a scavenger. How could Charlie not? And for what was in those black cases?

"But, sir!" the boys had protested. "But how, where . . . ?"

A preliminary answer you've witnessed in Taxi No. 1031. Rajeesh and I and the black cases were on our way to Mr. Kim and Charlie. My last tv-simple plan had hooked Charlie. So far, so far.

At the same time, my plan had also hooked my big mouth. I was so proud of my solution that I wanted to brag and bully, too —to tell Charlie that he'd fooled me and robbed me yet he hadn't shut me up. *I'd have my say.*

Vanity is such a silly sin.

Now you know most of the truth. The reason I was in the back of a ginseng-smelling van bouncing to rendezvous with Korean ops-for-hire was vanity, Charlie's and mine. Rajeesh, why was he there? Vanity too, I suppose, ask him, we were going to rescue our girl, we thought, who didn't really need rescuing, we thought.

I told you, these are my bad moments. I had figured everything but what was about to happen—a lesson in unvanity, sometimes called death.

For the further truth of it was that, while I had solved the case, I had not solved Charlie and the desperation of his partner-in-crime, his "little yellow woman," his devoted first wife, aka Mary Song, aka Rosemary Yip, aka dear Rosie.

5
Mr. and Mrs. Kim & Company

IT WAS RAINING AT INJE. The teenagers imitated the staginess of their favorite tv shows by blindfolding us with knit caps, then handcuffing us with flimsy-feeling bracelets.

Rajeesh bumped along beside me, passing cheeky remarks such as, "Hungry now? I told you to eat," and "They're bleeding virgins. It's like the university. I age and they never do."

"You've been grabbed like this before?"

Rajeesh was insufferable. "Relax, Tip."

I tried, "You can see pretty good through a blindfold. It's mostly a special effect, isn't it?"

Rajeesh teased, "They're bleeding virgins. And you're a carried-away mother superior."

We mucked blindly through rainwater and ducked into a cozy, funny-smelling room. The funny smell was a mixture of herbs, cured meat and the barnyard.

Correct. We were in the storage room of the apothecary shop at Inje, where, four days before, I had watched Captain Kim Ilwon and a policeman beat the fingerless ancient apothecary.

Again, expecting everything, I felt it was all in slow motion. I also remember thinking that *slow* wasn't right, that crime shouldn't be so predictable. I was smart, I thought, but was I this smart? To have figured out everything?

I bluffed myself again. I thought: I kept it simple; why blame them because they are simple? I'm right, I thought, so far, so far.

Lila provided entertainment. There was the thump of a door opening above us. Then there was an unmistakable squawk and footsteps down to our level.

"Great, just f——ing great," Lila began.

I turned my blind head to her clatter. "Happy to see us, Lila?"

She yelled at the teenagers to free us. Since they couldn't understand her, she shoved them aside and yanked off the knit caps. "You're nuts!" she yelled. "All of you, nuts!"

I blinked. She looked tired and about as dramatic as usual, still wearing her black pantsuit, but now under a dull quilted jacket. We let her threaten us for a while.

"Bastards, do you know what's going on? Bastards . . ."

Soon she made substantive remarks. "It's Charlie, you know that? He's nuts, like you! Charlie! Charlie, he's completely lost it. Why is this happening to me? F——! Can I pick 'em or what? Jesus!"

Lila frightened the teenagers, and they backed off behind the big pots. She whacked at us in turn. The fearless captive was a peeved woman, and it took Rajeesh several tries to interrupt her.

"We do know, luv," he said, "you must get hold."

"Stuff your 'luv.' "

"We've come to put a stop to it," he said.

"You're in on this, you shit! Charlie told me!"

"Not quite," he said, "it's caught me up too."

I was jealous as she slapped Rajeesh around.

I interrupted, "Where's Charlie, Lila?"

Lila slapped at me, and I felt better.

"What do you mean, you *know?*" she demanded. "Why'd you leave me in the taxi? Do you know what I've been through? Two days with a madman and his wacko bitch and these punks!"

Lila spat "punks" at the teenagers, and they cringed and bowed. Holding her hostage here must have been punishment detail, hardly worth what Mr. Kim had paid them.

". . . the garbage I've had to eat!" she continued. "Albino

snake soup, pickled slime, bleehh! They kept me in a closet! I
haven't had a bath! They don't understand a word! And every
now and again my nutsoid brother-in-law pokes in to giggle at
me."

Lila turned on the grinning U2. "You think it's funny?"

U2 reacted a mite hostilely, reaching into his pocket.

I made myself her target. "We've come to take you home."

"Oh yeah, I can see that. How do you call for a cab in handcuffs? And where the f—— are we? Jesus, these people are peasants . . . shit!"

She'd stumbled over the eleven black cases deposited among
the chrysanthemum roots and rice flour.

"What!" she demanded. "What!"

Rajeesh tried, "It's your ransom."

"How much is it?" She ripped into one of the cases and flapped
a pack of hundreds at me. "You'd better explain, fast."

Rajeesh and I glanced at each other. We wanted to calm her
down, not lose her to persecution mania. We risked encapsulat-
ing the high points. Yes, it's Charlie and Rosie; yes, they had you
abducted; yes, Charlie's very, very Charlie.

It did sound nutty in short form.

Lila flung down about fifty thousand dollars. Another woman
might have wept a little for emphasis, but not my Lila, our Lila.
She reached into Rajeesh's pocket for a cigarette. She was stalling
herself, trying not to trust smart guys like us.

"Tell me that again," she ordered us.

Rajeesh sighed. I sighed. Our handcuffs were clearly inconvenient and unnecessary. But the teenagers knew about tv, not common sense.

It also occurred to me that everything here lacked common
sense. U2 showed no control over us or his buddies. Their orders
had apparently ended with our delivery to the apothecary shop.
Not even the black cases seemed to interest them. They were
watching us, we were watching them, all of us were waiting for
Charlie.

"Uh, Raj," I said, "you get the feeling there's no one in charge
here?"

"Much like Charlie," Rajeesh said. "Laid-back, he calls it."

I suggested, "Let's get on with it."

"Might as well," Rajeesh said. "You do know the way?"

Lila demanded, "Know the way, what? Listen to me, Charlie's gone nuts—hey, do you know where we are? Hey!"

The teenagers were mumbling nervously.

I ignored Lila and them and led through the apothecary shop. There was probably a back way, but I kept to the sure route. Opening a door behind your back while wearing handcuffs isn't too difficult.

And then I was outside on the stoop.

It was mid-evening in Inje. The rain was a steady drizzle. The farmer's market was closed for the day. The alleyways looked utilitarian, worn, soggy—not base poverty, but not far from it, lit by oil lamps, naked bulbs.

I looked around for Jesse and Cole. But then, they wouldn't be doing their job if I could spot them. Where would captain spy-catchers conceal themselves in a Korean farm town?

Stupid question. The U.S. Army doesn't hide; it just parks itself like a Lab, and then it does its job.

Rajeesh stood in front of the apothecary shop like a man who needed a cigarette. "Our virgins've gone."

He meant the teenagers, who'd run away. Leaving us hand-cuffed.

"Hey, hey!" Lila demanded. She jumped in front of us. "What're you doing? Look, look, they've let us go. Come on!"

"You can go on," Rajeesh told her, "we'll be along."

Lila hopped in frustration. "Stop it! Stop! Whatever you two are doing, stop!"

"Lila," I explained, "I'm in a hurry, so listen. It's going to stop. Tonight, the end. Charlie has cracked up, and this is his *crazy* joke. We're playing along with it because we want to talk to Charlie. We came here to talk to Charlie. I know exactly where we are. I was here last Saturday along with MI. That's the High Noon boy to you. We're covered, Lila—left, right, Amex."

"Yeah?" Lila spun sideways as if caught in a prank. "Is that right?" she asked Rajeesh.

Rajeesh sounded speculative again. "Ask him."

I bragged for Uncle Sam. "We're Americans, Lila, we're al-ways covered."

Rajeesh used his worldly laugh.

"But those punks!" Lila protested. "They're dangerous!"

"Not to us," I said.

She squawked her theme song. "That's nuts!"

"It's Asia," I said, "and we're going home. But not without Charlie. I promised him I'd help him, and I'm going to."

"What! You're nuts too!"

No. I was all wet. Rather than waste more time appeasing the unappeasable, I gave Lila to Rajeesh's logical lies.

I stepped along carefully through Korean mud, into the alley, to the semi-attached hut behind the apothecary shop. The ancient, chubby witch, Mitsuko Koda, in her feathery white robe, was seated cross-legged at her low table. White is Korea's mourning color.

Mitsuko Koda's performance was well under way—drumbeats, chanting, candles and incense, the usual shadowy flimflam. As I ducked inside, Mitsuko Koda was dropping a flaming taper into her big brass urn next to the rack of small bells. Her husband, the ancient apothecary, was seated behind her at a scroll-covered wall. He was lazily beating a tiny two-faced drum, using a stick at one end and his fingerless palm at the other.

Translucent screens subdivided the hut, which tonight resembled a carnival act.

I sat on the straw mat opposite Mitsuko Koda. "Where's Charlie?"

More chanting and drumming, another lit taper into the urn. Remember, she was a professional witch. She was midway in the *kut*—her most high-priced hoodwink, designed to either summon or banish troublesome spirits.

I knew the old folks understood English, so I was rude. "You can't spit on a smiling face, Mr. Kim," I said. "I'm smiling. Start talking. Where's Charlie?"

No recognizable reaction; I got ruder. I told them that the last time I was here, they wanted two million won. Now I'd brought them six million bucks. But I still wanted the same thing. "I'm helping Charlie," I said.

More chanting, something like "Baa-baa, black sheep." Mitsuko Koda had a dark alto—too many cigarettes, too many years scamming the public.

"Stop the hooey," I said, "and call Charlie."

Lila and Rajeesh ducked into the hut and shook off the weather.

"Is that the witch?" Lila asked. She was a little better informed, thanks to Rajeesh.

I answered Lila "know-it-allingly." "Meet Mr. Kim. The two of them, Mr. and Mrs. Kim & Company." I introduced them like dolls in a diorama. "Grandma Koda's the old brains, and Grandpa Koda's the old rhythm. They're pensioned-off creeps now. But once upon a time they ran a reliable errand service. She handled the accounts receivable. He drove the taxi, fingers on the stick, stump on the wheel."

Lila knelt beside me. "They're it, these two? Spies?"

"Nope," I claimed. "They *were* an errand service. Work for hire. Whoever paid them. In the espionage racket, the fancy word is contractors. Right, Raj?"

"Yes, yes," Rajeesh said. He was working to shuck his handcuffs and not paying close attention. "We call them dustbinners. You can hire them anywhere, Lila, it's—"

"Shit," said Lila. "Are they Japanese?"

"Nope," I claimed. "Koreans with Japanese names. They were slaves once, as far down on the pay scale as you can get in Korea."

"What're they doing?" Lila asked. "Magic?"

"It's Wednesday night around the con game. She's stony, but she's not afraid of us. A couple of tough ops. I stood here last Saturday, and they didn't flinch. I'd stumbled right on top of their operation, and they kept at it. Tough, smart, veteran creeps."

Lila peered into the brass urn. "Are you sure they're not dangerous?"

"Retired dangerous," I claimed.

Mitsuko Koda lit another taper. It was actually a twisted piece of paper, and it was meant as either a prayer for success or a pox on enemies.

I used my foot to rock the brass urn. "Call Rosie, creep."

Mitsuko Koda growled.

As if by magic, Rosie appeared from behind one of the silk screens. She looked wretched. Everything about her was stepped on and discarded. This wasn't my dear, loving Rosie. This was the frightened, enraged, miserable woman I'd first caught scavenging turkey outside my kitchen door.

"Hiya. I'm here for Charlie. Not your poison."

Rosie hunched and darkened.

I said, "Tiny mistake you made there, Rosie, using the same herbs on me that you used to fake Charlie's suicide."

If Rosie had been a witch, she would have whiffed me into smoke.

"How'd you do it, Rosie?" I asked. "Was it in the seltzer or the soup?" (Fussy Holmes demands details.) "I say it was the seltzer. You took a peek into my fridge at home and made me for a New York seltzer addict, and you know all about addicts, right, Rosie? So where is Prince Poppy?"

Rosie muttered, "He doesn't want to see you, Mr. Paine."

I said, "Who can tell with a doper?"

Rosie said, "Take Miss Schumann and go away, please, please." Rosie deepened her hunch. "Mr. Purcell's sick. Please, he doesn't know what he's doing. He doesn't."

(Rajeesh flung his hands out, free of the handcuffs. Rajeesh knelt behind me to work on my handcuffs; he whispered, "Maybe we should go, Tip, they're not in good shape, just an opinion.")

I pushed it anyway. "You're a fool, Rosie," I said. "Me, too. So what?"

"Tip," Lila said, "can't you see she's shaking? You're scaring her. Give her a break—okay, okay, I know, but, shit."

I knew Charlie was hiding behind the silk screens. He'd swallowed his uppers yet still couldn't face us. His pretty revenge was back in his pretty face, and he couldn't figure why.

This was exactly what I'd come to preach. I began at the beginning of Charlie's "terrible thing."

"This is a story of family and greed, Charlie," I preached to the silk screens.

"Once upon a time, it was 1974, and you fell in love with a girl named Mary Song. You were pretty, she was better, and the dope was good. Then one day you got carefree and married Mary Song, and she put two thousand bucks in your greedy hands—a dowry from her pals Mr. and Mrs. Kim & Company. You drank rice wine and walked along the Han River. Mary Song took your picture, you took hers. You got into the jeep you'd liberated from the motor pool and went riding. Along the way you did Mary Song and her family a strange favor. They didn't explain, you didn't ask. But Charlie, what you did know was that you went over to the other side that day. Saturday, August 10, 1974.

"Then it's 1981, in Singapore. You're prettier, and Mary Song's history, but you're still wondering about that day. You meet a smooth guy named James Bhagavad-Gita Bond. You brag, he smiles. Soon, a snapshot turns up on your desk in Singapore. You know what it is. From your wedding album. A picture of you on the other side with black ops.

"Then it's 1988. You're richer and greedier, but you're wasted paying off for that day you can't forget. You get out of Singapore for Tokyo, but you can't get out of the other side. You're trapped there, and only the dope makes you feel carefree. It gets worse, and you try to escape so far into the dope one day that you almost disappear from yourself. When you come down, you do what you've been avoiding all these years. You decide that to get away from the other side, you have to go back there and beg. Do you write Mary Song? Go visit in person? You know all about the apothecary shop in Inje, because Mary Song was born there. Because Mary Song's grandma and granddad live there. Your in-laws, the Kodas—Mr. and Mrs. Kim & Company."

"In-laws?" Lila puzzled.

Grandpa Koda missed no drumbeats. Grandma Mitsuko Koda lit another taper and dropped it into the urn. Granddaughter Rosie was vigilant fury.

"Then it's the spring of 1989, Charlie, and you're a Jersey taxpayer. Amazing to you, the other side has been silent for a year. That's right, the blackmail stopped after you begged the Kodas with your 'please, please, help me' act. There was more amazing news. You're prospering at the bank, since one big deal came your way in Tokyo, and you've brought it with you to New York. It's routinely greedy—robots, tricontinental M & A. Your secret clients like you, they tell you they're your friends. Of all things, they're bankers from Seoul, high rollers like you. Who are they? I call them the Long Termers.

"What happens next, Charlie? Suddenly one spring day a miracle walks through your Jersey door. She's older and dowdier, and she's calling herself Rosie now, but she's still Mary Song."

Lila laughed nervously.

"Rosie/Mary Song says she still loves you. She says if you'll take her back, she'll rescue you. If you want rescuing, if you want to get rid of the Tableau of Treason. It's just paper, but it's so very heavy. And so Rosie/Mary takes you in her arms and hums a Confucian proverb: 'Even a sheet of paper is lighter when two people lift it.' "

Lila couldn't shut up. "You, Rosie, you did this to us? I can't believe it! Why didn't you just tell me? I asked you if you were in love with him. You're his *wife*, Rosie, you could've told me. I would have helped you."

Rosie glanced at Lila. I saw fear, and I also saw the sort of hatred that lucky folk like Lila don't know about.

(Rajeesh flicked at my handcuffs again. "It's rubbish, I need more light," he said; and then he whispered, "Go slow, this could get dicey.")

I remember thinking, Yes, slow, yes, slow. What was wrong here? But I was well launched. I had to go faster.

"Here's the strange part for you, Charlie," I preached the more. "Rosie also says that she let her grandparents blackmail you because you'd deserted her. But now that you've asked for help, now that you need her, the blackmail is over. She doesn't tell you much about what she's been doing since you deserted her. Perhaps a mention of how she changed her name, something about faking clinic records in Seoul, fuzzy stuff. She goes on to tell you about how they worked the blackmail on you in Singapore—how James Bhagavad-Gita Bond sicced the Schumann and Soo sisters on you. How your family and friends have used you."

Rosie stabbed at Lila with her black, black eyes.

"Did Rosie also tell you that she was still Mata Hooker—a KCIA creep? Not right away, but maybe. When she does, she tells you she's protecting you from three nasty case officers. Named the three Lees. Who have been searching for you since 1974 for revenge. Rosie tells you—and this part scares you so badly you start sleeping with the pipes—that what you did that day you went over to the other side was collaborate in the murder of their family war hero, Colonel Lee."

"Oh shit," Lila said.

"Rosie tells you something else that's strange, right, Charlie? That you were safe from the three Lees as long as you stayed with her. It was all kind of twisted for you, but you went along because you trusted Rosie, needed Rosie. She said she'd never leave you; she said she'd help you get even with your family and friends.

"It's Christmas 1989, now, and you and Rosie have put together a much too greedy sting operation against everyone. But, shucks, what's greed, you're damn good at your job. Better yet, the robots are going to work. You'll be free of everyone. You only need one sap to set it all in motion. And he just happens to live downstairs. Named Tip Paine. What luck. Let's study his books. Let's use Mata Hooker on him, too. We'll get everybody all together in Seoul and rob them poor. And then, freedom."

I lowered my voice to make Charlie listen hard, an old exhorter trick. "But," I mumbled, "but, but, you're the one who's been robbed, Charlie, every day since Saturday, August 10, 1974. And now, poor Charlie, instead of getting free of the other side, you're going to spend the rest of your life owned by it."

I fired up my cords and shouted at the silk screens. "The devil's got you, Charlie; the devil's not gonna let you go!"

This was thick hambone; it worked.

Charlie bumped against a silk screen and landed in the room. He didn't talk, he whined. Whine, whimper, pout, pout, staggering toward me.

Rosie caught him gently. "No, no, dear," Rosie cooed, very tender and unstaged for once.

Lila cut through the emoting. "You bastard, you thought you could rob me!" Lila jumped at him, fists like small clubs. "For what? I didn't know, Pammie didn't, and your children, Charlie, what'd they ever do to you?"

Rosie shielded Charlie like the wall in No-Man's-Land.

Charlie's whining gave way to heavy breathing. He was dressed badly in baggy Korean punk. He wanted to make a speech, but it came out whine, whimper, whine.

Everyone but the Kodas was standing now, so I got up and paced, hands still cuffed behind my back.

"Let's review the strange parts, Charlie," I said. "Question: What do Charlie, Mary Song and your in-laws the Kodas have in common with Raj and the three Lees?"

Smart Rajeesh laughed.

"Answer," I said, "you're all working for the same bad guys. And they're *not* the North Koreans. Nope, I got that wrong. I was willing to blame that sorry tyranny to the north for things it can't ever afford. Your bad guys are also the good guys. Good, bad, who knows? It's all in the family, the Asian Miracle, the Republic of Korea. More like the Asian Crybaby from a planet of them."

"Please listen!" Rosie said. "Please stop!"

"More questions, Charlie." I didn't stop. "Who hired Grandma and Grandpa Koda to abduct Colonel Lee, Saturday, August 10, 1974?

"Who murdered Colonel Lee because he was an inconvenient crusader?

"Who retired the Kodas and arranged for Mary Song to change her identity to Rosemary Yip, governess for hire?

"Who set up the blackmail operation against you in 1981— Raj for the Singapore leg, the Kodas for the Seoul leg?

"Who telexed you for insider information?

"Who arranged for you to leave Singapore for your fancy new job at Horizon Pacific in Tokyo?

"Who broke off the telexes when they knew you were cracking up in Tokyo?

"Who sent the robots your way in Tokyo?

"Who sent you to New York to complete the robot deal?

"Who's made you the richest junkie in Inje?"

I turned around with the answer: "The Republic of Korea— the miraculous Asian Crybaby."

Charlie pushed Rosie aside. "It's a lie! Tell him, Raj!"

"Afraid not," Rajeesh said. "What Tip says makes sense. The South Koreans ran you and me both, and I never knew. What's choice, I thought I was dealing with the Reds."

I teased, "Hard to tell 'em apart, right, Raj?"

Rajeesh laughed. "When their money's good, why care?"

"Who are they?" Charlie whined. "Who?"

"Gee, Charlie," I said, "two of their bagmen are named Yon. Whoever the big bosses are, they're *masterful*. You don't go from sticks and stones to Seoul's gridlocked skyline in twenty years unless you're very *masterful*. These days, the masters just call themselves the Han-gang Long Term Investment & Securities Company. I call them the Long Termers. And you, Charlie, are one of their best long-term boys."

6
Social Security

CHARLIE POUTED. LILA FUMED. Rajeesh smoked his scepter of a cigarette. The Kodas bent to their weird tasks.

And Rosie, she ran away, slowly and morbidly, as if fleeing a fascinating horror. I don't know where she went. She ran out of the hut, and I was stupid to let her go.

Charlie only had eyes for Charlie. "Rosie, it's a lie," he called after her, "tell him!"

Charlie whined at me, "I've read your books! You lie your way out all the time. Lila, he's lying, tell him. Raj, he's got you to go along with him!"

Rajeesh blew smoke at a dim-witted student of black ops.

Charlie reached behind a screen, yanking out the Gladstone with Lila's and my yen. "Take your f——ing money back!" He heaved the Gladstone at Lila. "I don't need it. Take it and get out!"

Rajeesh stepped on my lines. "We want you to come with us, Charlie. You haven't really done anything to run away from.

There'll be a stink for a while, I suppose, but Charlie, they don't make martyrs out of such as you. Leave it to your attorneys."

Lila taunted, "You'll need lots of lawyers, Charlie. I've got one for Pammie, and he knows how to make a broken marriage contract pay off."

"F—— you," Charlie said; the banker in him was emerging from the whining. "I'm doing nothing you say, just get out. . . ." He cursed me some more, adding, "You'll get nothing from me!"

"Good speech, Charlie," I said. "Now I'm going to tell you why you'll get nothing from your in-laws either."

Mitsuko Koda rang the rack of bells.

"Let's review the review," I said. "What have Rosie and the Kodas done for you lately? Other than blackmail you?"

Charlie was eloquent. "Goddamn you!"

Mitsuko Koda rose abruptly to begin a lopsided dance to the drumbeat, flapping her feathery robe, chanting louder and harsher. It was more nonsense. Still, I should have paid attention. It was the part of the *kut* where the witch welcomes in demons from hell.

I maneuvered out of the witch's way and raised my voice over the drum. "Rewind to the strange parts. Ask yourself, Charlie, how did the three Lees get onto you? How did they get hold of the picture of you and Grandpa by the Han River? How is it that Rosie was working for the three Lees? How is it that you're not to worry about the three Lees as long as you do what Rosie says?"

Faster drumbeat, cruder dancing.

"The answer, Charlie, is that you've been set up again by your in-laws. You're their social security insurance. But creep style, family style."

"Get out!" Charlie screamed without punch, a needy command.

"I figure it this way," I said.

("I say," Rajeesh interrupted, "could this wait until later?")

I stupidly ignored everyone for my stupid, useless tale. "Once upon a time, the Kodas were top-quality creeps for hire, specializing in abductions. The Lee family was just a rival gang of creep. Until their war hero, Colonel Lee, started tracking down certain prominent Seoul citizens whom he labeled war criminals.

"Soon enough, the Long Termers gave the order to terminate Colonel Lee, before he scored someone too big. The Kodas were hired; they did their job, snatching and delivering Colonel Lee. Someone called 'the Fisherman' did the killing. Years passed; Korea got richer; the creeps remained the same.

"Then, in 1979, the KCIA failed in a coup attempt against the government. The reaction shook up the old creep network. The Kodas were retired back to their hometown, Inje. Mary Song became Rosemary Yip and went international.

"At the same time, the Lee family, long in disfavor, catapulted to creepy prominence. Yet the Lees had a family score to settle. They knew Colonel Lee had been murdered by their untouchable big bosses, aka the Long Termers. But they also knew that, to save face, they had to track down everyone who'd been there. The American soldier. The hooker. The taxi driver.

"Meanwhile, the retired Kodas knew that the Lees would find them eventually. They needed social security, some reason so that the Long Termers wouldn't give them up to the avengers.

"Solution? None. Until one day there was an inquiry from a 'foreign agent' at Singapore station that delivered up a long-lost son-in-law named Charlie Purcell."

(Rajeesh interrupted me again, "Yes, Tip, all very intriguing, but this might not be the time.")

I ignored him, though I did abridge some. "Get it, Charlie?" I said. "The Kodas came out of retirement to run you again. This gave the Long Termers an asset in the Singapore banks. And it gave the Kodas their social security. All in the greedy family."

(Rajeesh complained, "I don't like standing around here.")

"Okay, okay," I said, ignoring him, and continuing, "For nine years, the social security works. But then, you start cracking up on them. You get out of Singapore for Tokyo. You try suicide. You visit the Kodas to beg—"

("I'm insisting now," Rajeesh said. "Just look at him.")

What Rajeesh meant was that, while I preached and Mitsuko Koda danced to the drum, Charlie was sinking gradually to the floor, holding his hands over his face. He was way ahead of me. He knew the answers I was coming to.

I leaned over Charlie. "Let's get up-to-date. The Long Termers have put you in New York. They've called off the blackmail. They've put the robots in your pocket.

"And then, Rosie walks in the door. With a story to tell. About her grandparents. About the three Lees chasing you. About how you have to do what she says or the three Lees are going to hang you on fishhooks, and other horrors.

"But who put the three Lees onto you?

"The answer is Rosie.

"*Rosie gave them the snapshot from her wedding album, the Tableau of Treason.*

"You'd think the three Lees might have puzzled as to why Rosie should have such a thing, why she would give it to them. Nope. Three blind creeps. Rosie's 'the great patriot' to them.

"And why did Rosie put them onto you, Charlie?

"More social security. Creep style.

"Because once the robot deal was done, the Kodas were going to lose you as their protection. They had to bring you into their family in such a way that you could never leave.

"That's why Rosie ratted on you to the Lees. To drive you and your bank account to Seoul and Inje.

"As for the three Lees, they're left forever to watch a tree they can't climb. Last Sunday, they discovered that you aren't a target of opportunity. Rather, you're a 'permanent friend of Korea.' The three Lees can never touch you. Nor can they ever touch your wife and in-laws, who are permanent friends of a 'permanent friend.'

"As for the Long Termers, they're satisfied. Hence the black cases. Their payoff to you, Charlie. The Long Termers know it all and don't care anymore. What they mean is: 'Have a dopey life, get lost.'

"As for the Kodas, they're retired again in the splendor of their golden son-in-law's social security plan.

"And as for Rosie, she got her man, didn't she, Charlie? Or are you finally ready to wise up and walk away?"

I stopped talking. My mouth was paste.

Charlie sat there, crumpled, silent, lifeless. And then he started to sob. His "terrible thing" sob.

I'd told the truth, and it didn't seem to matter to anyone. I tried once more anyway. "Come home with us, Charlie. Vice isn't a reward, it's only a place to live. Move on. You're finished here."

7
Demons from Hell

IT WASN'T IMPORTANT that Mitsuko Koda never stopped dancing to beckon the demons from hell.

Nor was it important that Lila mocked Charlie's sobbing, "Crybaby, you're just another crybaby."

Nor was it important that there must have been huge holes in my counterintelligence. I'd made too much of intelligence, found malice when there'd likely been only contrary silliness.

What was important that, when I finished, I finally realized why I'd thought everything had been predictable and too *slow*. That is, they weren't going slow, I had been going too fast.

I had raced through my storytelling as if by words alone I could get everyone up to speed. But as soon as I shut up—and I must have talked for at least a half hour—I saw that what had made me so glibly brilliant was that I had been living on vanity. That's a bloody-minded high. When it leaves you, what's exposed is all the wrongheadedness that you've ignored.

I returned from speedy heroism to mortal Inje. Where I saw

that I was handcuffed, hungry, surrounded by strangers in a flimsy hut and threatened by unpredictable facts.

It was the fact of noise outside that alerted me. I heard faraway thumping that wasn't thunder, that had been masked by the drumbeats and my big mouth.

Rajeesh poked his head out the door. He glanced back and sounded tense. "Are we finally done here?"

I didn't respond. I knew I had gone too far.

"Lila," Rajeesh said, "we're leaving now."

"What is it?" she demanded.

"Nothing," said Rajeesh.

Lila felt Rajeesh's anxiety. "I told you," she said, "I told you they were dangerous, I told you, but no, you had to—"

Mitsuko Koda began singing with a wail. Grandpa pounded harder. There's supposed to be eroticism to the *kut;* Korean witches are usually female, because they exude a timeless pornography. Maybe I've got this wrong. Mitsuko Koda was acting vicious, that's sure, as in vice, as in here comes the part you won't like.

I edged beside Rajeesh and looked out into the rain. There was nothing to see but a watery alleyway and the sort of rural blackness that contradicts the Enlightenment.

The faraway thumping noise was moving.

"It's maneuvers," I tried, "it's choppers from the army war games that start tonight."

"Good, good," said Rajeesh, "still—"

"It's maneuvers," I repeated, "it couldn't be anything else."

Rajeesh lit a new cigarette. "Just the same," he mumbled.

I faked confidence. I told Lila to bundle up. I told Charlie to follow us. I told Rajeesh that the boys would pick us up as soon as we cleared the alleys.

Rajeesh asked, "Where precisely is our rendezvous point?"

I wasn't sure. What had Jesse said? The town hall? Main street? Why couldn't I remember? What's wrong with me? Why's everything now going too fast for me?

I moved my feet and hardly felt them. My spit was gone. "It's the March madness," I declared to no one. "What else could it be?"

Rajeesh said, "Trundle on to supper. Fine by you, Lila?"

"You guys are the heroes. I'm just the girl."

Rajeesh ditched his cigarette. On tv, that would mean he was resolved. It didn't seem that here. "Bloody," he said.

We three eased tightly into the alleyway.

Charlie hung back at the door of the hut. Why did you do that, Charlie? Were you waiting for Rosie?

Lila shouted back at Charlie.

Rajeesh said something bullier.

I wasn't listening to them; I was concentrating on the wrong silence in Inje in comparison to that background thumping of helicopters.

I argued with myself—it was Operation Team Spirit; this was foul weather for flying; the Army was risking another crash in the mountains. I told myself, Stop thinking.

The truth is that I don't know what happened. When you're the target of a black operation, you don't get a briefing.

There was the helicopter beat like a thousand vibrating drums. There was Rajeesh leading the way. There was Lila holding on to me and our Gladstone bag. There was Charlie trailing us like a child. And then there was a flash from the apothecary shop. Not an explosion—a burst of white heat that lit us up in profile. It also illuminated small, quick, silent figures racing at the edges of my view.

The alley returned to blackness. The helicopter descended right on top of us, an invisible dynamo pummeling the air.

I found I was on my elbows, Lila atop me. Rajeesh was down in front of us; he had to muscle up from the mud. "Stun grenade," he said.

I couldn't speak. Lila moaned for me.

"Get up," Rajeesh said. "Can you get up?"

I didn't want to. I rolled around to complain to Charlie, "This is wrong, it doesn't make sense!"

Charlie wasn't there. Instead, I saw the hunched figure of Rosie caught between us and the hut. She had her back to us; she was moving toward where Charlie should have been.

I yelled, "Rosie, tell them, it's wrong, it's maneuvers!" What I wanted to say was: "Why did you do this, Rosie?" But that's the sort of foolish question that doesn't work when you're flattened.

The second flash shut me up. After that, I couldn't see or hear anything clearly.

Rajeesh screamed something like ". . . that . . . back . . . run!"

We didn't run, we wallowed. We had no direction; we kept together up one alley, then down another that could have been the same one. I held us back, since you don't even wallow good when you're handcuffed. Lila might have been more help to me, but she wouldn't let go of the Gladstone.

I'll skip our panic. Again, whatever I'd learned from tv was useless. You don't think when you're scared, and you certainly don't act cleverly. You're just scared, and that's where you live and where you don't want to be and of course that makes you more scared. We crashed and scrambled, and soon we were on a mushy incline. There was much water nearby. Was it the river? How could it have been? It must have been a runoff from the downpour. I slipped often and begged for a halt. Behind us, where there should have been the town, there was nothing but a searchlight from the sky.

I remember continuing to insist to Rajeesh that this didn't make any sense.

Rajeesh sensibly didn't reply. He got us moving again toward a single light on a path.

It was a shack, and the light we saw was an open door. There was a raggedy farmer crouching in the doorway.

Rajeesh tried barter to get us inside. The farmer chose the Rolex. Then he let us into a smelly vestibule lit by a kerosene lamp.

"Great," Lila declared, "just great—don't worry, Lila—" She kicked at wood planks and sat on top of the Gladstone. "We're taking you home, Lila—what a joke."

Rajeesh asked the farmer for cigarettes by showing his soaked pack. The farmer sold one for whatever cash Rajeesh could find. The farmer grinned at his largess, eyeing us for more profit. We thanked him in English, and he bowed in Korean, backing out the door like a pickpocket. By then we'd realized that what we had purchased wasn't a shack, it was mostly a stock pen with all manner of creatures in from the storm. The pig smell was a ruination.

My panic made a speech. "I'm right, I know I'm right. The Kodas are just old creeps. The Lees wouldn't attack them, not as long as they've got Charlie. And Rosie wouldn't call them down, not on her own grandparents. You see, you see."

"I see pig shit on my shoes," said Lila.

I babbled, "Why would Rosie do that? It doesn't make sense."

Rajeesh lit his scepter, leaned against the door frame. "I'm in a pigsty," he said to no one. "I'm down to one smoke, and I don't know what time it is." The pro among us closed his summation, "Now I've to listen to a man get carried away again."

I appealed to him, "Rosie has Charlie, Raj, listen to me. She has him. Maybe he was coming with us, maybe he wasn't. Why is this happening? Who are they out there? What was that?"

Rajeesh blew smoke. "Just a guess, but I'd say it was whatever their SAS is called. You ever been skyjacked, Tip?"

"Gee," I said.

"It's like that when they hit a parked plane."

I asked, "Why *hit* an old witch and teenagers?"

"If you don't know, why should I?" Rajeesh said. His man-of-the-world tone irritated me. He excavated his irony. "It doesn't have to make sense."

This frightened me more than the stun grenade. "Doesn't have to make sense?" I whined. "No sense?" I whimpered. "It has to make sense!" I squawked. "Doesn't it?" I begged.

Rajeesh returned Cambridge phlegm. "Whoever they are, they let us out before they closed the gate. For now."

"Oh, 'for now,' he says," Lila taunted, "trying to get my attention, huh, Raj? 'For now.' Great."

"Yes, well, there's this," Rajeesh said. "We aren't on a level field. Your and my passports are different colors. I say, Tip, I can only hope that your analysis has some weight. These Lee buggers aren't going to look upon me with favor."

"It's not the Lees," I complained.

"Yes, it is," Rajeesh said. "You know it, I know it, get hold, you figured it out. You just didn't count on them not being as philosophical as you."

"What's that mean?" I asked.

"It's a bloody compliment," Rajeesh said.

"But it *doesn't* make any sense that it's the Lees."

Rajeesh blew more smoke. "Relax."

Rajeesh was patronizing me with the pigs and goats, the sneaky hint I got that he was planning another doublecross. Even when he was trapped, he couldn't lose Cambridge or his wicked black-opshood. Still, he had cause to fret. I should have been sympathetic. I wasn't. I was trying to avoid the cold truth that it was the

Lees out there. That Rosie had called the Lees to Inje, had called them down on her husband and her grandparents and herself.

No! No! It couldn't be the three Lees. Charlie was off-limits to them. They'd told me so. And so was Charlie's family. Forever.

If it wasn't the three Lees, then who?

Okay, say it was the three Lees. Why, then? Charlie was the tree they couldn't climb. They'd said so! Why would they hack him down now in a demonic rage? For face? But the Long Termers would take off their faces! No! It couldn't be the three Lees!

There I stood, among the pigs and goats, so scared I was double-talking myself. Presently, my double-talk started to fall apart. After a noisy, hungry, anxious wait, there was a knock at the door.

Lila gasped, and Rajeesh floated smoke. But I, dimwit, still believed that bad guys don't knock first and called hello.

Wrong again. The farmer swung the door back and went to his knees and then his nose.

A narrow beam lit us up. A stern fellow announced himself oddly. "Dr. Paine? Please listen. Come to the door. Please to the door, and please the hands out—up."

Broadway muggers used this logic on me once, and I've had a guideline since. Don't move, refuse a lot. "No," I managed.

Rajeesh ignited the black light in his brain and told Lila, "Out this way." He pulled her back toward the livestock.

I'll grant this to Lila, she didn't go without saying to me, "Tip, come on, Tip." Then again, she didn't refuse to quit me. The only proof I have that she wasn't a stinker like Rajeesh was that she left the Gladstone behind, something she never would have done if she were willing. There were animal sounds and scraping, and then I knew they'd gone out the stock hatch.

The stern voice revealed himself. "Please, Dr. Paine, it is your friend the Captain Kim Ilwon."

"Mighty Mouse?" I said.

Captain Kim Ilwon snorted. "Please, sir, identify the companions."

I had no companions anymore; I refused anyway.

Enough tough-guy charade. The beam came forward, and it was followed by Captain Kim Ilwon of the ROK MI, dressed tonight in fantasy combat garb. Behind him a field phone crackled; there was Korean chatter; several quick figures moved sideways to pluck the farmer from the floor and remove him like trash. Captain Kim bowed. "I apologize, Dr. Paine, it was to see that you were not the prisoner."

He was a show-off, and he strutted around the pen being solicitous. "You are not injured?" he asked. "You wish me to remove the binds?" he asked.

I repeated "no" for as long as it took the good guys to come bouncing up the road behind a ROK jeep.

I knew it was Jesse and Cole, because who else drives a beige Ford Tempo in Inje?

Cole leapt the hood of the car and delivered his enthusiasm. "Are you okay, sir? Where's the redhead?"

Cole was soaking in a plain beige rain slicker. Jesse gracefully shook the rain from his cap. No two cowboys ever looked taller to me.

I was so relieved to be rescued that I snapped at them, "Where've you been?"

Jesse yanked me to shut up. He addressed Captain Kim. "We're even for this, Captain."

"It is good to make us even, Captain," replied Captain Kim, "and it is good luck." Captain Kim turned to me. "I am to thank you for my father for the book you made the signature in."

Instead of thanking Captain Kim, I remembered to be rude. "Did the Lees send you, Kim? Is that what those choppers are?"

Captain Kim straightened his holster. "I am happy you are not injured, Dr. Paine."

"You leave the woman alone, Kim. You call off your goons."

Captain Kim bowed and handed the Gladstone to Cole.

Jesse yanked at me again. "We're leaving now, sir, *now*."

I obeyed. Cole flipped the Gladstone into the backseat of the Ford, and I followed it. Cole put the car in a gradual turn around the ROK jeep.

Jesse waited until we were clear of the ROKs, then addressed me feistily. "What I have to say is by the book. 'U.S. Military participation in intelligence operations is generally limited by the host government concerned.' Do you understand, sir? Liaison, liaison."

"You're saying I messed up."

"Sir, I'm telling you that we informed the ROKs this morning that we were coming here to interrogate Purcell. Eight hours later, they fly in a strike force. We don't know why."

I admitted, "I don't understand it, either."

Jesse said, "One moment, we were sitting in our car waiting for you to bring us Purcell. The next, Kim was standing beside us. The strike force hit. We sat tight and told Kim that you were in the strike zone. He offered to return a favor he owed us. We said, Return it."

"Return it," I mumbled.

"That's it."

I shifted around to let Jesse use a pick to free the handcuffs. With my hands free, I regained my contrariness. "Lila's back there," I said. "We can't go without her."

Cole sighed as he rocked the car through a rain ditch.

Jesse said, "Steady, Boneman."

"What about Lila?" I complained. "And that rat Rajeesh is back there."

"Sir," Jesse said, "we'll be good to take care of ourselves."

This seemed a queer statement until we rolled off the incline and regained Inje's paved main street. Cole eased the car into blackness. It wasn't poverty that darkened the town. They had cut the power to cover the strike. We eased by several military vehicles marked by glowing dashboards. We passed through a line of combat troops smoking cigarettes.

"Jess," Cole said, "they want me to stop."

Cole meant a roadblock ahead of us, two military vehicles turned sideways onto the shoulders of the street.

Jesse said, "Steady. Just show ID."

We stopped. Stout young soldiers with big M-16s crowded close. Their leader used a flashlight on our faces. Cole showed his ID card; Jesse showed his. The flashlight fixed on me. Sharp Korean followed. A soldier opened Cole's door.

"Steady," Jesse repeated; he clicked on the car radio and dialed it to Armed Forces for easy-listening rock 'n' roll.

I asked, "I've gotten you in trouble, haven't I?"

"No, sir," Cole said. "We're earning our pay."

Sentries surrounded the car. An officer was called, but he didn't speak English either. They definitely wanted us out of the car. The officer stuffed his face close up to my window and tapped the glass with his baton.

I patted the Gladstone; I asked Jesse, "How about a bribe?"

"Negative," said Jesse.

Cole pulled field glasses from beneath his seat; they were the fancy infrared kind that can see fireflies breathing. He scanned stem to stern. "Lots of firepower out there," Cole said. "Two tracks about ninety meters ahead. Command chopper over the river." Cole turned back to me and asked, "I thought there was just that old couple, sir, and the teenagers? Was there anyone else? What did they have in that hut?"

"Witchcraft," I said.

The boys grunted.

"It doesn't make sense that the Lees did this," I complained to them.

Jesse and Cole ignored me with MI's "silence approach." ("The silence approach may be successful when employed against either the nervous or the confident-type source.")

"You think that I pushed Rosie too far, don't you? That I was taking Charlie away from her, so she called the Lees down? That I did this?"

"No, sir," Cole said.

"I did cause this, didn't I?"

Jesse reminded me, "No, sir. It's their country, sir."

"Yes, yes, but—"

My blithering was useless. The fact was that we were trapped, and it was an unpredictable fact, and it was further the kind of fact that you don't talk or figure your way out of. Even fear is pointless when you're as trapped as we were. I forgot about my breathing and bowels and watched Jesse and Cole more carefully than anyone but their mothers ever had. I made a deal with myself that I wouldn't start crying or screaming until they did. Yes, I would. I make this confession, too—the fairy tale that says every man gets to choose to die like a man, kind of brave and clean—well, in the Ford Tempo, I decided I was going to meet my demise cowardly and dirtily. I'd try to lie my way out of it if I ever got to St. Peter.

Soon enough, I saw that I was going to have to deal with a few demons on my way to dealing with paradise.

Behind us, walking slowly and confidently up to the Ford Tempo, came three men dressed by Barney's and, tonight, wearing Burberry's finest. The soldiers backed off.

Grandfather Lee poked his head into the open door to look at me. He glanced back to Lee Nam Paik.

Youngest Lee was next. "Dr. Paine," he said, "it is possible to speak?"

Jesse nodded to give me permission to parley.

Youngest Lee squatted down to my eye level. His face was radiantly ugly to me, good teeth and a politely foul mouth. "We wish to thank you for your assistance in the national security matter."

I was wretchedly dumb.

Youngest Lee said, "The cooperation is complete." He brought his hand from his pocket and reached past Cole's shoulder to offer me something small that was dangling on a string. "You will please to return this to Mr. Purcell."

It was a cheap gold wedding ring. And that wasn't a string. The ring was tied on a fishing line. I'd never seen the ring before, but then, there were lots of things about Rosie I wouldn't look at because I wanted to love her and did love her for what I made believe she was. ("Good of its kind, Rosie?" "Bad, bad," she'd said of Hollywood acting, "why don't they just pretend?")

The fishing line was sick malice by the Lees.

(Now you've seen as much as I can show you. I murdered her. I did it. And though I've tried to prepare you, it doesn't matter. Nor does it matter that I can't explain why the Lees attacked Inje. I do know I was right: Charlie was protected from them, and so were his family, the Kodas. The Lees never could touch the Kodas or Rosie. They were wrong to. I was right, and saying so is as much as it's worth.)

Youngest Lee started again with a mock-sober tone. "For Miss Rosemary Yip, there is no family, Dr. Paine. And there must be the funeral. Is it your wish that you attend to this?"

I should have preached. I thought of myself and said nothing. When it came to it, I showed myself to be a stinker like Rajeesh.

All you brave folk, listen, here's what I learned at Inje. You don't make deals or peace with the devil. You don't figure it's "just business" and the devil has to put food on the table, so he can be negotiated out of his rages. No. The devil has no sense (cf. Korea, Vietnam). The devil does what he wants stupidly, brutally, senselessly.

The Kodas were vicious creeps; in the end, they trapped themselves for nothing. Rosie was a vicious victim; in the end, she quit for nothing. The three Lees were vice itself; in the end, they murdered for nothing.

And I was a vicious coward who, that night, said nothing—not about the Kodas, Rosie, Charlie, Lila, Rajeesh or sense.

I pocketed Rosie's wedding ring. I took a hard breath and smelled the brimstone in the rain.

The Lees ordered the soldiers to stand clear.

Cole put the car into gear. Jesse pulled his raincap tight.

For no sense, you see, the devil let us go.

8
Six Trick Questions

THE THREE LEES LIED. I waited four days in Seoul, and I could have waited forty years but wouldn't have gotten Rosie to bury.

I spent the daytime debriefing for MI into a GI tape recorder. I retold my story so often, and with so many variations to keep myself focused, that I began to think that the only game I'd ever play again was court tennis.

At night, sleeping badly at the Royal Chosin, I suffered serial nightmares about "the Fisherman." I still don't know anything about him and that's probably why my nightmares seized him as the villain. What I can recall is that I was naked in a large body of water, and somewhere out there was the Fisherman. Meanwhile, this large body of water turned into a bathtub. I was a child in a bathtub. Downstairs, Mom and Dad were racing around getting ready to go out. Mom and Dad turned out to be Lila in black and Rajeesh in that hideous lemon tie. I didn't want them to leave me. I was sure the Fisherman was going to rise out of the bathwater and get me. There was also a detail that Rosie was beside the bathtub, scrubbing me down and humming lullabies.

What a mess—woozy mind-doctor hokum: monsters, sex, abandonment, helplessness. Whoever the Fisherman had been, dead or alive, I didn't want him in my nightmares, and I swore off seafood until I got out of the Asian Crybaby.

I only had to make one trip to Uncle Sam's house—that is, low-budget MI headquarters—to meet with Jesse and Cole's commanding officer. His name was Major Wally Howe, bucktoothed, knobby and younger than me. He acted the high school disciplinarian. This fit the ambience; the Army goes for the homeroom style circa Ike.

Wally Howe plopped me in his tiny office and bathed me with bombast. "You got lucky, mister," he said repeatedly. "We could've lost you as easy as we didn't. And then you're ruining careers here, mister, careers."

He meant his, but I understood it would have been Jesse's and Cole's as well.

Wally Howe also tried to slap paper on me, some ad-hoc document that I must sign to swear I wouldn't write or sell about my work with MI.

I laughed at him. Hey, Wally, even a piece of paper is lighter if you huff and puff and blow it off the table.

Sunday morning, Jesse, Cole and I attended the first service at the Youngnak Presbyterian Church. We left a check with a tiny assistant pastor named the Reverend Kim. It wasn't a big check. I didn't want to show off. I wanted something that suited Rosie. She wasn't good, she wasn't bad, she had forty-two years to mess up and should have had, like her grandmother, twice that.

The Reverend Kim recommended a scholarship fund for orphans. I said okay and tried not to feel sorry for myself. I did say a prayer during the liturgy. For me and Rosie, mostly for me. What I get out of Presbyterianism is "Thy will be done," even though I am never going to know why.

I did know I had a plane to catch Sunday noontime. Her name was Lila.

Jesse and Cole had the same plane to catch. His name was Charlie.

Charlie had disappeared from Inje and maybe Korea. There was a vague chance that he was dead, but then again, that wouldn't be the worst-case scenario. Operation REDLEGS remained "all nominal." It was MI's job to find Charlie.

Jesse and Cole were the advance team, dispatched to gather all the facts about Charlie. Others would judge. What this actually meant was Jesse and Cole would have to do mind-numbing reiteration. Start again, ask questions, ask again, ask again. They were going to be on the road for a while.

Lila's red head was first on their list.

Then it would be on to Jerry Kepler in Singapore, where they were going to ruin his day and make him wish he'd put his head in a snowbank at Jackson Hole. Honest Helen Solatoff was due a promotion.

Not to forget Jimmy Flowers in New York, where the boys were going to ruin his curls, his year, maybe his place in the century, one done Dartmouth Indian.

They couldn't interrogate Rajeesh again; he was out of bounds to Uncle Sam. Rajeesh does, indeed, have a great squash game, and, in the end, he'd found a way to win.

As for me, Jesse and Cole were disgusted with me. Trust was gone with Charlie. They didn't say it. It was obvious in the fact that they sat quietly at the back of our jumbo jet, Seoul via Hong Kong to Singapore, and didn't once come forward to visit.

Alone in first class with Hong Kong traders, I tried to cheer myself up by chasing the Imperial fleet. I didn't get close. The xenophobic thrill was gone. Eventually, I called up my "Goldilocks" file to review my tomfoolery.

Remember the six trick questions I asked you?

1. Who's Mr. Kim? Answer: Dead.
2. Why did he do it? Answer: Charlie.
3. How did he do it? Answer: Charlie.
4. Where's Lila? Answer: Back home.
5. Where's Rosie? Answer: Dead.
6. Where's Charlie? Answer: Who cares?

No, that wasn't the truth. I cared. I'd promised Charlie I'd help him. I keep my promises, it's the amateur in me, I just can't stop until I get to the end I've promised myself at the beginning.

We landed in Singapore's heat about 5:00 P.M. I didn't call

ahead. We rented another Ford, dropped my bag and laptop at the Kublai Khan (the boys were on Uncle Sam's slender chits and refused to bunk on my credit), then drove to Lila's.

Cole was excited by Singapore. He was finally going to meet the beautiful rascal. Jesse, I could tell, wanted to slap her in irons and Federal Express her to Leavenworth. It was a character trait with him; he didn't like the rich.

I agreed with him. I didn't like me much either just then.

Jesse was squinty-eyed at Lila's front door. "Captains D'Ambrosi and Cole from United States Military Intelligence to see Miss Schumann," he told the Chinese houseman.

The houseman blinked. The boys were not in uniform. Dressed conservatively in PX suits, tan with cuffs, white shirts, dull ties. That wasn't why the houseman was frozen. His slack face showed that he'd been expecting us, or something like us, and he was trying to remember what he was supposed to say.

Jesse maintained stern orthodoxy. He waved his ID and declared, "This is official business. We'll return with an embassy officer if it's necessary."

"Miss Schumann," the houseman said, "is at home, sir."

Certainly I knew by then that Jesse wanted me in irons with Lila. His sense of humor went missing at Inje.

Perhaps you've missed that I wasn't merely their companion anymore. I was now a suspect in a U.S. government national-security investigation, and my cooperation was obligatory. My file at Fort Meade was fattening by megabytes. It's just computer time, true, but it makes you feel unattractive.

Lila didn't look any better. We found her convalescing on the screened veranda overlooking the back lawn and the Johore Straits. She was wrapped in a caftan and smoking a long cigarette. There was a perfect Singapore sunset coloring the shoreline. The spring scent was Singapore splendor. Lila still smelled great. The clear change was that her smile was gone, and she'd let her hair get ratty.

"I guess this is it," she said.

"Hiya, Lila," I tried. "I'm fine, thanks. Rosie's dead."

Lila didn't illustrate her upset. All damage was going to be internal and come later. "I wanted to call," she said, "to see if you were okay."

"I did call to see if you were," I said. "Your luggage is en route by now, care of your office."

I laid her deed on the table by the tea set. "All in order," I said, "if you're curious." I laid the check for her share of the Gladstone swag beside it. "I left it in yen."

"I did try to call you once," she sniffled, brushing her long nose for emphasis. This was good dramatics; she was playing it for her memoirs. "The hotel said you were out—"

"Your office said you were home recuperating," I interrupted.

"—I knew that meant you were all right," she finished.

"Lucky," I said, finding myself using Wally Howe's voice, "we were real lucky, Lila."

Lila didn't ask for details. It was written in my wardrobe that we'd parted paths; I was back to my blazer and Panama.

Cole propped the GI tape recorder on the table and pointed the directional microphone at Lila. "I'm Special Agent L. B. Cole, ma'am, captain, United States Army, and this is my partner, Special Agent Jesse D'Ambrosi, captain, United States Army. We hope we're here at a good time?"

Lila nodded fragilely.

Jesse opened his notebook. "We're investigating the disappearance of Mr. Charles Purcell. Your brother-in-law. We have questions, Miss Schumann. And we'd appreciate your cooperation."

"I guess I understand," Lila said.

Jesse gestured to the house. "If you want to call your lawyer, Miss Schumann, that's fine by us. We can do this here or we can do it at the embassy."

"Am I under arrest or something?" she asked.

"No, Miss Schumann," Jesse said. "We don't have police powers. We're investigators. And we have reason to believe you have information about the disappearance of Mr. Purcell."

Cole continued with his part of the "Mutt and Jeff approach." "I'm glad you're okay, Miss Schumann. It was very brave of you, when you tried to help in Seoul."

"I screwed up," said Lila, trying a smile at Cole, falling into the approach just as she was supposed to fall.

"Mr. Paine," Jesse addressed me, "now that Miss Schumann is cooperating, it would be best, sir, if you—"

"I was just going for a walk," I said. "I'm sure you'll call me if you need me."

"Yes, sir," Jesse said.

Lila arranged her legs attractively. She was wisely thinking of herself just now and directed a good question to me.

"Am I in big trouble, Tip?"

"Yes," I said. "Me, too."

My consolation didn't work for either of us. I took a long stroll by the water while the boys did their job. I gave them an hour, and when that wasn't enough, I sat in the dark on the wharf watching for snakes in the grass and blaming myself. That failed; it still came out the same. Was I in love with Lila? Stupid question. When she'd tricked me into helping her, I'd thought she was a lovely pain. When I'd tricked her into helping me, I'd thought her a lovely pleasure. But now, after she'd lied, cheated, double-crossed, run away, chosen Raj over sense, used Charlie for everything he was and then put herself in a position to plunder everything he was worth—shucks, this was a woman to adore. In love with her? *She made me crazy.* It would never work; this counts for a lot with me. I could never sit here in the evening smoking my pipe and listening for her loud mouth calling supper. That downy red tail would never turn over to me. Lila was impossible. You say fare thee well to that. I wanted to make her a statue. And I might have, too, if the sculptor wouldn't have had to cast it so that the redhead's foot rested on a dead governess.

Later, Jesse and Cole called me back. I walked out of the dark and into the bright lawn lights. My pipe had scared off the major bug bites, but I was happy to get back inside the screens.

Lila had gone inside to change her scent after the sweating that comes with interrogation.

Jesse and Cole watched me closely. I was still thinking of them as "the boys," because it made them less intimidating to me. The truth was they were much more mature than I was.

"How'd it go?" I asked.

Cole directed the mike at me. "It isn't necessarily bad news, sir."

Jesse scratched a note. "How do you think it went, Mr. Paine?"

"I suppose," I double-talked, "that it matters that she tried to help, sort of."

Jesse and Cole were blank, back to the "silence approach."

I changed direction. "Okay, so her love life is black ops. Rajeesh Nehru is the bad guy. And Lila didn't know that before."

More blanks.

"You go that direction," I said testily, "you'll get a world of those who do it and those who want to do it. And you guys keeping score."

Cole puzzled, "Do what, sir?"

"The fancy term is 'misprision of treason,' " I said. "I figure it about covers everything Charlie ever did, meant or thought about."

Jesse reacted, "Mr. Paine, you said that you knew about us. Then you know it isn't ours to keep score."

Right. Jesse had me and he knew it. A tired man once said that if you can't prove it, it's politics. Another one said that, in politics, there are no permanent friends or enemies, only permanent blame.

Whoever was keeping score out there, Lila had several marks against her, and it was up to her to decide what to do. Did Lila want her passport or her squash champ? Did she want her country or her house? It was rotten that it was the same choice Rosie had made so badly, choosing both and getting neither.

Presently, Lila returned in fake control of herself. "I called Pammie," she began to me. "She's in L.A. with my mother." It must have occurred to Lila that I didn't care. She finished quickly, "Whatever happens to me, I don't want her and the children in this. She's starting the divorce. I want you to know that she's finished with him."

Tv would have me rescue the girl by marrying her. Rather, I gave us both a nasty chance to even up with the scorekeepers. "Tell them the truth, Lila."

"Leave me alone," she said.

"Tell them that when you bedded Charlie, when you handed him over to Pam, when you helped Pam suffer goldilocks, you weren't working for Raj."

"That's nuts," she declared, brushing her ratty hair out of her eyes.

"Tell them that when you bedded me you weren't protecting Raj. That when you stalled me an extra day in Singapore to give Raj time to get back from London, that when you sent me off to Seoul alone so Raj could get Charlie on the phone and bully him, that when you diverted me last Sunday afternoon to cover Raj's scheme to lose Charlie, that when you helped Raj get out of Korea (and that must have been hairy and sexy, huh?)—that you weren't working for the other side."

She wouldn't look at me. "You know that's bull."

"Tell them you're finished with Raj."

"Shit," she said and turned to the Johore Straits.

"You've got to say it, Lila," I demanded. "And say it like you mean it. They're here to help you, if you want it. They're not some slick liar who hides behind Cambridge and works for thugs. Jesse and Cole work for the good guys—they are the good guys —and you haven't gone over yet. Come back. Tell them you're coming back. It won't fix it, but it'll make you feel better while you sit here forty more years."

She came back toward me. "What's that make you?"

"The hero," I lied.

"Do you believe I knew what Raj was doing, that I set up my own family for him, that I knew about Rosie—any of it?"

I preached the truth. "No, I don't. It doesn't add up. I think you're very smart, and so you had to want to stay stupid. I think you're a first-rate woman who kinda *likes* guys who cheat you. Then again, I'm wrong a lot, and I've heard it claimed that love isn't arithmetic."

"You know shit about it," she said. "Get out of here."

"Sure, pal," I said.

Because I was frustrated, I pushed Lila as I'd pushed Charlie and Rosie.

"One more detail, Lila, it'll make me feel like a hero. Tell them where Raj put Charlie when he came crying back to him. Yesterday? Friday? Just tell them the truth."

Lila passed my trick test. She didn't shout or explain; she slugged, a stealthy left. Love talk. It hurt too, both of us.

"Gosh, Lila," I managed.

Lila marched back inside, trailing that red hair.

I loved her the more because she wouldn't choose between greed and family. To hell with my coin. To hell with the score-keepers. What was most important to her was what she wanted when she wanted it, and that didn't mean the truth, unless she wanted it, too.

Jesse and Cole stood on alert.

Jesse sounded impressed. "You know where Purcell is, sir?"

I looked where Lila had looked, the Johore Straits and Malaysia's jungle.

"Sure," I bragged.

9
Good-bye Charlie

PONTIAN KECHIL WAS A STEAM BATH on the sort of night that encourages spy fantasies.

Jesse and Cole were earnestly uncomfortable. Their bald-eagle IDs meant nothing in Malaysia. We were across a water border from Singapore, and their first backup was at our bases in the Philippines.

Perversely, this made me and Lila confident, since our first backup was in our billfolds, a situation that pleased the larceny in me and encouraged the boss in her.

Yes, she'd come along. Lila wouldn't ever leave herself out.

I hadn't protested. Neither had Jesse. His job was to find Charlie, not to control the uncontrollable. We'd even taken her renovated lemon Jaguar, instead of our rented Ford, because the border guards would pass it and her speedily.

Lila parked among the chickens. There was a Malay on the stoop, mending a fishing net, and I laughed at myself. I pointed out where I thought the tail had parked when Lila and I had visited.

Jesse said we were to stay in the car. He said that he and Cole were going to take a look around.

If you're wondering what sort of jeopardy we could find in a medieval fishing village, so was I. Then again, Rajeesh was chief of his Singapore station, and Charlie had eleven black cases the last we saw him at Inje. Six million cash could buy a whole coastline on Planet Asia.

Lila punched the radio to the BBC world service out of Singapore, the nine o'clock news hour. The dollar was up, the pound down, the yen sideways, the Germans were petting the commies, the commies were tendering more laughingstock. Out east, China was pouting, Mongolia was rearming, Vietnam was pan-handling, Burma was still changing its name on the stationery, North Korea was backfilling mass graves and tunnels. Welcome, Red boys, to the ranks of the disenchanted.

"We should take them to dinner," I told Lila.

"Here?" she asked.

"Later," I said, feeling cocky, "one of the nightclubs on the Orchard Road, where you can get a cellular phone at the table. We can make long-distance calls together. What time is it in London?"

She laughed. "Lunch." She laughed again. "Raj has lox on Sundays." She threw out her cigarette. "You're dreadful."

Jesse and Cole returned.

"It looks clear," Jesse announced through Lila's window.

He addressed me. "I must repeat to you, sir, that we don't have authority here. If Purcell is here, and if he wants to talk with us, then we proceed. But if there is any challenge, we leave. Do you understand me, Mr. Paine?"

"I am a cooperative and friendly source," I said. "Lila is a neutral and nonpartisan source. And Charlie is Charlie."

"No threats, sir," said Jesse, "and no deals."

"Affirmative," I said.

Lila whispered to me, "What's he mean?"

"All nominal," I answered.

Lila and I got out of the car like a posh couple, and we led Jesse and Cole into the tobacco shop. I bought gum from the Chinese counter girl. An ancient doper was hanging at the cur- tain near the stairs. The shop was poorer than I remembered, one step from nonexistence.

I addressed Jesse. "You're going to be disappointed. We didn't beat them, we outlasted them."

Cole was on rear guard at the door. He rearranged his beefy muscles and smiled sweetly at me to provide the sort of reassurance you get out of the law.

Jesse scanned the faces of the peasants. He was beyond my storytelling. If you have a story, call Jesse and Cole. They'll listen, they'll help you, and if you're lucky they'll believe you. When they stop listening, it means you're safe for a while.

We climbed upstairs clumsily on the narrow steps. The *fumerie* was the same foul opiate fog. The men were in underwear; the women were far away. The same teenage girl we had tried to buy out of hell approached us.

Lila spoke tenderly. "We're here for Soo Yu-Yi again."

The girl pointed the same way, as if it had only been minutes since we asked before.

Lila gave the girl money.

Lila said, "I hate this, Tip, I can't help it, I hate it. You tell me I didn't do it, but I did, somehow, I did, didn't I?"

I couldn't answer. I did know where Charlie was and went forward through the dopers to the cribs. I stepped up the ladder to look in.

Soo Yu-Yi's ghost was on the straw mattress, and she had Charlie's ghost in her arms like a child at the breast.

He was naked. No, he did have Pam's wedding ring and his dream life. And I suppose you could say he also had the one empty black case they'd left him for a pillow.

It must have been the opium that made me think I heard Soo Yu-Yi speak.

"Thank you," I imagined her ghost said. She embraced Charlie's ghost harder. "Thank you for bringing him to me."

I was holding my breath, but I wanted to talk to him and that needs air. The stink shocked me. So much, that I forgot about Rosie's wedding ring. I also forgot to be kind. "Good-bye, Charlie," I said.

His ghost took about forty years to turn to me. And I promise you it's the truth that the eyes were yellow-gold just like a cat's.

About the Author

John Calvin Batchelor was born in Bryn Mawr, Pennsylvania, in 1948. He is the author of seven novels: *The Further Adventures of Halley's Comet* (1981), *The Birth of the People's Republic of Antarctica* (1983), *American Falls* (1985), *Gordon Liddy Is My Muse, by Tommy "Tip" Paine* (1990), *Walking the Cat, by Tommy "Tip" Paine: Gordon Liddy Is My Muse II* (1991), *Peter Nevsky and the True Story of the Russian Moon Landing* (1993), and *Father's Day* (1994). He lives in New York City with his wife, son, and daughter.